D0312193

WITHDRAWN
FROM
COLLECTION

THE

EPIPHANY

MACHINE

ALSO BY DAVID BURR GERRARD

Short Century

THE

EPIPHANY

MACHINE

DAVID BURR GERRARD

G. P. PUTNAM'S SONS • NEW YORK

PUTNAM

G. P. PUTNAM'S SONS
Publishers Since 1838
An imprint of Penguin Random House LLC
375 Hudson Street
New York, New York 10014

Copyright © 2017 by David Burr Gerrard
Penguin supports copyright. Copyright fuels creativity, encourages diverse voices,
promotes free speech, and creates a vibrant culture. Thank you for buying an authorized edition
of this book and for complying with copyright laws by not reproducing, scanning, or distributing
any part of it in any form without permission. You are supporting writers and allowing
Penguin to continue to publish books for every reader.

ISBN 9780399575433

Printed in the United States of America
1   3   5   7   9   10   8   6   4   2

Book design by Gretchen Achilles

This is a work of fiction. Names, characters, places, and incidents either are the product
of the author's imagination or are used fictitiously, and any resemblance to actual persons,
living or dead, businesses, companies, events, or locales is entirely coincidental.

For Grace, my parents, and my brother

Remember your epiphanies on green oval leaves, deeply deep, copies to be sent if you died to all the great libraries of the world, including Alexandria? Someone was to read them there after a few thousand years, a mahamanvantara. Pico della Mirandola like. Ay, very like a whale.

—JAMES JOYCE, *Ulysses*

This tattooing had been the work of a departed prophet and seer of his island, who, by those hieroglyphic marks, had written out on his body a complete theory of the heavens and the earth, and a mystical treatise on the art of attaining truth; so that Queequeg in his own proper person was a riddle to unfold; a wondrous work in one volume; but whose mysteries not even himself could read, though his own live heart beat against them; and these mysteries were therefore destined in the end to moulder away with the living parchment whereon they were inscribed, and so be unsolved to the last.

—HERMAN MELVILLE, *Moby-Dick*

Enlightenment comes to the most dull-witted.

—FRANZ KAFKA, "In the Penal Colony"

Words are like weapons: they wound sometimes.

—DIANE WARREN, "If I Could Turn Back Time"

THE

EPIPHANY

MACHINE

THINGS TO CONSIDER BEFORE
USING THE EPIPHANY MACHINE

1. The epiphany machine will not discover anything about you that you do not, in some way, already know. But think for a moment about surprise. What is surprising is never what is revealed but the grace with which it has been hidden.

2. The unexamined life is often entirely worth living. If there is nothing gnawing at you, put this pamphlet down and never think of us again.

3. If there *is* something gnawing at you, that means you're delicious. That gnawing is the universe trying to get at the tasty juice inside of you. Your entire unsatisfying life is just the rind. When you look at our device, think of it as a peeler.

4. When most people look at our device, it reminds them of an antique sewing machine. Others think it looks like the fossilized jawbone of some extinct, single-toothed great cat. We could sit around and psychoanalyze you based on what you think it looks like, but that would take decades and cost you tens of thousands of dollars. Using the epiphany machine takes about fifteen minutes and costs a hundred bucks.

5. The machine does not tell your future, or even specific facts about your present. It does not know who will win the World Series or whether your wife is having sex with your neighbor. Or if it does know, it has yet to display any propensity to tell.

6. We limit each user to one tattoo. The device's value lies in its limits. Any more than one epiphany and you might as well consult the vast libraries that are already available to you and that have clearly not done you any good.

7. **CLOSED OFF** is a common epiphany. This is often cited as evidence that we are charlatans. We would argue that many people are closed off.

8. There is only one manner in which you may receive your epiphany: a tattoo on your forearm. The machine's design demands it; the jaw, as it were, can open only so far. You may want your epiphany on your stomach, but no matter how much you diet, your stomach will not fit. You can argue that the machine is less than perfectly designed for the human body; you can argue that the human body is less than perfectly designed for the machine. You can argue, you can argue, you can argue.

9. In no way is the placement of the epiphany tattoo on the forearm intended to mock or otherwise evoke the Holocaust.

10. We do not shy away from tough questions, including those about Rebecca Hart. Ms. Hart murdered her three children about a year after using our device. What the machine told her: **OFFSPRING WILL NOT LEAD HAPPY LIVES.** This was a logical deduction derived from a reading of Ms. Hart herself, and we certainly take no pleasure in deeming it an accurate one.

11. This case aside—and despite malicious rumors—there are absolutely no circumstances under which your epiphany or any other personal information will be shared with law enforcement, direct-marketing companies, or any other persons or organizations. Though we are generally agnostic on political questions, this is a principle that we consider sacrosanct. Your secrets are as safe with us as they would be with a priest, therapist, or lawyer, give or take the necessity of acquiring a wardrobe full of long sleeves.

12. If you believe that you do not need to use the machine, but that your husband or wife or mother does, you may be right. Are you?

13. Some of you are here because of a lover, parent, sibling, or child. You are here because someone you care about came to us and got an epiphany tattoo that changed or clarified his or her life. You are here to investigate our facilities and prove to this person that the epiphany machine is bunk, that he or she has been, in the term you will probably use, "brainwashed." (We plead guilty to scrubbing the thick film of self-deception from the thoughts of our users, but this is probably not what you mean.) We welcome you as we welcome all other visitors. We merely encourage you to ask yourself: Why? Why am I so suspicious of the newfound happiness or self-knowledge of this person about whom I claim to care? Am I truly committed to this person's well-being, or do I miss the comfort of feeling unshakily superior? These are uncomfortable questions to ask yourself, so you might consider asking the machine instead.

14. We have little interest in defending the device, and less in explaining it. If you are intent today on thinking of the machine as a kind of Magic 8 Ball, then today you will think of the machine as a kind of Magic 8 Ball. We will risk being cheeky by inviting you to ask again later.

15. One way to think about your life is as an extended freefall. An epiphany may help you see better as you fall. Rather than a meaningless blur, you will see rocks and trees and lizards. An epiphany is not a parachute.

16. If you believe that the epiphanies you have seen tattooed on the arms of your friends suggest that your friends are better, luckier, smarter, or more virtuous than you are, bear in mind that many disreputable establishments offer counterfeit epiphany tattoos that are no more indicative of a person's innermost mind than is a vanity license plate.

17. Then again, your friends may simply be better, smarter, or more virtuous than you, though they are probably not luckier. It is unlikely, though certainly not impossible, that the machine will remark on this. While always bracingly honest, the machine does display a certain quality that we might anthropomorphically describe as tact.

18. Your epiphany may be removed as any other tattoo may, which is to say: imperfectly.

19. You already know what the machine will write on your arm. That lie you've been telling yourself—you know what it is. That blind spot is not really a blind spot—you're choosing to look away. Perhaps more to the point, you already know whether you want to see it. You already know whether you're going to use the machine. So why are you still reading this?

TESTIMONIAL #101

NAME: Rose Schuldenfrei Lowood
DATE OF BIRTH: 12/19/1947
DATE OF EPIPHANY MACHINE USE: 01/06/1972
DATE OF INTERVIEW BY VENTER LOWOOD: 01/10/2017

In those days I had contradictory feelings about almost everything, so I was delighted to find that I was only delighted to be bringing bad news to Adam Lyons, the notorious huckster behind the epiphany machine. Even the potholes and the slush that the cab driver did not try to avoid made me feel like I was a bold adventuress on a dangerous road. Granted, instead of a sword I was armed with a manila envelope full of legal papers, but one makes do with the weapons of one's time.

Usually, when I was delivering envelopes like this one, I couldn't stop myself from thinking about how it would feel to be sued, how it would feel to be forced to stand respectfully before a judge who was probably going to take your money away for no better reason than that you were a sleazeball. I sympathized with sleazeballs, since if you didn't sympathize with the sleazeballs you were left with the nuns, and years of Catholic school had taught me not to sympathize with *them*. But Adam Lyons combined the worst aspects of the sleazeballs and the nuns, so he unquestionably deserved what I was delivering.

The driver pulled up into a filthy winter puddle at the address the client had given. The client was suing Adam over the tattoo on her arm, **GIVES AWAY WHAT MATTERS MOST**. Her fiancé, having goaded her into getting the tattoo in the first place, interpreted it to mean that she was marrying for money, and he consequently dumped her—her family was almost as rich as his was, but somehow that didn't seem to matter. The client's father interpreted the tattoo to mean that she had been having sex with her fiancé prior to marriage, and was furious that somebody who lived in old converted maid's quarters on the Upper East Side had scrawled this fact on his daughter. So the family was suing Adam Lyons for $40 million. A spoiled rich girl was certainly not someone I would have envisioned myself feeling honored to fight for, but I admired her refusal to go away without blood under her fingernails. And her father actually had the resources to go up against Adam Lyons, or more accurately whoever was propping up Adam Lyons. Though there were rumors about a real-estate heir, nobody knew for sure how he could afford the legal bills from various lawsuits, or why he was permitted to run a tattoo business out of his apartment, even though tattooing was illegal in New York City at the time and you're not supposed to run any business out of your apartment.

"Spending the morning with your boyfriend, Blondie?" This question from the cab driver confused me, because I had forgotten for a moment that I had dyed my hair blond. The driver was digging his thick fingers into the passenger seat and baring his yellow teeth at me. I said yes, I was spending the morning with my boyfriend. One of the worst things about men is that they make it dangerous not to lie to them.

I handed him a wad of bills, stuffing the five that was going to be his then generous tip back into the pocket of the fox fur coat I had bought for the same reason I had dyed my hair blond—because it was something I normally wouldn't do. I was usually quite clumsy, but, maybe emboldened by the coat, I leapt from the cab over the puddle and onto the curb with an elegance that could only be described as foxy. Not a trace of slush on my coat or my shoes, not the slightest totter on my heels, a safe several inches from any of the dog shit that sits for weeks in the New York City slush.

The driver, seeing that I had stiffed him, called out the name of a body part that it was unlikely he had been permitted access to ever since he exited one, and he tried and failed to splash me as he pulled away. I gave him a little four-fingered wave and felt ready to make the wicked bleed.

Adam's apartment was only one flight up, but the time it took me to climb that flight proved enough for all my self-confidence to evaporate. I think it was the sight of my coat against the dingy stairs. Something, anyway, turned me from feeling good about the coat to feeling horrible about the coat. Your grandmother had told me that the coat was a betrayal, a waste of what we needed to survive, especially given how little money we had with me going to law school at night. I could have answered that the reason I was going to law school *at night* was that I had, ahem, a mother to support, and that if we wanted to talk about bad money decisions we could start with her decision to marry a man who drank his salary every week for several decades prior to drinking himself to death at the age of fifty-seven. Or maybe we could start with her decision to give up the excellent radio-factory job she held during the war to become an ordinary housewife, forsaking the construction of complicated machines that fostered communication among millions so that she could spend her life talking to two people she would never understand. But if I had said any of this, she would have pointed out that she had done all of this for me, which would have left me in the silly position of pointing out that I didn't ask to be born, an unassailable point that only an adolescent would take seriously. Or she might have told me yet again that all of her friends had told her it was a waste of money to send a daughter to college, at least a daughter who wasn't an obvious genius. Worst of all, I would have been inclined to agree, since it was humiliatingly easy for my mother to make me feel stupid and worthless. And if college had been good for anything, it should at least have given me the ability to outsmart a woman with an eighth-grade education. Rather than open any of this up, I just apologized for buying the coat, and then apologized again, and then apologized *again*. The conversation ended with my thanking her for forgiving me.

I arrived at Adam's door raging at my inability to confront my mother, or at my inability to confront the extravagance and irresponsibility that she had diagnosed in me. I found myself hesitating to knock, overwhelmed simultaneously by a sudden rush of understanding for the anger and confusion that leaves people desperate enough to seek out a magic tattoo, and by an equally powerful and equally sudden rush of intense hatred for anyone stupid enough to actually go through with it.

I was still hesitating when the door opened to reveal a man who looked like an egg, an egg with a thick head of black hair, an egg with a beard—a beard better groomed than the Moses/Manson model—an egg with a short-sleeved, button-down shirt open two buttons to show a great deal of black hair on its eggy chest. He smiled, showing me the missing tooth that, he would later joke, was "the open window through which the truth rushes into my body."

"Your name is Adam Lyons and you live in this apartment?"

"Two true statements. Let's see if we can get you a third. Come in."

He had confirmed his identity, so this was where I was supposed to just thrust the manila envelope into his hands and be on my way. But I followed him through the door.

The foyer of his apartment, which was also his shop, was overstuffed with books, mostly thick, well-thumbed works about philosophy and religion. There were a lot of books by and about Kafka, whom I had discovered at a bookstore when I was twelve, and who had made me secretly dream of becoming a writer for a few years, until I realized that becoming a lawyer was a more practical way to spend your life staring at sentences.

Adam said that he would pour me some whiskey, gesturing to the bar that I was surprised to find at the center of a tattoo-parlor-cum-church. I responded that it was ten in the morning. Men need to be reminded often that it's too early for oblivion.

"Have you ever gotten a tattoo before? It's going to hurt. I'd suggest a drink." He poured some whiskey and threw in a couple ice cubes with his tobacco-stained fingers.

"No, thanks."

"Suit yourself," he said, and put the glass down. "So what brings you here today?"

I knew that if I answered his question with any words at all, rather than with a manila envelope dropped silently into his hands, then sooner or later I would give him my arm. I started talking anyway.

CHAPTER

—— · · ◆ · · ——

1

The first time I asked my father about the epiphany machine was also the only time that he hit me. What made an impression on me was not the actual physical contact, a gentle slap only slightly more abrasive than the wind that was blowing very hard for an October day. My father seemed no more likely to slap me than to slit my throat and watch me bleed out into the leaf-clogged gutter, so for all I knew that might come next. In my young mind, for him to have hit me at all meant that something must have been unlocked in him, something that would have remained boxed up had I not liberated it with the magic words "the epiphany machine," and that would now never cease to pursue me until it had achieved my destruction.

He knelt down and looked me in the eye. "You have no idea how much I've gone through to protect you from that horrible thing."

This made me sob.

"If you're old enough to know about the epiphany machine, then you're too old to cry."

This only made me sob harder.

"Venter, you need to tell me who told you about the machine. Was it your grandmother? She promised me she wouldn't say anything about it until we both agreed that you were old enough."

"It wasn't her. I just heard about it on TV."

This was not technically a lie. One night, after I was supposed to be asleep, I had heard my grandmother weeping while watching an eleven-o'clock news report suggesting that the epiphany machine might be responsible for the spread of HIV, another thing I had never heard of. I connected this to the time when my father had made an excessively big show of not freaking out over the cover of a copy of a magazine that had been left on the table at a coffee shop: "Did a Tiny Cult in New York City Help Spread HIV?" But these events had happened weeks earlier—which might as well have been decades according to my sense of time—and were not why I had asked about the device. I had asked because, at recess that morning, I had heard one teacher whisper to another as I passed by, "His mother got a tattoo from the epiphany machine." Now I wanted to know what it was. I was also wondering whether the epiphany machine had something to do with the tattoo on my father's forearm—**SHOULD NEVER BECOME A FATHER**—that he had sat me down to talk about shortly before I was old enough to read it, claiming he had gotten it as a stupid prank when he was very young, long before I was born.

"On TV!" my father said, laughing. "My brilliant boy, I'm sorry I slapped you. Let's take a walk." We walked past the crematorium across from our house to the cemetery two blocks away. (Queens was and remains a city of the dead with some halfhearted gentrification from the living.) The wind continued as we maintained silence for several rows of what my father and grandmother called "nails on a sum," aping what they said had been my attempt, at the age of three, to say that gravestones looked like thumbnails. I got myself together and stopped crying, but then I suddenly realized that my father must be taking me to see my mother's grave—that this was how he was going to tell me that my mother was dead, and had not merely run away. I started sobbing again. This time my father did not scold me, but he did not comfort me either. He just looked out at the traffic. Finally, he spoke.

"Do you know why your grandmother and I think that 'nails on a sum' is funny?"

"Because it's silly?"

"Because it's *not* silly. Because it's actually exactly correct. They've told you in school what a sum is, right?"

"That's in adding."

"Exactly. Can you give me an example of a sum?"

"In two plus two equals four, the sum is four."

"Good, my brilliant boy!"

This made me feel very, very good, as the fact that I hated him at the moment did not make me long any less for him to think that I was a genius.

"The sum is what things add up to," my father continued. "Everyone wants his or her life to add up to something. All the people in this cemetery, all the people that we're walking on, they all did lots of stuff, hoping to make the sums of their lives go higher and higher and higher. Maybe a few of them had sums that were very high, most of them had sums that were not so high. In every case, the gravestone is like a nail on that sum—not like the nail on your thumb, actually, but like the nails in a roof, the nails that say: no, house, you're not going any higher. Gravestones are like nails on a person's life, keeping the sum from getting any higher."

Often, he couldn't tell exactly at which level to speak to me, and so said things that made no sense on any level.

"I don't understand," I said.

"Okay. In a baseball game, there's a score, right? At the end of the game, each team has gotten a certain number of runs. The sum that I'm talking about in a person's life, that's like a score."

Something was stirring in me, a mature and morally serious version of the most childish emotion of all: impatience.

"Dad," I said. "What is the epiphany machine and where is my mother?"

"I'm getting to that," he said. "So the sum of one's life is the sum of everything you've done. And as you get a little older you start to realize that sooner or later you're going to end up here, in this cemetery or one exactly like it, and you want to make sure that your sum is as high as possible. The problem is that life is more confusing than a baseball game. In a baseball game, a run is a run and that's that. In life, sometimes you're not sure what counts as a run. Also, you don't know what the teams are. Or whether you're even playing. Sometimes you think you're playing and you're actually just sitting in the stands, watching other people play."

"Dad."

"Okay. All this means that you have to make up your own way of scoring. You have to decide what's important. For a lot of people, it's money. For a lot of other people, it's some kind of religious fulfillment. You know what the most important thing is to me?"

I shook my head. I knew what he was going to say, but I wanted to hear him say it.

"*You* are the most important thing to me. So whenever something good happens to you, or whenever I see you smile, or whenever you learn how to do something, that's like a run for me. When something bad happens to you, that's like a run for the other team. That's why I had to do what I did just now. Even though I didn't really hit you—it was really just a love tap, wasn't it?—I still felt horrible while I was doing it. I felt much worse than you felt, believe me. But the epiphany machine is very bad and I have to do whatever it takes to keep you safe from it. It's the sort of thing that could cause you to lose the whole game."

"What?"

"I'm saying that figuring out what's important in life and how to go about getting it is very difficult. Sometimes you get confused and you get tempted to just let other people make the rules. And some people are really happy to make the rules for other people. Adam Lyons, the man who runs the epiphany machine, is one of those people. There was a time when I let myself get confused enough that I let him write those words on me that you know aren't true."

"The epiphany machine writes things about people on their arms?"

"Exactly, my brilliant boy! I figured out that the machine was wrong. Your mother, on the other hand . . . well, Venter, it told her that she **ABANDONS WHAT MATTERS MOST**. You weren't born yet so she didn't know what matters most. Then you were born and she abandoned you."

"Why did she listen to the machine if you didn't?"

"That's the first question you should ask her if you meet her."

"I don't ever want to meet her."

"That shows that you are a very smart boy."

If I had actually been a very smart boy, I probably would have kept asking questions. At the very least I would have recognized his persistent flattery as a shutting-down of my curiosity no less violent than the slap. But I wanted his praise more than I wanted the truth.

That night I went downstairs to see my grandmother, who had laid out pound cake, my favorite. She was sitting in her recliner, knitting an afghan.

"Grandma, what do you know about the epiphany machine?"

I was expecting her to stop knitting and look up at me with fury, but she didn't even slow her rhythm. My father had obviously warned her. She was silent for a moment, filling the room with the sound of her plastic needles hitting each other.

"The epiphany machine is why I no longer have a daughter and why you no longer have a mother. It is for people who are lonely, gullible, and numb."

"What's 'numb'?"

"'Numb' is when you can't feel anything. People who can't feel anything do weird things to get their feeling back. They spend money they don't have on a fox fur coat. They want the coat to make them feel warm and elegant, they want the coat to make them feel like a real somebody.

Then the coat doesn't make them feel anything. So they let some stranger put a needle in them, hoping *that* will make them feel something. Then they can't feel the needle. That's when they decide they don't care about anything. They don't care if the sight of their tattoo makes their mother sick to her stomach. They don't care if they leave their mother, their husband, their son. They don't care about anything because they can't feel anything. Do you understand?"

I didn't say anything.

"Okay. If your tongue were numb, you couldn't taste pound cake. So there would be no point in me giving you pound cake. You can either be a pound cake boy or an epiphany machine boy. Which is it going to be?"

"I'm a pound cake boy," I said.

I ate pound cake every night for months afterward and never once asked about the epiphany machine. I even pretended that I didn't know that parents, terrified of AIDS, were telling their children to stay away from me, though of course I started hearing this every day at school. I pretended, too, that I had no idea that this was why we moved away from Queens to an affluent town in Westchester, in the hope that no one there would hear of our connection to the machine. It's even possible that I flattered myself about how good I was getting at pretending not to know things, one important life skill at which I was most likely outpacing my peers.

CHAPTER

——— · · ✦ · · ———

2

W hen we arrived in Westchester, I was under strict orders never to say anything about the epiphany machine to anyone. I was supposed to tell anyone who asked that my mother had abandoned the family, and say that I didn't know anything more than that. This worked, and I was avoided because I was weird rather than because I was dangerous. It often occurred to me that I would have preferred the latter to the former, but for years I never said anything. I didn't want my father and grandmother to move us again. (There was not a chance anyone would discover the tattoo on my father, since he wore a suit on the Metro-North platform, a sport jacket to the grocery store, and stayed clear of pool parties.)

Throughout these same years I don't think I asked my father or grandmother a single question about the machine. I had decided not only that I knew what it was, which I didn't really, but that I knew what it meant, which I didn't at all. The machine was for people who were lonely, gullible, and numb, and believed in by people who stayed that way. My mother was one of those people. I said the words "the epiphany machine" only to my father or grandmother, and only when I wanted to please them by saying:

"The only people who use the epiphany machine are lonely, gullible, and numb."

Those were the three words I used when I finally did mention the epiphany machine at school, on the playground in fourth grade. There were a few boys who liked to bother me about the fact that I didn't know where my mother was, chanting things like "Venter's mother is a slut," a word they knew despite likely having no more than the dimmest idea what sex was. Eventually I said: "My mom's not a slut, she's lonely, gullible, and numb." I felt superior when they didn't understand that the word "numb" wasn't just what novocaine made your mouth when you went to the dentist.

"It's a figurative use of the term," I said, having heard my father say "It's a figurative use of the term" once and deciding that it applied here. (To taxonomize myself, I was one of those smart children who wishes he were much smarter, and so compensates with a smug attitude toward other children and a toadying one toward adults. Honestly, I was probably bullied less than I deserved.)

These kids and others kept pushing me to explain what I had meant, and finally I said: "My mother used the epiphany machine!" I think I feared that we would be tarred and feathered and sent out of town, "tarred and feathered" being a phrase I had heard in movies I watched with my grandmother. But the kids hadn't heard of the machine. I discovered slowly, over the next few months, that some of the parents had heard of it, but for the most part thought it was something to snicker over, not to fear. (I later learned that the link between HIV and the machine had been definitively debunked—the institute that had posited the link in the first place turned out to be a right-wing Christian operation unhappy with the strange theology of Adam Lyons.)

I am not sure that I actually *felt* the absence of my mother, a woman I had never meaningfully met. To be honest, the times I missed my mother most intensely were when a teacher would ask me whether I missed her. And even then the emotion I felt was probably a desire to impress the teacher with the depth of my emotion, itself an emotion strong enough to cleave a child in two. And there *were* those moments when other kids, with varying degrees of subtlety, would harass me, first for not having a mother and later for having a mother who had joined a cult. Approval and protection were the only things I wanted from a mother. Maybe these are the only things a mother can give. I wouldn't know.

Or maybe that's a self-pitying way for me to describe my childhood. After all, I did have a mother in my grandmother, who cared for me by moving slowly but all the time. The signal sound of my childhood was of her shuffling feet, which would take her around the house with great noise and over the objection of her aching joints. She cooked goulash or lasagna or pot roast for us almost every night (resorting to spaghetti only when she was unusually tired), often changing a lightbulb or a roll of toilet paper on the other end of the house while the water was boiling. I should have helped, no question about that, although in my defense she adamantly refused my help on the (admittedly rare) occasions that I offered it. It didn't take the genius I hoped myself to be to realize that doing everything for me was my grandmother's way of redeeming herself for failing as the mother of my mother. Her more conscious attempts to revise her parenting style were less successful. "I gave your mother too much freedom and let her watch too much TV, so you can only watch three hours a week," she often said, but in practice she gave me an essentially unlimited amount of freedom and let me watch an essentially unlimited amount of TV. We also watched a lot of movies together, mostly riches-in-the-midst-of-the-Depression musicals and gangster movies, as we tried to pretend that we truly enjoyed each other's company and were not trying to distract ourselves from our mutual loneliness.

If my father was lonely as well—he appeared to have no social acquaintances—he did a remarkable job of channeling this loneliness into a stream of staggering productivity that would suggest a man operating at an unsustainable pace save for the fact that he sustained it. In addition to the infamous hours of a partner at a corporate law firm, Isaac Lowood worked obsessively on his private passion, privacy, and wrote an influential book on the subject, *Polaroids, Pac-Man, and Penumbras: Technology, the Supreme Court, and the Future of the Fourth Amendment.* He boasted of a colleague who had referred to him as "a legend in his spare time." Other colleagues complained of all the time he spent on extracurricular pursuits, but he could always point to the fact that he billed more hours than they did. My grandmother made sure I knew that none of this would have been possible if she did not drive me to and from school and see to one hundred percent of household chores, but it also wouldn't have been possible if my father slept more than five hours each night and worked fewer than sixteen hours each day. (His workday began the moment he stepped on the train in the morning, when he would remove files from his briefcase and start reading.)

It is also true that it would not have been possible if he had spent much time with me. I'm not sure what we would have done together, other than maybe watch sports that neither of us liked. My father did the best he could, which as a description of human behavior sounds like a tautology but is actually true of very few people.

CHAPTER

◆

3

The epiphany machine only truly came into focus for me around the same time that I met Ismail. If one or both of us had not been assigned to Ms. Scarra's ninth-grade Global Studies class, then you might be watching a play written by Ismail rather than reading a book written by me. I fell in love with Ms. Scarra as soon as I walked into class on the first day, and I was determined to lose my virginity to her, a goal I probably chose because I had seen the scenario in a few of the nudie movies I had only recently discovered on late-night cable. At the very least, I was determined to make her think I was a genius. So I was annoyed that her early favorite was another boy. Though unreligious, I had a great interest in the world religions we studied early in the year, and would have been the star of any other class. But Ismail's command was undeniable. He was extremely knowledgeable about not only Islam, his own religion, but also Judaism, Christianity, Hinduism, Buddhism, and particularly Zoroastrianism, of which his late father had been a scholar. When I say Islam was Ismail's own religion, I mean it was his own religion in the way that Judaism and Catholicism were my own religions, ambiguously inherited from parents who had not themselves been believers. Ismail made it very clear one day that he thought that religion was "stupid" and that "anyone who doesn't hate thinking knows there's no God," which angered a lot of the other kids, most of whom had already embarked on lifelong careers of believing in God whenever they needed comfort or forgiveness that they did not want to ask another human being for. The nasty tenor of his remarks gave me some hope that I would become the teacher's favorite despite being outmatched, hope that was bolstered the next day when Ms. Scarra asked him to stay after class, maybe to lecture him about respecting the beliefs of the other students. Then she asked me to stay as well, so I got to listen as she praised Ismail effusively and he looked on with a barely respectful smirk, almost certainly harboring the same fantasies about Ms. Scarra that I did and appearing to have at least a slightly higher likelihood of fulfilling them. Finally, she turned to me and said a couple of nice things about me—not as nice, I thought, as what she had said about Ismail—and asked us to serve as co-presidents of the Coexistence Club, an afterschool group that would be devoted to harmony among religions. Ms. Scarra said that religious intolerance was cultural intolerance, and that since between the two of us we had cultural ties to the three major monotheistic religions, we were the ideal co-presidents. I think Ismail was as unhappy with the situation as I was, since there were strong flavors of tokenism, condescension, and illogic in the whole endeavor. We might have asked her about the arbitrary focus on monotheism and why she didn't want to include a co-president who was actually religious—the idea of two atheists coexisting seemed strange. We might also have asked what she might possibly have thought the purpose of the club was. But Ismail and I both said yes, since the club was obviously going to look good on the college applications we were already looking forward to filling out. More important, Ms. Scarra was a female who was willing to talk to us.

In addition to co-presidents, Ismail and I were also the only members of the Coexistence Club, so we would just sit in Ms. Scarra's room after school on Thursdays, she would bring doughnuts, and we would talk, occasionally about issues connected to religion. I think we had been doing this for six weeks or so when she brought up the epiphany machine.

Not that the machine was an entirely random topic to bring up at the time. This was the fall of 1995, and the second Rebecca Hart killings had occurred the previous June. Even those who considered Adam Lyons nothing more than a huckster now felt the suspicion in the back of their necks that the man was touched with genuine black magic. Other kids' parents who saw me at the grocery store looked at me like I had somehow cheated death, which was not something done by a trustworthy person.

"Venter," Ms. Scarra said after she had said the words "epiphany machine" to me for the first time. "Your mother used the epiphany machine. What's your opinion of it now?"

"It's something that people resort to when they're lonely, gullible, and numb," I said. "That was my mother. Some people who are lonely, gullible, and numb are also capable of murder. That was not my mother."

"I don't think it's much of a coincidence that the two women were named Rebecca Hart," said Ismail. "The second one happened to be crazy, too, and she was probably obsessed with the first Rebecca Hart and decided to be just like her."

"But then," Ms. Scarra said, "how did she get the same tattoo?"

"I'm sure that whatever he says, this guy Adam Lyons will give you whatever tattoo you want if you pay him enough."

Ms. Scarra gave Ismail a pitying smile that I found weirdly erotic. "That's the skeptic's perspective. Which is only one among many."

"It's the correct perspective," Ismail said.

"A lot of people who aren't crazy and who aren't stupid have used the machine," Ms. Scarra said. "John Lennon used it. You don't think John Lennon was lonely, gullible, and numb, do you?"

"I have no idea what John Lennon was like," Ismail said.

"You don't think there's any reason why people who are not lonely, gullible, or numb, but are as wise and full of feeling as any of the three of us, might realize that it's in human nature to be self-deceiving, to not see important things in our own lives, and so seek external guidance to correct that?"

"I'm not self-deceiving," Ismail said. I could see in Ms. Scarra's eyes that she thought this was naive, but I admired how confidently Ismail had spoken. I said that I wasn't self-deceptive either, though I may have stammered a bit.

Ms. Scarra retreated to her desk and picked up a manila folder, from which she produced two photocopies of two chapters from an idiosyncratic 1991 book called *Origins and Adventures of the Epiphany Machine*, written by a reclusive writer whose real identity was unknown and the subject of much speculation, but who went by the name Steven Merdula.

"*Only the Desert Is Not a Desert* is Merdula's masterpiece," Ismail said. "I read it last year and loved it. I hear this one is crap."

"Just read what I photocopied," Ms. Scarra said. "I'm going to get some coffee."

I had been firmly forbidden by my father and grandmother from ever reading this book. But I was ashamed now of having complied, and I certainly wasn't going to let myself look cowardly in front of Ismail and Ms. Scarra. So I read the strange and mutually contradictory chapters, feeling as I read each sentence as though I were being pulled by something malevolent into the sea.

Let's say that the epiphany machine was invented by a Nazi rocket scientist. Let's call him Wernher, not because I'm thinking about Wernher von Braun, but because Wernher is the first German name that comes to mind. Wernher was sitting with his wife one night, trying hard to focus on the story she was telling about the time at their wedding—*Hochzeit*, or high time, is the German word, meaning that nothing will ever be as good again—when Wernher's mother accidentally, or maybe on purpose, stuck her with a hatpin. But Wernher was not listening. He was too distracted by what he was always thinking about: rocket trajectory. His wife noticed that he wasn't paying attention to her, so they quarreled, but he couldn't pay attention to their quarrel, and naturally this made her even angrier, and she stormed off to bed.

Wernher was, despite making weapons for the Nazis, in no way a heartless man, and it upset him to upset his wife. He found that he could not concentrate on his work, and decided to clean the closet, on the pretense of making things easier for his wife but really as a way of doing what he was always doing: creating a certain kind of weapon. *See what a good husband I am, I even do the work you are supposed to do, what do you have to complain about?* He removed a few coats he would never wear again, and then he removed an old pair of rain boots from the floor, and underneath these he saw the sewing machine that his mother had given his wife as a wedding gift. This was the sewing machine that Wernher had spent many childhood hours watching his mother operate, torn between feeling annoyed that she was not playing with him and feeling enthralled that she was transforming nondescript pieces of cloth into dresses and pants. The impulse to imitate his mother—the impulse to create things that would envelop, overpower, and define human bodies—is what led him to rocket science.

But perhaps rockets were, well, too airy. Perhaps the true place for him was here with this sewing machine; perhaps this sewing machine would lead him to what he was destined to invent. There was no reason for him to believe this, but suddenly he did. Where the idea for the tattoo came from is anyone's guess, though the use of tattoos to mark a person's worth was an idea that was, shall we say, not foreign to Nazi culture.

For the next year or so, he tinkered with the machine every day after work, not really knowing what he was doing, but driven by something, something that he was convinced would lead him to complete a work of genius and that, in any case, completed his neglect of his wife. Either he was aided by some supernatural force or he wasn't, but he turned the sewing machine into the epiphany machine. Perhaps he discovered what he had created only after his wife, finishing some cross-stitching, asked him to pass her a book—*Mein Kampf*, if we are being nasty, or even if we are simply playing the odds, since *Mein Kampf* was given to every German couple on their wedding day during the Nazi years. He reached across the machine, accidentally activating it. His wife watched as the needle found his arm and dug in, and certainly she was horrified, though perhaps, also, she thought that he deserved it. He screamed, terrified of the ink forming on his arm; he must have thought that it was God's retribution for the Holocaust, which he must have known about even if he did not know about it. Then the needle disengaged and he saw what was written on his arm, and he saw that he was right, that it was God's retribution.

Now the question is: What did the needle write? Let's say it wrote: **IGNORES WIFE FIXATED ON MOTHER AND WORK**. An accurate assessment of Wernher, one that might even have led him toward a more fulfilling relationship with his wife. Possibly, if you're in a generous mood, you might say that it served the purpose of distracting Wernher from his work for the Nazis. The epiphany machine may have saved the world from the Nazis, and would therefore have to be counted as the greatest-ever technological boon to humanity. And yet the tattoo itself is clearly monstrous. In lieu of any serious engagement with Wernher's culpability for the evil in which he participated, the tattoo mediates a turgid Oedipal dispute and tells Wernher, incorrectly, that there are more important things than work. It ignores completely the nature of that work, which, so far as the tattoo is concerned, might as well be the construction of a toaster.

In the last years of the nineteenth century, with the dark decades ahead not yet visible, Andrew Blue and Richard Reid were classmates at Eton. Andrew and Richard were famous for the vigor and erudition of their debates over military history, a subject about which they knew much more than any of the other boys, all of whom knew a fair amount about military history. Red and Blue, as they were called, even though Richard's last name was pronounced "reed," treated the question of when and how war should be fought as a sacred inquiry. Much blood had been spilled into the earth, almost all of it needlessly, and yet there were undeniably times when blood *belonged* to the earth, and to keep it locked up and sloshing around in the bodies that lurked above it was nothing more than cowardice. On the list of terms that Andrew and Richard wanted never to be applied to them, "coward" was a close second to a cluster of terms they preferred not to think about. The conversations between the boys would last long into the night, and they spent their summers together at Andrew's estate, where they swam, played tennis, read on the lawn or in the capacious library, went riding, and—though they would not have used this word, or any word at all—gave each other handjobs. The handjobs occurred after their daily swim, and afterward they put their hands in the stream, watching their semen stretch and join and separate and disappear. Theirs was hardly an unusual arrangement among Etonians in any aspect other than the depth of their feeling for each other, and neither of the boys felt it necessary or permissible to acknowledge that they would one day face a choice between what they wanted and what they were permitted to want, and that that day would come soon.

Richard was brooding on this subject in the middle of an August night when he woke at three and could not find a way back to sleep. A change had come over Andrew over the last several days—he had started to talk a great deal about God and was not interested in swimming. Richard worried that they had already embarked on the unlivable life that awaited. For lack of anything else to do, he walked through the woods at first light. In a mostly futile attempt to revive a feeling of innocence and guiltless curiosity, he took a stick and, just as he had when walking through the woods as a small boy, cut worms in two or three. Several worms into this pastime, his stick struck something metallic. He poked some more, enough to determine that whatever it was was large and buried deeply. He rolled up his sleeves and removed handfuls of dirt until he had determined that it was a sewing machine. Odd that one of Andrew's servants had buried a sewing machine out here. Perhaps it was broken, and whoever had broken it did not wish to have the cost of replacement garnished from her wages.

Richard decided that he was going to carry it back and determine who was responsible, not because he cared but because he felt an urge to ruin someone's life for no reason. He pulled at the device and then pulled again, and tried one angle and then another. Finally, he reached the neck (or the arm, or whatever metaphor we wish to use) of the machine, and this is when the needle tore into his forearm. He screamed, but there was no answer; he tried to pull away but the needle merely dug in further, sliding down the neck of the machine and dragging itself down his arm. Deeper into the flesh, deeper and deeper and deeper. His arm belonged to the needle now, and he realized it must intend to kill him, whatever it was, most likely as punishment for his unnatural love for Andrew.

Finally, the machine fell silent and the needle stopped moving, just sitting still in his arm as though it had gone to sleep. The desire to remove this horrible thing from his skin outweighed the terror of what would happen once he did, and he ripped his arm free to find these words inscribed on him:

WILL NOT CHOOSE WAR

He sat there in the dirt, looking at this tattoo. He was crying, not because of the pain, though the pain was considerable. The message was vague and had no meaning at all, and certainly had no special meaning for him, except that of course it did. He pushed dirt back onto the device and then returned to his room to lie down.

At supper, Richard spoke to Andrew only enough to make it clear that they weren't going to have any kind of fight over Andrew's recent distance. The boys took their meals together for the remainder of the summer, but in the balance of their time, they read in their own rooms.

Many years went by, and both Andrew and Richard found success. By their early thirties, they were respected journalists whose work was rumored to be read by the most important members of Parliament. The tattoo on Richard's forearm precluded any leisure activity that might have required him to bare his arms, and it certainly precluded marriage, a shame given that Richard had matured beyond the regrettable predilections of his adolescence and would have fully been prepared to be a man were the presence of a tattoo not certain to repel any woman worth having. But his social isolation left more time for work.

Richard and Andrew often dined together, and one occasion when they did so was shortly after the assassination of Franz Ferdinand. Richard had spent many hours over the past days alone in his flat, naked or close to it, staring at his tattoo. It had always seemed to mock him, but never more so than now. The idea that this tattoo contained any magical knowledge was patently absurd; it was clearly some kind of Gypsy trick. Looking now into Andrew's sharp yet gentle eyes, Richard thought that there was no clearer moral duty than to fight, even when fighting went against reason.

"Any serious man has to admit that there must be war," Richard said.

Andrew turned his gaze down and chewed his steak thoughtfully, and when he finished chewing, he wiped his mouth and spoke softly. "I don't believe that England should be party to any war that results from any of this."

Richard was shocked. "Why?"

"You'll have to read my column."

Richard tried to discern whether the reference to a "column" was some sort of double entendre, an invitation to return to school days. Such a double entendre seemed more likely than the one that Richard feared: that he would not learn of Andrew's thoughts until they were coming off on everyone else's hands.

"I know you too well," Richard said. "If you truly had any serious arguments, you would subject them to my scrutiny."

"Richard, however much you've always enjoyed arguing with me, I'm afraid I've never enjoyed arguing with you. Not even when we were boys."

The statement was presented so bluntly that Richard found himself, much to his own surprise, having to fight back tears. This fight, like the war, was one he would choose, his tattoo be damned. He told Andrew that his mental acuity had peaked at Eton, and that persuading a mob of idiotic, cowardly members of Parliament to behave as idiotic cowards could hardly be considered an impressive feat, should he manage to pull it off. He left with his eyes dry and his dignity, he was reasonably certain, intact.

Andrew remained at the table for some time, fighting back tears of his own. Surely his friend must have seen through that preposterous lie; arguing with Richard constituted one of the very few genuine pleasures of Andrew's life. And yet evading the conversation had been the only option. Richard would have had a very easy time dismantling any points Andrew could somehow manage to cobble together against the war, a war Andrew considered self-evidently necessary. But he was going to do everything he could to make a convincing case against the war, and everything he could was usually quite a lot. He certainly wasn't going to tell anyone the truth: that God had buried an instrument on his family's estate for Andrew to find, and, using that instrument, had written on his arm the instruction not to choose war.

There was another reason Andrew stayed at the table: he did not want to return home to Elizabeth, who would see through him.

Elizabeth was the only other person who knew about Andrew's tattoo. He disliked that she knew about it, or knew anything about him at all, though he did everything he could to forgive her for wasting her life on him. He had entered into the marriage in some-thing approaching good faith; they had gotten along very well, and he certainly enjoyed talking to her more than he had ever enjoyed talking to anyone who was not Richard, even if her opinions on Napoleon were fairly pedestrian. He thought he would find it rela-tively easy, when the time came, to show her the tattoo on his arm. On their wedding night, after they had arrived in their marital suite, she excused herself to use the washroom, and he began to unbutton his shirt. He hesitated and moved slowly, but he would have gotten his shirt off if she hadn't emerged from the washroom naked, throwing him off completely. He no longer felt equipped to take his shirt off at all, and when she moved to do this for him, he stopped her. He did manage to get his pants and underwear off and launch a credible assault at consummating their marriage, but the whole ordeal proved too much, and the night ended in failure. So did several succeeding nights, on each of which he took his pants off but kept his shirt on. Eventually, they stopped trying altogether. Elizabeth kept asking sweetly whether there was anything she could do, and he hated this so much that her sweetness seemed like an obscure threat.

This was not terribly far off. Though proudly still a virgin, she had been looking forward to sex for many years, with fantasies of the erotic bliss that awaited the only effective defense against the stirrings inside of her. She had always felt contempt for girls who were scared of their wedding nights, the ones who had to be instructed to lie back and think of England. And here she was, married, with nothing to do at night but lie back while Andrew talked of England. At long last she confronted him, saying she did not understand why he would not at the very least completely disrobe. After some grumbling he agreed to take off his shirt, warning her in advance of his disfigurement.

Elizabeth was puzzled, but she was also relieved. The marking was unsightly, perhaps, but not terribly so, and she could not understand why thus far he had chosen the shame of a sexless marriage over the shame of showing it to her. If it was true that he **WILL NOT CHOOSE WAR**, if he felt a commitment to pacifism so strong that he had once felt a need to display it to the whole world, or at least the tiny portion of the world that might see him without his shirt, then this made her very glad. Britain was always launching stupid and pointless wars, and she was happy to have a husband who might persuade the men who made the decisions not to send her future sons to die. But not to be on the side of war seemed to make him nervous, so it was her duty to calm him. She was attempting to do just that when he told her that he believed his tattoo was a direct message from God.

"I don't know what it means yet," Andrew said. "But whatever it means, this message is the most important part of my life."

Elizabeth's husband now displayed two qualities—impotence and insanity—that would each justify an annulment according to even the strictest standards. But Elizabeth found, perhaps oddly, that she loved him anyway, and she promptly kissed the tattoo on his forearm, lingering on and finding adorable the tiny mole in the

upper left-hand corner of the second *W*. When this did not immediately lead to further intimacies, she decided to give their sexual
difficulties the only thing she had: time. This did not prove enough.

That she would never have sex with Andrew became clear only
very slowly, and by the time it did, she had already given herself
over to becoming a novelist. Perhaps Andrew *was* on a mission
from God, even if that mission was merely to descend into a celi-
bate madness, and perhaps she had a mission of her own. Not having sex, she started to believe, would prove a major advantage for
her writing, as the erotic energy built up in her body would have to
find its way on to the page. Even more important was that one thing
she had, which she would now have more of. All the time she would
save by not being poked at until people started tunneling out of her,
people to whom she would be expected to devote all of her time to,
all that time now stretched out before her, and she could put it all
into her work.

After all, there was one more thing she had in addition to time:
language, the true love of her life, even if she loved language too
much to put it quite that way. Every morning she sat in her room
with pen and paper, putting sentences down. But the sentences did
not come out right, they did not express what she wanted them to
express, and she found it difficult to concentrate. It occurred to her
that perhaps she wasn't writing well because she wasn't getting
what she needed from her husband; this thought made her hate
Andrew, but it made her hate herself even more, since it meant that
she had already failed in her work and was looking for excuses.

At some point—perhaps because she was hoping to meet publishers, perhaps because she was looking for distraction—she had
become a hostess, apparently a prominent one, and before long this
was her only source of enjoyment in life. Though she rebuffed the
men who made insinuations to her—the words "for worse" had
been included for a reason in the promise she had made to God—

she nonetheless found these insinuations agreeable. She was frustrated that she could not seem to make the brilliance she summoned in conversation stick on the page, but, though it caused her pain to think explicitly in these terms, the adoration of her friends was worth much more than the veneration of hypothetical people who would read her hypothetical work only long after her decidedly nonhypothetical death.

All of this meant that Andrew was correct: his opposition to this imminent war made Elizabeth furious. Not that any good would come from this war—which looked, if anything, even more transparently pointless than most—but she could already see that the war was going to happen no matter what, and that all their friends would support it. Since Europe was going to be set on fire no matter what they did, they might as well choose the path that would not cost them all their friends. Since he had given her no sons to lose, Andrew owed her at least this much. But Andrew's mind was made up, and within a few months they had in fact lost all their friends, including even round-faced, pockmarked Richard. Mutual friends had hinted to Richard that he must change Andrew's mind or break off contact with him, and Richard, having brought himself to choose war once, simply could not do so again, and acquiesced to the general will. He felt guilty, but he need not have. No longer seeing Richard brought with it a certain kind of peace that Andrew had not known since childhood, a peace that he ascribed to defying the general and indeed correct consensus in favor of the error that was God's obscure plan for him.

Of course, the consensus changed, the war was almost universally deemed a catastrophe, and by the early 1920s, Andrew Blue was regarded as a prophet, invited to give lectures in the most prestigious halls and the most exclusive salons. Very often, men and women would stop him on the street, and tell him that England should have paid him heed when it had the chance, for if it had, then their sons would still be alive. In the years that followed, London pricked up its ears at his every utterance.

Over these same years, Richard found his reputation falling. His support for the war had not distinguished him from virtually any other journalist, almost all of whom had supported it as well, but most of whom did not have any pathological tendencies that might have caused them to remember this fact. Richard felt sheepish about expressing opinions after having been so wrong, and suspected he should be silent on questions of state; as a result, he was trounced in arguments and his prose read as pusillanimous and watery. As the twenties became the thirties, Richard also discovered that he had a strong physical resemblance to Adolf Hitler, an embarrassing fact that might have had any number of effects; the effect it did have was to make Richard feel all the more humiliated simply to exist. It seemed to Richard that Hitler should be stopped—in fact he *hated* Hitler—but he did not have the will to choose war against his friends by choosing war against this man, his hatred of whom was probably just an expression of his hatred of himself.

Andrew, for his part, was predisposed to admire Hitler. He thought that the Nazis were absolutely right about the Jews. Everything he had learned recently suggested that Jews had been responsible for the Great War. Someone needed to keep them in line.

But should they be kept in line by *this* man? Andrew found himself staring for long nighttime hours at newspaper clippings of Hitler's strange round face, which seemed to circle the Earth like an angry moon. As everyone remarked, Hitler looked a great deal like Richard, and Richard was so evil that he had tempted even a man as virtuous as Andrew toward unnatural acts. Andrew felt something intense for both men, and of many possible names for this feeling he chose "hatred."

It pained Andrew to advise any action that might benefit the Jews. Further, the message that he had received from God had been unambiguous in its directive that he not choose war. On the other hand, that message was now fading; the **NOT** in particular had grown so faint that it seemed possible God had erased it. Perhaps his tattoo now said **WILL CHOOSE WAR**. Andrew had to squint a bit to see the message this way—when he squinted another way it looked like **ILL HOO WA**—but of course any message from God could be deciphered only by labor, discipline, and faith.

The logic was clear: it must be war.

Elizabeth and Andrew did not discuss Hitler, or anything else— by this time they had essentially not spoken in years, except in the company of others, though they continued to live in the same house. When Elizabeth read Andrew's column calling for war— which deployed an elaborate metaphor of the importance of destroying monsters in adolescence, before they have reached adulthood—she considered taking a letter opener, finding him in his study, and slitting his throat. Their social position was better than it had ever been, and now he was once again endangering it. She tried appealing to his madness, telling him that he was on a mission from God and that he must fulfill it. But it was no use; he merely said that he had made up his mind, and that he had nothing to add to his column.

As soon as she left his study, Elizabeth resolved to write a memoir about the lunatic who had imprisoned her in his delusions, the lunatic who believed that God had issued a kind of pacifist Eleventh Commandment on his forearm, and who then decided to defy this commandment. For the first time in years, she locked herself in her study and began to write. But each sentence that sounded brilliant in her head sounded stiff and leaden as soon as her fingers hit the keys of her typewriter. The truth was that she no longer had any idea what good writing was. She had tried reading the newer writers, Joyce and Woolf and a few others, but the language was so strange that she could only conclude that no one had anything to say anymore and that these writers were going to extraordinary lengths to disguise this fact. Either that, or time and language had gotten away from her, just as everything else had.

That she never finished her memoir turned out for the best, for she was soon known as the wife of one of the most brilliant men in England, one of very few men who had been right about both wars. Everyone wanted to see them now. Andrew even seemed eager to entertain—rather than taking one drink with guests before retiring to his study, as he had always done in the past, Andrew now merrily chatted long after Elizabeth felt drowsy. In his twilight years, he considered it his duty to share his wisdom with the vigorous young men who sought it. When he thought about his own life, the fading tattoo played only the most minor of roles. It no longer seemed likely that the tattoo was a message from God; it seemed even less likely that the message had influenced his thinking on war, which, after all, had proven more sophisticated than anyone else's thinking and could not be distilled into a simple slogan. What had influenced his own thinking had been his own learning and insight, his own strength and independence of mind, his own—there was no point in denying it—genius.

One evening, while Andrew was being treated to dinner by a group of those vigorous young men and Elizabeth was alone, a visitor called. Elizabeth gasped when she opened the door to find Adolf Hitler, who, having somehow escaped from Berlin, had shaven his moustache and arrived at her threshold. She apologized immediately, mortified not to have recognized her husband's oldest friend, but even as she led him into the parlor, it was difficult not to see the man who had murdered millions. She squinted at him as sympathetically as possible, but he still looked pallid and hunted.

"Elizabeth," Richard said. "Did your husband ever mention playing some sort of prank on me when we were boys?"

Elizabeth responded, quite truthfully, that she had no idea what he was talking about.

"Did he bury some kind of unholy Gypsy device on the grounds of his estate, something that looked like a sewing machine, so that it would defile me and lead me into ruin?"

At this he moved to undo his cufflinks and push up his sleeve. She knew what she was going to see before she saw it. The tattoo was just as faded as her husband's, though with a liver spot serving as an ungrammatical period:

WILL NOT CHOOSE. WAR

"Why did he do this to me?" Richard asked. "How did he predict exactly what effect this would have on me, and how did he know which war would be worth fighting?"

This was a man who had suffered greatly. This was a man who deserved compassion. "Oh, Richard," she said. "You know the answer. He was smarter than you. That's all."

Richard broke into sobs, letting his forearm dangle like a useless penis.

"But you don't understand," he said. "Andrew and I had . . . something."

She was going to make him say it.

"We were in . . ." He drummed his fingers on his tattoo, which did not contain the word he was looking for.

"You were in . . ."

"I can't. I can't."

"Richard. You have been wrong about a great deal. So what? Plenty of men are wrong about a great deal. It's hardly some sort of deep secret that flooded your life with shame and drained it of joy." She had lost too much not to enjoy herself a little. "I'll tell Andrew you stopped by. My love to . . . oh, I'm sorry, you live alone."

After he was gone, she poured herself some Scotch. She wasn't sure what she had learned, exactly. Perhaps she had learned that her own misery could have been avoided, or that all men are governed by obscure longings and failings. Perhaps she had learned something about the absurdity of lengthy, agonized debates over war, since war is as natural as sex and, like sex, will be engaged in enthusiastically barring humiliating dysfunction, even if it is often regretted later. But of course she had always known all of this, and knowing it had not gotten her anywhere. Perhaps she had learned that if she had used this device, she too would have received the tattoo **WILL NOT CHOOSE WAR**, and that this is what linked her to these unhappy men. But really she had learned nothing other than that a perfectly good sewing machine had been wasted on the task of informing two men of the obvious fact that they were cowards.

CHAPTER

✦

4

Ismail, a faster reader than I, started complaining about the Wernher story before I had reached the third paragraph. He was particularly bothered by the obvious inconsistency of a German scientist inventing a machine that, by all accounts, wrote exclusively in English. My problem was more with the whole thing, which was transparently ridiculous. Also, no matter how much I hated the machine, I didn't particularly like the idea that my parents had been defaced by the Nazis.

The other chapter made Ismail far angrier. He had read many of Andrew Blue's essays, which he said were full of great intellectual clarity and even greater moral decency; *these* were the qualities that led to Blue being right about both wars. Merdula had no insight into Andrew Blue whatsoever.

"The only reason anybody reads Merdula's epiphany machine book," he said, "is because everybody loves *Only the Desert Is Not a Desert*. But now that I've read these two chapters, I'm wondering whether I was wrong about *Only the Desert*. It can't be that good if it was written by this idiot, whoever he is."

He said a lot more, but I wasn't really listening. The two chapters could not both be true—if the machine was invented by a Nazi, it was not discovered on a British estate at the turn of the twentieth century, and vice versa—which suggested to me that neither chapter was worth paying attention to. I was focused on the questions I wanted to ask Ms. Scarra when she returned, beginning with whether she had used the epiphany machine. I was pretty sure, though I could not be certain, that she was wearing a long-sleeved blouse that day. It was possible that she exclusively wore long-sleeved blouses; I had no idea, since even though I had paid great attention to her breasts, her eyes, her lips, her hair, her neck, her ass, I had never noticed her arms.

We waited in her classroom for forty-five minutes, but Ms. Scarra did not return, and eventually we were chased out by a janitor. By this point Ismail and I were engaged in a long conversation about what it meant to be right or wrong about history, devising many insights that seemed brilliant to us both at the time, and we continued the conversation as we left school. If Ismail had not invited me to come over to his house, everything might have been different for him. But he invited me and I accepted, and that's just the way things happened.

Ismail's mother worked at a pharmaceutical company in Armonk, so the house was empty. As soon as he reached the kitchen, he offered me some Entenmann's pound cake.

"Your mother likes that?" I asked. "My grandmother loves it."

"It's the blandest thing I've ever bitten into," he said. "But you have to offer something to guests, and this is all we have."

He sliced off a piece for me, and I wasn't finished chewing the first bite when I suddenly realized that it was in fact as bland as he said, and that I had convinced myself that I liked it because I wanted to make my grandmother happy, as she had invested so much in the idea that she provided me with food I craved. I felt annoyed with and constrained by my grandmother, and felt retroactively justified for having recently noticed her only when she accidentally kicked me off an online chatroom by picking up the phone. My father had been taking her to the hospital a lot over the past several months and I had hardly asked why, a fact that had made me feel guilty but that now struck me as a necessary distancing of myself from my grandmother. I couldn't spend my entire life pretending to like pound cake.

Or maybe I did like pound cake but didn't want to look unsophisticated in front of Ismail, and so was renouncing this mass-produced pleasure.

Ismail took a pen and notebook out of his pocket and jotted something down.

"What are you writing?"

"When I think something is funny or weird, I write it down."

"What was funny or weird just now?"

"You had this look on your face like deciding whether or not to eat a piece of pound cake was tearing you apart."

"Was that funny or weird?"

"Um, both?"

I didn't want to think about any of this, so I put the cake aside and suggested to Ismail that we play chess. As we did, he talked more about Andrew Blue. Every word that Merdula had written about Blue's homosexuality, insanity, and anti-Semitism was pure libel. That Ismail obviously disapproved of homosexuality made me feel morally superior to him, which itself made me happy, because his knowledge of Andrew Blue had made me feel intellectually inferior, as did the fact that within a few moves it was clear he was going to defeat me soundly at chess.

After Ismail won and suggested that we try for two out of three, then beat me again and suggested three out of five, I started to wonder whether in fact he was attracted to me, and was denying Andrew Blue's homosexuality in order to deny his own. And I wondered if I was attracted to him as well. But if either of us was attracted to the other, neither of us tried anything, even when I started going to his house nearly every day to do homework, listen to music, and watch *The X-Files*.

The Coexistence Club never met again after that afternoon with the manila envelopes—Ismail wrote to me in an email once that "our friendship kommenced after the krash of the koexistence klub." Ms. Scarra was out for a week after that day, and we had a substitute who visibly struggled to refrain from putting on an offensive accent when discussing Confucius. Then, all of a sudden, Ms. Scarra was back one morning. Before class, when I had a free period and was wandering the halls, she pulled me into the teachers' bathroom. I thought this was bizarre, of course, but I wasn't exactly unhappy about it, given that Ms. Scarra was the closest thing I had either to a sex object or a mother figure—or at any rate a mother figure of childbearing age—and with Ms. Scarra on top of a bathroom sink was one of the virginity-loss permutations I had imagined.

"Do you know what I'm about to show you?" she asked as she unbuttoned the sleeve of her blouse. I must have, and yet I remember being surprised when she rolled up her sleeve and held out her forearm to me as though it were a rack of lamb:

DOES NOT UNDERSTAND BOUNDARIES

"If it weren't for this tattoo," she said, "you would be in trouble right now. Do you understand?"

"No."

"If I hadn't gotten this tattoo, I would have been able to convince myself that I was capable of controlling myself around you. Now I know that I'm not. So I'm going to leave. I'm going to get in a car and drive away. Mr. Thompson will be your substitute for the rest of the year."

"Okay."

"Okay? It doesn't bother you that I'm leaving?"

Whatever my feelings, it was becoming clear to me that Ms. Scarra was crazy.

"I don't know," I said.

"You don't know. I guess I deserve that. The point is that I understand that I don't have boundaries with you. I only invited Ismail to be part of that stupid club because it would not have been appropriate to ask you to stay alone. And I would not understand any of that if I did not have this tattoo. But before I leave I have a question. What do you know about your mother?"

"She was lonely, gullible, and numb."

"What makes you say that?"

"Because people who join cults are lonely, gullible, and numb."

"Which you say because . . ."

"It just makes sense."

"You're a smart kid. Do you really think that's a persuasive argument? Why do you think that you think that people who join cults are lonely, gullible, and numb?"

"I'm going to be late for math."

"Late for math? I'm trying to teach you how to add two plus two. You say what you say about cults because that's what your father and your grandmother tell you to say. So what do you think that makes you?"

The answer, when it occurred to me, really did feel like a slap in the face. She tore off some brown paper towel and handed it to me for my tears.

"It's all right," she said. "Something you should always remember is that you should only feel shame before you feel shame. Once you feel shame, you know that you have to change. When you feel shame, you should really feel relief. You should say: 'Hurray! Now I know what I have to change.'"

"Yes, of course, I see that now," I said.

"'Yes, of course, I see that now'? Look at how eager you are to prove to me that you understand. Before you can prove that you understand, you have to actually understand. Say what you are. Say it."

"Lonely, gullible, and numb."

"Now say: 'Hurray! Now I know what I have to change.'"

I tried to, but instead I got caught in great, noisy sobs.

"Come on, Venter. We can't stay in this bathroom forever, however much I want to."

"Hurray!"

"Come on! Give it to me, Venter. Give it to me. Give it to yourself."

"Now I know what I have to change."

"And is that a good or a bad thing?"

"Hurray! Now I know what I have to change."

"Good! Good, Venter. I knew you could do this. I wish I could stay around and watch you use the machine and flourish, but I'd probably wind up ruining your life by having sex with you. So: good-bye!"

After she left, I ducked into a stall to continue crying. She was crazy, of course, but she had revealed something to me. Then again, I reminded myself, she had revealed something to me, but she was crazy. I kept on reminding myself that she was crazy, and eventually this crowded out the fact that she had revealed something to me. By the end of the day, I was more certain than ever that I would never use the epiphany machine.

CHAPTER

— · · ◆ · · —

5

For most of high school, Ismail and I were best friends, obsessed with the great things we would do as adults but also wanting to freeze time in a place when we could believe ourselves geniuses without having to prove it. Failure was something that might happen, but probably to other people, and death lay in a future so remote we would be long dead by the time it arrived. Once, he was driving us over the Tappan Zee Bridge when he noted that if he were a believer, now would be a time when he would have to pray. With the sunset drenching the Hudson in red, it wasn't hard to figure out where Mecca was, so he closed his eyes, took his hands off the wheel, and started to pray in that direction, letting the car swerve toward the next lane. Every car around us honked, and Ismail interrupted his praying to remark that it sounded like the call to prayer. I grabbed the wheel and straightened the car, cursing at him. Finally, he opened his eyes, took the wheel, and laughed. "Killing us both would be one way for me not to have to become a doctor." I was indescribably angry, but somehow I found myself laughing, too. The whole thing, I had to admit, had been a rush.

"Never forget," Ismail said, "that there's an infinitesimal chance that we are the first invincible people ever born, and that chance will be there until one of us dies."

Invincible is how we felt when we were acting, which we started to do together near the end of freshman year. I was delighted when I was cast as Jim, the romantic lead in *The Glass Menagerie*, and he was cast as the secondary Tom, at least until I figured out that the play was actually about Tom learning to name the lies he was surrounded with, and that Jim was just a sweet but clueless catalyst for the lies to fall apart. For a few days, it looked like we were both going to fall in love with a girl named Laura, who was playing Laura, but instead we both fell in love with a girl named Leah, who was playing Laura's mother, Amanda. Leah brought such intensity and commitment to a character who refused to admit the truth that she seemed the embodiment of truth itself. Obviously, it's impossible for me to definitively chart the evolution of my feelings and even harder for me to chart Ismail's, but I'm fairly certain that we thought she was the embodiment of truth before we thought she was the embodiment of beauty. In any case, it wasn't long before she was the only thing either of us thought or talked about. The unlikelihood of her actually dating either of us—she seemed exclusively interested in the lackadaisically predatory twenty-year-old guys who worked at the coffee place or the deli—was the only thing that stopped us from openly fighting over her, and led us instead to tacitly agree to just follow her around.

Our savage servility slid by in *Grease*, in which Leah played Sandy and we were stuck doing tech, since neither of us could sing. When Ismail was cast as the director in *A Chorus Line*, I was undeniably jealous, and I was also unnerved, because this—unseen, making judgments and rationing out fates from the back of the theater—was how I imagined Adam Lyons, the man who ran the epiphany machine, and it was also how I imagined my mother. I was stuck doing tech once again for the play, and Leah sang "Tits and Ass," changed by our drama teacher to "This and That." After rehearsals, the three of us would often hang out and smoke behind the auditorium, twenty minutes or so that I lived for and that seemed like the greatest pleasure imaginable, even if afterward I always hated myself for not making a move on Leah. Eventually, Leah started joining us at Ismail's house to watch *The X-Files*. We were also joined by Ismail's mother, a stern scientist who made us all laugh by identifying strongly with the skeptical Dana Scully, constantly insisting that the show would be much better if it "dropped all the alien nonsense" and were actually about Dana "doing the things Dana should be doing." Once, as we were walking to our separate cars complaining about the absence from that week's episode of the smoking man, who seemed to have some great secret knowledge that would explain the whole world, Leah turned to me and asked, very seriously: "Do you think his mom is worried about Ismail hooking up with you or with me?"

"I mean, I don't think she'd be happy with either one. She's cool and everything, but I think she's kind of conservative."

"She just wants him to be a doctor and doesn't want him to get distracted by us arty kids. Smart lady."

I drove home trying to figure out whether through thick layers of sarcasm Leah had paid me a compliment by calling me an arty kid.

CHAPTER

———··◆··———

6

Our junior year, the three of us took a humanities class. In April, our teacher, Mr. Sullivan, announced a unit on epiphanies in literature. He asked us to define "epiphany," and almost everyone in class looked to me for the answer. I was surprised to find that I couldn't quite put it into words.

"Maybe this will help," Mr. Sullivan said, passing out photocopies of a passage from James Joyce's *Stephen Hero*. I read the passage several times but couldn't figure out what it was supposed to say. It appeared to be saying that an epiphany was when you looked at a clock and saw that it was a clock. If an epiphany was realizing that a clock was a clock, it didn't seem like you needed such a fancy name for it. On the other hand, this was Joyce, who I knew could be difficult to understand, so perhaps the fault was in me, a possibility I didn't particularly like to entertain.

"This passage," I said. "It's brilliant."

"Really?" Ismail asked. "It sounds to me like it's just saying that a clock is a clock."

"Isn't it saying that a clock can have an epiphany?"

"Yeah, I thought that, too, for a second, but I think it's saying a clock is a clock."

Immediately I felt that Ismail was right, and I felt foolish and I wanted to agree, but I feared losing face in front of the class. "Only on the most superficial level."

"Oh, fuck you, Venter," Ismail said.

This made the class laugh—including, infuriatingly, Leah—and earned only the mildest rebuke from a clearly amused Mr. Sullivan. I felt angry and ashamed, but most of all I felt that I had been justly rebuked: I had been wrong and Ismail had been right to point out that I had been wrong. When still nobody in class had an answer for what an epiphany was, Mr. Sullivan asked us to do an in-class writing exercise explaining the concept.

"Sometimes your pen knows what your tongue doesn't," he said.

I wrote two pages about how, even when we think we know what something is, we don't really *know* it. I also made a reference to Krzysztof Kieślowski, whose films about identity and connection Ismail and I had recently rented at the Blockbuster where he was working a part-time job, sending most of the money he earned to charities that supported Muslims afflicted by war in Bosnia and Chechnya. (He had been inspired to do so, he said, by Andrew Blue's stirring essays exhorting his readers to fight fascism in all its forms.) I was the first to volunteer to read aloud to the class, which met what I read with silence occasionally interrupted by sighs. Even Mr. Sullivan was clearly not paying attention for the last several paragraphs.

Nobody else volunteered, so Mr. Sullivan called on Ismail, who said that he did not read incomplete thoughts out loud. Mr. Sullivan was annoyed but didn't argue. He was about to move on when Leah volunteered.

She read a moving account of her part-time job at a pet store, a job she had taken because she needed the money and loved animals, but which required her to try not to realize that all the animals came from abusive puppy mills. When two Yorkies were nipping at and rolling over each other, pretty much the cutest possible sight, she was not supposed to think of their mother, who was probably poked to produce yet another round of these adorable creatures. So all Leah could do was look at the clock and wait for the shift to be over. That was the epiphany that Joyce was referring to, she said, that was why he had chosen to illustrate epiphanies with a clock: life was waiting for life to be over.

This ending was unquestionably teenager-maudlin, but Mr. Sullivan loved it anyway, and so did I, despite my anger that someone had done this assignment better than I had. Ismail pulled out his notebook and wrote furiously; I pulled out the mostly empty notebook I had bought in imitation of Ismail, but wrote nothing, since I was too embarrassed to admit on paper that I had been completely bested and couldn't think of anything else to say. As we were leaving class, Ismail and I each tried to elbow the other out to tell Leah what a great job she had done.

"Oh, that?" she said. "I don't even care about those puppies. I just figured Mr. Sullivan would like it."

This made me even madder, and also more in love with Leah, since she had now outmatched me in the two things at which every teenager wants to excel: caring and not caring.

I went to Ismail's house with a new sense of purpose, determined to use my family history to understand epiphanies on the deepest possible level. Our assignment was to read two stories in *Dubliners*—"Araby" and "The Dead"—and then write something in response. "Araby" left both Ismail and me a little cold—we both thought that the kid was being overly dramatic about buying something for a girl at a fair, the racial connotations of the word "Araby" made me uncomfortable in Ismail's presence, and overall we just did not see how that story might relate to anything we found intellectually engaging. But "The Dead" was something else. Neither of us interrupted the other with commentary or with thoughts on something unrelated, as we usually did. Neither of us wanted to talk, particularly as we read the last few pages, as Gabriel Conroy lustfully scoops his wife, Gretta, up from the party, hoping for a rare night of middle-aged sex, but instead discovers that his wife has essentially spent their marriage pining for Michael Furey, a boy who had loved her and who had died when they were seventeen, having ignored his illness to brave the rain and see her. After we both finished, we found that neither of us *could* talk.

"I'm glad Mr. Sullivan made us read this," said Ismail, finally. After a few minutes of silence, I simply stood up and all but ran to my car. As soon as I was in my car and driving, and certain that no one could hear me, I shouted out loud: "DEATHBED! DEATHBED! DEATHBED!"

I made a promise to myself to whisper this underneath my breath every moment for the rest of my life.

The bed I was thinking of was not really my deathbed. It's not that I thought I was immortal, exactly. I knew that swerving into the other lane would kill me, and the prospect of dying in a car crash held the same glamor—or maybe just the same safe impossibility—for me that it held for Ismail. But the bed I was thinking of was my present one, which was so empty that it felt—in wordplay I was so impressed with that I pulled over so I could jot it down in my notebook—"like the grave."

I thought about driving to Leah's house, kissing her, and telling her I loved her, but I wasn't quite seventeen enough to do that.

Instead I went home and—in a fit of inspiration I still struggle to replicate—stayed up all night writing. Ismail, Leah, and I had recently added *Buffy the Vampire Slayer* to our TV-viewing regimen, and I rewrote "The Dead" to make Lily, Gabriel's aunts' servant, into a Buffy-like vampire slayer on a mission to kill Michael Furey, in my version a vampire who is attempting to kill Gabriel Conroy and reclaim his lost-love Gretta. To the story's first sentence, "Lily, the caretaker's daughter, was literally run off her feet," I added the phrase "by vampires." There was a piquant new meaning when a harried Lily exclaims, "The men that is now is only all palaver and what they can get out of you." Lily and Michael have their final battle in the graveyard outside the Conroys' hotel room, and Lily puts the stake through Michael's heart as Gabriel looks out the window contemplating disappointment and death; and though Gabriel does not see Michael, Michael sees Gabriel and feels an instant of kinship as he draws his last immortal breath. Naturally, I called the story "The Undead."

I volunteered to read an excerpt aloud in class the next day and Mr. Sullivan loved it. More important, Leah loved it, too, so much so that she followed me out the door of class to tell me how much she loved it. Ismail followed close behind, saying that I had missed the point of both *Buffy* and "The Dead."

"Buffy isn't afraid of sex," Ismail said. "Whereas Lily clearly is. Michael Furey didn't show up at Gretta's house in the middle of the night because he was in love with her—it was a booty call that went bad. And Gretta *ages*. If Michael Furey were a vampire, he'd be looking to bite some young hot flesh. Like Leah's." He tried to pinch Leah's neck, but she batted him away.

"That's a cynical way of looking at it," I said.

"She was worth dying for *in her youth*. Now she looks old. Joyce even says so himself." He dug in his bag for his underlined copy, knocking into a couple of people who were hurrying to class. "Sorry, sorry. Here. 'He did not like to say even to himself that her face was no longer beautiful, but he knew that it was no longer the face for which Michael Furey had braved death.'"

"Right," Leah said. "*Gabriel* is thinking that. Arrogant, full-of-himself Gabriel is the one who sees his wife as no longer beautiful. Hot vampire Michael would be happy to feast on Gretta, just like Venter says."

Ismail sputtered. I, of course, was enjoying this. "You'd rather believe pretty things than the truth," he said, finally.

"You don't know things anywhere," she said, quoting her character in *The Glass Menagerie*. "You live in a dream; you manufacture illusions." She batted her eyes at Ismail in the mockingly flirtatious way she had that I had been in love with for most of high school, which is to say most of my sexual life.

"One day you'll see the world for how it is," he said, before disappearing into a classroom. When he was gone, she rolled her eyes and asked me if I could believe him. Then she said something I definitely could not believe:

"Will you take me to use the epiphany machine?"

"Sorry?"

"I know both of your parents used it. I read Steven Merdula's book. It's really not his best work, nowhere near as good as *Only the Desert Is Not a Desert*, but it still made me curious about the machine. Also, I've been reading a lot about John Lennon's experience with it. I want to use it. Will you take me?"

"Well, I, um . . ."

"I can't make it this weekend," she said. "Take me next weekend."

"Okay."

"Great. It's a date." She kissed me on the cheek and walked away.

By the time I got home and was pulling into my garage, I was convinced I had a girlfriend. When I heard my father bounding down the steps—he was not usually home at this time—the first thought that crossed my mind was that he was coming to congratulate me on my upcoming date with Leah.

"We're getting you a cell phone," he said with exasperation, as though he had been arguing for years that I should get a cell phone, which in the late nineties were still rare.

"Move over," he said. "I'll drive."

"Dad, what's the matter?"

"Your grandmother's in the hospital. They're putting her on palliative care."

"What? I thought she was just a little sick."

"Yeah, well, she's a little more than a little sick." He shooed me into the passenger seat, and I obeyed.

"Why didn't you tell me how sick she was?"

He was pulling out of the driveway now. "She's been sick for years. If you wanted to know, you would have known."

"That's not true," I said, "and you're an asshole." What I was actually thinking was that it was true and that I was an asshole. I had noticed that my grandmother was sick and had paid no attention. I had barely even asked what was wrong with her.

"You've never had much talent for paying attention to the world around you," my father said.

For a man who often seemed hardly to think about me, my father had a way of knowing exactly what I was thinking at any given moment.

We said very little for the rest of the car trip, and even less as we walked through the halls of the hospital. He led me to my grandmother's room, where a doctor who was just leaving greeted us and told us that she was doing much better.

"We're going to keep her for a couple days," he said. "Hopefully, you'll be able to bring her home on Monday."

My father thanked him, and for a moment seemed to collapse with relief.

"It would have been impossible to raise you without her," he said to me.

We sat together silently as she slept until we both felt awkward, and he got up to take a walk around the hospital, leaving me alone with her. After a few minutes, she roused from her sleep.

"Nick," she said.

"I'm Venter, Grandma."

"I know who you are. I know your stupid hippie name. Nick is the man I should have spent the last years of my life with, rather than taking care of the son my daughter abandoned after giving him a stupid hippie name."

"Grandma, I know you're suffering. I know you don't mean the things you're saying."

"This is the first time since I married your grandfather that I've said what I meant. And you're going to listen to me."

NAME: Theresa Rose Schuldenfrei

DATE OF BIRTH: 11/25/1915

DATE OF EPIPHANY MACHINE USE: N/A

DATE OF INTERVIEW BY VENTER LOWOOD: 04/24/1998

My own mother died in 1934, before I had turned nineteen. She had never been much of a mother to me—during Prohibition she spent all night at speakeasies, supposedly working as a waitress, but I think my father knew that she went for the men. Because of the Depression, I had long since dropped out of high school and already had a job cleaning houses, a job I was lucky to get. I had saved up enough money to get my own place with a few other girls, but my father told me that I couldn't move out, because now that my mother was dead I had to stay home and take care of him. He wasn't completely wrong; he probably would have starved to death staring at the stove before he figured out how to light it. Totally helpless, just like you and your father will be now without me. And I thought, well, if he can't take care of himself, that means I have to take care of him. I also took care of my older brother, Harry, who spent all day at the gym and called himself a "bodybuilder" to cover up the fact that he was an unemployed bum.

Being so busy gave me an excuse for why I wasn't dating, but deep down I was certain that I wasn't dating because I was ugly. Bucktoothed and fat. There was a boy named Nick I chatted with a little whenever I would see him working at the grocery store, and he took me out a couple of times, by which I mean he walked with me around the block while we surreptitiously nibbled on whatever candy he could swipe without his boss noticing. Once we were sitting on a stoop and he wiped some chocolate from my mouth and kissed me. It was heaven, honestly. Then one day he wasn't in the grocery store, and I stopped hearing from him. He was totally gone. I was sad, very sad, but I couldn't spend days crying because of a breakup, unlike kids today—and unlike my brother Harry then. Every time things didn't work out with a sweetheart, Harry would spend days crying in bed while I brought him soup. Me, I just got back to work. Years went by like that, until my father got remarried and his new wife started treating me like a servant. By then, I had spent everything I'd saved on Harry and my father, and I couldn't afford my own place anymore. So I had to live with them, and now I was breadwinner, housekeeper, and cook for three people rather than two. When Harry finally did get married, he told me I wasn't allowed to be in the wedding party because I was too ugly. He actually said those words to me. I showed up to the wedding in a black dress, got drunk very quickly, and when I gave a toast, I said: "I give this marriage six months!" Turns out I underestimated the marriage. It lasted eight months. Joke was on me, though, because he moved back in, totally dependent on me again until the war started and he got drafted.

The war was the best thing that ever happened to me. Not only did it get Harry out of the house; it opened up a job for me on the assembly line of a radio factory. The girls on the line could tell I was smart and tough, so they made me union representative. I went down to Washington to negotiate a better contract. The night before the meeting the men took me out drinking, probably thinking they could take advantage of me in more ways than one. Well, I drank *them* under the table, and the next day they were hungover, and I came back to my girls with a very good contract. Plus, I loved the work that we did, I loved seeing the radios come together, one after the other. And I made enough money to move out and get away from my father and his wife. I wanted the war to go on forever so the men would never come back.

Of course, the war ended, and with it any hope I had of rising to a top union position. I could have kept working, maybe. Could have been one of the first career girls. Instead, I decided to listen to Ellen.

The conversation that I never should have had with Ellen took place at the same grocery store where I had met Nick all those years earlier. Ellen, who was fourteen at the time, told me that she needed a mother, so I should marry her father. I knew the family from around the neighborhood; I'd known her father since we were children. Her mother was one of those people who's always making huge swerves in life, trying to get away from themselves. First she had gotten engaged to Ellen's father; then she broke it off to become a nun; then she dropped out of her training to marry Ellen's father after all; then after Ellen was born she left them both to run away with a neighbor. Ellen's father, William, had been a single father and was supposed to get a draft deferment, but the draft board had no idea what to do with single fathers, so after fighting with them he just gave in and enlisted in the Navy, leaving Ellen to bounce around between aunts and cousins for the rest of the war. Now her father was back and she wanted a mother and a home, so she invited me to dinner that night.

To my surprise I said yes to dinner. William didn't know what his daughter was up to, but I think he was happy for adult female company, and we had always gotten along well. He cooked sauerbraten; a man who cooked anything was amazing and wonderful to me. We ate and laughed until late that night, and then around ten or so Ellen said she had some homework to finish before bed, so it was time for her father and me to go ahead and get engaged. Her father looked at me and said that he'd be honored to have the most beautiful woman in Ridgewood, no matter how strange their engagement was. I said yes. Okay? I said yes.

Three months later we were married; I got pregnant on our honeymoon. I think Rose was two before it became obvious that William would always be a very heavy drinker. The sauerbraten was never repeated. He hardly even ate the sauerbraten I made. He went to work, he went to the bar, he came home only to pass out. Ellen gave me a little help with Rose, but she met a boy—an army boy—and got married when she was nineteen. They moved around various army bases in the South, and I practically never saw her again. She was the whole reason I married your grandfather, and I practically never saw her after she was nineteen. Eventually she even took her own mother in and cared for her in her old age. That really made me mad.

Anyway, I did my best to raise your mother, even though she was a malingerer who pretended to be sick all the time. Not that that was her fault, exactly; the nuns told her that her father and I were going to Hell because he had gotten remarried after a divorce. She was smart and preferred to read books on her own rather than listen to ignorant people tell her horrible things. But what they said got to her anyway. She admitted to me once that she prayed for her father to die so I could go to confession and be saved. I slapped her and tried to hide that it made me cry to learn how much she loved me. I did try to keep from her that her father was a drunk, but I'm not a magician.

Around that time, I saw Nick again, back in that same grocery store. He asked why I had never returned his phone calls. What phone calls, I asked. Apparently, he had left abruptly when we were teenagers because of a sick relative in California, and he had called a couple of times because he wanted me to go with him. Turns out Harry hadn't given me the messages, since he didn't want me to get married and stop supporting him and my father. I was never going to speak to Harry again, that was for sure. Nick asked me to go away with him now, and it was the most wonderful thing anyone had ever asked me. Then he said I would have to leave my daughter behind, because he didn't want to take care of another man's child. I decided on the spot to say "yes," but when I opened my mouth, the word that came out was "no"—I wasn't going to abandon Rose. This time I cried for about two days.

William's drinking only got worse, and he kept on getting demoted at work, so I had to make do with less and less money. Being a housewife is a lot like running a business whose finances you have no control over. Rose offered to get a job when she was fourteen, but I wanted her to devote herself to her schoolwork and to all those books she read. She still planned to be a secretary, like every other girl she knew, but she had one teacher who told her that she was smart enough be a lawyer, a doctor, a writer, an architect, whatever she wanted. She came home that night and told me she was going to be a lawyer. It annoyed me that all the encouragement I had ever given her had had no effect and she just listened to a teacher, a man, but that's the way it was. Eventually, she went to college, using the small inheritance I received from my father when he died. *Before* he died, by the way, I had spent a couple years essentially as his nurse, since his second wife had died long ago. I also had to referee his constant arguments with Harry, who had lost his job and was once again living at home, and whom I now saw all the time despite my promise never to speak to him again. And believe me, every single time I saw Harry, I saw the life with Nick that he had deprived me of. Then Harry got cancer, and I felt guilty for hating him, and he and your great-grandfather died within weeks of each other. All the time that I spent caring for the two of them as they died made my relationship with my husband even worse, if that was possible. By now, he was drunk and angry whenever he wasn't sleeping.

I decided to divorce my husband the summer after Rose graduated from college, but he died before I could do that. That was my first thought when I heard that he had had a heart attack in the middle of the street: "Damn it, now I can't divorce him." My second thought was that now there would be no income at all.

Rose got a job as a paralegal, eventually going to law school at night. She started to resent me very quickly, annoyed that she had to spend her youth supporting her mother; she denied it, but it was easy to see. I was no longer employable, and the alternative to living off of her was living on cat-food casserole. Then one day she comes home and shows me that tattoo on her arm.

ABANDONS WHAT MATTERS MOST

When I saw it I burst into tears, because I knew that God had meant it for *me*, not her. The daughter for whom I had abandoned everything that mattered most had obviously wasted all the money I had spent on her college tuition, because she was still stupid enough to join this wacko cult run by an obvious liar.

I called Nick to see whether he would still have me, but by this point, he had a wife and children of his own. Between that and the fact that it was too late to have a career, there was no question of my getting back what was most important. So I continued to be supported, first by your mother, who dropped out of law school and quit her paralegal job to become assistant cult leader, and then by your father, who eventually went to law school and, unlike your mother, actually finished. And eventually your mother and father left the cult, though they were still sufficiently influenced by it to give you your stupid name. I think they thought you were the ventilation that let their spirit free or something.

Shortly after you were born, Rose asked me if I would take care of you for a few hours a day, so that she could get some work done. I had no idea what kind of work she was talking about, and I don't think she did either. I said absolutely not. I was done caring for other people. Then, the night before we were going to throw a little party for your first birthday, she came to me in tears, saying that she had abandoned what was most important to her in order to take care of someone. Yes, that would be you, buckaroo. I thought she meant that the most important thing to her was the epiphany machine, which made me want to throw her out of the house her husband was paying for me to live in. But Rose said no, what was most important to her was not the epiphany machine. She didn't know what was most important to her; she still needed to find out what it was.

People of my generation laugh at talk like this, but I thought about how much I regretted leaving the radio factory, and I told her that she had to live a life that fulfilled her, even if that meant leaving you to cry in your crib. I didn't mean that literally. I meant that she should stay up a little later at night to work on whatever she wanted to work on, and that if you started to cry, she should just ignore you. I certainly didn't expect her to leave a note the next morning essentially saying: "Good-bye forever, I hope Venter grows up okay!" I felt so guilty that I threw myself into caring for you, even though you have no sense of gratitude and don't seem to notice me or anything else.

That's why, Venter, my dying wish is that you use the epiphany machine. You have to learn who you are before it's too late. The big mistakes
people keep making in life—the pattern is so obvious to everyone except
the people themselves.

Now, please—get out of my sight. Don't make me die while I'm taking
care of you. I'm throwing you to Lyons.

CHAPTER

—— · · ✦ · · ——

7

When she spoke, my grandmother's breathing was labored, so her sentences were shorter than the ones I've written above. And I wasn't taking notes, of course; the only thing I wrote down was Adam Lyons's address, which she gave to me. Also, I've fleshed out what she said with bits and pieces that she'd told me over the years. And I've made some things up. But I think that you get that strangest of things: the gist.

I had little to say in response, and said none of what I did have to say. I just looked into her eyes, which were asking me what I was going to do, and then I turned around and headed through the hallways and elevators that seemed designed to lead you to the suffering of people irrelevant to you. Eventually, confused and lost as I was, I found my way to the parking lot and my father's car, which I drove to the train station. There were some people I recognized on the platform, but fortunately they didn't see me, or didn't want to talk to me any more than I wanted to talk to them.

It was close to nine when I arrived at Adam Lyons's apartment and rang the unmarked buzzer. I realized as I did so that it was possible, even probable, that the address had changed in the last several decades, or that my grandmother had remembered it wrong. Almost immediately a gruff voice said, "Hello."

"Hello, I'm here to see Adam Lyons."

The buzzer sounded and the door opened when I pulled it. Two short men in business suits were drunkenly walking down the stairs, one leaning on the other.

"I'm not **DEPENDENT ON THE OPINION OF OTHERS**," said the one doing the leaning. "Right?"

What a sad and pathetic man.

Almost as soon as I started to climb the stairs, I could hear music—*Magical Mystery Tour*—and I could smell pot. Thoughts of my grandmother and even of the machine fell away, and my head danced with the idea that I had found a slice of the secret and therefore the authentic Bohemian New York I had been dreaming of gaining admittance to since the first time I'd listened to *Rent* on CD.

The door to apartment 7 was opened a crack by a muscular guy in his mid-forties who looked like the bouncer he seemed to be, or maybe seemed to have been ten or twenty years earlier. On his forearm was written **DOES NOT STAND GROUND**. "Password, please," he said.

"Password?"

"Anyone unaccompanied by an epiphany alum is required to know the password."

"I'm not here to use the machine," I said, though all I had been thinking about on the train was using the machine. "I'm here to speak to Adam Lyons."

"Adam Lyons does not speak to those who have already decided not to use the machine, though he wishes you well in your decision. There is no point in opening a door to a closed mind."

I thought about pushing my way through, based mostly on a hope that he would indeed not stand his ground. But he was awfully muscular. Plus, for me to believe that he did not stand his ground might be an admission of sorts that I believed in the machine. Plus, he was awfully muscular.

"Maybe I'll use the machine after speaking to Adam Lyons," I said.

"Very well. The line is right behind me."

I couldn't see very far into the apartment, but nonetheless I could see that the line to use the machine was long.

"It's Friday night," I said. "Why are so many people here?"

"On Friday nights, people either distract themselves from the serious questions about their lives, or they decide not to distract themselves."

"And which one of those is drunkenly getting a tattoo?"

"If Adam Lyons's guests just wanted tattoos, they could find more aesthetically pleasing ones elsewhere."

"Fine. Look. I'm just here to ask Adam Lyons some questions about my mother. Her own mother is dying and I would like to find her so that they can reconcile." I hadn't known that that was why I was there until I said it out loud, but it sounded reasonable, even noble, certainly the reason I *should* have come.

"So you're not here to use the machine."

"I'll make up my mind later."

"Why would Adam Lyons know where your mother is?"

"She used the machine and then went to work for him. Then she abandoned me."

"Your behavior does not flood me with confidence that you're going to wait in line."

"My grandmother is dying, I would like her to see my mother before she dies, Adam Lyons may be able to help me find her, and I do not want to wait in line."

People waiting in line now looked back at me and then quickly turned their heads forward, as though I were the poorly adjusted one.

"Why do you think you use such hostile language?"

"Because you won't let me in."

"I'm sorry, but I never said anything like that. I merely asked you to wait in line like everyone else."

"I'm not like everyone else."

"Why not?"

"Because I'm looking for my mother."

"And you consider this unusual?"

"I consider it different from being a loser who would actually pay for a tattoo saying that he doesn't stand his ground. I consider it different from being a loser who *would actually hold that tattoo up* to people when he's getting in their way."

I tried to push through, but he blocked me without ruffling a single salt or pepper hair.

"So you're saying that you're not a loser?"

I straightened my shoulders, since I had read somewhere that you should keep your shoulders straight in a confrontation. "That's exactly what I'm saying."

"And you want to cut in front of all these people whom you consider losers. Are you sure you want to cut the line because you think you're better than everyone, and not because you think you're worse?"

"All right, George," said the gruff voice I had heard on the intercom. "That's enough." A heavy man with close-cropped, mostly white hair and a close-cropped, mostly white beard—as well as unruly and completely white chest hair sprouting from the plaid short-sleeved shirt he had buttoned no more than halfway up his torso—appeared from around a bookcase. He smiled, showing a missing tooth. "You've made us sound like a cult," he told George, "which you want to watch out for. That thing about open doors and closed minds was over the top. And what the hell are you talking about, password? There's no password."

It annoyed me that I hadn't noticed until just now that everyone kept on looking off to the side, obviously at the man whom I had come here to see.

"But I need to learn to be firm," George said. "Otherwise I'll never be able to say no to my son, and I'll keep letting him lie on the sofa playing video games all day."

"And it's good that you stood your ground with this kid, a decent stand-in for Ian, though you should remember that Ian has a considerably stronger will. Ian won't tolerate the cult stuff; you'll have to win him over with the force and plausibility of the dark portrait you'll paint of the future he has in store if he keeps doing nothing but playing video games."

"I should be a better father already. I should already know how to stand my ground."

"Does it sound to you like you're doing justice to your epiphany? Go home and . . ."

I wedged myself between them. "Adam Lyons, my name is Venter Lowood. I'm the son of Isaac Lowood and Rose Schuldenfrei."

"I know who you are, Venter. I could tell from your voice when you buzzed up; you sound just like your father, who also had a tendency to interrupt important conversations."

"I need to talk to you now."

"You've managed to make it seventeen years without doing the due diligence of coming to see me. You can wait a few more minutes."

"My grandmother is dying and I need to find my mother."

"It can't be news to you that your grandmother is mortal. Your sudden urgency is hypocritical." He turned the hairy back of his neck to me; if I had a razor I would have cut off the hair and the neck. "Now, George. Practice saying no to your son. Go upstairs, and if he's playing a video game, suggest that the two of you sit on a sofa together, each with your own book, and read."

"I hate reading."

"Good! Then stop reading your epiphany over and over again as though it's eventually going to say something different. Put on workout clothes and go for a late-night jog with your son through the Upper East Side. Run down through the Lower East Side, and across the Williamsburg Bridge. Run all night and come back at dawn. You'll be shocked at the way you see the city, and each other, afresh."

"But then what am I going to do tomorrow?"

"What were you going to do tomorrow?"

"Work on remodeling my kitchen while Ian plays video games."

"And what are you going to do now?"

"Ian likes video games. He showed me an article with convincing evidence that playing video games is beneficial to the mind. I should encourage that kind of active approach to making a case for himself and what he wants to do."

Some people in line snickered at this.

"Hey!" Adam yelled inside to the crowd. "This is where you will all be after using the machine, if and only if you're as committed to change as George is. I know you are all frustrated that I am observing George rather than attending to you, but you would all do well to practice patience. If you think you're frustrated now, just wait until after you've gotten your tattoo and you try to improve your life. You think you just get the tattoo and you're different?"

The crowd was quiet.

"George! Sorry we keep getting interrupted. Just keep trying to be honest with yourself about your tattoo. One common mistake my guests make is to assume that whatever is on their arm is *necessarily* what they need to change. Sometimes the tattoo points you in the direction of what you most resent about yourself and think you *should* change, but is in fact the best part of you. Maybe what your son needs is for you not to stand your ground. I certainly don't know that. I don't know anything. The machine doesn't know anything. Only you know. Your tattoo is there to help you know what you know."

George started weeping with the force of something having been settled or released, even though, as far as I could tell, nothing had been settled or released. He gave Adam a deep hug, and then took slow and weepy steps up the staircase. Adam finally turned his attention to me by putting his dirty fingers over my lips until he heard George's door close.

"Venter Lowood," Adam whispered finally, hugging me tightly with his tattooed arm. "Sorry, George is my new superintendent, so it makes my life a lot easier to keep him on board with what I do. Your mother was great with the super back in her day. I used to tell her that she was super with the super, and she even forgave me for that pun. Quite a woman, your mother. I don't think I understood before she came to work for me that the epiphany machine really does make everyone's, absolutely everyone's, lives better, regardless of whether they've even heard of me. The ripple effect, you should read about it. God, I miss that woman. Not as much as you do, of course, although maybe I miss her much more, since unlike you I actually knew her."

There was some grumbling from the line.

"Oh, pipe down!" he called inside. "You'll get your tattoos in a minute. Ignorance is bliss, so enjoy it while you can. How much time does your grandmother have, Venter?"

"Probably a few days. Maybe a week or two." The doctor had seemed to think she was going to be fine, but I was not convinced I was lying.

"I would do anything to talk to your mother once in a while. At the very least I'd like to have some idea of what she's doing. But I have no idea where she is."

"There must be something you can tell me. You were her confidant, or her confessor, or her boss, or whatever."

He took a step into his apartment, and when I followed, he put his hand up to stop me. "You know, I caught a glimpse of you when you were a baby," he said. "It was after your parents told me to go stick my dick in my own machine. Your mother was pushing you in a stroller through Central Park, and I happened to see her and say hello, and then I leaned down to get a look at you. She pivoted you around and started running, furiously but not very fast, like your stroller was a wheelbarrow and you were a bag full of gold coins she had stolen. 'Never come after him,' she called behind her. I responded that I would never, under any circumstances, come after you."

"Let me in," I said.

He lowered his hands and stepped aside. I looked at the people in line, their hungry and worried faces and their waiting forearms. I looked at Adam's tattoo and thought of several interpretations of **FIRST MAN TO LIE ON**. Then I thought of several more. Then I entered his apartment.

CHAPTER

——— · · ◆ · · ———

8

Adam sent away most of the people waiting in line, telling them to come back later or not at all.

Even after the last of them had filed out, I didn't get to see Adam right away; he agreed to see those who had been waiting in line for ninety minutes or more. So I picked up a copy of the pamphlet "Things to Consider Before Using the Epiphany Machine" from the bar and sat down to read it on a stool in a corner of the apartment that served as a waiting area. After I read it I put it down and picked up a book, but my head was too full to read a book, so I put the book down and read the pamphlet again, and then again. The pamphlet had been only lightly revised since the seventies version I included at the beginning, but two differences were significant. The entry on Rebecca Hart now referred to Rebecca Harts, plural, and the entry on sharing epiphanies now read as follows:

11. Our position has not shifted: under NO CIRCUMSTANCES will epiphanies be shared with law enforcement.

Adam had to nudge me awake when he was finished with the night's final epiphany. As soon as I had roused, this last customer kept me awake by saying: "This is not true! This is just not true. **PLAYS MARTYR TO**

EVADE RESPONSIBILITY! What does that even mean? It's so general that it doesn't mean anything at all! I would never have come here if I wasn't so devoted to you, Amy!"

"Let's just go," said the woman I assumed was Amy.

"See what I did to try to become a better husband? Defaced myself. Or disarmed myself, or something."

"Okay, John."

John continued berating Amy as they walked out the door. Once they were gone, Adam lit a joint, then looked at me and chuckled.

"There's no way his tattoo could be that accurate unless you were guiding the machine," I said.

"Except in the unlikely event that I'm telling the truth." He offered me the joint, but I declined. The apartment felt very empty, with almost no sound save for a faint whirring that I thought might be the machine but was just the air conditioner.

"So what other steps have you taken to find your mother?" he asked.

"None. My father and grandmother didn't want me to find her. My grandmother *really* didn't want me to find her."

"But she does now."

"I don't know. I don't think so, actually? But family members are supposed to reconcile when one of them is dying, right?"

"Supposed to? According to whom?"

"I don't know. People."

"And why do these people say that family members are *supposed to* reconcile before one of them dies?"

"So that they can die at peace."

This was the first time that Adam gave me one of his wild-eyed that's-the-stupidest-fucking-thing-I've-ever-heard shrugs. The Adam Shrug. "You think that seeing her daughter now is going to help your grandmother die at peace? After Rose forced her to raise you?"

"She did not force her to raise me. Wait, how do you know she forced her to raise me?"

Adam grinned. "I ran into your dad once. Manhattan is a small town."

I looked at his yellow teeth, at the chipping paint all over the room. The door to another room was open, and through it I could see a very unassuming-looking bed, as well as a nightstand on which there was nothing but an alarm clock and a book. A TV and a computer monitor appeared to be propped up on the boxes they came in. If this were an underling's quarters, that might have made sense. But it was clearly where Adam slept. This did not look like the apartment of a man who had gotten rich peddling lies.

"I'm not going to use the epiphany machine," I said.

"Nobody asked you to," he said. "And frankly I don't think you should. But it can't surprise you that most of the time when people say that to me, they're no more than an hour away from asking to use the machine."

"The machine is self-help bullshit and it took my mother away."

"I'm not sure what you mean by 'self-help,'" he said. "Could you be more specific?"

"Everybody knows what self-help means. It's something that . . . you know . . . tries to help you make yourself better."

"And you think that's a terrible thing."

"I mean, not when you put it like that."

"You put it like that," Adam said.

"Stop trying to confuse me."

"You've been sitting here for a long time, reading that pamphlet when you weren't sleeping. Your mother wrote the original version. Epiphanies are not necessarily actionable. We tell people who they are. Sometimes that helps people become better. Often not."

"I don't care. I just want to find my mother."

"Do you consider your mother to be your servant?"

"I consider my mother to be my mother."

"And if she sees herself differently?"

"She has obligations. She wasn't supposed to just abandon me."

"And you think your life would have turned out better with the daily presence of a mother who did not want to be your mother?"

"Do you have any idea how angry this is making me?"

"Some. But you're controlling it well, considering how tired and emotional you are. I'm proud of you."

"What do you mean you're proud of me?"

"I mean that I'm proud of you."

"You're my real father, aren't you?"

Adam looked at me for a second and then guffawed. With some difficulty—his joints did not appear to be in the best shape—he crouched down by my stool.

"No, Venter. Your mother was very attractive, and I would have gladly had sex with her, but I guess her tastes ran toward men who buttoned their shirts."

"Stop talking about my mother having sex."

"Difficult subject to avoid when you're trying to establish your paternity."

I was, I had to admit, relieved. Whatever problems I had with my father, I did not want to stop thinking of myself as his son.

"So my mother has never tried to contact you, and you have no idea where she might be?"

"Cross my heart and hope to die, stick one of my needles in my eye."

"Then I guess I'm wasting my time with you. I should be spending this time with my grandmother."

I stepped off the stool and briefly cast a shadow over Adam.

"Why *did* you come here?" he asked. "You couldn't really have thought I could help you find your mother, at least not in time for her to see your grandmother."

"Why not?"

"Because I have to imagine that if you had thought that I had information you could use, you would have tried harder to get it out of me."

"My grandmother told me to come here."

"Why? Does *she* think I know where Rose is?"

I searched his face for any sign that he knew why my grandmother had sent me here.

"She told me I should use the epiphany machine."

Adam let out some kind of cough in disbelief. "Rose's mother is doing recruitment for me now?"

"It seems to be her dying wish."

"I definitely did not see that one coming. Guess I'm not much of a prophet."

I peered through the foyer into the room beyond, at the far end of which was the purple velvet curtain that shielded the room with the epiphany machine. "Was that curtain up when my parents used the machine?"

"The very same one."

"Does it have some kind of meaning?"

"Meaning?"

"Like ritualistic significance or whatever."

He laughed. "No. No ritualistic significance. Although my mother did sew it, so that might sound like significance to you."

"So when am I going to use the machine?"

Adam put his hand to his mouth, evaluating me. "You're seventeen."

"So?"

"Tattooing is finally legal again in New York City, but you have to be eighteen. I've found my way into the light of the law, and just as I'm blinking and my eyes are adjusting you're asking me to scurry back into the darkness. Come back on your eighteenth birthday."

"My grandmother's not going to live to see my eighteenth birthday," I said. I hadn't realized this until I said it, and the knowledge reduced me to sobs.

"Good," Adam said. "I'm glad to see you're upset. Up until now I've wondered whether you have a heart at all. To be honest, I've been worried that you're just going to get a **CLOSED OFF** epiphany, which would be a waste of my ink and your arm."

"Please," I said. "Can I just use the machine?"

Adam gave a different shrug, a more shruglike shrug than the Adam Shrug.

"I'm just a boy who can't say no," he said.

He led me over and around the piles of books on the floor, and through the purple velvet curtain. On the other side of the curtain was a small room that looked like a medical office. In the far corner there was a dentist's chair; closer to me were white cabinets that hung above a sink. I noticed that there was a device obscured from my view by the dentist's chair, and as I walked toward it, I could see that it really did look like an antique sewing machine.

"Do you want the tattoo on your right arm or your left arm?"

"What do most people say?"

"Most people want it on whatever arm they don't favor. It's like wearing a watch."

"I'll take it on my left arm." I rolled up my sleeve.

He tugged the device around on its rolling stand and told me to sit in the chair. He hit a button on a CD player and "Instant Karma" started playing. He washed his hands, put on a pair of latex gloves, and unwrapped a needle. He put an oven mitt on one hand. Then he was by my side, lifting up the arm of the device and sliding the needle into it. He pointed to a track on the underside of the arm, and explained that the needle would slide down the track to give me my tattoo. He told me to put my arm on the base and I complied. I was still getting used to the cold feel of the metal slab when he lowered the arm of the device, and then the needle was inside me, hurting me and telling me things. I *was* the needle and the ink, somehow; together, we were some sort of trinity that had come together to save me. I was also the paper in my own polygraph test. The metaphors were endless and so was the machine. I knew that my epiphany would be

LONELY GULLIBLE AND NUMB. Or maybe it would be **CLOSED OFF**, because it was true, I was closed off, I didn't know the first thing about myself and I made it impossible for anyone to tell me. Or maybe it would be **CARES NOTHING FOR ANYONE OR ANYTHING EXCEPT BEING THOUGHT A GENIUS**, and this one in particular seemed so terrible that I was certain it was going to be my epiphany.

Thoughts about myself and who I was were enough to distract me from the pain until they weren't. I saw what was happening, a foreign object was ripping open my skin and leaving behind a trail of ink that would never come out. The needle zagged and dragged and finally froze.

When the machine stopped whirring and Adam lifted the needle from my arm, the pain did not subside. My eyes were closed now, and I wanted to keep them closed because I didn't want to see that horrible word **GENIUS**.

This was what I actually saw when I opened my eyes:

DEPENDENT ON THE OPINION OF OTHERS

"No, no, no," I said. "This is the one I saw on the guy who was leaving as I was coming in. This must have gotten stuck in the machine or something."

"It applied to that guy, too."

"But this is the worst possible thing you could say about someone. I'd rather be a monster than a sheep."

"If Rose were here, she would explain more delicately than I can that the worst possible thing you could think of to say about someone will almost certainly be your epiphany."

"Why isn't she here? Why hasn't she been here all my life?"

"I've never been a big fan of mother-blaming, but what do I know?"

For the second time that night, I burst into tears.

"Epiphanies tend to cause the most anguish to the most intelligent," he said.

"Really?"

And this was the first time he looked at me sourly. "What do you think it says about you that you're so happy that I just suggested you were intelligent?"

I knew where he was going with this, but I couldn't take it.

"I'm getting tired of being asked leading questions that are designed to get me to admit that I suck."

"Good!" he said. "Good. That's an impulse to cultivate. But be careful, because it can also lead you back into servitude. Now, for the sake of the Christ who never existed, stop worrying about what I think of you and get back to your grandmother. Do you want gauze or Saran Wrap?"

Later, I was to learn that Adam was conscientious about needle protocol, but mostly indifferent to hygiene as soon as the machine had done its work. The room was well stocked with soap and two options for anyone who wanted to keep their tattoo safe from the elements in the hours after using the machine, and Adam intermittently insisted that one of the two options be used, but usually showed limited interest. I would also learn the politics: guests who were proud of their tattoos, or who wanted to appear proud of their tattoos, chose Saran Wrap; guests who wanted to shield the tattoos even from their own eyes (or who were truly serious about hygiene) demanded gauze pads; still other guests were so upset that they fled before either option could even be offered. Adam's lax attitude should have led to infections, but it was surprisingly rare that infections were reported to Adam. This could have been because, as Adam liked to not-really-joke, "The god in the machine keeps the tats clean," or it could have been because those who had gotten infections were afraid that if they came back they would have their minds further fucked with, so decided to just go to a doctor and get some antibiotics.

My first instinct, of course, was to ask for a gauze pad. But then I realized that if I asked for a gauze pad, I would be showing Adam that I was worried what people would think about me. And I was determined never to worry about that again.

"I'll take the Saran Wrap," I said.

NAME: Joshua Sternberg
DATE OF BIRTH: 10/02/1967
DATE OF EPIPHANY MACHINE USE: 04/03/1994
DATE OF INTERVIEW BY VENTER LOWOOD: 01/30/1999

If anyone else had gotten the epiphany tattoo that I got, it would have ruined Adam Lyons. Maybe the fact that it went to me, rather than to someone who would have gone public with it, was a stroke of luck for him. Or maybe I got it because it was actually meant for me.

Growing up, I went through the motions of honoring my faith and my ancestors. I studied the Talmud and was encouraged to become a Talmudic scholar, but really I was just a talented and insightful reader of whatever text was put in front of me; I didn't really *care* about what I was reading.

By my mid-twenties, I was putting my powers of textual analysis to good use as an associate at one of the top law firms in New York, reading through thousands of pages to find a stray phrase or two that I could deploy in the service of some brilliant argument that might help one multibillion-dollar company extract money from another multibillion-dollar company. The work was engrossing, but I lived for the vanishingly small amount of time that my associate's hours allowed me to spend with Julie. Julie was an associate at another firm, so she understood my schedule. We did our best to see everything the Met put on and to eat at every new restaurant that was either ostentatiously healthy or ostentatiously full of pork, but that wasn't the core of us. The core of us was what we would do in bed on Sunday, assuming neither of us had to work. I'm not just talking about the inventive, heroic, athletic love we made, though of course I am talking about that. I'm talking about the way it felt to be with her when we weren't touching, or even talking. This, like, warmth between us. The way it felt to have her head resting on my chest.

Eventually, I proposed to her. She wanted to get married in a Christian ceremony to make her mother happy. Since it didn't matter to me, I said sure, get a priest, or a minister or whatever. Get a priest *and* a minister. Get two of each. Could not matter less to me. I told my mother, and she cried— we're talking hard-core, sloppy sobbing, wailing about how she had always dreamed of continuing the Jewish line. But eventually she got it together enough to tell me she was happy for me.

I recoiled at what I thought was my mother's racism. I thought she didn't want me to marry a Korean. But I think she would have been delighted if Julie had converted. She just wanted me and any grandchildren she had to be Jewish.

A few weeks before the wedding, I started getting terrible stomach trouble. Worse than anything I had ever experienced. I saw a gastroenterologist, who told me that I had either a parasite or wedding jitters.

"Of course, a wife sometimes *is* a parasite!" he said, laughing heartily in the way of unfunny men. I didn't take this well; I loved that girl. But he said: "Look, let me just roll up my sleeves and show you something."

CAN TOLERATE WIFE was written on his forearm.

"Before I got this tattoo," he told me, "I never knew that I could tolerate my wife. I mean, I love her, but we argue all the time. I thought I would have to be miserable forever, or get a divorce, which would also make me miserable, since I love her. But after I got this tattoo, I knew: I can tolerate my wife. No question. When she yells at me for not cleaning the kitchen, or for putting forks tines-up in the drying rack rather than tines-down the way she likes, I think: I can tolerate this. So I do."

He gave me the business card of the Rubicon Epiphany Corporation, and as soon as I left his office, I tossed the card into an already overflowing sidewalk garbage can. When I got home, I scratched out the gastroenterologist's contact information from my datebook. No way was I going to trust my stomach to someone who had joined a cult.

I couldn't sleep that night. I thought about Julie, looking beautiful in her dress, but standing with me in the shadow of a Christian minister, who would of course talk about Christ. I thought about our children, who would not know whether to be Jewish, or Christian, or nothing. I woke Julie up to pick a fight with her about Israel, which however contemptuous I was of Jewishness I would always defend. She told me that she agreed with everything I was saying about Rabin and the peace process. I told her that as a non-Jew she couldn't understand, so that even if she agreed with me she agreed for the wrong reasons. She told me she had a 7:30 deposition and did not have time for this.

If I kept on letting the Jewish thing get to me, I knew, I was going to call off the wedding. So I had to do something that would keep me away from Judaism forever.

It's not true that you can't be buried in a Jewish cemetery if you have a tattoo, but tattoos *are* banned by rabbinical law. Well, *maybe* they're banned by rabbinical law. Like all law and particularly like all strict law, the more attention you pay to it, the harder it gets to know exactly what it's telling you not to do. The relevant passage in Leviticus reads: "You shall not make gashes in your flesh for the dead, or incise any marks on yourselves: I am the Lord." The wording leads some scholars to believe that only tattoos that took the Lord's name in vain were supposed to be forbidden. There was an obscure Jewish king named Jehoiakim who got a tattoo on his dick, either "Yahweh" or the name of a pagan god, either of which would be a pretty clear offense against Judaism, if also pretty badass. Most scholars think that it's the permanent alteration of the flesh that's the crime. That makes sense, right? God gave you this beautiful gift, and you want to draw on it like it's a diner placemat and you're a kid with a crayon? Tattoos are terrible, totally offensive to God; if that wasn't the final rabbinical interpretation, it was, at the very least, mine. I was trying to run away from Judaism, so I decided to run to a tattoo parlor. A pagan tattoo parlor, actually, where the golden calf basically shits into your skin.

I remembered the address on the card. I remember everything I read.

Nobody was waiting to use the machine when I arrived, so it was just Adam, doing some sweeping. The emptiness of the place gave me pause. I never really liked going to temple as a kid, but you always feel like less of a schmuck when there are other people around doing the same ridiculous things you're doing. I cleared my throat and said I was there to consult the epiphany machine.

This made him turn around and give me that big, tobacco-stained, missing-toothed smile.

"'Consult'? Now you're making us sound fancy."

He poured me some whiskey, and even though I had come for the straightforward purpose of getting a tattoo that would distance me from Judaism forever, we got to talking. Eventually I told him about Julie, and my reservations about marrying her, and he did this very distinctive but also very Jewish thick shrug and said: "There's more than one person for everyone. But not that many more. You've already given God your foreskin, you don't owe him the rest of your dick."

I laughed at this and told him that this wasn't about God, whom I didn't believe in anyway, but about my mother.

"So you owe your mother the rest of your dick?"

Another good line, and I'm not sure what I said in response, but in a sense I did owe my dick to my mother—and to my father, and to the two sets of grandparents who had kept their children alive through the Holocaust by leaping frantically from country to country when no country wanted them, and to whichever of my ancestors had made bricks with their hands for the pharaoh while dreaming of the laws they would follow once they were free. My dick and what I did with it had been a gift from all those people, and no gift may be used just as one pleases.

This is the epiphany I needed from the machine, and sometimes I think I should have just thanked Adam and walked out right then. But I had had similar thoughts before that hadn't stuck. So I'm glad that I let him lead me through the curtain into the back room, and I'm glad that I didn't let myself get too freaked out by the device, which, when you see it close up for the first time, is a very grisly thing.

He put on latex gloves and an oven mitt as I collapsed into the dentist's chair.

"Sterile for the devil, cushion for the pushin'." The hand covered only by a latex glove he put on the needle; the hand with the oven mitt he put on the arm.

I asked him if there was any truth to the rumor that he had tattooed Arnold Schwarzenegger.

"I'm less an eighties war guy than a sixties love guy. Not 'Come with me if you want to live' but 'Live with me if you want to come.'"

"That's a little gross, man."

Again I saw the shrug. "So is this."

He's very conscientious about easing your arm onto the base of the machine and making sure you're ready before lowering the arm. Worse than the sting—for me, anyway—was the feeling of losing control of my arm. Something very elemental in me wanted to gnaw it off, like I was a fox in a trap. Apparently, a lot of machine users report this feeling. Adam would say, wrapping his profundity in bluster and nonsense as he often does, that until we use the machine we are all gnawing at our arms in the trap of ourselves. Eventually this feeling fell away and I stared at the ink. I couldn't read it from that angle, but something about it made me feel sharp. Then it stopped and I had nothing to focus on but the pain.

"Careful not to brush your arm against the neck of the machine," he said as he lifted it. "It's very hot."

When he saw what was written he brought his hand to his mouth and bit his latex-covered index finger.

"Remember, there are a number of ways to interpret this."

DIRTY JEW

"I know what it means," I said. A neutral observer would probably have thought I had been the victim of an anti-Semitic hate crime. But you have to remember that the only person who can really understand an epiphany tattoo is the person who gets it. The machine was telling me that I had dirtied my Jewish heritage and that I needed to clean up.

The first step was to break up with Julie, which I did that very night, after I asked her to convert and she said she didn't think she could. So maybe breaking up with her was the second step. The second step, or the third step, was to have the tattoo removed. God had wanted me to get the tattoo so that I would see why I needed to get it removed.

My stomach trouble went away immediately. Within the year, I was married to a Jewish woman. Now she's pregnant with our second spectacular son. I've thought about leaving corporate law and going into non-profit law, or maybe belatedly becoming a Talmudic scholar, but with the uncertain future of the American economy, abandoning a corporate law job would be tantamount to abandoning my family.

I did run into Julie once, in a clothing store. She tried to pretend she hadn't seen me, ducking behind a mannequin that was wearing jeans and a sweater with a much-too-big turtleneck. It reminded me how she used to hide underneath the kitchen table or under the comforter in our bed, depending on where we were in our foreplay. I'm not articulate enough to give you any sense of how great she looked, so I'll just say she looked great. I tried to walk out of the store without acknowledging her, but in the course of trying to avoid each other, we wound up face-to-face. I told her that I was a husband and father now, and she told me that she was doing fine, incredibly fine, unbelievably fine, and then we talked about mutual friends for a couple of minutes before saying good-bye.

Sometimes, when I'm walking down the street, I still get the strongest image of Julie's ass in the air as I entered her from behind, or the look on her face when she would flip over after we had both come, this look of being completely exhausted and done but still ready for more, and it just stops me, like that was the purest image of himself that God would ever give me, and I rejected it. And, of course, if that were true, rejecting God is what would make me a dirty Jew.

But that's just God testing me again. After all, the real trials of Job don't begin until after the Book of Job is over, when Job is confronted with a new wife whom he has to compare to the old one. Maybe Julie, I mean my new Julie, my Jewish Julie, I mean my wife, isn't quite as right for me as the other Julie was. She doesn't challenge me as much, we don't laugh as much, and our sex isn't as good. But this Julie challenges me almost as much, we laugh almost as much, and our sex is . . . fine. Julie and I might have been a little happier than Julie and I, but Julie and I are still happy.

The question becomes: How much is an increase in happiness worth? Is it worth the very survival of your people? Maybe for you it is. For me, it's not. And I'm not sure I would have ever figured that out without the epiphany machine.

9

A Metro-North trip through Westchester late at night was usually a dreary thing, with packs of drunk, loud teenagers conducting experiments alongside packs of drunk, loud middle-aged men to see whether drunkenness became more or less obnoxious with age, each one, like me, exiled from a city that had deemed them too unserious to spend the night. But the tattoo on my forearm seemed to infect the world with interesting things, things that I had been too **DEPENDENT ON THE OPINION OF OTHERS** to notice. Now I felt happy simply to observe the people around me, not worrying, on the one hand, about what they were thinking of me, and also not worrying, on the other hand, about how I could distance myself from them so that imaginary other people would know that I was better than these loud, drunk, obnoxious losers. The gaggle of bankers who were all agreeing with one another that if the police had one problem it's that they treated black people too gingerly: these racist idiots were not irretrievably awful; they could be guided toward a less-obstructed view of the universe. All they had to do was receive and heed messages on their forearms, rather than wave around beer cans the size of their forearms. And if they could be redeemed, then certainly so could the teenage girl wobbling around asking for aspirin through the shields that solo passengers had constructed for themselves out of newspapers. All it would take to get this girl to stop chasing the desiccated remnants of fun available to a society that was simultaneously decadent and repressed was for the epiphany machine to tell her that that was what she was doing.

"Excuse me," she said. "I'm talking to you."

This was when I realized that she was in fact talking to me, rather than to the dozing woman in the row behind me.

"Do. You. Have. As. Pir. In."

"No," I said, remembering my decision not to hide from anyone ever again. "But I do have this!"

I rolled up my sleeve and held up my arm. She laughed so hard that she stumbled and had to catch herself on the back of a seat.

"Did your mom make you get that so that girls will know that you need her permission to go on dates? Because I don't think that's going to be an issue."

"It means that my natural tendency is to be too worried about what people think of me to show my true self. But I can use this tattoo to fight against that natural tendency, even when I probably shouldn't, like now."

"Oh, shit!" she said, shrieking and raising her hand to her mouth. "Is that an epiphany tattoo?"

"That's exactly what it is."

"That changes everything. I was afraid you were a freak."

After some burpy laughter she toddled on her way, like the childish pre-epiphany person I had been a few hours earlier. Shame sloshed around in my stomach, as it always did after I had been mocked, and reflexively I looked around to see whether anyone in the car was laughing at me. But even though I noticed two or three people who might have been actively averting their eyes rather than simply not looking at me, I did not care as much as I usually did, because I knew that I was on track to not caring what people thought.

Rather than continue to engage with strangers, which I was probably not ready to do, I tried to focus on the physical pain that the needle had left me in, since physical pain is a famous cure for concern about the opinion of others.

From the train station, I drove straight to the hospital and somehow kept taking the wrong turn in every hallway. Eventually, I found my father sitting with a stack of papers in a lounge in a part of the hospital completely different from the one I was trying to get to.

"You took my car without asking," he said without looking up at me.

"I'm sorry."

"Your grandmother is dead."

"What? But I just left a few hours ago."

"Right. When you leave someone who's about to die, that person might be dead by the time you come back. That's the way it works."

"But I thought I'd have more time."

"I have no trouble believing that you thought that."

He still wasn't looking up, and I felt emboldened to make him hate me. "She asked me to use the epiphany machine," I said. "And I did."

I rolled up my sleeve and received the same exasperated look I had seen as a child when I told him I had broken something. I thought he would scream or laugh or maybe be silent forever, never speak to me again.

"The worst epiphany of all. The one that tells the world you can't think for yourself. A son who would think for himself is all I ever wanted, though Adam is right that I don't have one. He was also right that I never should have become a father. Whatever else he is, the man is certainly perceptive." Then he looked back down at his papers.

For the second time in nine or ten hours, I turned around and walked out of the hospital, or through it and around it and finally out of it. I drove straight home and lay in bed until the sun came up, thinking about a time when I was small and I asked my grandmother if we could stay up all night until the sun came up, and she told me that I was too young to stay up all night, but she promised me that we would do that one day, or one night, maybe the summer after I graduated from high school. I thought that this should make me sob, but it did not.

I called Adam Lyons at a number he had given me. He did not sound surprised that I was calling.

"You do important work," I said. "I want to come work for you. Be your assistant."

"Like mother, like son?"

"I just want to help you do what you do. I don't want to go to college, or even go back to high school. I don't want to do anything except help you."

"I am not letting you drop out of high school. The biggest mistake I made with your mother was letting her drop out of law school to work for me full-time. This would be a lot worse than that."

"Part-time, then. Let me do something."

It occurred to me that the best thing I could do to address my own epiphany was to stay away from the machine, since remaining near a source of advice and reassurance might keep me **DEPENDENT ON THE OPINION OF OTHERS**. Adam took a long time to respond, possibly thinking this as well.

"Okay," he said. "I think I have something."

Honestly, I probably would have agreed to become some kind of hit man for him; I would have hunted any enemies he had. Instead, he just suggested that I become the official oral historian of the Rubicon Epiphany Corporation; essentially, my job would be to take down the stories of people who used the machine. I would come on Friday and Saturday nights, "salon nights," when people who had used the machine over the years would hang out, smoke, drink, and discuss how their tattoos had affected their lives. If so inclined, they could bring potential new users, and sometimes those new users would wind up using the machine. Many nights, salon nights and otherwise, were like the one I had just witnessed, with so much traffic that a line formed. (I would find that there were also often salon nights on Thursdays, Tuesdays, whenever Adam felt like it. And guests would come to use the machine at all hours on all days. Adam never really closed.)

"Who knows," he said. "Even Rose might show up eventually."

I accepted the position before he had finished explaining it.

CHAPTER

✦

10

My grandmother's funeral was on Monday and I returned to school on Wednesday. On Tuesday, all I thought about was Leah. At first, I told myself that I was just using Leah to distract myself from the pain of losing my grandmother, but then I kept thinking about her. I also wondered whether she, not my grandmother, had been the real reason I had gotten a tattoo, and this started to seem more and more likely. I thought about calling Ismail and asking for his advice, but I didn't want to be **DEPENDENT ON THE OPINION OF OTHERS**, and besides, he probably wanted Leah for himself. In any case, the first thing I did on Wednesday at school was find Leah.

"I got an epiphany tattoo," I said, dragging her onto a bench between buildings and rolling up my sleeve in one gesture. "Just like we talked about. I can take you this weekend and you can get one, too."

She looked at my tattoo for a while, then took a deep breath. "I'm really sorry about your grandmother, Venter. That must have been really awful. I can see how it might make you do something rash like this."

"I was trying to honor her by getting this tattoo," I said, though at this moment it definitely felt as though I had gotten it just for Leah. "It was her dying wish."

"People say strange things when they're dying. My dad kept asking me to give him his hat back, and I had no idea what he was talking about, because I had never seen him wear a hat. Actually, one of my dad's college friends, who comes to visit my mother and me every once in a while, does laser tattoo removal. As a favor to us, he might be willing to do the procedure for you for free."

"Why would I want it removed? The entire point is for it to stay there and remind me what my flaw is. I thought you were into this."

"It's just . . . you know how before you paint a wall you're supposed to hold up one of those little cards, to see how the color will look? I sort of wish you had done that with this tattoo."

"I don't care about how I look."

"It says right there on your arm that you do! Everybody cares about how they look, but they don't want to be reminded that they do. That's one reason people are going to hate you when they see that tattoo."

"If that's the price, then I'm willing to pay it."

"Another reason people are going to hate you is that you're going to say self-righteous shit like that. And it's really going to bother you that people will hate you."

"You're right. I am **DEPENDENT ON THE OPINION OF OTH-ERS**. I guess I forgot just now, but seeing that tattoo every day will remind me. Now it's your turn to learn about yourself. We can get you a tattoo next weekend."

"Venter. I want to be an actress. I'm never going to get a tattoo of any kind. And if I did, it wouldn't be an epiphany tattoo."

"But you said you wanted to get one."

"I was just *talking*, man. Words aren't supposed to last forever. That's why you should call that friend of my dad's."

She reached for her backpack for something to write his number on, but I was already walking away.

The day was over and I was rather melodramatically smoking by myself outside the auditorium when Ismail approached me.

"Go away," I said, hoping he would stay and praise me for being so much more honest than Leah, so much more willing to face unpleasant truths.

"I can't believe you joined that cult," he said.

"It's not a cult."

"Fine. 'Religion.' I thought we agreed that all religion is bullshit."

"It's not religion."

"What would you call it, then? Magic science?"

"It doesn't matter what I call it. What matters is what I do with it."

"I know you're grieving over your grandmother, but this is not the way to do it."

"I'm not grieving over my grandmother. This is the first time in my life that I've actually paid attention to her." I tried to ignore the fact that I wasn't sure whether I had gotten the tattoo because of my grandmother or because of Leah. "It's like the first time she's ever been alive for me."

"You sound brainwashed, Venter."

I dropped my cigarette and made a big show of walking away. When I got home, I pulled out my notebook, intending to write down my observations about what happened, but I wound up just getting lost in my own thoughts.

By the next day, word had gotten around to the entire school that I had joined the same cult that my mother had joined, but that was fine with me. My thoughts were not with school.

CHAPTER

♦

11

Armed with a tape recorder and microcassettes, I showed up the next Saturday night, prepared to ask users if they wanted to be interviewed. If they said yes, I was supposed to take them into Adam's bedroom, sit with them at a desk he had set up, and have them give their testimonials. Adam told me to aim for a total of one hundred testimonials, "an arbitrary but suitably large number."

I did not immediately take to the job. Talking to people has never been my strength. Instead of anxious, most people on salon nights were relaxed, only in part because of the joints that Adam continuously circulated. I would later discover that there are many parties, particularly in New York, where everyone is stoned or otherwise intoxicated and still a nervous wreck, because everyone is worried that everyone else sees through them to their deepest, most secret flaw. That worry was nonexistent here, with those flaws all out in the open for everyone to read. (There was an unspoken rule that salons were short sleeves only.) "We're all like criminals who have been caught," somebody said once. "We can finally get a full night's sleep." Not everyone claimed to be living a perfect life, of course, but everyone who attended—meaning machine users who had chosen to come back for salon nights—thought the machine had been a mostly positive experience, and had directed their energy away from trying to deny what was wrong with them and toward fixing or accepting it. Of course, if I had been paying attention, I would have noticed the intense rivalry among members, each of whom wanted to be Adam's favorite, the most improved user of the epiphany machine. But I still felt too suffocated by my own need to make a good impression to notice anything beneath the surface.

"So I've really accepted the fact that I'm **DEPENDENT ON THE OPINION OF OTHERS**, and I'm trying to get better about it," I kept finding myself saying within a minute or two of starting a conversation. I say that I kept finding myself saying this, but actually Adam pointed out that I kept saying this, and for some reason I couldn't stop myself from saying it even after he pointed it out. For a while, I tried not introducing myself to people, and just hanging around and eavesdropping instead. There was one guy who said that his marriage had been saved by his tattoo—**DISTRACTS HIMSELF FROM WHAT MATTERS WITH STRING OF EPHEMERAL OBSESSIONS**—not only because it told him that his wife was what mattered, but because it made him realize that he did in fact have a string of consuming crushes on female coworkers that he made his wife feel crazy by denying; his wife confirmed this, and said that she had felt so grateful and inspired that she too used the machine, which told her that she **FOCUSES ENERGY ON OLD RESENTMENTS**, a tattoo that helped her stop obsessing over her husband's obsessions once the obsessions stopped. This seemed very interesting, but when I introduced myself and asked them if I could record their story, they looked at me as though I had asked to record them having sex, which, in a way, I suppose I had.

"I'm not sure I'm right for this job," I said to Adam one night after everyone had left. I had told myself that I was wasting my time by listening to people talk about their boring lives in the faint hope that one day my mother might walk through the door; really, I just wanted to avoid talking to people.

"Like Shakespeare said to Nathan Hale, I always get my man," he said.

When I arrived the next evening, Adam told me, with a self-consciously lascivious grin, that a woman was waiting for me in his bedroom.

"This is Catherine," Adam said. "You've probably read her books."

I did recognize Catherine Pearson, though I had not read her books. I had read a review of her last book in my father's copy of *The New York Times Book Review* that called her the heiress to Chekhov, and a review in my father's copy of *The Village Voice* that called her "a hack who repeats herself, constantly resorting to the same epiphanies, all as cheap as the one that adds her arm to her list of disfigurements." (I would much later read an essay or a blog post condemning this reviewer as misogynistic, citing this review and many other examples.)

"Ms. Pearson!" I said. "I'm a big fan of your work."

"Everybody I meet tells me that," she said. "You must have something more original to say if Adam picked a child to do something as important as record the oral history of the epiphany machine."

I looked at Adam and got an Adam Shrug in return.

"I don't have anything to say," I said, figuring this out as I was saying it. "I think that's why Adam picked me. Ma'am."

"Hey, that's not bad. Now tell me about the tattoo on your arm."

"It says that I am **DEPENDENT ON THE OPINION OF OTHERS**, which I know is not exactly the best epiphany for me to have, given that I want to be a writer, since obviously it's even more important for a writer to have his—or her—own opinions than it is for other people, since obviously we're supposed to see the world in our own way, but given that I do have this problem, I think it's good that I know now, so that I can correct it and not waste time deny—"

"Adam, are you sure you're not making a mistake?" Catherine asked.

"You were on the right track a little earlier, Venter," Adam said. "When you said you didn't have anything to say."

"So you just don't want me to talk?" I asked.

"Not exactly," Catherine said. "Who's your favorite writer? Don't say me, because you obviously haven't read a word I've written."

"Am I not supposed to answer the question?"

"Not answering a direct question is rude."

"Steven Merdula," I said.

Catherine shrieked with laughter and looked at Adam, who already looked furious. I had known this would bother him; I had said it mostly to see his reaction.

"You like Merdula?" Adam said. "You hate your mother enough to like Merdula?"

"I'm sorry?"

"Your mother used the machine. Fine, maybe she turned against it. But if you like Merdula, you're basically saying that your mother—and now *you*, I might add—used a device invented by the Nazis."

"Oh, lighten up, Adam," Catherine said. "You know that that's not what Merdula says. That was one chapter in a book that imagines *many* different scenarios for how the epiphany machine came to be."

"Yeah, and they *all* make the epiphany machine sound evil."

"Go write a doctoral dissertation about the bigoted representation of the epiphany machine in Western literature."

"It could have been worse," Adam said. "He could have said Carter Wolf."

"That *would* have been worse. I might even have walked out if he'd said Carter Wolf. But since he didn't, why don't you pipe the fuck down so I can do what you invited me here to do and educate this young man?"

"Fine," Adam said, and left the room, slamming the door on us.

"Is he never going to talk to me again?" I asked Catherine.

"Who cares? Don't be so **DEPENDENT ON THE OPINION OF OTHERS**. But he'll be fine. Adam gets mad sometimes, particularly when somebody mentions Steven Merdula, but he always settles down. He even likes it when people talk to him that way; he's the **FIRST MAN TO LIE ON**, meaning that he's very easy to lie down on. He gives up quickly. But all of this brings us back to the question that I asked you and to how you should have answered it. Remember that if you're going to be interviewing people about their epiphanies—and I really don't know why Adam asked you to do this job, rather than somebody who has at least finished college—then your interviewees, even if they've used the machine and have gotten something out of it, are going to be looking for excuses not to talk about anything important. 'Who is your favorite writer?' is a question that allows you not to talk about anything important. It leads either to a boring argument like the one we just had or to completely brain-dead agreement. Reading Fitzgerald is an important experience; standing around at a party saying how much you love Fitzgerald, trying to look smart and interesting by saying you prefer *Tender Is the Night* to *The Great Gatsby*—that's just a waste of your time on earth. Remember your objective, which is what?"

"It's . . ." I felt as confused as I had long ago with my father in the cemetery talking about baseball.

"You're coaxing people to talk about what the epiphany machine has meant to their lives. That's important, and nobody wants to talk about what's important. The only way to get people to talk about something important is to leave them with no other option."

NAME: Catherine Pearson

DATE OF BIRTH: 11/15/1966

DATE OF EPIPHANY MACHINE USE: 11/15/1994

DATE OF INTERVIEW BY VENTER LOWOOD: 06/01/1998

Before I used the epiphany machine, I was essentially Carter Wolf's aman-
uensis. Not literally, exactly. It's not as though I took dictation from him.
But I did organize my day around making sure that he had no distractions.
I made him oatmeal for breakfast and brought it to the corner of the bedroom that he called his "study"; I made him a peanut butter sandwich—no
jelly—for lunch, and brought that to his study, too. Sometimes he would
join me for dinner, usually not. Theoretically, I had all the time in the
world to do my own writing, but somehow preparing meals and cleaning
a house and seeing to someone else's needs, whether or not you care about
doing these things well, almost invariably takes up the entire day.

Maybe that's an excuse. Maybe the reason that I couldn't do any of my
own work was that I just didn't have anything to write. Or maybe I was
suffocated by a genius. I married him when I was very young, twenty-four.
The funny thing is that we met after he sent *me* a fan letter. He read a story
I had published in an obscure literary journal and he sent me a two-page,
handwritten fan letter. My heart stopped for pretty much the entire dura-
tion of those two pages. When I accepted his invitation to meet, I knew I
would probably sleep with him, but I never would have thought I would
marry him. *Middlemarch* was one of my favorite novels, and I had no intention of becoming a Dorothea to a Casaubon. The difference, or one
difference, is that Carter, unlike Casaubon, was sexually vital and insanely
productive. He would get up two hours before me to write his one thousand morning words, then come back to bed for a morning fuck, then

write another thousand words, then an afternoon fuck, then read for hours, on most days devouring an entire book, before fucking me one more time before we fell asleep. I didn't think I would suffer from the problems that Dorothea suffered from. I thought, okay, all that typing will inspire me to type stuff of my own. Instead, it just paralyzed me. I wanted to blame it on the noise, but really there was no noise. Carter was a very soft typist. Just knowing that he was typing made it impossible for me to type. In my college circle, and even in my MFA program, I had unquestionably been the best writer—it had even kind of turned me on to know that I was so much better than the boys—but I knew that what Carter was writing was just on another level entirely from what I was writing.

What I just told you is a Carter-friendly version of this story. It's not completely inaccurate—it's how I understood our situation for most of the time we were together—but it leaves out the part where, after I gave a reading at a bar that only my friends showed up to, he said: "At least only your friends heard that piece." It leaves out the part where, even though I responded with copious comments on every draft he showed me, he had only this to say on both occasions I showed him a draft: "Early drafts often look like this." As it often is, it's hard to say whether he was being honest or just being a dick. I hated everything I wrote, and I was also invested in thinking that I was tough enough to accept any truth about myself and my work, so I chose to believe that he was being honest.

On the morning of my twenty-eighth birthday, I remember thinking that my writing was finished for good, and I also remember missing it. Physically missing it. I think I used the epiphany machine mostly to get words back into my body. I also got the tattoo to humiliate Carter, I guess. He was receiving an award at a dinner that night, so that was how we would be spending my birthday, and he had mentioned he wanted me to wear a sleeveless gown. That's what I would have worn anyway, most likely, but it bothered me how blatantly he was letting me know that he thought of me as the pretty wife two decades his junior to be shown off to all his friends and admirers. He wanted to say: Not only do I have the Prestigious

Award, but I also have this hot, sexy girl. Well, I thought: I'll show you. I'll show up with an epiphany tattoo, and essentially tell all your friends and sycophants that the hot, sexy girl you married is a cult member.

There were a lot of people here on the day I used the machine. People were chattering all around me, looking for reassurance that they weren't crazy. I offered the little grunts of sympathy that are useful for getting people to tell me things, meaning that they're useful for finding the raw material for stories. Only while I was waiting in that line did I realize that this was a major reason why I was so successful writing fiction in college: because people were eager to empty their secrets onto me. Three a.m. confessions fueled six a.m. writing sessions at least four times a week, back when my body could support my philosophical aversion to sleep. Now this was almost exactly the same situation. All these people standing around, telling me their stories, telling me what had led them to the epiphany machine and what they hoped to learn. What they feared they would learn. I would listen to what they were not telling me, and whole short stories would emerge in those gaps.

By the time I got to the front of the line, I didn't want to sit down and use the epiphany machine. I wanted to rush back home and start writing again. But everyone was looking at me, both the people behind me in line and the people who had already used the machine and were taking their first confused steps toward understanding their tattoos. All of these people were expecting me to use the machine, and I worried that if I told their stories without using the machine myself that I would be using *them*.

I don't know why I let that bother me. A man wouldn't let that bother him. Carter, if he had been in my situation, would have happily walked out of line and opened his laptop at the nearest coffee shop. He probably would have danced the white-boy shuffle on his way down the stairs. In any case, I didn't get out of line, and I got a tattoo.

That's how I got this tattoo that you're scared to read out loud. **DOES NOT LOVE HUSBAND**. That I already knew this, but did not know that I knew it, is only part of what makes the machine so valuable. The machine doesn't just tell you what's wrong with your life; it forces you to change it. You can't really avoid a divorce when you have a tattoo on your arm that says **DOES NOT LOVE HUSBAND**. But I guess I still wanted some sort of revenge, because I called Carter and told him I would meet him at the dinner rather than beforehand to toast my birthday as we had planned. I got there early, and by the time Carter arrived, I was already at our table, absorbing the stares of all the writers in line for the open bar. I was also being hit on by a writer even older than Carter. When Carter saw the tattoo, he looked at it and asked what he had done to deserve it. As soon as he used the word "deserve," I knew that he and the word "deserve" were the two things that were keeping me from what was mine.

As far as I know, he hasn't been able to finish anything since, while I have written two books in four years, the second of which won the award Carter won that night.

CHAPTER

———— · · ◆ · · ————

12

Talking to Catherine did not change everything for me. The biggest challenge with trying to get testimonials at salon nights, I discovered, was that even though the announced intention of salon nights was for people to come in and discuss their experiences, in practice, people talked about what people always talk about: serious matters like gossip, trivial matters like the fate of the planet. They also wanted very much to talk about and to Adam.

Something that nobody who knew Adam could deny: he was an unparalleled conversationalist. After his standard introduction ("Madam, I'm Adam"), he would often begin talking about something inappropriate, not infrequently his enthusiasm for breastfucking, which he considered the supreme form of heterosexual sex, as it carried no possibility of impregnation, was substantially easier to execute than anal sex, and, unlike oral sex, made possible mid-coital conversation. Guests would be so disarmed by his candor—and so eager to point out that nobody actually wants to talk in the middle of sex, or that breastfucking is no fun at all for the woman—that they would feel a little bit less worried about divulging whatever was most repellent in them. When I write this down it sounds offensive; somehow, said in his warm, blustery manner, it wasn't. I have never met anyone with more infectious openness than Adam Lyons. Adam was quite amenable to being kidded—"Only on our arms," I remember one obviously adoring acolyte saying, "is history written by a loser." Even Adam's own epiphany, **FIRST MAN TO LIE ON**, could be read as a product of his openness; even those who regarded him as a giant fraud had to give him credit for not letting the theory that he was a giant fraud become an elephant in the room. He loved to explain that his tattoo meant that his purpose was to provide his guests with someone to lie on. "I am the great bed of humanity," he liked to say. "You can sleep on me when you need to recharge, or even better you can toss the coats of your self-delusion and shame onto me while you go join the party." Over the course of any given salon night, Adam might tell a story about a late-night pizza run with John Lennon in 1978, pitch the machine to a first-time visitor, list a few reasons why Steven Merdula was a terrible writer who didn't understand the first thing about the epiphany machine, then tell a story about procuring cocaine for a famous photographer whose name he wouldn't mention so that the photographer could snort the cocaine off the arm of the machine while she was receiving her tattoo.

Prying one of Adam's fans away from all this to tell his or her life story to a teenager was difficult, and I never really did figure out how to do it. Eventually, Adam started pointing to people and telling them that it was their turn to give me a testimonial. Almost every one of them complied, although in many cases they were too drunk or stoned for their testimonials to be usable. Either that, or their problems and solutions bored me— maybe they were too clogged with op-ed-style pontification or irrelevant detail for me to find any essence to distill, or maybe I couldn't relate to a given speaker—and I would procrastinate on transcription until I had lost their tapes.

In theory, my hours were from six p.m. until midnight; in practice, I worked from six p.m. to six a.m. One night shortly after the school year ended, I passed out on the floor next to Adam's bed, and by the time I woke up, a little before one in the afternoon, Adam was already seeing guests, so I took a shower and helped out. We didn't discuss it, but I basically lived there for the rest of the summer. (My father didn't care that I was gone.) Adam had a huge collection of videotapes of old movies, not that different from my grandmother's, and sometimes when there were no guests we'd watch *My Man Godfrey* or *Bringing Up Baby*. We would have long chats, wherein he would defend himself and the epiphany machine.

"Sometimes people say, the first Rebecca Hart, that was understandable, but the second Rebecca Hart, you should have known better. How was I supposed to know that there would be *two* batshit-crazy women named Rebecca Hart? What was I supposed to do, prevent anyone named Rebecca Hart from using the machine? Wouldn't that be discrimination? I mean, *now* I don't let anyone named Rebecca Hart use the machine, but that's only to keep people off my back. Basically, I'm just being a coward. But at least I'm not enough of a coward to deny the machine to people who *aren't* named Rebecca Hart. Really, any doubts that anyone had about the machine should have been completely laid to rest after the machine accurately predicted that those two women would kill their kids. Some people are convinced I'm a fraud but *still* want me to share epiphanies with law enforcement, as though that position makes any sense."

Sometimes he would get on one of these jags while we were exercising in the park. He would jog very slowly and I would pretend to jog as well, even though I could easily have walked and kept pace. For the most part we kept to the East Side, but when the weather was nice he couldn't be nudged away from cutting through to the West Side, where we would inevitably come within sight of Strawberry Fields, the memorial for John Lennon across the street from the Dakota, where he was murdered by Mark David Chapman.

"I remember Chapman; I'd probably remember him even if he hadn't done what he did. I was shocked when he got the same tattoo that John had gotten. I was afraid that John would be mad. I was afraid that John would think this meant I was a fraud and was making fun of him. Oh, John. That was the closest I ever came to smashing the machine. But John would have wanted me to keep going. He told me that the epiphany machine was capable of doing more good for humanity than anything else that actually existed in the world, apart from his music."

I doubted that Lennon had actually said any of this, but it didn't matter. There was something incredibly beautiful about this old man gliding down the path, passed every few seconds by younger, fitter bodies, contemplating whether his life's work had been, on the whole, good or bad.

Like many teenagers, I was certain that the biggest questions were the most important ones, and that I was going to answer them. I thought about my future, enriched by the testimonials I was recording, the thoughts on life and how to live it that I had the rare privilege of listening to, and it seemed to me that I would make fewer mistakes than most people.

I suppose I have to mention Si Strauss. The heir to a real-estate fortune, Si was the reason that Adam was able to run a business out of his apartment that would have been illegal even if he had run it out of a storefront. (Though there was little to no enforcement, tattooing was illegal in New York City from 1961 to 1997, due to a hepatitis B scare.) Strauss—through an organization he called Friends of the Epiphany Machine—paid the bills for Adam's many legal troubles, and for much else. Adam's defense for the zoning issue—that those who used the machine were his guests rather than his customers, and that the fee was a voluntary donation to defray costs—wasn't exactly untrue. Indifferent to the concept of "inflation," he never charged more than a hundred dollars for the use of the machine, even though there were many who would have paid thousands, and he never refused service to anyone who did not pay. But most people wanted to give him some money before he put a needle in their arm; most people wanted it to feel at least a little like a business transaction. How Adam evaded the illegality of tattooing remained a mystery to me, partially because tattooing had already been legalized by my first visit; I suspect it was largely due to the many high-ranking city officials who were rumored to have received tattoos and, of course, to the influence of Strauss.

For the most part, Strauss was quiet and never talked to anyone. He did not wear short-sleeved shirts; in fact, I never saw him not wearing a suit, even on days in August when Adam's air conditioner was broken. One night, after I had been coming for nearly a year, I managed to cajole him into giving me a testimonial. When Adam found out about this, he insisted that I destroy the tape in front of him. But this one I had already transcribed.

NAME: Si Strauss
DATE OF BIRTH: 01/25/1935
DATE OF EPIPHANY MACHINE USE: 05/02/1966
DATE OF INTERVIEW BY VENTER LOWOOD: 03/10/1999

When I'm here and somebody who just used the machine is crying and screaming their head off that they're going to sue, I'm not too concerned. Even the ones who actually start legal proceedings, most of them drop their cases after a few weeks. If I weren't intimately familiar with Adam's supply chain, I would say that there's something magic in the ink itself. Something that in a robust teenager such as yourself reaches the heart almost immediately, but takes longer to work its way through old blood. Young people absorb what the machine tells them faster because young people absorb everything faster. That's why I have my baseball charity; I love to watch young boys as they learn. Their eyes get so intent and focused, and you can see what they're learning go through their entire bodies. When older people use the machine, you can almost see them trying to block the path their epiphanies are taking from their arms to their brains. But just as blood keeps circulating until you're dead, no matter how old you are, your epiphany gets to every part of you eventually.

Growing up, I wanted to be a center fielder, and through high school I was just good enough to keep that fantasy going. Sometimes I would stay out practicing until my hands bled, and when I got home my father would tell me I was lazy for not working in his office after school to learn the family business. I was spoiled, he said, lost like a typical self-indulgent American to the pursuit of a pastime, rather than to the cultivation of buildings, where people would live and work. Often he would yell at me for an hour. By college, it became clear that I'd never make the big leagues, but

I still wanted to work in baseball. My father, one of the biggest guys in New York City real estate, could have bought a team for me if he had wanted to. But he definitely did not want to. He told me that there were men built for baseball and men built for buildings, and I was the latter. I agreed to go to work for his firm, telling myself that I wasn't doing it because my father forced me to, but because I was going to be a slugger one way or another, and if I couldn't use baseball bats I was going to use skyscrapers.

To get to the top of those skyscrapers, I started out low man on the totem pole, even though in practice everyone knew that I was the boss's son and was extremely deferential. Almost immediately I missed baseball. I made a habit of getting drunk and smashing parking meters with baseball bats. Twice I got arrested; both times the charges mysteriously got dropped as soon as somebody saw my name, and I was back at my office the next morning.

Mostly my job was making sure that tenants were paying on time, and kicking out anybody who wasn't paying market rate. Obviously Adam stuck out as an easy target. Not only was he running an illegal business, he was illegally running it out of his apartment. I had my lawyer send him an eviction notice and figured that would be the end of it. A couple of weeks later Adam mails me a photograph of my lawyer, who's holding up this letter that, if you squint, you can see is a resignation letter. But it took a while to notice the letter, because I was more focused on the tattoo on my lawyer's arm, which he had rolled up the sleeves of his shirt and jacket to display: **NEEDS TO STOP SPEAKING FOR OTHERS**.

Pretty obvious, to me anyway, that the tattoo was intended for me even more than for my father. I don't think this term existed at the time, but I had what today would be called "anger management issues." This lawyer was smart and hardworking, but he was generally inclined to be easier on tenants who didn't belong in our buildings than I was, settling for getting them out in two years rather than fighting to get them out in two months. He had gotten used to doing things his way. I yelled at him. I yelled at him *a lot*, I guess. My father was always firm but gentle and soft-spoken with the people who worked for him, reserving his yelling for me. And I knew my father would take his anger at the lawyer's resignation out on me, particularly given the circumstances.

I put the photograph down and walked to my window. The floor I was working on was still low enough that I could make out the outlines of the people. I remember I saw a few little kids pass by wearing Yankees caps, the hats of their heroes. Those kids, their faces, the way they moved, that's what life was about, and I would never have that life again. I picked up a baseball bat signed by Willie Mays that I kept in my office, told my secretary to cancel my afternoon meetings, and drove straight to see Adam.

When I buzzed number 7, Adam asked who it was, so I told him who it was and I told him to meet me outside so he could act like a man. He asked why he should act like a man when, like everybody else, he was doing his best to become a god. I told him to just fucking come downstairs, and he stopped answering. I had forgotten my keys to the building, so I smashed the glass door. Yeah, I definitely had anger management issues. I cut my hand up, but I was still prepared to break down the door to Adam's apartment, and probably would have if he hadn't left it open for me.

I entered slowly, thinking maybe he had a gun or something. Instead, he was holding a drink, and he kind of smiled at my bloody hand before gesturing to his ice bucket and asking me if I needed some ice.

I looked at his missing tooth for a while before answering.

"Not only are you running an illegal tattoo parlor, but you're selling liquor without a license?"

"I'm not selling the liquor," he said. "Or the tattoos. My guests are my guests."

"Nelson is a good lawyer," I said. "He wouldn't have gotten that tattoo if you hadn't brainwashed him."

"Maybe he wouldn't have worked for your family all these years if your father hadn't brainwashed him. Your father sounds like a son of a bitch."

I agreed with him about my father, but that didn't stop me from smashing a bottle of Scotch with the bat. It broke the bottle and drove a tiny shard of glass deeper into my palm.

"That was good Scotch," Adam said. Without asking permission, he plucked the shard from my palm, and then offered me a rag to use as a bandage. I hesitated, but took it.

"This building belongs to my family," I said.

"And so do you."

"What are you talking about?"

"I think you know," he said, "but just to make sure you don't forget, let's get it in writing."

And that was it. A little more wrangling back and forth, and I agreed to use the machine. Everyone says that the machine hurts, and maybe the only reason I didn't notice the pain is that I was already in so much pain, but honestly I think I was just completely relieved. Relieved and awed. All the wisdom in the universe was being shrunk down to a scale model of itself that would fit in my forearm. I don't want to say that the actual tattoo was a disappointment, exactly, because it definitely wasn't. **BURNS WITH DESIRE TO MAKE A DIFFERENCE** immediately felt right, felt true. What was important to me was to make a difference in the lives of kids like the ones who had passed underneath my office, not necessarily to work in the sport they enjoyed.

When I was leaving the building, an elderly tenant was standing in the doorway, weeping over the broken glass.

"Those animals are taking over this city."

I wasn't under any illusions about what she meant by this. She was just an old racist. But she was right about what a handful of rich families, including my own, were doing to the city, had been doing for a long time. And you know who serves his family and doesn't care about anyone else? An animal.

"Not if I can help it, ma'am," I said, a bit grandly, of course, but I was really excited about the prospect of helping people. The first thing I did when I got back to my office was to call somebody to install a new door in Adam's building. The second thing was to quit. By the end of the year, I had used much of my share of the family money to start Friends of the Epiphany Machine.

Supporting and defending Adam has easily been the best thing I could have possibly done with my life. There were some other things I sort of wanted to do—every once in a while I feel the urge to cash out Friends of the Epiphany Machine and buy a baseball team, and I still wake up from dreams where I'm a ballplayer wondering what might have happened if I had practiced even harder, or if I hadn't given up in college. I look at what I've done with myself instead of playing baseball and I see that I've essentially been the pitching coach for the greatest metaphysical pitcher who ever lived. Or maybe I am the team owner after all. Pick your own damn metaphor, as Adam says sometimes. I also started a charity to help inner-city youths get involved in baseball, and that's enough baseball for me. Seeing those kids slide through the dirt, my God. Those kids. The point is that I've made a difference, through Adam and my charity, and that's the best life anybody can hope for.

CHAPTER

——— · · ◆ · · ———

13

Si's tattoo probably should have made me suspicious, since nobody gets a tattoo that good. But it didn't.

There's somebody else I have to mention at this point. One guy who often came to hang out was thirtyish, with boxy glasses, an untraceable European accent, and, quite noticeably, no tattoo. Usually, Adam would sidle up to quiet, untattooed people on their second visit; if they weren't tattooed by their fourth, he would shut them out of conversations. This guy got to stick around, tattoolessly chatting with Adam at salon after salon. He didn't say much, and didn't register much emotion either, except when Adam called him "Douglavich," which would make him briefly narrow his eyes and turn his nose away as though he had smelled something bad. He never talked to me until one day he did.

"It's impressive that Adam Lyons likes you so much," he said. "A lot of people want his attention, but you're the only one who seems to have it. Everybody else is just a customer."

"I don't know if that's true." I was pretty sure it *wasn't* true, and yet I wanted it to be true so badly that hearing it out of someone else's mouth seemed to magically make it true. "And we call them guests."

He smiled at this term to let me know it was dumb. "How would you like to help me bring the epiphany machine, a device that you and I both believe helps everyone who uses it, to people who can't afford a trip to New York?"

"What, like a tour?"

"No. I don't want to move the machine. I want to make new machines. Mass production."

"How can you do that when not even Adam knows who built it or how it works?"

"Of course he knows who built it. He built it. And of course he knows how it works. He makes it work by making people think it works."

"So you're just a skeptic."

"A skeptic is the last thing I am. The epiphanies aren't magic, but that doesn't mean they aren't real."

"So you want to put random tattoos on people to guide their behavior?"

"It seems just as likely to make the world a better place as anything else that's been tried."

"Why would you need Adam Lyons to do this?"

"Because because because because becauuuuse . . . because of the won- derful things he does." I thought that his accent enhanced that song's most sinister qualities, and then I chided myself for being influenced by bad Hollywood movies with vaguely European villains. "He's why people think the machine works."

"In that case, what would be the point in mass-producing it? Not everyone could meet him."

"And not everybody who buys Nikes can meet Michael Jordan. But every Nike customer feels Michael Jordan on his feet."

"So you want to stock the machine in Walmart and put Adam's face on the box?"

"Not exactly. But Adam's endorsement would be helpful."

"And you think I can get that for you."

"I think you might be able to get that for me."

"I believe in the machine," I said. "Not just in Adam."

"You believe it's supernatural. You believe that there's a literal god-in-the-machine who is guiding the tattoos."

Put this way, it sounded silly. But by this point I was coming to realize that I was so impressionable that I could be convinced of anything, and therefore I might as well continue believing what I currently believed. So I just said: "Yes."

"Not even my father was quite that stupid."

"Excuse me?"

He put up his hands as though he were surrendering to my idiocy. "I should get going. Nice chatting with you."

As soon as he was out the door, I found Adam near the bathroom. A skinny bald guy who was there a lot was leaning over to tell the story of his life, and Adam was nodding along.

"I need to talk to you in private," I said to Adam.

The skinny bald guy looked up at me. "I was just in the middle of something."

"Oh, please," I said. "I'm sorry for interrupting you while you tell Adam for the thousandth time about how sorry you are about being someone who **CHOOSES GLAMOUR OVER CHILDREN**. Maybe you can address that issue by actually going home and hanging out with your kids."

This made Adam laugh, maybe not only because I was quoting verbatim from something he had said a few weeks earlier to a guy with an identical tattoo. The bald guy had that crestfallen look that people get in the few seconds before their personality decides for them whether they're going to get sad or angry. He looked like he was tilting toward sad, so Adam took a puff on his cigar and slapped the man's back.

"The epiphany machine is worthless to people who can't take advice," he said. "So my advice is not to be one of those people. Now go home to your kids."

"Can I explain why I don't think that's a good idea after you talk with Venter?"

Adam did not hide the rolling of his eyes. "Fine."

As soon as we were alone, Adam said to me: "That was good, man. Keep talking to people that way. Ward off other people's opinions with your own."

"The guy who was just here," I said. "Be careful around him. He wants to mass-produce the machine."

"Oh, you mean Douglavich? He talks that nonsense all the time. He's harmless."

How could you have been so stupid, Venter? "I should have realized that. He was pretty obviously just a crazy guy who could never have anything like that kind of money."

"No, he has a lot of money. A lot. He could buy and sell me. He could buy and sell Si Strauss. His name is Vladimir Harrican. You should read about him; he's an interesting guy. But don't worry, we're not selling out."

I was, if anything, even more sympathetic than the average teenager to any argument against selling out, and to the argument that there was no difference between selling and selling out. But that's not what I was concerned with.

"It wouldn't be possible to sell out, right? Because the machine is the machine and can't be copied once, let alone mass-produced."

"Anything can be mass-produced," Adam said, "as long as you don't care about quality."

The next day, I went to the library and was pointed to a recent (and rather lurid and gossipy) book about post-Soviet Russia that included a chapter on Vladimir Douglavich Harrican and his family. Vladimir's father, Douglas Harrican, was a famous British violinist who defected to the Soviet Union in 1965. The book reported that Douglas may have used the epiphany machine while he was living in New York and that his tattoo might have inspired him to leave his fiancée and the West. (Adam refused to explicitly confirm to me whether Douglas had used the machine, saying only that he couldn't be expected to remember every British tourist with some musical ability who wandered in looking for some divine advice in American spelling.)

Virtually the moment Douglas arrived in Moscow, a provincial party leader named Anton Vasiliev, sensing an advantage in an alliance with the prominent, dashing convert, introduced him to his beautiful daughter, Anya, and, it seems, all but forced a marriage between them. Anton prepared a lavish concert that was sure to enhance his status in the party. But on the eve of the concert, Douglas announced that he was not going to perform, at that engagement or ever again. His tattoo was **MUST MAKE DIFFERENT USE OF HANDS**, which Douglas read to mean that he had to work in a factory rather than play the violin. The party, which had relished the thought of parading this violinist around the Western capitals he had renounced, was greatly displeased, but it was decided that coercing, jailing, or expelling Douglas would be ineffective at best and counterproductive at worst. Someone in the party who had evidently read about the machine and had a sense of humor put him to work in a factory that assembled, among other things, sewing machines.

Anton's status in the party was greatly diminished by the episode, and he himself was sent to work in the same factory. Anton and Douglas worked side by side on the assembly line, cursing at each other under their breath all day in a mix of English and Russian, and then returned home to yell at each other all night. Vladimir's early childhood was dominated by screaming matches among his father, grandfather, and mother, replaced by screaming matches between his father and grandfather when his mother died shortly after Vladimir turned six.

After several years, Douglas grew tired of making repetitive motions with his hands that did not require talent or skill, tired of his coworkers, most of whom took Anton's lead in hating this strange tattooed Englishman who had appeared in their ranks, and he tried to return to playing the violin. But by now his hands were mangled. He had broken three of his fingers and worn the rest down, and he was judged unsuitable even to teach the violin to children. Finally, when Vladimir was thirteen, Douglas decided that the different use he must make of his hands was putting a gun into his mouth and pulling the trigger.

Anton remained furious with Douglas, even then. But he was a cunning, resourceful, and determined man, not the sort to give up. Slowly, he rose to become manager of the factory, and he used this position to become, at the apparent prodding of Vladimir, one of the first to smuggle personal computers into the country, an endeavor that proved much more successful than even he could have imagined. As the Soviet system collapsed, Anton and Vladimir used their considerable and retroactively legitimate wealth to take control of a number of formerly state-owned companies. Anton died of a heart attack in 1995, leaving Vladimir a billionaire and his grandfather's presumed successor at the pinnacle of the new Russian system. But Vladimir detested Russia and moved to New York, using his billions to make investments, mostly in the tech sector, which had made him more billions.

All this left me with many questions, not least of them why someone would want to invest in the mass production of a machine that looked like a device that his father had stood on an assembly line mass-producing until he killed himself, or why he wanted to hang out with the man who had given his father the tattoo that had led him to that assembly line in the first place.

His strange and dark upbringing, his complex psychological reasons for both hating and being fascinated by the epiphany machine, and the perfect English he had learned from his father all left me with a theory that I knew was far-fetched, but that I kept on thinking about and filling in details for: that he was Steven Merdula.

In any case, I intended to ask him many more questions the next time I saw him. But after that night he had talked to me, his frequent visits suddenly ceased, and I never saw him at Adam's apartment again. I wish I had never seen him again at all.

That instant was I turn'd into a hart;
And my desires, like fell and cruel hounds,
E'er since pursue me.

—WILLIAM SHAKESPEARE, *Twelfth Night*

There was nothing inside the head of Rebecca Hart. The mind of a woman who murders her children can never be opened, and what can never be opened is empty.

There was nothing inside the head of Rebecca Hart. Her father told her this many times. My princess can't seem to figure out how to play the piano no matter how many lessons we pay for, but that is for the best, because men do not like women who make a racket. My princess doesn't seem to be taking well to her French lessons, does she, but that is for the best, because one language is all a woman needs. My princess is not the sharpest knife in the drawer, is she, but that's very good, because a man does not want his woman to be a knife, sharp or otherwise, but rather a drawer, in which he can store what he needs.

There was nothing inside the head of Rebecca Hart. Fearing her father, she told her mother that she did not like to be called a princess. Only a very stupid little girl would not like to be called a princess, her mother responded. A princess was the best thing a little girl could be.

There was nothing inside the head of Rebecca Hart. She read books about Greek and Roman mythology. Long after she was supposed to have gone to sleep, she would read under her blankets, pretending that she was in a tent with Ulysses, plotting strategy against the Trojans. She did almost no schoolwork.

There was nothing inside the head of Rebecca Hart. Her mother insisted on taking her to see *Sleeping Beauty*, then insisted on taking her to see it again, and a third time, and then her mother had the gall to complain to her friends that Rebecca was forcing *her* to see it.

There was nothing inside the head of Rebecca Hart. Rebecca *did* envy Sleeping Beauty her good fortune in getting pricked by a needle and sleeping for a hundred years, waking up to find a different world. When Rebecca pricked *her* finger with a needle, she found nothing but blood, and not even very much of that.

There was nothing inside the head of Rebecca Hart. One boy followed her home whispering rude things. She could provide the heart, he said, and he could provide something else. That was clever, she told him, that pun on her name, and she told him another pun on her name: "Hart" is a little-known synonym for "deer." She told him the story of Actaeon, who spied on Artemis, the goddess of hunting, as she was bathing in the woods; in vengeance, she turned him into a deer, a deer who was then torn apart by his own hunting dogs. The boy turned away and left her alone. As her father often said, men do not like women who pose a threat.

There was nothing inside the head of Rebecca Hart. Her guidance counselor told her he did not have time for girls who wanted to attend college, particularly girls with academic records as spotty as hers. She was not certain she disagreed; she was not certain she belonged in college. Perhaps she belonged in jail, having killed her guidance counselor. She did not kill her guidance counselor and went to college instead.

There was nothing inside the head of Rebecca Hart. This was almost the first thing that Elliot told her. The results of her tests and her work suggested that she was not likely to do much better than a B. The pleasure she took in Homer and in Athenian drama was admirable, but divorced from an ability to master the languages, her pleasure offered no hope of a future career in classics. Maybe she could be a high school drama teacher somewhere, make kids love Sophocles. But that seemed like it would be a shame; she was so beautiful that she should be a movie star. She was more heart than head, if she did not mind his saying so.

There was nothing inside the head of Rebecca Hart. Otherwise, she would have cursed at him and left his office. It wasn't even *his* office. He was just a graduate teaching assistant.

There was nothing inside the head of Rebecca Hart. Otherwise, she would not have taken his words as confirmation, even for a moment, that there was indeed nothing in her head. She certainly would not have agreed to go back to his apartment with him.

There was nothing inside the head of Rebecca Hart. Otherwise, she would have found a way to find a doctor who would perform an abortion.

There was nothing inside the head of Rebecca Hart. Otherwise, she would not have left school.

There was nothing inside the head of Rebecca Hart. Otherwise, she would not have agreed to marry him.

There was nothing inside the head of Rebecca Hart. Otherwise, she would have insisted that Elliot help out around the house in some way. Instead, whenever she asked him to so much as take out the garbage, he grumbled, "I'm an intellectual," and refused to budge from his armchair. Seven months pregnant, she took out the garbage.

There was nothing inside the head of Rebecca Hart. Otherwise, she would not have been fooled even for a moment into thinking that she could be happy caring for this red, screaming thing.

There was nothing inside the head of Rebecca Hart. Otherwise, she would not have been surprised when the only permanent job Elliot could find was at a tiny college in a tiny town.

There was nothing inside the head of Rebecca Hart. Otherwise, she would not have calmed herself with a pursuit as mundane and as stupidly female as sewing.

There was nothing inside the head of Rebecca Hart. At faculty dinners, it was easy enough to watch professors and their wives come to this conclusion as soon as they saw her.

There was nothing inside the head of Rebecca Hart. And her head, already empty, somehow got emptier every time she wiped up spit or put her fingers over her eyes as though this would make her gone.

There was nothing inside the head of Rebecca Hart. Hunched over her sewing machine, she resembled neither Helen nor Penelope, who had neither machines nor thoroughly worthless husbands.

There was nothing inside the head of Rebecca Hart. She pricked her finger and wished that that pricking would put her into a sleep from which she would not wake up, even in a hundred years.

There was nothing inside the head of Rebecca Hart. But there was another thing inside her womb.

There was nothing inside the head of Rebecca Hart. Babies were supposed to be pleasant to look at. The first time around, she thought that maybe she just happened to get a rare ugly baby. Now she knew that all babies were ugly. Slightly less ugly than adults. But louder.

There was nothing inside the head of Rebecca Hart. Two children, two years, no sleep. Any mind she once had was gone.

There was nothing inside the head of Rebecca Hart. That did not mean that she did not know that Elliot was having an affair with the coed who was in the living room, listening to him tell her how he envisioned her playing Antigone in a major Broadway production.

There was nothing inside the head of Rebecca Hart. Jobs and rumors of jobs. Now there was a rumor of a job at Cornell. He was trying to get to Ithaca. Ha, ha, ha.

There was nothing inside the head of Rebecca Hart. For Elliot's interview, they left the kids with Elliot's parents and took a car trip to Ithaca. A large part of Rebecca hoped that a monster would devour her and Elliot en route.

There was nothing inside the head of Rebecca Hart. On the way back, they spent several nights in a hotel room near Central Park. The intent was to rekindle their relationship. They did have a lot of sex, granted by Rebecca mostly to interrupt Elliot's monologue about how the faculty had set him up to fail so that they could hire somebody's unimaginative nephew.

There was nothing inside the head of Rebecca Hart. On their last night in New York, Elliot fell asleep early and Rebecca went for a walk. Each step she took was a step away from Elliot. She could stay in the city forever, or get on a bus and by morning be in a town she had never heard of.

There was nothing inside the head of Rebecca Hart. Otherwise, she would have kept walking when a man tapped her on the shoulder and told her she looked lonely and sad. She would have run away when he unbuttoned his sleeve and pulled it up to reveal a tattoo that said **FIRST MAN TO LIE ON**. She certainly would not have once again followed a man back to his apartment.

There was nothing inside the head of Rebecca Hart. Otherwise, when she went home with this strange man, she would never have used his machine, no matter how much she wanted to believe that there was something within her that, if only she could find it, might offer a way out of herself.

There was nothing inside the head of Rebecca Hart. Otherwise, she would have seen **OFFSPRING WILL NOT LEAD HAPPY LIVES** for what most of us agree it was: a fortune-teller's guess.

And maybe that's how she did see it. Maybe that tattoo had nothing to do with what happened. Nine months after that trip to New York, she gave birth to a third baby, and three months after that, she drowned that baby in the bathtub along with his two older brothers. Maybe, as some have speculated, Adam Lyons was the baby's father, and she felt shame for cheating on her husband. Most likely, something happened to the chemistry of her brain that left her with little of what we would call choice.

There was nothing inside the head of Rebecca Hart. Maybe when, in Adam's apartment, she saw her tattoo for the first time, she felt elated. She returned to the hotel, taking a comfortable stroll with no knowledge of what was already growing inside her. She had every intention of telling Elliot that she was leaving him. She would also be leaving Greek myths. There would be something for her beyond benighted people doing bloody things. She did not yet know what that was, but she would figure it out as soon as she was free of this man whom she had punished herself into marrying for reasons she could not even remember. But maybe she intended to tell Elliot she was leaving only after seeing her children one final time and giving them the sweetest news that a mother can truthfully give: that their unhappy lives were just beginning.

CHAPTER

— · · ◆ · · —

14

I will never forget the first time I saw someone receive a **DOES NOT UNDERSTAND BOUNDARIES** tattoo. I was assisting Adam in the epiphany room, and to the extent that I had noticed anything about Peter Stevens before seeing his tattoo, it was that he seemed to be a type of guest I was starting to recognize: the midlife-crisis guest. In his mid-forties and marked by a deep tan, Peter had driven in for the night from Hartford, where two decades earlier he had taken a job in the insurance industry in the hope of becoming the next Wallace Stevens, "a spiritual ancestor though not a literal one." Peter's poetry hadn't thrived, but his insurance career had. He told me how he wished he were still writing about nothing happening beautifully and living in a hovel like this one rather than making bets about terrible things happening expensively and living in a mansion that he called "the opposite of poetry." If I wanted his advice, he had told me while he was waiting in line, I should follow my dreams, because that way I would not have regrets. Then he started talking about the influence of Wallace Stevens's poem "The Idea of Order at Key West" on the Beatles' "Lucy in the Sky with Diamonds," saying that they were both about water and women, "two things we can't live without that are impossible to grasp." I lost the thread of his argument and started thinking about whether believing it was important to "follow my dreams" meant that I was **DEPENDENT ON THE OPINION OF OTHERS**, given that everyone else seemed to believe that, too.

"Excuse me," he said. "Are you even listening to me?"

He was an overtanned middle-aged rich guy in a polo shirt, looking like an actor who had gone from playing the rich asshole who loses the girl to playing the rich asshole who is the father of the girl, but he was still a human being, and therefore deserved to be listened to and not to be lied to. I decided to lie and say I was listening to him, but I don't think he listened to my lie.

"John Lennon was drawn here because he was a visionary," he said. "There are always going to be people who destroy visionaries."

We kept chatting until it was his turn to use the machine. I nodded along as Peter explained for a second time his theory about "The Idea of Order at Key West" and "Lucy in the Sky with Diamonds" ("The woman is the same! In the first she's in the sea, in the second she's been exiled to the river!"). I comforted him when the needle pierced his skin and continued to comfort him when he started screaming. I was getting gauze from the cabinet when I heard Adam make an unhappy grunt I'd never heard him make before.

"**DOES NOT UNDERSTAND BOUNDARIES**," Peter said. "I love it! It's true that I don't understand boundaries. Nor should I. Boundaries are for the timid."

"How is your relationship with your children, Mister Stevens?" Adam asked. He didn't call anybody "Mister" unless he hated them.

"Very good," he said. "I want to show them everything."

"Uh-huh. And what do you mean by 'everything'?"

"Excuse me?"

"I'm pretty sure you know what I'm talking about."

"Um, no, I don't."

"Do you have a daughter named Lucy with whom you like to be alone? Is that why you're strangely obsessed with that song?"

"I have a daughter I named Lucy because I like the song. Are you suggesting that I behave inappropriately with her?"

"I would suggest that you do *not* behave inappropriately with her. Unfortunately, the machine believes that you are behaving inappropriately with somebody's children, if not your own."

Peter grabbed the gauze from my hands and held it to his tattoo. I was too shocked and confused to do anything. "I'm leaving. And I'd like my money back."

Adam flung some bills from his shirt pocket onto the floor. "There. Maybe use it to pay for a hooker so you leave kids alone."

Peter took a hard swing at Adam, for which I couldn't exactly blame him. Adam fell back into the epiphany machine chair and I held Peter back from taking another punch. He struggled free easily, but he calmed down a little.

"I don't know what your deal is," Peter said, "but your arm is certainly right that you're the first man to tell lies. You'd better not spread this completely baseless bullshit around." He stomped through the curtain, leaving the bills on the floor.

"What was that?" I asked Adam. "Do you know him?"

"I've never seen him before, and I hope never to see him again."

I pulled out another gauze pad to apply to Adam's lip.

"So why did you freak out like that? That tattoo seemed pretty harmless."

"Only child molesters get that tattoo."

"What are you talking about? My freshman-year Global Studies teacher got that tattoo, and she's not a . . ." I stopped myself, thinking about what had happened in the bathroom when I was fourteen.

"She? Your freshman-year Global Studies teacher? Michelle Scarra?"

I was surprised that he knew her name, since I had never mentioned her. "She told me she had gotten that tattoo, and then she left school so as not to be tempted. But honestly, if I was traumatized, it was only because nothing happened."

"That's jejune bullshit, Venter." I tried to put the gauze on his mouth but he waved me off. "An adult should not be making advances on a high school freshman."

"But 'boundaries' could mean practically anything. Why do you think that tattoo meant that Peter is molesting his kids?"

"Because every time somebody gets one of those tattoos they turn out to be a child molester. This is the fourteenth time it's happened. Fifteen if you count Scarra. I was hoping she'd be okay."

"And you're sure it's every time? That's not a common epiphany?"

"Fifteen instances is pretty common."

"But aren't epiphanies open-ended?"

"As far as I know, every epiphany is open-ended except for this one. If I could ask the god who's writing these things why this particular tattoo has been chosen for this particular purpose, I would. But I know that these people are child molesters, so I do something about it."

"How do you know they're child molesters?"

"I pay attention to these tattoos. There have been arrests. Now I don't wait for the arrests."

"So what do you do? Report them to the cops?"

Adam laughed, which hurt his mouth. "I would never report anyone to the cops. I have principles."

"Call Child Protective Services?"

"I don't think they take calls from people they consider cult leaders."

"So what *do* you do?"

"You don't need to worry about it," he said, walking to the curtain to let in the next guest. I blocked his way.

"What do you do?" I asked again.

"I call a friend."

"And what does your friend do?"

"Whatever he thinks is appropriate."

"Adam, are you killing people?"

"You think if there were a bunch of corpses that all had the same tattoo, that wouldn't get attention? Trust me, you would have heard about something like that. What happens to guests with that tattoo is what happens to all my guests: they are given an opportunity to change. It's just that in their case, the importance of changing is impressed on them more firmly."

"So you're going to have somebody beat Peter up?"

"That man is a pervert."

"Adam, this is totally wrong and unethical."

"You think I don't know that? Nobody cares more about privacy than I do. Except maybe your dad, and he's a freak. A man's tattoo is his own business. But this is different, this is kids."

"But isn't this a slippery slope?"

"Yes. So we'll just have to work harder to keep our balance. The other option is not doing anything at all, and just allowing kids to be abused. Is that what you want?"

There was no evidence that Peter Stevens was a pedophile; he was just somebody who liked to bore people with his half-baked theories, and if we were going to start killing everybody in New York who did that, the skyscrapers would soon be returned to the vines, an image that would be phallic if there were any men around to see it, which there wouldn't be. And yet the thought of what I would say to a kid who had been molested, whom I not only hadn't helped but had actively stopped from being helped, made it impossible to say anything. Except for one thing:

"Don't do anything to Ms. Scarra, okay? She never touched me. She left her job so she wouldn't touch me."

"I'm not going to have a woman beat up."

And that was it. He disappeared through the curtain and brought another guest in. A few days later, while we were cleaning up, we heard a story on the radio about a Hartford insurance executive who had been assaulted in a parking lot. Adam gave me the smallest of smiles before turning the radio off.

People who are not famous think that fame means many things, some good, some bad. John knows that fame means one thing: arms. Arms everywhere and all the time. Arms at his face, as though his eyes are diamonds to be snatched. Arms at his chest, as though there is a famine and his heart is food. Arms at his belt, as though every girl who fucks a Beatle wins a spot on the last bus to God. Arms holding pens, sign my notepad, sign my guitar, sign my program, sign onto my program, sign this contract, sign my soul.

An army of handlers to keep him from arms and hands.

An armored van saved this man from the arms and ardor of his fans.

Now, at this stadium, in heat that would be oppressive even without the sweat and skin of other people, there are more arms than ever: 111,200. All of them reaching out to John. Girls screaming, weeping, grabbing the batting cage like refugees trying to flee themselves and their lives in search of whatever they imagine John can give them.

On his way to the stage, he tosses a pack of Gauloises cigarettes—an *empty* pack of Gauloises cigarettes—and he watches what the pack does to the arms and what the arms do to the pack. What the pack does to the pack. John is nearly blind without his glasses but he can see enough. The arms push each other, slice at each other. The arms would do any harm to each other or the people they're attached to to claim the great prize of John Lennon's garbage. These people may think they're people, but their arms know better. Either you're John Lennon, or you're a thing that grabs for things touched by John Lennon. And in the process of grabbing, you turn John Lennon into a thing.

He wanted to be the king and was the last to learn that the king is a thing of nothing.

As soon as he has shaken the clammy hand of the undertaker who embalms the music of the young, John feels tempted to do his cripple routine, hobble around the stage with his arms curled up into grotesque claws. He's been doing this act all his life. As a child, he imitated cripples on buses. Any joy he feels in performing has this mockery at its root. He thinks about doing this for the entire show and not playing any music. But John the cruel bully is not the John for which these arms have pressed cash into other arms.

Then they start to play, and everything is better. The John who places his arms at the service of his guitar, his lungs at the service of the song, and his entire being at the service of the group, this is the John that he is supposed to be, and it is much more fun to be this John than any John wants to admit. Singing with Paul and clowning with Paul is obviously what he is here—here in this stadium, here in the universe—to do, and he wishes that he could do these things and only these things and make every other aspect of his life and of his mind disappear. There are even moments when he succeeds, even tonight. At one point, introducing a song, Paul gets confused about which record it came from, their last record or the one before that, and John throws his arms in every direction, and the crowd laughs, and it is wonderful. The show would be better if John were doing air traffic control for the planes that periodically fly overhead, since the screaming makes it impossible for anyone in the crowd to hear anything. He could spend the entire concert telling everyone to go fuck themselves—he could actually speak the thoughts in his head—and no one would know the difference.

Maybe he could have more fun if it weren't for the arms in this stadium. It looks like a vision of Hell, a mountain of limbs stacked high.

Girl after girl rushes onto the field, running with arms extended for the stage. John beckons them, mostly for the fun of seeing pair of reaching arms after pair of reaching arms get enveloped by the meatier arms of the cops.

But one girl almost gets through. It takes him a moment to realize that it *is* a girl, because her head is shaved and there is a tattoo on her arm. Her bald skull transfixes him.

The mountain of arms, which cheered the other girls, jeers this one. The cops embraced the other girls eagerly, probably the closest the cops have come to fucking in years, but they approach this one diffidently, as though she might bite. One almost has her, but she slips away. There is a piece of paper in her hand.

At this point she is so close that even blind John can read her tattoo. Or almost. He is actually misreading it, slightly. What he reads is **HORRIFIED TO CREATE LOVE**.

This is the woman for him. All this love he has created, and he is horrified by it. Together they will create more love to be horrified by. She will jump on stage and John will ask if there is a preacher in the house—surely there must be one—and then they will be married. Technically it will be bigamy, but Cynthia can be dealt with later.

Inches from the stage, the girl is caught by cops. She kicks and kicks and flings the piece of paper on to the stage, where it lands at John's feet. He reads her tattoo over and over as she is dragged away, and he picks up the piece of paper between songs. The words "The Epiphany Machine" are written below a drawing of a sewing machine. Below that is an address, not terribly far from their hotel.

He puts the paper in his pocket and he feels elated for the rest of the set, casting his guitar aside and banging madly on the organ throughout "I'm Down," not playing anything coherent, not thinking of the army of arms—no one in the audience can hear the music over the screaming anyway—but thinking only of the night ahead.

After the show, he asks to be dropped off at the address on the paper. The others don't want to hear it—they suggest that someone be sent to bring the girl back to the hotel—but he is not in a mood to be denied.

To his surprise, the door is opened not by the girl but by a bearded, paunchy man about his own age—exactly his own age, they will later discover, born on the same day. The man has large, half-moon sweat stains under his arms. His arms themselves are matted with sweat; on one of them is written **FIRST MAN TO LIE ON**.

"Your sister in?" John asks.

"My sister?"

"The bald, tattooed lady. She your wife? I'm afraid I can't let you stay in the room during the act, if that's your thing."

"Are you a sheriff?"

"Excuse me?"

"Your badge."

John looks down and sees that he is still wearing the Wells Fargo badge that all four of them were given after the ride in the armored van from the helicopter to the stadium.

"No, I'm not a sheriff."

"I was joking. You don't have a sheriff's air of authority. You look desperate and lost, like almost everybody else who comes to use the epiphany machine. Do you want some whiskey?"

To his own surprise, John follows the man inside. "I'm not here to use the epiphany machine. I'm here to use—see—the bald girl."

"Lillian?"

"Is Lillian bald? Is she here?"

"Want to take off your jacket? It's very hot."

"I'll leave it on. Do you know where Lillian is or not?"

"No. She came by yesterday for one of my flyers, said she was going to a concert. The Beatles, I think. Is that where you met her?"

"Yes. Great show."

The bearded man gives a long and heavy shrug. "I'm much more of a Dylan fan."

So, to John's annoyance, is John.

The bearded man pours two glasses of whiskey, and then he pulls out some rolling paper and a bag of marijuana.

"You know, I got high with Dylan," John says.

"Oh? Do you work somewhere he performed?"

"I'm John Lennon."

"Who?"

"You've heard my name."

"Oh, are you one of them? The only name I can remember is Ringo."

"I'm a big fan of Ringo's. No Dylan, but he's still pretty good." He takes a drag on the joint that Adam has just rolled. "Thanks for this, but if you don't know where Lillian is, I'll be on my way."

"You didn't come for Lillian," the bearded man says. "You came for the epiphany machine."

"What *is* the epiphany machine?"

"It's the universe, when the universe wants to hold your hand."

"You do know my music."

"I can't get away from your music, just like I can't get away from inane giggling babies. That's what you and your friends sound like to me, inane giggling babies. Don't you want to be more than that?"

"Who the hell are you?"

"Adam Lyons. I'm the guy who, very shortly, will operate the epiphany machine while it tattoos the truth about you onto your arm."

"So, that's what the girl's tattoo was. Well, let me tell you right now that there's no way I'm using your daft machine."

"As you might say: yeah, yeah, yeah."

They talk for hours, but John knows already that he will use the machine.

It is two o'clock when John finally removes the tan jacket he has been wearing all night, and which is now drenched with sweat. He settles into Adam's chair and gives his arm to Adam and the needle.

The pain is tolerable. What is not tolerable is what he starts to think of as he stares at his arm: hitting Cynthia. He is able, often, to forget for weeks, months, years at a time that he has ever done so, but now, now that he keeps on looking at his arm, he cannot deny that that arm is his and that it has hit Cynthia. That he has hit Cynthia.

SEES NOTHING FROM THE TOP OF THE MOUNTAIN

Of course. Of course. For a long time—forever?—he has focused on how little other people see and has not focused on how little he sees. He has a view of the world that almost no one else has ever had, and from that view he sees nothing.

The nothing that he sees all looks different now. All the arms that reach for him, they are not reaching for him, they are reaching up in surrender, not surrender to him but surrender to something that has no name. What could be more beautiful? Those 111,200 arms crowded together to become one with each other, and with everything else. That is what he has to offer: through him, the universe brings all of its wayward children back to it. Until now—*until now*—he has been left out. Now, now he is no longer selfish. Now he no longer has a self. Now he is what everyone is and should be: a Beatles fan.

CHAPTER

— · · ✦ · · —

15

O nce school started again, I didn't have any time to spend at
Adam's, but I spent all my time there anyway. I chose my classes
mostly to avoid seeing Ismail and Leah, and though it was impossible to avoid them completely in the hallways, it was easy to keep our
conversations perfunctory. Occasionally, I would have to field rude questions from near-strangers about my tattoo and/or the cult I had joined—a
good way, really, to break myself of being **DEPENDENT ON THE OPIN-
ION OF OTHERS**, since these people all thought I was a wackjob and I
thought they could go fuck themselves—but this was rare and got rarer as
the year progressed, so mostly I would spend my classes thinking about
the epiphany machine, and then I would get on a Metro-North train and
be at Adam's by 4:30.

The stream of guests was fairly steady during the week, usually around
ten per night, even on nights that were not salon nights. My reputation was
growing among former guests, and sometimes they returned just to tell
me their story. These people mostly had the most boring stories to tell,
canned and self-congratulatory, their tapes for all intents and purposes
lost before they had finished speaking.

One Saturday morning, I saw a *New York Post* cover about Michelle Scarra, a high school teacher in upstate New York who had been arrested for having sex with a fifteen-year-old student.

"Did you have anything to do with this?" I asked Adam, who was already smoking a cigar.

"That headline? 'Hot for Teacher'? I could have done better than that."

"Did you report her?"

He took a puff. "I had a guy look into what she was doing. Found her in bed with this kid. My guy would never have called the cops. He was just going to talk to her. I don't mean that as a euphemism; he was really just going to *talk* to her. But she called the cops on him when she caught him outside her window. When they arrived, she stupidly told them everything about the kid she was fucking. The whole thing's a shame, but predators are predators, buddy."

"How do you know she was harming this kid? He probably liked it."

"He probably loved it. She still belongs in prison."

"Sounds awfully puritanical for a guy smoking a cigar and drinking Scotch at ten o'clock in the morning. This is a woman's life."

"Which she shouldn't have thrown away by fucking teenagers."

"Teenager. One. She resisted the urge with me."

"Venter, I hate to break this to you, but there were probably others. You should consider yourself lucky that she found you resistible."

"She quit her job because she couldn't trust herself around me! She wanted to do the right thing. She tried to do the right thing."

"If trying to do the right thing were the same as doing the right thing, nobody would ever feel the need to use the machine. But a lot of people do feel that need, and a lot of them are coming today. So would you like to help me get ready?"

I argued for a bit longer, but I already knew I was going to give in, and I did.

I have to admit it was always fun to watch Adam field a difficult question from somebody who had come only to ask Adam a difficult question.

"If you've figured out the secret to life," one guy asked, "then why aren't you married?"

Adam put out his cigar and rubbed his palms together. "So many assumptions in one simple question. Venter, would you like to enumerate?"

"He's assuming that it's you rather than the machine who's doing the figuring out."

"Boom!" He put up one finger. "That's the first assumption. What's the second?"

"He's assuming that what's being figured out is one thing, rather than many things."

"Nothing but net!" He put up a second finger. "Now let's make it a hat trick, whatever a hat trick is."

"He's assuming that what's being figured out is about life in general, rather than the specific life of the specific guest."

"And that is . . . correct! Now, do you want to take your winnings and go home, or do you want to try our bonus round?"

"He's assuming that the machine deals in secrets, rather than in truths so obvious we can't help but forget them."

"Shazam! Brilliant. Speaking of which, you've left out the most obvious one."

"That enlightenment necessarily leads to marriage?"

"That's good, too, but I was thinking of something more obvious."

"Just because you've used the machine, and just because you own the machine, you've benefitted from it?"

"There we go. You see," he said, "I make no claims to knowing anything more about myself than anyone else knows about themselves. You never really know yourself, even if you've used the epiphany machine, worked hard to understand what it has told you, and then worked even harder to adjust your behavior to account for what your tattoo has revealed as lies, evasions, and nasty delusions. Even if we do all this, our sense of ourselves will still be far from perfect. Even in the best outcome, I will still be the missing link in my own evolution."

He took a long drag from his joint, and then looked at the man who had asked the question. "So," he said. "The needle or the door?"

Later that night—maybe another night, almost certainly another night, the nights blur—as I was vacuuming the epiphany room as Adam had requested, he stood in the threshold, draping himself in the velvet curtain, and stared at me.

"Am I vacuuming wrong?" I asked.

He laughed a gently mocking laugh I had never heard before. "I'm amazed at just how much like themselves people can be."

"Would you rather I not vacuum?"

"Can you tell me something?" he said. "Are you any closer to finding your mother than you were the first night you came to see me?"

"No," I said. "I guess not."

"What have you done to find her?"

"Very little."

"Very little is not nothing. Give me an example of what you've done."

I tried to think, one of my favorite ways of not thinking. "I always hope when I interview somebody who used the machine in the seventies that they might have kept in touch with my mother or something."

"Do you ask them if they know your mother?"

"I figure that if they do, they'll tell me."

"It doesn't sound like you're trying to find your mother."

"I guess I'm not sure if I want to find her. If she were worth finding, she would have returned to my grandmother before she died. I don't know how she would have known my grandmother was sick. It's not rational. But I don't have to explain to you about believing things that aren't rational."

"So why do you keep coming here?"

"I guess I'm hoping that if I see enough models for how people have used their epiphanies, I'll figure out how to use my epiphany."

He gave me a look that told me he liked this answer. Maybe the search for this look from authority figures has always been the major search of my life.

"More of my guests should think about *using* their epiphanies," he said. "Too many people think they can just come here, get something written on their arm, and their lives will magically change. You're a very special young man, Venter."

I was not sure that I had learned anything from other people's epiphanies; in fact, I was sure that I had not. But I said nothing about this to Adam. His faith in me was misplaced, but not unwelcome.

When it became clear that I was not going to respond, Adam continued. "I don't think anyone has understood the machine so well since your mother."

This made me cry, even though I wasn't sure what it meant. Adam lifted his arms into something other than a shrug and embraced me.

"Your mother was the smartest person I've ever met. You should have heard her observations about the people who used the machine. I should have written them down. She should have written them down."

Adam's feeling for me was starting to come into focus: he had been in love with my mother and therefore regarded me as his son.

"Be honest with me," I said. "Do you know where my mother is?"

"I have no idea," he said. "If I did, I would tell you."

"How about Si Strauss?" I asked. "He must have been paying her salary, right? She must be making money somehow, if she's still alive. Maybe he's still giving her money."

Adam released me from his embrace. "I paid Rose with my own money."

"But that money was provided by Si, right?"

Now Adam was angry. "People who want to destroy the machine always exaggerate Si Strauss's role in what I do. I could be doing all of this without him. The wild conspiracy theory you're spinning sounds like something out of that goddamn Merdula book."

I looked at Adam and felt sorry for him, that his dreams were dependent on a rich man's whims, though I knew that that was true for almost everyone.

But this was an opportunity to ask a question I had been wanting to ask for a long time.

"Is Vladimir Harrican Steven Merdula?"

"Douglavich?" I could see in his eyes that he suddenly found this plausible. "He would have been around twenty when Merdula started publishing."

"Not impossible." I still had vague hopes of publishing my first book when I was around twenty.

"It's not worth thinking about," he said, headed again for the velvet curtain. "Get back to vacuuming. Nobody wants to hear from the heavens when there's dirt on the floor."

One more story and then I'll have to get to the day Ismail came to Adam's apartment. On a night when I had missed the last Metro-North train, Adam and I walked to a drugstore to get some candy. Another aisle over was a guy shopping for shampoo, a beefy guy with thick, messy white hair and a tattoo on his forearm that depicted his own head with a snake wrapped around it. (The hair in the tattoo was equally messy, but black.) I saw him see Adam and keep on glancing over while Adam was deciding between a bag of M&M's and a bag of Kit Kats.

"Another fan," I said.

Almost as soon as Adam looked up, he grabbed a Toblerone and threw it at the guy, missing and knocking some Head & Shoulders from the shelf.

"Counterfeiter!" Adam yelled. "Fraud!" He was shaking, something I'd never seen him do.

The white-haired guy picked up the Toblerone off the checkered floor, calmly unwrapped it, and took a bite before deliberately dropping it again.

"I'm the fraud? People come to you for the meaning of life and you give them tattoos. People come to me for tattoos and I give them tattoos."

"Goddamn it, Goldberg. Don't you realize that these are people's souls you're playing with? Doesn't that make any difference to you?"

"Doesn't it make any difference to *you*? Nobody expects to leave my shop knowing any more about themselves than they did when they came in. Though they often do leave knowing more. You'd be surprised how much people can learn about themselves just by discovering what they ask for."

"You're asking for it, all right."

The only term for what happened next that feels either accurate or fully immersed in the context of the moment is that Adam lost his shit. That is what I thought while Adam pulled Twizzlers and Skittles and Hershey's Kisses from the shelves: "Adam is losing his shit." The security guard would have been entirely justified in calling the police, but, out of generosity or laziness—the two most underrated human qualities—he just looked at me and said: "Can you control your old men, please?"

I said I would, and that I would clean up the candy. Adam was settling down, like a toddler after a tantrum, and I sent him home. Goldberg stuck around to help me pick up the candy. And of course he told me his story.

NAME: Daniel Goldberg

DATE OF BIRTH: 10/05/1942

DATE OF EPIPHANY MACHINE USE: N/A

DATE OF INTERVIEW BY VENTER LOWOOD: 07/15/1999

Most tattoo artists hate the epiphany machine, and for good reason. It's a cheap perversion of what we do. If Adam Lyons were peddling some kind of magic dance that healed your soul, don't you think choreographers would hate him? If he ran a magic barbershop, don't you think barbers would start daydreaming about what they'd do with their scissors if they could get him in their chair? Furthermore, the epiphany machine negates the most important aspect of tattooing: choice. Real tattoos are a kind of marriage vow you make with your current self; you're saying that who you are is who you will always be and what you want is what you will always want. A lot of marriages go bad, but there's still something beautiful in marriage. There's something beautiful in saying: My heart has stopped in exactly this position and will stay in this position until it stops for good. Epiphany tattoos are arranged marriages, except without the consolations of community. They're like being fixed up by a stranger with another stranger on a blind date that lasts the rest of your life.

But I've always loved the epiphany machine because, boy, is it good for business. At the height of the epiphany craze, in the late seventies, before Chapman and AIDS, over eighty percent of my business was epiphany-related. A lot of people came to me asking for tattoos in the epiphany font saying things like **LOVES HIS WIFE DEEPLY** or **DOES NOT MISS HER CAREER** or—let me see if I can remember this one verbatim—**WOULD ABSOLUTELY PUT HIS FATHER IN A BETTER NURSING HOME IF ONLY HE HAD THE MONEY**. Some of them, like that last one, have to be written in a font too small for other people to read them, but I guess other people are not the point. My favorite—and we got some variation on this probably twice a month—was **EVEN BETTER IN BED THAN HE THINKS HE IS.**

Adam—or, rather, Si Strauss—sent a bunch of lawyers after me to harass me, since tattoos were illegal in New York City at the time. Si and Adam did permanently shut down a couple of other places that did what I do, so I guess I should be grateful to him. I had to move my shop around a lot, but they kept sending henchmen to find me. A henchman and a henchwoman, actually—there was this woman who always wore a fox fur coat, even in May, and her boyfriend, who had a Jew-fro—and they were always finding people with my tattoos and tracing them back to where I was operating. Finally, I moved to Jersey for a while. I thought that would be enough to get them to leave me alone, but then they went after me for copyright infringement, which is pretty rich considering that Adam claims to be taking dictation from God. But I survived.

I want to say that I survived because I'm stubborn, made of harder stuff than Adam or Si. And I do think that's true, but I'll never really know because the big reason I was able to survive is that my sister was a lawyer. A brilliant lawyer. She loved me and she hated the machine, and she was fucking brilliant. She argued that my service was completely different from Adam's. He offered the judgment of a higher authority, while I offered slogans, advertisements for oneself. The beauty of it was that of course Adam was a lying tank of ink, of course he was offering the same thing I was, but he could not say that. The only difference between what Adam offered and what I offered is that if you came to me, you got to choose what was written on your arm, and if you went to him, he got to choose. That's a pretty big difference, but it's not one that Adam should be proud of.

Sure, my staff and I mocked the tattoos we were making for people. I bet that prisoners making vanity license plates make fun of them, too. Human vanity is always funny, and if you paid attention either at Friday-night services or in life, you know that all is vanity. But at least my customers made the choices about what they put on their bodies. It wasn't Adam sitting up there in his rent-controlled, landlord-coddled tower sitting in judgment. I mean, honestly: fuck that.

The only person who ever really took me seriously as a craftsman was my sister. She used to sit watching me work for hours—hours that no lawyer has. She was convinced that I was a great artist. Sometimes that was almost enough to convince me that I was a great artist. In my youth, I used to have artistic pretensions, which is why I have this stupid tattoo on my forearm of my own head as an apple squeezed by a snake. I had dreamed of doing the best tattoos in the world, of just completely altering the way people thought about what could be on their bodies. Any out-of-shape forty-year-old could be my Sistine Chapel. I loved being a rebel who worked in an art form more or less banned by my religion. I wanted to be famous, I wanted to be anonymous, all that stupid stuff. Slowly I came to accept myself as a hack, meaning that I created what people wanted me to create. As though that's something to be ashamed of.

All of this doesn't even mention that I did a serious public service for the people who knew my clients. Somebody gets a tattoo saying **COMPLETELY OPEN AND HONEST**, you know not to trust him. Your husband comes home with a tattoo that says **NOT CHEATING ON WIFE**, you start to think, Maybe this asshole is cheating on me. On the other hand, if Adam Lyons talks to a guy, decides he's hiding something, and then gives that guy a **HIDES WHAT MATTERS MOST** tattoo, what does that tell his wife? Seeing that tattoo every time you make love or soap up your husband in the shower or brush your teeth side by side is going to make you suspicious. No matter how much you try to banish the thought, it's going to make you think: What is he hiding? But what does it really tell you? It tells you that Adam Lyons made a judgment, a judgment that could be right or could be wrong. In other words, it tells you jack shit.

And yes, it's true that when Adam gave some guy a **HIDES WHAT MATTERS MOST** tattoo, that guy might come to me. That particular one is tricky grammatically. A **CLOSED OFF** tattoo, you can just add a **NOT** in front, but with a **HIDES WHAT MATTERS MOST** tattoo, you have to do something like **HIDES WHAT MATTERS MOST FROM EVERY-ONE WHO IS NOT IMPORTANT**, or something else that sounds stilted and is not going to fit on everyone's forearm. You can get a tattoo or a bunch of tattoos over it, but aesthetically that's going to make you wince every time you look in the mirror, and you can usually make out the original tattoo underneath anyway. You can tattoo a black bar of redaction over it, but that looks suspicious. So you interpret the tattoo to make it go away. You just say that **FROM EVERYONE WHO IS NOT IMPOR-TANT** is implicit in **HIDES WHAT MATTERS MOST**. Now you're in the realm of trying to read something so that it says what you want it to say, which I guess is the realm everyone has been in since the invention of writing.

What I'm saying is that once you've made the mistake of seeing Adam Lyons, there's really nothing I can do for you as a tattoo artist. Your tattoo can truly be erased only by the worm that will one day eat it, or by the fire that will one day turn it into ash.

CHAPTER

◆

16

By the time Goldberg was finished talking, we were finished picking up the candy, and the candy display was the same as it was before we had come in. This story had made me as angry at Goldberg as Adam was—Goldberg was the enemy of life and knowledge, he was selling plastic fruit in the Garden of Eden—and I wanted to hurt him. But I needed to find out if he knew anything about my parents.

"Wait," I said. "That couple that you said harassed you. The woman had a fox fur coat. Tell me more about them."

"They would just track me and find me, yell at me to leave, call the cops, then repeat until the cops kicked me out. They made my life miserable for a couple of years and it didn't seem to bother either of them. I tried to engage them in conversation a few times, real conversation, but they were too brainwashed to reveal anything about themselves."

"Did they seem like they were in love?"

"In love? They often stood outside my places of business making out, but I'm pretty sure that that was just to annoy me. Brainwashed people can't be in love."

"Did you notice their relationship changing at all?"

"They kept on harassing me until I left the state. When I came back to New York, they weren't around anymore. That was pretty much all I noticed. I wasn't a marriage counselor or a Peeping Tom."

"What do you think your epiphany would be, if Adam tattooed you?"

"My epiphany? Oh, it would obviously be **WASTED HIS ARTISTIC GIFTS** or whatever Adam thought would hurt me the most."

"What if you never had any artistic gifts at all? What if you've always known that? What if **HIDES FROM LACK OF TALENT IN CYNICISM AND LIES** would be your epiphany?"

"Then it would be just like everyone else's epiphany: something that could apply to anyone."

I decided to try one last thing. "What if your sister could have done more valuable things with her law degree than help you keep your shop? How many people who needed her help did she not help so you could inscribe people's delusions onto their own skin?"

This question had, to my surprise, precisely the effect I hoped it would, and for a moment I thought Goldberg was going to knock all the candy over again. "Actually, I don't have to wonder about that. Years after the legal trouble faded away, my sister got an epiphany tattoo. She was depressed; she had cancer. She gave a fake name, and since her hair was gone and she looked very different, she didn't think Adam recognized her. But of course he did. He wrote **WASTED LIFE TRYING TO MAKE SOMEONE ELSE HAPPY** on her forearm. She had always been much smarter than I was, but those chemicals must have made her dumber, because she thought that that proved the epiphany machine was real; it had proved that she had wasted her life idolizing me for no reason. I guess Adam figured that would be pretty solid revenge against me. What he doesn't know is that before he gave her that tattoo, she asked me to choose a tattoo for her, so that she could live out her final months knowing what I thought of her. I refused, because choosing tattoos for my customers is not my bag, but what popped into my mind was **WASTED LIFE TRYING TO MAKE SOMEONE ELSE HAPPY**. So all Adam did was save me some ink."

CHAPTER

— · · ✦ · · —

17

kay. Ismail now. One hot Sunday morning the summer before I was to enter college, Adam was sitting in the corner when I arrived, and he was still sitting there two hours later, ignoring the line that had formed, ignoring the people leaving the line, ignoring the people arguing over whether Adam sitting on a stool was just some kind of cult mindfuck, or a sign that they had actually done something wrong, or a sign that the epiphany machine was broken. Finally, I asked him what was wrong, and he just sat on his stool and stared impassively. It wasn't unusual for Adam to stare impassively, but now he was missing that glint in his eye that told you that he was just going to let you argue with him until you started arguing against yourself.

"You're going to leave me, you know," Adam finally said.

I looked into Adam's eyes and saw true terror and pain, which both touched and bemused me. The thought of no longer working for him had not occurred to me.

"What? What are you talking about?"

"It's the natural way. The natural way always leads to death. In this case, the death of you and me."

"I'm going to Columbia. I'll just be uptown. It'll be much easier for me to get here than it is now."

"You're going to be ashamed of me. You're going to be hanging out with lots of cool young people, and you'll decide that you're too cool for me."

"Nonsense! I'm not too cool to hang out with anyone."

"Sure, but you won't want your classmates to find that out."

"Hey, Adam. Let's stop sitting here feeling like crap. Let's go see a movie. Way downtown."

I was expecting him to say something about not being able to leave his post, but instead he slapped his knees and said: "Okay. Let's go."

"I'm sorry?"

"I said let's go. You name the movie."

Taxi Driver was playing at Film Forum, so that's what I suggested. The fact that he accepted wound up ruining at least one life.

Adam so rarely left the Upper East Side that he had never even heard of MetroCards, and he wanted to use a token instead, but I insisted that he learn.

"This is terrible!" he said. "This is even worse than making epiphanies public. I'd rather have the government know who I am than where I am!"

If he could still get mad, I thought, he must be more or less okay.

"Everyone in this car is going to use the machine," he said, almost as soon as we stepped onto a train. He didn't seem to notice that a woman was reading Steven Merdula's *Only the Desert Is Not a Desert*, but that was just as well. "But only after we lose control of it. It's going to be taken from me, and then they'll use it."

"You mean Vladimir Harrican? The machine chose you, not him, and so did I."

"In a few years, no one will care what you or the machine think. There will be tattoos, but they will be fake, assigned, the way that people think that I fake and assign tattoos. Whatever god speaks through the machine will return to silence and will be replaced with the chatter of false prophets. But maybe that's just what these people need! What's wrong with a golden calf? It's made of gold! Who wouldn't choose that over two hunks of rock with words tattooed on them?"

He was speaking loudly, and though the twenty or so people in the car were all practiced in ignoring people who spoke too loudly on the subway, a few necks gave snap-swivels of attention at a couple of points in the speech. I looked for a friendly arm but they were all clean. As we got off the subway, I was starting to see myself through the eyes of the people around us; I was starting to wonder what I was doing with this crazy old man. The hot walk down Houston did not improve my mood. I hoped an afternoon at Film Forum would make us both feel better, despite the fact that we would be watching a movie about a disturbed man who thinks he is on a mission to save the city.

We had to line up outside, and I wanted to make sure that Adam was okay and didn't need to lean against a wall, which may be why it took me a couple of minutes to notice that Leah and Ismail were standing in line a little ahead of us. To my shock, they were holding hands. In a moment, Ismail was smiling and Leah was punching him, and when a guy is smiling and a girl is punching him, you know that they're in love.

"Venter!" Leah said, gesturing for me to cut the people ahead in line and join her and Ismail, and I complied, since either cutting the line or refusing her invitation would have been rude and I tend to err on the side of doing what I'm told. "We haven't seen you in so long." Actually, I had seen both of them at graduation little more than a month earlier, where we had barely acknowledged each other. If Leah and Ismail had been dating at the time, I certainly hadn't noticed. I was surprised that Leah was being so friendly now, and I couldn't tell whether she was magnanimously treating me like an old friend or consciously rubbing her love for Ismail in my face.

"I've been spending a lot of time with this guy right here," I said, gesturing for Adam to come save me from an awkward three-way conversation. "Adam Lyons, this is Leah and Ismail."

They each shook Adam's hand, warily. Then Ismail grabbed my shoulder and looked into my eyes like a cop trying to figure out whether I was on drugs. "I've missed you, dude," he said.

"I didn't know the two of you were dating," I said. "Mazel tov."

"We haven't told a lot of people," Leah said. "Ismail's mother would not approve."

"And you're rebelling against your mother," Adam said. "Very American of you." I wanted to kick him for this condescending remark.

"I know extremely little but have very strong opinions," Ismail said. "So I am *very* American."

Leah laughed and beamed, like she thought she was dating Lenny Bruce.

"Adam, I've read and heard a lot about you," Ismail said. "Venter and I had a teacher who was obsessed with your machine. Do you think it's true that Wernher von Braun invented the machine?"

"Where'd you hear that nonsense? In that garbage Merdula book?"

"The Wernher in the story wasn't Wernher von Braun," I corrected Ismail. "That was just a hypothetical Wernher." Of course he knew this, and was just trying to—to use an appropriate metaphor—get under Adam's skin.

The line was moving now, so we were moving, too. I started thinking about Ms. Scarra and how she was doing in prison, but I made myself stop.

"You give your life to something important," Adam said, "and people will make up lies about it."

"You tease a man very gently," Leah said, "and he will pronounce important principles very solemnly."

I tried to think of something to say to preempt whatever offensive thing Adam was going to say next, but instead he laughed, rather heartily, I thought.

"I'm right about Merdula," Adam said, "but I'd rather be wrong than solemn."

We all chatted amicably after that, and Adam laughed throughout the movie, mostly at inappropriate times.

I think it was during the confrontation between De Niro and Albert Brooks that Ismail whispered in my ear that he wanted to talk to me about something after the movie. I wasn't in the mood to hear any kind of lecture about how it wasn't too late for me to be deprogrammed from this cult, so I gave a noncommittal answer.

"The part where Bob shoots off the guy's finger," Adam said, as we were walking out. "Originally, Marty was going to use that for Harvey's death scene. But the night before they were going to shoot that scene, Marty, Harvey, and Bob all got drunk and came and got epiphany tattoos. Harvey didn't want to lift his arm the next day because it was too painful."

"Are you kidding?" Leah said. "There are literally thousands of actors you could have chosen for that lie who would have been better than Harvey Keitel. He's naked on screen, like, all the time."

"Ever hear of post-production?"

"You're saying that in *The Piano* and *Bad Lieutenant* and probably a million other movies the tattoo on Harvey's arm is blurred out, but so seamlessly that the audience can't notice?"

"Filmmakers are very good at hiding the truth. And so are people who remove tattoos. Why do you think Harvey is more compelled to display his body than any other male actor? You don't think that his need to show off his epiphanyless body is psychologically suspicious? Look closer at his arm the next time you watch one of his movies. And why do you think Marty and Bob made *Cape Fear*, if not to show Bob's epiphany tattoo by not showing it, by showing so many other tattoos? They both felt a need to display Bob's body as a palimpsest."

Leah clearly thought Adam was crazy or lying or both, but she couldn't help asking the obvious follow-up. "So what did their tattoos say?"

"I'm not going to tell you that. That would be a violation of my personal code of ethics."

"Which is what?"

"Not to disclose information about my guests."

I tried to catch Adam's eye so we could have a silent chat about what he had done to people with **DOES NOT UNDERSTAND BOUNDARIES** tattoos, but he did not look my way.

"Didn't you already violate that by telling us that the three of them used the machine?" Leah asked. "Shouldn't you keep that a secret?"

"You don't believe me, so I haven't divulged anything. As far as you're concerned, I'm just some crazy guy making shit up."

"You give your life to something important—like, say, making one of the greatest movies ever made—and people will make up lies about it."

Adam laughed again, and I decided that he was back to normal. The fact that I registered this annoyed me; if I were as strong as I should have been, I should have been less focused on the fluctuations of an old man's mood and more focused on the fact that my best friend was dating the girl I was in love with. Or my former best friend was dating a girl I had once been in love with. I had barely thought of either Ismail or Leah in more than a year, except to be annoyed with them for not believing in the machine, but my total lack of justification for being upset only made me more upset.

"I want to see the epiphany machine," Leah said.

I had thought that she was, at best, humoring Adam, so I was surprised when she said this, and also personally offended. "You hate how epiphany tattoos look," I said.

"I didn't say I wanted to see epiphany *tattoos*," Leah said. "I said I wanted to see the epiphany *machine*."

"You don't like how the tattoos look?" Adam said. "Most people do. Maybe something is blocking you from seeing beauty."

"Or maybe, unlike our mutual friend, I'm not **DEPENDENT ON THE OPINION OF OTHERS**."

"Nobody *thinks* they're **DEPENDENT ON THE OPINION OF OTHERS**," I said.

"Which is why, Leah, you should come uptown now and get a tattoo," Adam said.

"Hold on, that's not what I said." I was mad at Leah, but I did not like the idea of her giving her arm to Adam.

"It wouldn't matter if that *was* what you said. I wouldn't get an epiphany tattoo."

"Then why do you want to see the machine?"

"I like attending Catholic Mass with my Catholic friends. I like the ceremony. That doesn't mean I have any intention of taking Communion. I like to observe religion, not let it into my body."

"I'm not usually a fan of fans," Adam said. "I prefer people who want to get involved. But maybe a body as beautiful as yours should be left intac—"

"*Adam*," I said.

"Don't bother showing me your teeth, Grandma," Leah said. "I *am* the fucking wolf."

"Leah," Ismail said, "why do you want to see this thing? I don't understand."

"I want to see just how desperate people are for meaning. Plus, I want to do things that are interesting, and seeing it is more interesting than not seeing it. Plus, I'm a Lennon fan, just like everybody else."

Leah enjoyed showing Adam how to use his MetroCard, since of course he had forgotten in the time since I had shown him. I expected Ismail to be concerned for Leah, but instead he again whispered in my ear that he wanted to speak with me privately when we had the chance.

We were hardly inside Adam's apartment when Adam rolled a joint for Leah, who happily accepted.

"Where is everybody?" she asked. "I want to see somebody use the machine. Aren't cults supposed to have, like, followers?"

"I don't know what the machine would tell you, but I'm tempted to tattoo **NEEDS TO BE FUCKING PATIENT** on you myself." He was smiling broadly as he said this, unself-consciously displaying his missing tooth and clearly enjoying being teased by Leah, and I felt a surge of jealousy, maybe not because Adam was behaving lecherously toward Leah, but because he was treating her with a kind of cantankerous deference, like she was his daughter.

"Venter, let's go take a walk," Ismail said.

"Yeah, Venter, go take a walk," Adam said. "Some exercise might help with your nerves. It can't be good for your health to hang out with an old man in a cramped, smoke-filled apartment all day."

I didn't see any way to say no, so I did not say no. Many of the biggest decisions we make in life, I've observed, are the ones we barely make at all. The ones where we just get maneuvered into doing something we're barely aware of doing, or do just to be accommodating. Or maybe it's just me.

On the staircase, Ismail tried to engage me in a conversation about *The X-Files*, but I wasn't having it.

"Aren't you worried about what Adam is going to do with Leah?"

"Leah can take care of herself. I need your advice on something."

"*My* advice?"

"Don't sound so surprised, dude."

"I thought you weren't **DEPENDENT ON THE OPINION OF OTHERS**."

"I'm not. That doesn't mean that no one else's opinion is ever useful. Even the opinion of somebody who is **DEPENDENT ON THE OPIN-ION OF OTHERS** can be useful on rare occasion."

"You're really making me want to help you, brother."

"You know why the machine is so popular?"

"Okay."

"'Okay,' you know why it's so popular?"

"No. 'Okay,' I'm giving you an opening for you to spin your theory."

We were in the lobby now, and as I opened the door to the vestibule, we caught each other's eye and smiled.

"We should definitely be pleased with ourselves and these ballbreaking, verbally dexterous characters we're playing for each other," Ismail said. "Speaking of which, I need you to break up with Leah for me."

We were on the sidewalk now, abreast of each other and abreast of garbage.

"What? Why?"

"I just don't want to be with her. And we're teenagers! I shouldn't have to explain myself."

"Except that you want me to break up with her for you, so you should probably explain yourself to me."

"Leah's your friend, too. Do you want her to be with a guy who doesn't want to be with her?"

"Fair point," I said, though it wasn't, since it wasn't clear that Leah was still my friend. "But why are you asking me to break up with her instead of breaking up with her yourself?"

"You distracted me earlier, so I never got to tell you my theory about why people use the epiphany machine."

"Okay."

"Let's not start that again," Ismail said. Two men, no matter how intelligent, can talk for only so long before they start to sound like Vladimir and Estragon in *Waiting for Godot*, or like Abbott and Costello doing the "Who's on First" routine.

"I don't think people use the epiphany machine because they want to learn about themselves. I don't think that anybody, deep down, wants to learn about his or her own stupid, tiny soul. I think everybody's hoping that the machine will break up with people for them. 'I'm too **CLOSED OFF** for you.' 'You wouldn't want to be with someone who is **ADDICTED TO DISSATISFACTION**, would you?' 'Sorry, baby, I'm **DEPENDENT ON THE OPINION OF OTHERS**, so you're better off without me.'"

"You are just so good at talking me into helping you."

"See? This is what happens when you're honest with people."

"It doesn't sound like you're asking me for advice. It sounds like you're asking me to do something you're too cowardly to do."

"You got me."

"Let's get some pizza and talk about it."

It's true that in that moment—and, I think, only in that moment—I was wondering what treacherous thing I could do to Ismail. But it's not as though I tricked him into thinking that he was still in love with Leah when he wasn't or that the epiphany machine was the only way out of his predicament. By the time we found a pizza place a couple of blocks away, Ismail was deep into a discussion of how staying up all night sewing a dinosaur costume with Leah for a production of *The Skin of Our Teeth* had been one of the greatest experiences of his life, but the time had come for that kind of silliness to end. He was going to be pre-med in college, and, in a decade or so, as a young doctor, he would have his pick of women.

It seemed obvious and obviously unfair that he would have his pick of women and I would not, just because he was going to pursue a necessary career that required great skill and I was basically a caretaker for a tape recorder, with a dream of becoming a writer that might very well remain a dream.

"Sounds to me like you're in love with Leah," I said.

Ismail took a bite that pulled all the cheese from his pizza, and then told me that I was very smart. When you summarize what people say back to them, they often tell you that you're very smart. Still, I liked to hear him say it.

"But we can't be together," Ismail said. "We just can't. You have to tell her that."

"Why do I have to tell her?"

"Because I want to be with her and I won't be convincing."

"Why can't you be together?"

"Because I can't date a non-Muslim. My mother won't allow it."

"What does she care? She's not a believing Muslim."

"It's not about believing. Heritage is complicated."

"Why can't you disobey your mother?"

"Because," he said, taking a long, stringy bite, "disobeying your parents just leads to misery. Clear, firm guidance, even when it's wrong, is better than stumbling around with no idea about how you're supposed to live. Look around you and you can see that that's true. The machine is a parent for people who think they're too good for their parents."

"Didn't you have a different theory a few minutes ago?"

"I am a multitude-containing motherfucker."

"Have we talked about how dickish it is to say 'I contain multitudes' when somebody catches you in a contradiction?"

"I do contain multitudes, though. That's why I got that part-time job at Blockbuster to send money to Muslims in Bosnia and Chechnya, even though I don't consider myself a Muslim any more than my mother does."

"Do you still have that job?"

"No. It was taking away time that I wanted to spend with Leah."

"It sounds to me like you want to use the machine."

"I take it back. You're not very smart."

"When I was a little kid and I wanted something," I said, "the most important decision I had to make was whether to ask my dad or ask my grandma. When I wanted to watch TV, I asked my grandma, since my dad hates TV, but when I wanted a toy, I'd ask my dad, since my grandma would take any request for a purchase as an excuse to talk about the Depression."

I wasn't sure whether this was actually true—I could think of plenty of times when my father had turned on the television for me and then retreated into his den, and plenty of times when my grandmother had bought me a toy I hadn't known I wanted until she bought it for me. But this was not a story that was supposed to contain multitudes; this was a story that was supposed to have a point.

"So my point is . . ."

"That I need to ask permission from the right source," Ismail said. "And you think the right source is the epiphany machine."

Ismail's quickness annoyed me.

"But there are other issues," he said. "I'm going to Stanford and Leah is going to NYU."

"I'm sure if we sit here for another ten minutes you can come up with twenty more excuses."

"Tattoos are forbidden in Islam. That might sound like an excuse to you, given that you have no meaningful connection to any religious community, but it means something to me."

"If the tattoo tells you to be Muslim, you can always get it removed in order to become the Muslim it tells you to be. I talked to a Jewish guy a while back who did that."

"What if it just tells me that I shouldn't be with Leah?"

"Then it will be on your arm and you won't forget," I said.

In the years that followed I spent a lot of time trying to figure out exactly why I suddenly wanted so badly for Ismail to use the epiphany machine. Maybe I wanted to hurt him. I was annoyed with the smugness and condescension of the stuff he had just said about "religious community," especially given the smugness and condescension with which he had treated religion when we first became friends, so I wanted to ruin any future he might have had with Leah and/or ruin his relationship with his mother.

Or maybe I did not want to hurt him, and just wanted to make myself feel better. Maybe I thought if he used the machine, I would know for a fact that I had not been a fool to use it myself.

Or maybe I honestly thought I was helping my friend. Maybe I thought that using the machine would clarify things for him, would set him on a clear path for the rest of his life. If this is what I was thinking, I was not exactly wrong.

Ismail slammed his waxed paper cup on the table and wiped some grease from his mouth. "Let's do it."

There you boys are!" Leah said when we returned. "Adam was just telling me about a Secret Service agent who got a tattoo in the early seventies. This agent had been jogging alongside the car when Kennedy was shot, and he told Adam *with one hundred percent certainty* that Oswald was not the only shooter. He caught a glimpse of a gun on the grassy knoll a few seconds before the shooting, but, despite his training, he thought it was a cigar until it was too late. If Adam would go public with what he knows, then this great question of American history would finally be *answered*."

"No, it would not," Adam said. "Because no one would believe me. It would just be: 'Blah blah blah the huckster who hypnotized John Lennon is telling this wacky lie about the Kennedy assassination.'"

"We still wouldn't know who the second shooter was," I said.

"Nobody cares about that," Adam said. "Not really. What America needs is acknowledgment that a bullet cannot be magic."

"But a needle can be," Ismail said.

"When God wants to alter the trajectory of a life, he doesn't alter the trajectory of a bullet. A gun is just man's sorry attempt to build his own epiphany machine. Marty told me that that's what *Taxi Driver* is about."

"What was the tattoo?" Ismail said. "The Secret Service agent's tattoo, I mean."

"**TAKES TOO LONG TO NOTICE WHAT'S IMPORTANT**," Adam said, making us all laugh. "He hugged me and thanked me, told me that he had been ignoring the fact that his wife was unhappy with their humdrum lives and that he was immediately going to take her on the trip to Europe that he had been too depressed to take ever since the assassination. He rushed out of this place on his way to a travel agent."

"Aren't you breaking that rule or code or whatever you were talking about earlier?" Ismail asked. He had taken a place next to Leah and was stroking her back.

"Again, you think I'm making it all up. Nobody is as free from all bonds of law and custom as a crazy old crank. You all have something to look forward to."

"Don't worry, Ismail," I said. "Whatever your epiphany tattoo is, it will be completely safe with us."

Adam and Leah expressed surprise in unison. Also in unison, they told Ismail that he could not use the machine.

"Ismail is going to use the machine so he can be told to stay with the woman he loves."

"Wait, what?" Leah said.

"Venter, what are you doing?" Ismail said.

"You're already in danger of forgetting everything you said at the pizza place. That's why you need to have it written on your arm."

"Venter is practicing his salesmanship," Adam said. Adam was an excellent conciliator, though this was one of the hardest things to notice about him. "The sale shouldn't be quite this hard, Venter, and besides, your friend is a little young to use the machine."

"Maybe I *should* wait awhile and see if I still want to use the machine," Ismail said.

I got the sense from everyone in the room that I was pushing too hard, that I should relax. But I wanted to keep pushing, in part because I also wanted to do what they wanted me to do and stop pushing, and yielding to *that* impulse would once again demonstrate that I was **DEPENDENT ON THE OPINION OF OTHERS**.

"If you wait to use it, you'll never use it. You'll just keep saying that one day you're going to use the epiphany machine. You'll probably even tell the maternally approved woman you're not all that psyched about marrying that you're going to use the epiphany machine one day, and she'll nod her approval and tell you that you can use the epiphany machine whenever you want to, and you'll both know that the only reason she's telling you this is because you both know you'll never do it."

Adam grunted in approval and put his hand on my shoulder. "If I didn't know better, I'd think you were actually listening to those testimonials you record. But you should test your skills out on somebody who's sure about using the machine."

"I am sure," Ismail said. "Venter just convinced me."

"You're not actually thinking about doing this," Leah said.

"I'm not thinking about it. I've made up my mind."

"This guy is a lunatic and the machine is bullshit! We're here because it's *funny* bullshit, and we both like funny bullshit. I thought we were on the same page about that."

"If I weren't a hardened, soulless huckster out to defraud humanity," Adam said, "that might hurt my feelings."

"I want the machine to tell me that I have permission to keep seeing you," Ismail said, ignoring Adam.

"Do you hear yourself? You need the machine's permission to keep seeing me?"

"I mean I'm not getting my mother's permission."

"Why do you need anybody's permission?"

"Everybody needs somebody's permission," I said. "Everybody is **DEPENDENT ON THE OPINION OF OTHERS**. That's what is going to make me a great writer. The great problem that stares us all in the face is written on my arm."

"*Easy*, buddy," Adam laughed.

"This is the guy whose advice you want to follow?" Leah asked Ismail.

"You want me to follow your advice instead? All I want to do is what I want to do, but I don't know what I want to do because everybody keeps talking. Maybe *that's* the point of the epiphany machine: to shut everybody up."

"So you're telling me to shut up."

"No, I'm not! You're just trying to find any excuse to keep me from getting a tattoo because you don't like how the tattoos *look*. Maybe you're just a very shallow person."

It was essentially in one movement that Leah gasped and turned around and walked out. Ismail ran after her, apologizing desperately, and they stopped just outside the door of the apartment to argue. All we heard was murmuring, not the words they used. But a great truth that writers try not to understand is that precise wording is never important for understanding something; precise wording is only important when you're trying not to understand something.

"Should we drink whiskey to your success?" Adam asked.

"Fuck you."

"I'm serious. You wanted to break them up, and you succeeded."

"I wasn't trying to break them up."

He took a sip of whiskey and licked his lips. "There it is. The look I've been waiting for."

"What look?"

"The look of disgust with me. It's what I was talking about earlier."

I was annoyed with him, but I couldn't help finding his fatherly fear of abandonment endearing, especially since I had seen so little of it from my own father.

"I'm not going to abandon you, Adam."

"We'll see."

The door opened. It was Ismail, who did not meet my eye when he passed me.

"Where are you going?"

"To use the machine, obviously. Now that I've apparently broken up with my girlfriend over it, I at least want to see what it has to say."

He walked past Adam and through the purple velvet curtain.

"I don't think he's ready," Adam said. "I don't want any part of this."

At this point, I think—though of course I can't be sure—that I wanted Adam to throw Ismail out. But instead Adam just stood there, probably testing me, to see what I would do. It annoyed me to be tested, but I followed Ismail through the curtain.

Ismail was hunched over the machine, examining it like it was a puppy he was thinking of buying.

"It looks exactly the way you described it," Ismail said. "That's disappointing."

"Would you like me to describe it poorly in the future?"

"So Adam doesn't have to be the one to operate it?"

"I've never seen anyone else operate it. Adam keeps the machine steady, and I don't think anyone wants it to shake."

"But you can operate it? I think I'd trust it more if you operated it."

I looked over my shoulder, expecting Adam to walk in, but it was quiet on the other side of the curtain. I reloaded the ink and told Ismail to have a seat in the dentist's chair—the chair we're all trying to reach as soon as we leave the womb, Adam liked to not-really-joke. Ismail settled in and let his arm float upward and to the side, in the direction of the machine. I put on latex gloves, and unwrapped and loaded a needle. This was going to happen. I was going to learn whether the machine was real, or whether Adam composed the epiphanies himself.

"All right, Sorcerer's Apprentice, step away from the machine." Adam popped through the velvet curtain. He didn't seem mad that he was being usurped, he didn't seem nervous that he was about to be exposed as a fraud; he just looked happy to get back to work. He took my place, ran his finger along the machine, and, not pausing to put on latex gloves, pressed it down into Ismail's arm.

The pain took Ismail immediately, and he did not like it.

"Why didn't you tell me how much this was going to hurt?"

"Think your thoughts," Adam said. "Now's the time."

He said this frequently while tattooing, and now I understood why. Thinking, like any other drug, can be a useful distraction from pain, as long as it's carefully managed and does not become an addiction.

Maybe I should have been angry that I had been robbed of my opportunity to see whether the machine was real, but all I felt was awe. As Ismail groaned and squirmed, and Adam composed or channeled, the machine dragged and looped its needle along Ismail's arm like a calm figure skater. If Adam was a charlatan, if he did in fact design and build the machine himself, he was underrated as an engineer. The machine was either made by God to write a final testament onto the rotting bodies of his creations, or it was a testament to human grace and skill. Either way, only the small of soul would decline to worship it.

The whirring slowed and quieted, and Adam lifted the arm. Ismail looked up and met my gaze for a moment, still in pain and probably not wanting to look at what the machine had written. I wondered again why the machine wrote in English, and I wondered why I had learned English, or any language, since surely the point of words is something other than to understand them. I wished that I did not know the meaning of the words the machine had written on me, and I wanted Ismail never to learn the meaning of the words on his own arm. I wanted each of us to be like a kid with a "Kick Me" sign taped to his back who had no idea what the words "kick me" meant, who just enjoyed the sensation of a slip of loose-leaf paper flapping against his coat.

But Ismail did look down at his arm, of course, and his eyes widened in bewilderment, just as I had seen so many eyes do. I was waiting for the scream, for the refusal, for the useless threats of lawsuits. Instead, he jumped in the air and embraced first Adam and then me.

"Thank you so much for making me do this!" he said. "This epiphany is perfect." He stretched his arm out for our reading pleasure.

WANTS TO BLOW THINGS UP

I looked at Ismail's epiphany, or more precisely, I looked at the brown skin around Ismail's epiphany. My first thought was that Adam had committed a hate crime.

"This is telling me exactly what I need to hear!" Ismail said. "It's telling me that I need to go to NYU, not Stanford!"

"What?"

"I don't want to be a doctor. I want to work in the theater. But I couldn't admit that to myself, because it will alienate my mother. But I *want* to alienate my mother, if that's what it will take to live the life that I want. If I have to blow up my relationship with my mother, then so be it. Relationship blown up."

"Now you're talking," Adam said. "This is exactly what the epiphany machine is supposed to do."

"Okay, but can't you be a theater director if you go to Stanford?"

"It will be easier if I'm in New York. Plus, this will send a clear message to my mother. I know that if I go to Stanford, she'll keep wearing me down to take pre-med courses until I give in and become a doctor. The only way to do this is just to do it."

"I didn't even know you applied to NYU."

"I kept it quiet. Sent in deposits to both NYU and Stanford."

A teenager deciding between colleges, ecstatic that the choice had been made for him. That's what Ismail was.

"Ismail, you've restored my faith in my own machine," Adam said. "I'll be first in line for your first play on Broadway."

"I guess this means you'll be close to Leah," I said.

"Oh, I don't care about Leah. We broke up outside and we're not getting back together."

I could tell from the way he said this that they'd be back together by the end of the week.

"So you'll both be going to college in the city," Adam said. "Two young men on the edge of a millennium."

Sometimes I try to picture how Ismail and I must have looked to Adam in that moment. He probably did not register Ismail's quixotic attempts at a moustache or the scabs that my incompetent shaving left on my cheeks and neck; what he saw was the word "promise" written all over our faces in invisible ink. And despite everything that happened afterward, it can't be said that we lacked promise.

The epiphany machine was forged sometime in the middle of the eighteenth century, on a plantation outside Charleston, by a slave employed, in a manner of speaking, as a blacksmith. There is no way to know his name, and in any case his name would not be his, but he is often called James. As a child James had, at the greatest possible risk, taught himself to read and write using a Bible that he had—to use a word that casts all words into confusion—stolen. After the Bible, James stole other books, mostly works of science and philosophy, often when called upon to make repairs to the furniture in the vast library in the main house. James hid his literacy from Richardson Johnson, the man whom the law designated his master. Richardson Johnson did not notice or care about the missing books—unlike his deceased mother, who had acquired most of the collection, he found reading dull—but he did take notice of James for his precocious gifts in carpentry. James had not turned seventeen when Johnson sent him away to be taught blacksmithing.

James quickly established himself as a star pupil, able to concentrate on his work despite the constant prattling of the white man assigned to watch him, and—it was made very clear—whip him if he showed any sign of indolence. Despite having seen much of the world while serving in the British Navy, the man assigned to watch over him had almost nothing of interest to say, a fact that did not stop him from talking.

If what James created was used to sustain, defend, or decorate a society of the greatest evil, that evil seemed somehow quarantined from the act of creation itself. Only in iron and fire was there reprieve from violence.

After three years, James was returned to the Johnson estate to set up a shop, and soon his horseshoes—or, as they were known, Richardson Johnson's horseshoes—were widely agreed to be the most dependable horseshoes that could be acquired in the Carolinas. His larger-scale work was even more impressive, and the gates and balconies that James forged for the Johnson estate earned Richardson the envy and admiration of his neighbors.

Occasionally, another slave would suggest that James build weapons; he always declined, believing Richardson Johnson to be a fundamentally decent man who had been led astray by the satanic forces that ruled this region of the world. Richardson Johnson and his family did not deserve horror. Richardson Johnson's young son, also named Richardson Johnson, often approached James and sweetly offered to help. True, this was a monumental hindrance to James's work—he could not refuse the boy's offer, and every offer meant a wasted day of tedious supervision. James was unsure whether he would be hanged if the boy slipped up and hurt himself, and he certainly had no intention of finding out. But even at his most innocently destructive, the boy was so eager, so curious, so impressed with what James was able to do. The boy treated James like a valued teacher, even like a second father. At times, James was able to forget himself and the world and see the boy as his son. In the boy's eyes, James saw a future in which there was no slavery, and everyone respected each other. This respectful, openhearted boy could grow up to be a respectful, openhearted man. What Richardson Johnson's family needed was education.

James daydreamed about approaching the older Richardson with a branding iron that would inscribe **MUST END BONDAGE** on his master's flesh, a message that might burn the demons away and help Richardson see clearly. But James was not a fool and knew that the whites would see this not as what it was—the only hope to save Richardson's soul—but rather as an act of the purest aggression. He feared being hanged even for thinking it. And yet the thought would not go away.

One day, heating metal in the furnace, James felt that the fire was speaking. This was not so unusual—he often felt that fire and metal were having a conversation, and that his job was to translate, as the Bible had been translated. But today he felt as if the fire were speaking to *him*. As soon as he started to listen, though, the fire's speech was drowned out by the neighing of a horse waiting to be shod. In his anger, James stared at the horse, and then noticed something in the shape of its skull, and looked more closely.

Within a month, James had crafted an object, the beauty of which Richardson Johnson could not deny, but the use of which he could not discern. James said that it was merely for decoration, rather than for sustenance or defense. Richardson said that he felt some primal urge to touch it, and of course James was not going to tell his master not to obey his urges.

Richardson touched the top of the neck (or the arm, or whatever we want to call it), and said that it was very cold. He touched the base and said nothing. Then he touched the needle, and then he lifted it, and then it was in his arm and he was screaming.

Finally, the needle stopped and sat in Richardson's arm. James lifted the needle, and Richardson muttered about having James hanged, until he read what was written on his arm.

"**MUST END BONDAGE!**" Richardson said, his voice joyful. "Of course! God Himself has sent this message to me. Thank you for serving as the messenger."

James bragged to the other slaves about what he had done, rejected their skepticism, and waited for word to arrive that they would all be free to go. But this word did not come. Only slowly did James realize that Richardson had formed (or possibly merely joined) a group that sought representation for the American colonies in the British Parliament and had invited the other members to use his device, which he said had been "prepared" by his slave. Each of Richardson's friends received tattoos stating that they **MUST END BONDAGE**, and they were grateful for the reminder that they must free themselves of the tyrant King George. Richardson told James that he would not let his important contributions to Richardson's work go unrewarded and that he would make special provisions in his will for James to be freed upon his death.

Angered though he was by the way white men interpreted the message that he had coauthored with God, James nonetheless maintained hope that, once liberation from King George had been achieved, slavery would indeed be ended. After all, as the eighteenth century wore on, very intelligent white man after very intelligent white man came to use his machine: Washington, Jefferson, Madison, Franklin. (It is rumored that the trail of black ink up his arm inspired the rattlesnake Franklin drew for his famed "Join, or Die" print, though the timing on this is fuzzy.) Surely anyone—surely *one person*—with that message on his arm would come to understand that **MUST END BONDAGE** meant **MUST END BONDAGE**, and that this could not possibly refer to the freedom of white people.

James waited for the white man who would realize this, and continued to wait.

Years went by and James forced himself not to lose hope. During the war, believing that freedom was at hand, James made weapons to be used against the British, rather than, as James's friends continued to suggest, Richardson Johnson. In the unsettled years that followed the victory at Yorktown, James distracted himself by crafting balconies. He could have constructed the balconies poorly, and white people overlooking their slaves could have been surprised to find themselves falling, but nothing could have tempted James toward shoddy work.

One night, James received word that Richardson Johnson had died. He expected to receive the freedom that Richardson Johnson had promised would be written in his will. But weeks passed and no word of freedom came. Finally, Richardson Johnson's son, Richardson Johnson III, came to take a look at a gate that James was working on. This Richardson asked questions about the tools James used, obviously out of nostalgia for his own childhood, rather than out of any continuing interest in the tools themselves, and certainly not out of any interest in James. James asked about his freedom, and Richardson sucked in his lips.

"Being on your own at your age would be nothing but frightening and confusing," Richardson said. "This is what's best for you. Don't worry if you feel overworked. In a few years, my son will assist you, just like I did."

James hardly saw Richardson for more than a year after that—most of the work he was ordered to do came through overseers—until one day Richardson burst into James's shop with the glorious news of the ratification of the United States Constitution. Richardson did not mention that this Constitution perpetuated slavery, but he did not have to.

"To commemorate this occasion," Richardson said, "I would like you to mark my breast with the phrase **AN AMERICAN AND A GENTLEMAN OF SOUTH CAROLINA**."

"Your breast?"

"Over my heart."

"I can't choose the marking."

Richardson laughed—warmly, he probably thought—at James's foolishness. "Of course not. You cannot even read what it writes. But now that bondage has ended and we are a free people, I am confident that God will choose this marking for me."

"My device cannot open wide enough to write on your chest. Only your forearm."

"I'm sorry. I must have misheard. It sounded as though you called it *your* device."

James put down the hammer he was holding. "I am sorry. The Johnson Body-Pen."

"That's better. Now, I expect you to resolve any minor difficulties quickly. I will visit you again on the first Monday of next month to receive the marking I have requested."

James looked at the device that he made so many years ago with so much hope. He attempted to lift it, with the intention of hurling it into the furnace along with himself, but his strength was not what it once had been. He turned to the furnace with nothing in his hands. He would not fit into the furnace, of course, but this was—how to put it?—one of those minor difficulties. He could feel the heat of the flames on his hands when he got a better idea.

For the next days, he ignored the agony in his joints as he shaped and molded and twisted iron. One need not be at one's best to do one's best work.

When the day arrived, Richardson Johnson III did not notice that this device was significantly larger than the Johnson Body-Pen, or if he did, he did not seem to care. The things white men failed to notice would fill the world they had ruined ten thousand times over.

James had laid some linens over his worktable and otherwise cleared it save for the device.

"I hope that those linens have been laundered," said Richardson Johnson III.

"Of course."

Richardson removed his shirt, and, with James's assistance, lay down with the machine tucked underneath his left shoulder blade.

"Now," James said. "The machine will tell you who you are."

He tapped the neck or the arm of the machine and the needle pierced Richardson's chest. It slid in, just as the needle of the smaller device did. Richardson protested that it hurt; James responded that it was a needle, after all. Desperately, Richardson ordered James to stop.

"If I stop it now, the message will be incomplete," James said. "I'm sure your father could have withstood the pain."

"Set me free!" Richardson shouted. As soon as he had done so, the needle stopped. Richardson could see—more or less, given that he was reading upside down, and the machine was still lodged in his chest and obstructing his view—that the machine had written exactly what he had asked: **AN AMERICAN AND A GENTLE- MAN OF SOUTH CAROLINA**. Perhaps, as he read the script, he realized the irony of telling his slave to set him free. Unlikely, granted, but there are essentially no limits to the moral truths a person is capable of understanding for the few seconds it takes to forget them. We will never know what Richardson knew or for how long he knew it, though, because almost immediately the needle began to move again, rewriting **AN AMERICAN AND A GEN- TLEMAN OF SOUTH CAROLINA**, and then rewriting it again, each time cutting deeper and deeper into his flesh. "Set me free! Set me free!"

Richardson kept screaming, and James could not quite say he was happy to be watching the man die. But there was more truth in the ripping of his repulsive pink skin than there could be in any words James's device could possibly have written, more truth in the ink stains that formed on Richardson's muscles as the needle tore them apart than there could be in any words the ink could possibly form.

Richardson continued to scream, and white men arrived to come to his aid just as the needle was cracking Richardson's breast- plate on its way to puncturing his heart. Their first objective was to free Richardson from the needle in time to save his life, which they would not be able to accomplish; their next would be to hang James.

The time had come to thrust his arms into the furnace. He took one last look at his beloved device—his true device, the one that could contain only an arm and the truth, not the cumbersome murder weapon that he had designed for a single use, the murder weapon that would have to be cracked open and destroyed to free the corpse of Richardson Johnson III. As the fire began to write on his forearms, James said a prayer to the God for and with whom he had created what neither called the epiphany machine. Whether the prayer requested that his device one day be used by those who could heed it, or whether the prayer requested that his device curse all who use it—or whether either prayer was heeded, or even heard— all of these questions are of course impossible to answer, and for James, they were perhaps even irrelevant. All that was relevant in the last seconds of his consciousness was that his arms were aflame and were embracing an overseer whose body would soon be ash, and that what had been written on the chest of Richardson Johnson III would soon be read by worms. All that was relevant was that James had brought to these uneducable people some tiny fraction of the misery and horror they deserved.

CHAPTER

✦

18

Now we come to what I have always thought of as the Suitcase Feeling.

As I had told Adam, since I was going to Columbia, a short bus ride from his apartment, there was no reason for me to stop working for him. It would be no more inconvenient than many part-time jobs or other extracurricular endeavors. And I would certainly be more useful to him: studying at Columbia provided me with the opportunity to recruit my classmates to use the machine. Adam never brought that subject up, and I had no reason to think he had ever thought about it. But it did provide me with the cover I needed to renounce him while I was packing.

A caveat here: I'm not at all sure that I *did* renounce him while I was packing. It's impossible to know at what point you decided to do something, though that rarely stops us from constructing stories about when we decided to do something. So, my story is that I stared at the stack of short-sleeved shirts in my suitcase and felt the Suitcase Feeling.

What was the Suitcase Feeling? Naming our emotions is of course one of the most important things we do, and I do not know whether I felt revulsion or fear.

The case for revulsion: I was packing for college, which I understood to be the time and place to ask fundamental questions about myself and the world, and yet I had aligned myself with a device that promised a shortcut around those questions. Worse, I was in a position to lure my classmates into that same shortcut if Adam ever asked me to, which he had not yet but might, in such a way that I would probably not register the request until I had already complied with it. Revulsion took over my body, revulsion with Adam, with the machine, with the entire apparatus of attitudes behind the machine. So I dumped all my short-sleeved shirts out of my suitcase and packed long-sleeved shirts instead.

The case for fear: I would be entering college with a tattoo on my arm that advertised that I was **DEPENDENT ON THE OPINION OF OTH-ERS**. If you need other people to think well of you, advertising that fact will guarantee the opposite result. And beyond my specific tattoo, my association with Adam would brand me as a follower, a weirdo, someone to whisper about rather than talk to. So I dumped all my short-sleeved shirts out of my suitcase and packed long-sleeved shirts instead.

But all of this happened very quickly in my mind, and I can't give an accurate accounting.

No matter why I did it, my father walked into my room just as I was doing it. He looked at the short-sleeved shirts on the floor and gave me a look that I hadn't seen from him in a long time: one of compassion and concern. "Venter," he said. "You think you'll be the only Ivy League freshman who's **DEPENDENT ON THE OPINION OF OTHERS?**"

"I'm not hiding the truth about who I am. I just tend to get cold easily."

The temperature was warm during orientation week, so I was even more uncomfortable than I likely would have been otherwise. But the long-sleeved shirts did allow me to hide my tattoo even from my new roommate, Cesar Solomon.

Cesar and I became good friends right away, talking endlessly about Kafka and Borges and Radiohead, conversations so absorbing that I barely noticed that I was ignoring emails from Adam about when I would visit.

Cesar talked about his reverence for Merdula's *Only the Desert Is Not a Desert* and had a couple of half-baked theories about Merdula's identity; I was grateful when he didn't mention the epiphany machine book. Then one night, just before we were supposed to go out to a party at a bar that would require fake IDs, I took a shower to freshen up. I was supposed to meet Cesar in somebody else's room, so I thought I was safe, but he came back in while I was shirtless and drying off. I threw on a T-shirt but it was too late.

"Holy shit! You have an epiphany tattoo."

"Yes."

"You're a big fan of the machine that killed John Lennon?"

"Mark David Chapman used the machine before he killed Lennon. It didn't make him do it."

Cesar pounded out a few bars of "Working Class Hero" on the keyboard that he had brought and that took up most of our room. "Merdula's epiphany machine book is crap. Doesn't hold a candle to *Only the Desert*. *Only the Desert* gets to the heart of man's essential isolation; the epiphany machine book is just a bunch of random stories that don't add up to anything. The portrait of Lennon is two-dimensional and unconvincing. So this is why you only wear long-sleeved shirts?"

I nodded.

"Why did you choose *that* tattoo? It's not going to be easy to hook up with girls if they see that thing as soon as you take off your shirt."

"I didn't choose the tattoo."

"Right, the dude chooses for you. What's his name? Adrian Lyne?"

"Adam Lyons. Adrian Lyne is a movie director."

"Right. *Fatal Attraction.* Like your attraction to a device that killed one of the greatest musicians of the twentieth century."

"We've been talking about music for days. I didn't even know you were a Beatles fan."

"I haven't talked about oxygen either, but I like it and I think it's important. I have to be honest with you: I'm a little weirded-out that my roommate belongs to a cult."

"I don't 'belong' to it. And it's not a cult."

"So you don't belong to it, meaning that you went to this place and got your tattoo and haven't been back since?"

"No, that's not exactly right."

"How many times have you been back? Once? Twice?"

"I mean, a bunch."

"So, like, once every few months?"

"More than that."

"Once every couple of months?"

"I worked for him for a while, okay?" I was surprised to hear myself talking about working for him in the past tense. "It's not a cult. It just offers guidance. It's not like it hypnotizes people into doing its bidding."

"So Mark David Chapman just happened to get a tattoo."

"He might also have listened to John Coltrane that day. That doesn't mean that John Coltrane is responsible."

"And we know that he was reading *The Catcher in the Rye*. A hit, a most palpable hit." This was a line from *Hamlet* that Cesar had already established a habit of quoting every time I made a decent point. "So why did you use it?"

"Both my parents used the machine, and I . . ."

"And you never really questioned it?"

"I questioned it all the time."

"But they forced you to use it?'

"No! I never knew my mother." At this point, I was more or less consciously using this to get him to back off. It didn't work.

"Okay. Your father forced you to use the machine."

"My father hated the machine, and so did I."

"Because you're **DEPENDENT ON THE OPINION OF OTHERS**. If he had loved the machine, you would have loved it, too."

"I'd like to think I'm smart enough that I would have seen through it if my father believed in it."

"Of course you'd like to think that."

I did not like being someone else's entertainment, but I felt that I needed to get through this so that he would continue to like me. Which obviously suggested that I was **DEPENDENT ON THE OPINION OF OTHERS**. But I tried to ignore that.

"Your parents are atheists and so are you," I said. "Does that make you **DEPENDENT ON THE OPINION OF OTHERS?**"

"A hit, a most palpable hit. But eventually you started to believe in the machine. Which must have been why, when you moved in here, your father set up your computer in silence and then left."

"My mother abandoned me because of the machine. I went to Adam Lyons because . . ."

"Because you felt like an orphan and needed his opinion of you."

"I wanted to find my mother."

"And did you?"

"He had no idea where she was."

"How do you know?"

"Because that's what he said."

"So what did you do to look for her after that?"

Cesar must have seen the answer in my face, because he laughed.

"So Adam Lyons diverted your mission to find your mother into a mission to, what, do some odd jobs for him, I'm guessing? This guy sounds like quite the magician. But instead of distracting you with a hot assistant, he distracts you with your own self-loathing."

"Fuck you."

"Look, Venter, I'm sorry for laughing. I'm sorry for laughing, because this is *serious*. I've talked to you enough in the last few days to know that you're a very smart guy. If Adam Lyons has made such an impression on you, he must be really dangerous. We need to break you free from him completely."

It's not exactly to my credit that I went along with him. But, like most people who lead us astray, he had raised some good points.

CHAPTER

—— · · ✦ · · ——

19

esar and I arrived to a crowded and boozy salon night. The joyful revelers celebrating their self-knowledge immediately looked like a bunch of pathetic drunks. I felt a pinch of anguish, because I was not completely oblivious and understood that my newfound scorn was mostly the product of Cesar's influence. I'm not even sure that the night was any boozier or more crowded than usual. Seeing what I saw now merely confirmed that I was **DEPENDENT ON THE OPINION OF OTHERS**.

"Venter," said a drunk guy who grabbed my arm. I recognized him from previous salon nights but didn't know his name. He was big and wore a big black fedora. I had previously thought he looked mysterious and wise, but now he looked like he was trying to substitute a *Blues Brothers* costume for a personality. "I want to give you my testament."

"Testimonial."

"Whatever. I want you to tell my story. I was born on November 15, 1956, and I used the epiphany machine on February 14, 1994."

"I don't have my tape recorder with me," I said. "I can't do this now."

"Wait, do what now?" Cesar asked.

"I knew it was my fault that Sarah had left me," the guy continued. "No, wait, it was Anna who had left me, or maybe I left her. Anyway, Anna and Sarah, I loved them both and I lost them both. I had just moved to New York and had just lost my job—no, wait, maybe I lost my job after I used the machine."

"It was nice talking to you," I said, "but I have to go find Adam."

Cesar stopped me and loudly read the tattoo on the guy's forearm.

WOULD RATHER BE RIGHT THAN HAPPY BUT IS USUALLY NEITHER

"If you're usually not right," Cesar asked, "how do you know you're right about this?"

"I'm not right," said the *Blues Brothers* guy. "The tattoo is right."

"Do you really think that's specific enough to mean anything?" Cesar asked.

"It might be true for a lot of people, but it's definitely true for me."

Cesar turned to me. "'It might be true for a lot of people, but it's definitely true for me.' Is that like a supplemental tattoo that everybody gets? Or does Adam proclaim it and convince everybody that they came up with it themselves?"

This was hardly a new thought to me, but I had rejected and repressed it. Hearing it out of Cesar's mouth made me feel stupid for rejecting and repressing it. But it had always felt small-minded *not* to reject and repress it.

"He is good at making people think what he thinks," I said.

"He's good at brainwashing people."

"Except for corners," Adam said, emerging from the backroom. "I can never get the corners of people's brains clean, no matter how hard I scrub." He elbowed the ex-boyfriend of Sarah and Anna out of the way, and then he looked at me and mimicked my unhappy face. "The prodigal son returns and is he ever pissed. Who's your friend?"

"This is my roommate, Ce—"

"You go to Columbia with this guy? I would expect a more sophisticated choice of words from an Ivy League student than 'brainwashing,' a nonsense term that people use to make themselves sound like they're not scared. Tell me his name again."

"Cesar Solomon."

"Don't tell him my last name," Cesar said. "I don't want to end up on any mailing lists for recruitment literature."

"Too late," Adam said. "I already have your name, so I'm going to start mailing out recruitment literature for the sole purpose of harassing you."

I felt an urge to be conciliatory that I couldn't explain, at least beyond the obvious fact that I wanted them both to like me. "It seems like the two of you are getting off on the wrong foot."

"That reminds me of the punch line to one of my favorite jokes," Adam said. "Have I ever told it to you, Venter? It's about two foot fetishists who are married to twin sisters."

Cesar laughed appreciatively, which surprised me.

"If this cult-leader thing doesn't work out," Cesar said, "you have a career ahead of you as a Borscht Belt comedian fifty years ago."

"Venter, your friend's remarks remind me a little of your friend Leah. But I have to admit that these stabs at witty banter are less appealing coming from a rude, smug eighteen-year-old boy than from a smart, open eighteen-year-old woman."

"Maybe I want to use the epiphany machine and I'm just nervous," Cesar said, "so this is a defense mechanism."

"Oh, I would say that's a strong probability. And admitting what you want under the guise of sarcasm is another 'defense mechanism,' if you want to call it that. Another thing to call it would be 'a boringly typical way for a teenager to hide.'"

"Why do you think I'm being sarcastic? Show me the machine and let me use it."

I looked at Cesar and tried to gauge whether he was serious. He seemed to be.

"The epiphany machine is not a joke," Adam said, "and I don't appreciate it being treated as a joke. Venter, please get this guy out of here."

"Why don't you want him to use the machine?" I asked. "Are you afraid he'll see that the machine is a fake? That he'll figure out how you've rigged it to write whatever you want it to write?"

"Oh, yeah. Of all the people who've used the machine over the last four decades, this kid is the first one I've ever been intimidated by. This is the child who will bring the machine to ruin! He is the Chosen One."

The salon-night crowd let out a loud laugh at this, a mob laugh, a laugh joined in even by people who were too far away to have heard what Adam said, but who did not want to be the only ones not laughing.

"Where's my mother?" I asked.

Adam patted his pockets, then dropped to his knees one creak at a time—a slow process that required some of his acolytes to step out of the way and look on nervously as they wondered whether to lend a hand. Once he was on the floor, he searched under the bar. "Rose? Are you down there? I think there might be an old bottle of rosé under here somewhere. Does that count?"

"You've taken advantage of me, dangling hope that my mother will one day reappear while I do all this work for you."

With some difficulty, Adam pushed himself back to his feet. "When have I dangled that hope? I said that it's possible she might come by at some point. That was true when I said it, and it's true now. It's certainly more likely she'll come to see me than it is that she'll come to see you. I've ignored my misgivings about you. As though anybody with a **DEPEN-DENT ON THE OPINION OF OTHERS** tattoo could ever be anything other than a sniveling, toadying coward. I always knew I would be punished if I ignored my own machine, and I guess that punishment is you. *Rose*, on the other hand, always knew how to read people. She got you right from the minute you fell out of her."

I imagined myself taking a lunge at him, but I didn't need an epiphany tattoo to tell me that I would just stand there as those words ate into me.

"Building you up and tearing you down is classic cult behavior," Cesar said. "He's trying to make you feel like shit so that he can control you."

"It sounds like *you're* trying to make him feel like shit so *you* can control him, Charlemagne Augustus or whatever your name is. It sounds like that's why you came here. And it sounds like that will be good for everyone. I thought that if Venter interviewed enough people he would see that everybody's foolish and nobody's opinion is worth listening to, but it's clear to me that he needs someone to tell him what to think, and I don't want to be the one to do it anymore."

I sputtered incoherently for about a minute before Cesar tugged at my shirt and pulled me out of the apartment.

"Good riddance!" shouted the *Blues Brothers* guy. "Don't come back and beg for forgiveness."

"Oh, shut up, Jim. Go back to Sarah or Anna," Adam said as Cesar slammed the door.

"This is good," Cesar said on the stairs. "You've closed the door, quite literally, on your pre-college life, and now you're open to what comes next. I'm proud to have you as a roommate."

This was so stilted that even I noticed how stilted it was, especially since I hadn't been the one who literally closed the door. Of course I can't be sure, but I think I had a premonition of what was to come over the next several weeks: Cesar would decide that the cult stench clung to me, embodied by my tattoo, and press me to get it removed, which I would refuse to do, and then he would lose interest in me entirely, abandoning me as a rehabilitation project and, instead, relegating me to the "weird roommate" he could count on to make for a funny story when I wasn't around.

I knew I wasn't going to get my tattoo removed. That was the one thing I knew that I would never do. Maybe I thought, without any reason to think so, that the tattoo served as some kind of beacon, and would one day lead my mother to me, assuming she wanted to find me. (I decided after the night I broke with Adam that I did not want to find her, if she did not want me to find her; this seemed nobler than simply being too lazy and diffident to properly search for her.) In any case, no matter how foolish I may be, I have some sense of when something has become part of my skin.

CHAPTER

— · · ✦ · · —

20

Over the first couple of months of school, I did my best to bury myself in reading, since, after all, I was looking at the great ancient Greek texts that addressed all the questions the machine purported to answer. Unfortunately, the great ancient Greek texts seemed to teach only that one should not have sex with one's mother or challenge a god, both of which seemed kind of obvious and, since I had neither a mother nor a god, irrelevant.

In November, a girl came up to me and asked whether I was the guy who had used the epiphany machine. I did not want to answer yes, but she was already at my arm and my sleeve had rolled up a bit, revealing most of the final letter, **S**. My embarrassment must have been pretty easy to spot as I pulled my sleeve down, because she put her hand on my arm and asked me if I wanted to get a beer. I had a lot of reading to do before meeting up with Ismail and Leah that night—the first time we would be hanging out since school started, as I had kept putting off seeing them ever since they had, as I had predicted, gotten back together. So I told the girl no, I had to get to the library, but kept walking with her.

She talked rapturously about a band I had never heard of, and it was fun to listen to her talk, until she asked me what my favorite band was. I was so nervous I could not even think of a band name.

"The Beatles," I said.

She laughed and clapped. "The Beatles! Of course. God, you're so natural, you're so . . . *yourself*. Most guys would try to impress me by picking some really obscure band, but *obviously* those bands aren't anywhere near as good as the Beatles. I asked you what your favorite band was, and you told me the answer and didn't worry about how it would make you look."

"Are you making fun of me? Do you already know my tattoo?"

"I've just heard you've used the machine, that's all. Can I see?"

"I'd really rather wait to show you."

"I get it," she said. "You're not that kind of girl."

I continued insisting that I had to go to the library, but we sat down at the West End, a bar at which I had dreamed of drinking ever since I had read in tenth grade or so that Allen Ginsberg and Jack Kerouac had once drunk there, as though drinking beer at this particular bar would constitute taking my place in the line of literary greats rather than simply taking my place in the line of college students who drink beer.

There was a lull in the conversation, and I couldn't think of anything to ask except for the most boring question of all. "What do you want to do with your life?"

"Let's see," she said. "For a little while I thought I was going to be a writer—a few weeks, my whole life, I'm not really sure—but I'm taking a fiction workshop this semester and I can tell my professor thinks I'm not very good, even though he won't come out and say so, and his negative comments are absolutely on target, so I'm never going to write again."

"That seems extreme."

"When you realize a great truth, you have to accept it and then act on it. You must believe that, or you wouldn't have used the epiphany machine."

"There's a lot of disagreement about whether you should or even can behave differently because of what the machine tells you. Adam Lyons contradicts himself a lot on that." I wished I could confront Adam on this contradiction, which made me miss Adam, which in turn made me annoyed with myself.

"What do you think?" she asked me.

"I think the epiphany machine is for losers who need other people to tell them what to do."

"I like things that are for losers," she said. "I don't like the way we think of winning and losing."

I recognized the way she was talking. Someone who wanted to be talked into using the machine.

"You could hail a cab and have a needle in your arm in, like, half an hour," I said.

"I feel like I've used it already, and I've gotten my one big important epiphany. There are other things I'd like to know, but I don't want to get greedy."

This struck me as a throwaway not-really-joke, so I didn't pursue it. Besides, an idea had just occurred to me that I did want to pursue.

"Listen, do you want to come downtown with me tonight? I'm getting drinks at nine with two friends from NYU."

This was forward of me, but I decided it would be more tolerable to hang out with Ismail and Leah if I wasn't wondering whether they were thinking that I was sexless and pathetic.

"Sounds fun! But I'm supposed to have dinner with my parents tonight. Want to come to that first and then we'll meet up with your friends?"

I looked at her, expecting her to tell me that she was joking, not not-really-joking. But she didn't.

"I mean, I guess I could," I said. "Even though . . ."

"Great! It would be depressing to spend tonight having dinner with no one but my parents, since it's my birthday."

"Oh. Happy birthday."

"Thank you. Since it's my birthday, would you mind coming back to my room with me and going down on me?"

She grabbed my hand, my answer being obvious.

Once we were inside her room, I barely had time to take in her bookshelf—Virginia Woolf, Catherine Pearson, Sylvia Plath, several books on mastering the craft of writing fiction, a prominently placed copy of Daphne du Maurier's *Rebecca*, and, yes, both *Only the Desert Is Not a Desert* and *Origins and Adventures of the Epiphany Machine*—before she pushed me down on her single bed. She took my shirt off and I winced as she read my tattoo, mostly expecting her to throw me out. And she did give me the disappointed look I was expecting.

"**DEPENDENT ON THE OPINION OF OTHERS**? Is that even an epiphany? Isn't that true of, like, everybody?"

This felt like exactly the sort of acceptance I needed, like I could just kiss her and the movie of my life would fade to black and the credits would roll.

I kissed her, and the movie continued.

She pulled down my pants and boxers in one unbroken movement, an act that felt as abrupt and strange as this entire afternoon, but as soon as she put my penis in her mouth, I was very glad that I had accompanied her home. Very rarely does life give you unambiguously positive feedback; in fact, I'm not sure that such feedback comes in any form other than oral sex. When my turn came to give her the same feedback, I pled for mercy by saying I had never performed oral sex before. (I decided not to mention that I had never received it either.) Her loud moans felt like the overly effusive praise one gives a fifteen-month-old child trying to walk across a room. She yanked at my hand until I figured out that she wanted me to put first one finger inside her and then another, and once she had control of two of my fingers she seemed to start genuinely enjoying herself. Once we were finished, her cheeks were a very bright red. I told her she looked like a lobster, and she giggled and covered her cheeks. We exchanged theories of the universe and then I went down on her again.

After her second, more subdued orgasm, I kissed my way back up her torso, hoping that this orgasm had been more genuine, and that I was fulfilling the sacred duty of lovers and Americans: Getting Better. But when I reached her chin and pulled myself up to make eye contact, she avoided my gaze and stared at the ceiling.

"I'm sorry," I said. "I'll keep working at it."

"That's not it," she said. "You should probably know my name is Rebecca Hart."

"You're not serious."

"That may be true. But it's definitely true that my name is Rebecca Hart."

"You must hate the machine."

"No, I'm grateful for it. It hasn't written on me, but it gives me my epiphany every time I write my name. I would kill any children I have, so I'm just not going to have children. And I didn't even have to get a tattoo! No tattoos, no children. Nothing permanent for my body."

"You can't actually believe that just having the name 'Rebecca Hart' makes you want to kill your children."

As I was saying this, she jumped out of bed and put her shirt back on. "I just met you, so I'll let it slide this time, but please never, ever tell me what I can and can't believe ever again. Now let's go meet my parents."

CHAPTER

◆

21

ebecca's father, seated at a table at the far end of the restaurant, saw us as soon as we came in, and he stood up and waved furiously. If he was dismayed that his daughter had brought a date, he showed no sign of it, and when we reached the table he commenced doing what fathers are supposed to do: state facts in a way that makes their children hate the facts, their fathers, and themselves.

"I see the birthday girl has brought a young man."

"Venter Lowood, sir."

"Don't call me 'sir.' Politeness is creepy in your generation. Call me 'Bob.' What did you say your name was again?"

"Venter. My parents wanted me to have a name no one else had."

He looked at his daughter. "Well, there's nothing wrong with having a name that other people have either."

I had not intended any comment on the history of the name "Rebecca Hart." It wasn't even true that my parents had wanted me to have a name that no one else had—this was just a breezy line I used to get out of talking about my name. I tried to think of a way to explain all this while Rebecca's father explained that Rebecca's mother was trying to find a parking space.

Rebecca, not having registered any unintentional insult from me and already in chiding-daughter mode, said that it didn't make any sense for them to have driven, since it would have been much more convenient for them to have taken Metro-North. It struck me as a major failure to learn that the first girl I had hooked up with lived in a town accessible by the rail system that fed commuters from suburban New York and Connecticut into the city and then spat them back out again; I had gone to college hoping for new experiences, but had formed my first real connection with someone who was, apparently, from the same place I was.

After saying that the train always made her mother sick, as Rebecca well knew, her father launched into a monologue about how lucky we were to be in college and how much he missed it. He was an ear, nose, and throat doctor, which, he told me, he considered a ludicrous specialty. It made sense in a way, of course—the medical profession had sound reasons for carving up specialties the way it did—but he said he couldn't help feeling that he had been tossed the leftover parts of the body, the ones the other doctors weren't interested in. He had really enjoyed reading Augustine in college, and in his dorm at night, he used to fantasize about becoming an Augustine scholar, even though there was never really a time when he was going to do anything other than go to medical school, and he was glad he had gone to medical school, since he had friends who were academics and they said it was a miserable life for all but a lucky few at the top. Anyway, he said, his point had nothing to do with wanting to be an Augustine scholar, it had to do with wanting to live the life of an undergraduate, and reading whatever you wanted to in a fun and superficial way, and making all sorts of plans that don't really mean very much, and that both Rebecca and I should enjoy this time while we could, and we should remember that every moment we weren't enjoying ourselves was basically a moment that we were adding to our own oblivion, and it would be pretty dumb to add any moments to our own oblivion, since our oblivion already extended into functional eternity in two directions.

Throughout this monologue, Rebecca tried to interrupt to get him to talk about something more interesting, but I appreciated the fact that I was not being called on to talk. Despite my extensive practice, I still wasn't very good at making conversation with a father who would prefer that I was not there.

When Rebecca's mother arrived, she took a deep, unhappy breath at seeing me, and then said she was delighted that I could join them for their private family dinner.

"It's New York, Mom. There's no such thing as a private family dinner."

Her mother collapsed into her chair and took Rebecca's comment as an invitation to complain about New York, particularly the parking. As we all shared some bruschetta, I noticed Rebecca's mother glancing at me, waiting for the right opportunity to strike and say something nasty. I told myself I was imagining this, until the right opportunity struck and she said something nasty.

"So, Venter, I hope you're ready to be portrayed unflatteringly in Rebecca's first novel."

"I'm not writing fiction anymore, Mom."

"What? But that's your dream."

"Was my dream. And that's all it was."

"Is this because you've been distracted by your boyfriend? You should never let that happen."

"I'm totally supportive of whatever Rebecca wants to do," I said. I was generally supportive of anyone's artistic inclinations, so I would almost certainly be supportive of Rebecca's specific artistic inclinations were I ever called upon to do so.

"Young lovers are never going to listen to us, Melanie," Rebecca's father said. "Lecturing them will only make them want to rebel."

"Oh yeah, everything I do is out of rebellion," Rebecca said. "That's why I'm dating Venter. Venter's favorite food is bacon. Bacon-wrapped shrimp is pretty much the only thing he eats."

"Rebecca likes to tease us," her mother said. "It's not as though we keep kosher. We're secular."

"Venter's not just secular. He is a *very bad Jew*. He's such a bad Jew he has a tattoo."

This obvious baiting of her parents was getting tiresome.

"The salmon looks amazing!" I said, pointing to a nearby busboy and lamely trying to recover the moment.

"Is that true, Venter?" her father asked. "Do you have a tattoo?"

"Daddy doesn't want Jews to have tattoos. He doesn't like the rhyme."

"It was a bad decision," I said. "I should never have gotten it. It's not worth alienating anyone over."

"Oh, now I'm disappointed," her father said. "You shouldn't care what I think. I certainly didn't care what Melanie's mother thought. She didn't approve of the fact that my father wasn't Jewish, but I certainly didn't apologize for my background, or for anything else I did. I'm not sure how I feel about my daughter dating someone who cares what I think."

"Whoa, looks like the epiphany machine and my dad agree about you, Venter," Rebecca said.

"Wait, what? You don't have an epiphany tattoo, do you?"

"Yes, I do."

"You understand that Adam Lyons ruined our daughter's life."

"Ruined her life? She's a freshman at Columbia."

"Her entire life, she's had to endure jokes about Rebecca the Heartless."

"I recall a different term," Rebecca said.

"So why did you name her Rebecca?" I asked.

"Rebecca is my grandmother's name and Melanie's grandmother's name, so we had other associations with the name 'Rebecca,' if you can believe that."

"I like my name!" Rebecca said. "Not that you've ever cared about that."

"So what does your epiphany tattoo say?" her mother asked.

"I'd rather not discuss it."

Both parents laughed at this. "He'd rather not discuss it," her father said. "He gets it tattooed on his arm for the whole world to see, but he'd rather not discuss it."

"Not the whole world," I said. "Just people who see my arm."

"People like my daughter."

"People like me," Rebecca said.

"So let us see it, too," her father said.

"Let you see it?"

"I didn't ask to see your dick. I asked to see your fucking forearm. If my daughter is dating a cult member, I'd at least like to see what the cult has told him."

I stood and shoved up my sleeve for him to see.

"Happy now? Because, uncharacteristically, I don't give a shit."

Within seconds, I was out of the restaurant and half a block away, trying to imagine how I would tell this story to Leah and Ismail in a way that would make me sound as heroic as possible.

"I'm sorry I used you as a prop against my parents," Rebecca called from a few steps back. "How about letting me make it up to you by letting you use me as a prop against these friends you're obviously trying to avoid?"

I mumbled something about how I wasn't trying to avoid them, but she hailed a cab and we were on our way.

CHAPTER

─ · · ◆ · · ─

22

The bar was so crowded that we found them only when Leah spilled her gin and tonic on the arm of my coat. She was very embarrassed until she saw that it was me.

"Venter!" she said. "I'm so sorry. Just think of it as me dousing you with Adam's holy water. The power of Lyons compels you!"

"He misses you, man," Ismail said. "We've missed you, too."

"Rebecca, this is Leah and Ismail," I told Rebecca. "Although I doubt those are the names on their IDs."

"I'm an actor!" Leah said. "I am everyone and no one. I am as much Rebecca Hart as I am Leah Marx." She pulled out an ID purportedly belonging to Rebecca Hart of Chicago, Illinois, born January 6, 1976. The Feast of the Epiphany. She turned to Rebecca. "It's kind of an in-joke. You probably don't remember this, but Rebecca Hart was the name of . . ."

Rebecca, to my surprise, laughed. "My name is actually Rebecca Hart. Maybe I should have gotten a fake ID that says Leah Marx."

"This is a funny girl, Venter, you should keep her."

"I *am* funny, but my name really is Rebecca Hart. It's not your fault that my name is a joke. But I'm not an actor, so I can't be anybody. I'm Rebecca Hart to the bottom of my heart."

"I can't be anyone either," Ismail said. "I can only be someone who **WANTS TO BLOW THINGS UP.**" He rolled up his sleeve. "No acting for me."

"Shut up," Leah said with a laugh and a punch. "You could act if you wanted to. You're much happier directing me and writing for me." She then turned to us. "He wrote this *amazing* monologue for me called *An Author's Undoing.*"

"The play's just okay. The one I'm working on now will be better, I think. But Leah is amazing in it."

I wondered whether Rebecca thought less of me because my college life was not as productive and adventurous as that of my friends. I also wondered whether Ismail and Leah thought that Rebecca was boring.

"What was it like to use the epiphany machine?" Rebecca asked Ismail.

"It made me realize I wanted to 'blow up' my relationship with my mother," Ismail said. "She was going to force me to go to medical school." I had forgotten how easy it is to get bored hearing people tell their life stories. "When I told her I was going to go to NYU to pursue theater instead, she tried to make me take organic chemistry, just in case I changed my mind and wanted to be a doctor after all. When I refused, she forced me to get a job as a gas station attendant in town for the remainder of last summer. I guess she just really wants me to stick tubes in things to get them to run."

Leah laughed, in love with her boyfriend's sense of humor, and then turned to Rebecca. "You should come to our show! Particularly since you're dating Venter. I mean, you guys *are* dating, right?"

"I'd love to come," Rebecca said, sidestepping the question. "Leah, do you do any of your own writing?"

"Writing's not my bag," Leah said. "Although I do want to do one of those testimonial things for Venter. Venter, do you have your tape recorder?"

I didn't, and I also thought about pointing out that I didn't take testimonials anymore. But I was curious enough about what Leah would say that I brought my tape recorder along to a coffee date with her the following week. In the meantime, right there in the bar, I imagined the four of us as the group of sophisticated, glamorous friends that I had always wanted, and I could already see how disappointing it would be to have it.

NAME: Leah Marx
DATE OF BIRTH: 04/10/1981
DATE OF EPIPHANY MACHINE USE: N/A
DATE OF INTERVIEW BY VENTER LOWOOD: 11/23/1999

I loved Coke when I was a child. The soda, not the powder. If I could get my hands on a can of Coke, I just popped it—I loved the sound of that popping—and then I pointed the bottom to the sky and I kept drinking until it was empty. I loved feeling overpowered by that particular blend of sugar and unholy chemicals. You can laugh if you want, but I think it's morally perilous to laugh at childhood joy, no matter where that joy comes from. Certainly my parents laughed about it, particularly about the fact that I would throw a tantrum if someone offered me a Pepsi instead. "I guess Pepsi *isn't* the choice of a new generation!" But even then, I could tell that the jokes weren't really jokes. My father told me I was going to get fat, then said he was sorry for saying something "so horrible." When I told him I didn't care if I got fat, that *really* scared him. He forbade me from drinking Coke, or any soda at all. Like any good heroine of any good love story, I was inflamed by my father's disapproval of my beloved. Nothing could stop me from drinking Coke now. Meeting in secret just made our couplings more intense. I spent a good portion of my first sleepover in the birthday girl's bathroom, pouring a six-pack down my throat can by delicious can. This probably should have made me a weird pariah; instead, the sugar gave me enough energy and verve to plunder the girl's mother's makeup, and that made me a fucking child celebrity. A couple of the girls tried to make fun of me for being fat, but I was too in love to care, and that love radiated out of me and made the other girls love me. And loving me meant bringing me to their houses, which, for them, meant latching on to my bold, sugar-fueled adventures, and, for me, just meant drinking Coke.

I don't have to tell you what I looked for in the vending machines the week my father spent dying in the hospital. Or what I drank almost non-stop for several hours after he took his last breath. Or what I drank more of than ever in the weeks and months after he died. I knew that I was supposed to deny myself the only thing I enjoyed in order to mourn this man who denied me the only thing I enjoyed—this man who tried to make me feel bad about taking up a little too much space on the planet. I knew that if he were alive he'd still be horrified at how much Coke I was drinking, and definitely at how fat I was getting, and I liked knowing that.

Then I had no taste for Coke at all. Starting around the time I turned eleven, it just tasted like water into which somebody had poured sludge. I didn't want Coke; I didn't want anything. I stopped doing my schoolwork, or even getting out of my bed without my mother physically dragging me out.

I took to acting, because you got to inhabit these weird fake people who were so artificially constructed that they *wanted* things, as though anybody in real life wants the same thing for more than like a minute or two. Judging from the reaction to my performances, people really believed that I wanted things when I was on stage, and that was really funny.

You know what I used for every emotion I showed on stage? I knew my love for Coke was dead, but sometimes I would get some other junk food from the vending machines, just to see if I could reproduce the feeling. Kit Kats, Doritos, whatever. I could never tolerate more than a bite or two. But every once in a while, whatever I had bought would get stuck, and *then*, at least for a couple of minutes, I would experience strong emotion. Desire, frustration, hope, anger, everything you see on stage. Nobody ever wants a person the way they want a bag of chips they've already paid for that refuses to fall at their feet. Or maybe people want people in exactly that way. Funny.

I snorted coke a few times, since that seemed like it would have some appropriate symmetry, and coke is supposed to make you want more coke, which at least is wanting something. But that kind of coke didn't do anything for me, and I would just kind of look at the other people doing coke, and they would all just be funny to me.

I got a job in a pet store, hoping *that* would make me feel something, since I did like dogs. The thing with the puppy mills, the thing I wrote about for Mr. Sullivan's class, made me feel sad, but not sad enough to make me do anything. The sadness of those dogs just reinforced the idea that life was a joke.

I was friends with you guys mostly because you were funny, and it amused me to watch you fall over yourselves for me. It even persisted into the beginning of the time I was first dating Ismail. The epiphany machine was funny to me, you were funny to me, Ismail was funny to me. I started dating Ismail because he was funny to me. And then Ismail got his tattoo and everything was different, for him and for me. I could see that he really did want to blow things up—not only his relationship with his mother, but, I don't know, every single convention of contemporary theater. He *wants* to destroy everything old and create something new, really *wants* to do it. And seeing him want to make great art makes me want him, and want to join him.

Here's the thing, though: I feel guilty that all I'm doing is helping Ismail achieve his own artistic vision. I feel guilty for not writing myself. And yet for some reason it feels *important* to me that the words I speak on stage aren't mine—I love being deluged by them, even gagging on them, in the same way that I loved being deluged by and gagging on Coke. Something's only mine when it's not mine, if that makes sense.

Maybe it doesn't make sense. But if it doesn't make sense, I don't want to know that it doesn't make sense. That's why I don't want to use the machine myself.

CHAPTER

✦

23

Just before winter break, Rebecca and I attended Ismail's play, which was terrible. Eighty minutes of Leah talking about nothing in several voices. This brought me no joy whatsoever; what I mostly felt was rage at Ismail for wasting all the energy that Leah brought to the small black-box stage. There was one moment in the play, when for some reason she was playing *The Odyssey*'s Penelope, doing what Penelope does every night—which is to say, sitting at her loom, undoing her day's work on her father-in-law's burial shroud—when I could *see* the loom, *see* the shroud that was being undone (though there were no props, only Leah, her black sweater, and her blue jeans), and most of all I could feel Penelope's anguish at having to undo the only thing she did all day, but what I could not do was understand what Penelope was doing in the middle of what amounted to an eighty-minute monologue about writer's block, or why Ismail had written an eighty-minute monologue about writer's block.

I was careful not to look at Rebecca, since she and I were the only ones in the audience and I was fairly certain that Leah would be able to see if Rebecca and I exchanged "This sucks" looks. When it was over, we both applauded as though we had just seen the twentieth century's final great work of art, and I waited until we were out on the street before I said: "Well, maybe his next one will be better."

"What are you talking about?" Rebecca said. "It was really good."

"Are you kidding? It was just about being blocked. Incredibly boring."

"Being blocked is everything."

"Do you want to talk about the fact that you're blocked?"

"I'm not blocked," she said. "I've given up writing."

"How do you know the difference?"

"I don't know, because I don't approach my heart like it's a jigsaw puzzle?"

"I could never give up writing," I said.

"Maybe you should. That story you gave me was shit, Venter."

"You said you hadn't read it."

She looked at me like she couldn't believe she was hooking up with someone this stupid.

"You lied to me? I don't think I can date a liar."

"You're going to break up with me because I didn't like your story?"

"I'm going to break up with you because you're a liar."

"You're going to break up with me because I didn't like your story, and you can't handle that. **DEPENDENT ON THE OPINION OF OTHERS,** man. There's a limit."

We argued for a few more minutes, in the course of which we both realized that we were each going to have to break up with someone for the first time in our lives. It was exhilarating and it turned us both on. We didn't wait for Ismail and Leah, and instead got on the subway and headed uptown, where we fucked in my room before vowing never to see each other again.

CHAPTER

——— · · ◆ · · ———

24

The vow never to see each other again was our official policy for winter break and for the first several weeks of spring semester; Rebecca and I appeared to have an unspoken agreement that seeing each other between the hours of midnight and five in the morning did not count. Then one morning I fell asleep in her bed after sex and we woke up at noon, after which we got lox and bagels and decided we might as well be a couple again.

We probably would not have stayed together very long if it hadn't been for Ismail and Leah, whom we started seeing three or four times each week. On days when they didn't see us, Ismail and Leah often saw Adam, and I suppose that part of the reason I wanted to see them was so that I could keep hearing about Adam. Leah mentioned a "creepy guy named Vladimir Harrican," who had come by Adam's one night and apparently asked about me; Adam had responded, "Get lost, Douglavich."

Mostly, Rebecca and I wanted to hang around Ismail and Leah for how they made us feel. Ismail and Leah would take us to plays, most of which were quite bad, and then we would get pizza or just two plates of French fries and make fun of the plays.

"I think the lead girl is my new idol," Leah said, after one ridiculous production. "Every time I give Ismail a blowjob from now on, I'm going to interrupt myself to look at the wall and deliver a monologue about how women are brainwashed by the media into thinking that male sexual pleasure is more important than female sexual pleasure."

Her mockery, she had explained to me, had a clear place in her scheme to stop finding everything funny: she was going to keep holding art to high standards and laughing at art that failed to meet those standards, while genuinely laboring to meet those standards herself. And her use of the word "brainwashed" made me miss Adam acutely.

"And then I'll be like the guy," Ismail said, "and apologize to the wall on behalf of all men, and then go down on you."

"I love that the author of the play was a man," Rebecca said. "You know that he was like, 'Holy shit, this is going to make all the girls ask me to go down on them.' Why don't you write a play, Leah?"

The shift was jarring, and Leah took a moment to recover.

"I'm an actor, not a writer," she said. "Why don't *you* write a play?"

"I'm neither an actor nor a writer," Rebecca said.

"So I guess we'll have to leave the writing to the boys," Leah said. "Since they're better at it, *obviously*."

This made me uncomfortable, so I was grateful when Leah continued speaking.

"You should write about Adam," she told Ismail. "And I'll play Adam."

"Why would you play an old man?" Rebecca asked. "Why don't you play a woman?"

"For the challenge. Why would I want to play myself?"

"I never know whether I want to slap you or salute you," Rebecca said.

"They're not mutually exclusive," Leah said, either play-flirtatiously or flirtatiously-flirtatiously. Rebecca looked a bit flustered, and maybe—if I was reading her right, always a big if—a bit turned on.

"Slap her!" Ismail said. "I'm too scared to do that myself. Write about

Adam. What a dumb idea." Ismail said this in a way that made it obvious that he had already decided to do it.

"Adam has been covered way too much," I said. "You should pick a worthy subject."

"'You should pick a worthy subject,'" Leah said, imitating me and making Rebecca and Ismail laugh and laugh.

After that conversation—and on many, many other nights that stretched out for the rest of the school year and through the next—the four of us wandered around downtown. Rebecca and Leah shared a particular fondness for Greene Street; they liked to do these stumbling waltzes on the cobblestones. Often, they would get far ahead of us and fall into what looked like intense conversations, and Ismail and I would hang back and try to guess what they were talking about, at least until we got frustrated and started talking Beckett or *The X-Files*.

As the sun rose, Rebecca and I would take a cab back uptown on the West Side Highway, exhausted by the knowledge that we were two young people watching the dawn light on the Hudson, and that clearly this was the best life could get, so we better enjoy it.

NAME: Georgette Hoenecker

DATE OF BIRTH: 12/10/1945

DATE OF EPIPHANY MACHINE USE: 06/15/1971

DATE OF INTERVIEW BY ISMAIL AHMED AND LEAH MARX: 02/11/2001

I had little choice but to fall in love with Douglas Harrican. I was nineteen, with no directive in life other than to marry a man my father would approve of. I wasn't raised to have any pursuit of my own, and for the most part I didn't have one. I did have a passion for French cuisine, which I was very serious about and to which I devoted a great deal of time from a young age, but this was regarded even by close friends as just my way to snare a man, no matter how I protested otherwise.

Douglas had very little money, at least by my father's standards, but he was a famous, and famously handsome, British violinist, and even though my father could not have cared less about classical music, he recognized that there was great prestige in being a famous violinist, in being handsome, and in being British, and prestige was what my father really cared about. If my father had ever gotten a tattoo, I think it would have been **DEPENDENT ON THE OPINION OF OTHERS.** In any case, I hated all the men I knew who had money, and I certainly hated all the men I knew who had old money, so when I met Douglas at a party and he was taken with me, I thought: He'll do. He was a genius, after all, not only a spectacular musician but staggeringly well-read and fluent in French and Italian and German and Russian. I thought that that made him my best option, even though his conversation was pedantic and tedious and I found him about as sexually compelling as a piece of cardboard. All the other girls swooned for him, of course, and they were all jealous that I was the one he picked. I pretended to swoon, too, since doing otherwise would likely have made me seem a sore winner. Of course, it was only because I was cool to him that he picked me.

We had been dating only a couple of months when he proposed, and I accepted, glad to be finished with what I had thought would be a lengthy game in which I'd have to pretend to be pretending not to be interested in him. I was also happy that we would be discussing wedding plans, which, boring though they would be, would be far preferable to Communist theory, the minutiae of which was the only thing he cared to discuss when we were alone. I couldn't figure out why. I would have liked to hear his thoughts on Bach and Schubert, subjects about which he had more than secondhand knowledge, but he said that he spent all day talking about music and that at night he wanted to talk about his true passion, the deplorable present conditions of the Western worker and the glorious future that awaited. I hoped that he would bring this up when my father was present, since that might have gotten me out of the engagement and at the very least would have been entertaining, but with my father, he spoke only of dining options in European capitals, leaving out any reference to the Communist parties that were then active therein.

Instead of wedding plans, Douglas moved from my acceptance of his proposal directly to preparations for the taking of my virginity. I was now his fiancée, and so he expected me, essentially, to put out. My father had impressed on me the importance of keeping myself intact until my wedding night. I didn't much care either way. I yielded to Douglas, thinking it could not be all that unpleasant.

It was very unpleasant. I had heard that there was often pain involved for the woman the first time, so I expected it to get better the second, third, or tenth time. It did not. The pain lessened, I suppose, but it was replaced not by pleasure but by discomfort. It felt like getting shoved out of the way on the street, over and over, only you were expected to make noises signaling how much you were enjoying it. The only part of our lovemaking I found tolerable was when he put his fingers inside of me, but despite my urging, he always rushed through this prelude on his way to the thrusting fortissimo. As inappropriate as I knew it to be, it was after one of these sessions that I said one of the only prayers I've ever said: that Douglas would take his time and finger me.

The wedding was coming up and I was trying to devise some kind of plan to get out of it when, walking home one night from one of his performances, we were all but literally shoved out of the way on the street. It took us a moment to understand what was happening: a completely bald man was shoving flyers at us. Then I saw that the bald man was in fact a bald woman, a girl about my age, with these blue eyes that, when they met mine, somehow locked my feet in place. We stood there staring at each other, and it took me a moment even to notice her tattoo, **HORRIFIES TO CREATE LOVE**, which struck me as very strange, not just because it was very unusual in those days to see a woman with any kind of tattoo, but because I did not understand how she could horrify anyone. Though I could certainly understand how she could create love. I think I was about to tell her this, consequences be damned, when she turned and continued down the street.

"The epiphany machine!" she called behind her. "Know thyself."

I looked at Douglas, thinking of how I would explain away what had been the most intense several seconds of my life. But he hadn't noticed. Instead, he was staring at the flyer. Or rather at the drawing on the flyer.

"We have to go to this address," he said.

Adam opened the door smelling of whiskey, which was more or less how I expected men to smell, and acting immediately like Adam, which was not how I expected men to act. I was mildly charmed, but mostly I was impatient for Douglas to stop talking about all of his doubts about whether the music of the dead was a waste of his life. I just wanted the right moment to strike for me to ask about the girl who handed us the flyers. But Douglas hardly stopped talking until he was in Adam's chair. It all happened so quickly that I barely had time even to figure out what the epiphany machine was. I pointed out to Douglas that letting a stranger put a needle in your arm could not be a good idea for a violinist, if it was a good idea for anyone, but he couldn't be dissuaded. When I saw his tattoo, **MUST MAKE DIFFERENT USE OF HANDS**, I blushed and thought of my prayer. Douglas jumped up and down and said that this was true, he had to emigrate to the Soviet Union so that he could work with his hands in a factory and join the liberated proletariat.

"Slow down," Adam said, laughing. "Sit with your epiphany; let it work its way into you. Don't make any sudden changes. And where are our manners? We should offer the lady a turn."

There was no way I was going to let that thing anywhere near my arm. But this was my opportunity to ask about the bald tattooed girl. And I didn't take it. I knew that if I asked about her it would change the course of my life, and I just wasn't ready. Not being ready cost me years of my life.

Douglas talked a lot about his plan with me that first night—he was going to defect during an upcoming tour of the Eastern Bloc—but he stopped mentioning it after that, and it never occurred to me that he was actually going to do it. I didn't think that this boy who was still so obsequious with my father had it in him. When I stepped outside one morning during the tour and saw his face all over the newsstands, tattooed with headlines accusing him of treachery, I felt happy for him that he had actually had the courage to do something, and much happier for myself that I wouldn't have to marry him.

The following months did not make me happy. I was the jilted fiancée of Comrade Harrican, and everyone wanted to interview me and/or tell me how sorry they felt for me. It didn't make sense to me why Douglas had done something so silly, but I could see now how fame could make you insane.

Speaking of which, around this same time John Lennon used the machine. Douglas's use of the machine was not yet known—I had no interest in telling anyone about it, and neither, apparently, did Douglas—so no one connected the two cases at the time. I had no interest in Lennon or his music either before or after his use of the machine. Lovesick boys who are mad in equal measure at war and at girls who don't return their affection have never held much appeal for me. But I did notice some reports that Lennon had been handed his flyer by a bald girl with a tattoo.

I thought a lot about going back to Adam's apartment and asking about her. There were times when I got in a cab and got out in front of his building. But I could never bring myself to ring the buzzer for apartment 7.

There wasn't much else I could bring myself to do, either. I had no purpose in life except to find a husband, and I knew by now that I would never have any interest in doing *that*, so I didn't have any interest in doing anything. For a few years after that, no one in our circle wanted to be seen with me, for fear that I carried some kind of Soviet contagion. I mostly lay in bed in my room in my father's penthouse, waiting to pass from sought-after prize to invisible old maid. I preferred that role, although I would have preferred no role at all. I read a lot of novels, less to find a model of a person to be than to experience life without being any kind of person at all. The world is such an interesting place to spend two or five or seven or ten decades, and it struck me as a shame that I had to spend those decades as one person, with particular proclivities and experiences. So limiting. So I tried to live without those things.

Eventually my circle's memory of Douglas wore off. By this time, my attachment to my books and my bed had grown enervating, just like, I thought, any long-term relationship.

Occasionally, my father insisted I go to dinner with the son of one or another of his friends, including a date with Si Strauss. I had heard rumors that Si was now funding the epiphany machine, but he was very cagey and would not admit his involvement. I wanted with my entire being to ask him about the bald tattooed girl, but instead I just let him talk the whole time about a youth-league baseball team he was coaching. Sweet but boring.

Another rich man's son I was compelled to let take me to dinner was Caleb. As far as I could tell he was doing nothing with his life, but he spent most of our first date talking about how much he despised the poor. When he ended our first date by proposing to me, I wondered what he thought our connection was, and then I suddenly realized that neither of us had anything to offer beyond our family's wealth, and that this was as strong a bond with another human being as I was likely to find. I wanted to cry, but instead I said: Sure, okay.

My father was happy, though he reminded me not to give up my virginity before my wedding night. I didn't mention that I had already lost my virginity to Douglas, and I certainly didn't mention that I would prefer never to have sex with any man again, either before or after marriage. I just said: Sure, okay.

Once again, wedding preparations. Caleb got very jealous very quickly. Every time a man looked at me I could count on Caleb flying into a rage. I told him over and over again that none of those men appealed to me, which was extremely true, but he refused to believe me. I did have a brief affair with a coat-check girl, but he didn't notice that. He started accusing me of marrying him for his money, which was absurd given my father's wealth. He started getting obsessed with Douglas, thinking I had never gotten over the man who had left me for Russia. Exasperated with this particular avenue of his paranoia, I told him that I had lost any interest I had in Douglas when he used the epiphany machine, a bizarre device for the dumb and credulous.

It turned out that Caleb was a devoted fan of John Lennon—a fellow pathologically jealous guy—and was ecstatic to learn that I knew where the epiphany machine was. He said that this could solve all of our problems. All I had to do was use the epiphany machine to prove to him that I loved him.

It's hard to say why I didn't just refuse and leave him. But breaking off another engagement would mean another round of pity and scorn from everyone I knew, and I just couldn't face that. So I agreed to go with Caleb to Adam's apartment.

Adam recognized me immediately and gave me a very gentlemanly, if probably mocking, kiss on the hand. This did not seem to make Caleb jealous, since this man was John Lennon's prophet and therefore his own.

My tattoo was **GIVES AWAY WHAT MATTERS MOST**, which I immediately knew was completely accurate and therefore made me completely
furious.

Caleb thought this was confirmation that I was marrying him for his
money and cheating on him, so he called off our engagement. My father
thought it was confirmation that I had had sex with Caleb, and he was
livid with me, but far angrier at Adam for tattooing on his daughter what
he took to be a declaration of her whorishness. He hadn't seemed to care
about Si's rumored involvement with the epiphany machine when he insisted I go to dinner with him, but now that his daughter had this filthy
thing on her arm, he was furious at the Strauss family for funding this
monstrous operation; he told me he wanted to sue. I was angry and adrift
enough that I agreed.

Preparing for the lawsuit gave me something I hadn't had in a long
time: purpose. I wanted to be as involved with the firm we hired as I could.
I especially liked one paralegal working on the case, a girl named Rose, who
tried hard to disguise her Queens accent and—I remember distinctly—
wore a brand-new fox fur coat. I was very surprised when she showed up
at my apartment one night and told me I had to drop the lawsuit.

She told me that Adam's work was important, and the epiphany machine had showed her who she was. She took off her coat and showed me
her tattoo: **ABANDONS WHAT MATTERS MOST**. I told her that this
was very similar to my tattoo and just provided evidence that Adam was a
charlatan, who made vague, interchangeable judgments.

"'Abandons' is very different from 'gives away,'" Rose said. "I don't
know you very well, but you seem like someone who gives away. I abandon."

I did not find this persuasive and asked her to leave my home. I was
saddened that Adam had brainwashed this bright, hardworking girl, and I
did not relish the prospect of calling the firm to tell them to fire her, but I
did so the next morning. They told me she had already quit.

A few weeks later, I came home to find Rose waiting outside my building. My first instinct was to call the police, but then she took a couple of

steps toward me and I saw a bald head and blue eyes behind her. I immediately recognized those eyes.

Lillian and I went to a coffee shop and stayed until closing. People
stared at Lillian, and I tried to shoo them away, but she told me that she
didn't care about the way that they were staring at her, because of the way
that I was staring at her. She had felt the same connection that I felt that
night with Douglas, and she had been waiting for the epiphany machine to
find me again. When Adam told her that I was the same woman who had
been engaged to Douglas, she knew it had finally happened. We walked
together all night. She told me she thought that the Beatles got at universal
longings that lay beyond personality, and it was her desire to get past personality that led her to adopt her androgynous, anonymous look. She was
proud to be the inspiration for Loretta Martin and Polythene Pam. To this
day I think that the Beatles get at nothing more universal than subjugating
women and stealing from black people—so, universal for heterosexual
white men—but the Beatles are still pretty much the only thing we've ever
disagreed about. She told me she had been working for a few years as a sous
chef in a French restaurant, and we immediately started making plans to
open a restaurant together.

I brought Lillian home to my father and told him we were in love, expecting that he would throw me out and we would never speak again and
I wouldn't have a penny to my name. That was almost what happened, but
he was so eager to get me out of New York and away from the eyes of his
friends that he gave me enough money to get started. Lillian and I opened
up a small French restaurant in Phoenix that is thriving to this day. For a
while, Lillian and I were the only employees; eventually we brought on a
third, but that's as big as the operation has gotten. I come to New York
every once in a while for business, but mostly to thank Adam. If my arm
were clean, my life would be so squalid.

CHAPTER

— · · ✦ · · —

25

The pressure to be constantly happy at the best time of our lives often made both Rebecca and me cranky and quick to find fault, particularly after we returned for sophomore year. We were two kids who liked to fuck and who hated each other.

Exactly why we hated each other was too difficult to decide. But Rebecca offered many ideas:

"I hate you because you have your head so far up your ass you don't even know why I hate you."

"I hate you because this isn't *Annie Hall* and I can't bring out James Joyce to tell you he hates you."

"I hate you because you act like you're a goddamn hero when you wash your fucking towels."

"I hate you because you put in just barely enough effort in bed to make me feel guilty for criticizing you, and literally no more effort than that."

"I hate you because this isn't *Annie Hall* and I can't bring out Steven Merdula to tell you he hates you." She was fond of this construction.

"I hate you because you joined a cult to search for your mother and then you barely bothered to try to find her."

"I hate you because you're scared of everything. And to be scared is to scramble the sacred."

To this one I responded: "Which self-help writer is that?"

"Do you have any idea how much I could be accomplishing right now if, instead of listening to you belittle me for reading self-help, I was doing literally anything else? I could be having much more adventurous sex, and with lots of different guys. I could be getting really *good* at sex. I could be studying my ass off every minute that it wasn't getting fucked if only I wasn't sitting around in your room dozing off to *Friends* or Fellini all the fucking time. I could be doing *so much better* in school. For the rest of my life, I'm going to regret every minute I'm spending with you."

"So then why do you spend so many minutes with me?"

"I don't know. I promised my therapist that I was going to break up with you. She told me she won't keep seeing me if I don't break up with you by the end of the month."

"Are therapists supposed to do that?"

"People do all sorts of shit they're not supposed to do, Venter. You'd know that if you weren't so fucking **DEPENDENT ON THE OPINION OF OTHERS**. Or maybe **CLOSED OFF**. That would be a good epiphany for you, too."

And so on. I said a lot of mean things, too, but I remember those less well. One night in the first few weeks of sophomore year I got so mad at Rebecca that I emailed Adam asking whether I could bring my girlfriend—I didn't mention her last name—to use the epiphany machine. By the time I woke up, Adam had already responded.

Hey buddy,

Things have been boring as hell since the Great Rift. I like to say sometimes that Hollywood is the real epiphany machine, and Hollywood is right on target that when you're my age and you've found a surrogate son, you can defuse three nuclear bombs before breakfast and then breastfuck three blondes at night, and it won't mean a goddamn thing if you lose that surrogate son. The other day, a guy came to a salon night, a guy who used the machine a few years ago and had gotten a tattoo that was something like **WILL REGRET NEGLECTING OFFSPRING,** and he came up to me and he had tears in his eyes and he kept thanking me over and over, telling me that because of the tattoo he had volunteered to coach his daughter's soccer team, and that now they were close, and he could hear an obvious difference in the way his daughter said "I love you," like she really meant it now, and he just kept on thanking me over and over again for breaking whatever it was in him that was keeping him from his daughter. He was exactly the reason I do what I do, and I just wanted to punch him in the face so bad. Why does he get to have someone who carries on his legacy, and I don't? Why did I sacrifice the most profound relationship I've had since John died? I should have been easier on you when you were trying to look cool for your friend. I hoped you wouldn't act like a teenager, which is too much to ask even of old men like me. Everybody likes to act like a teenager.

Anyway, bring your girl over anytime. Can't wait to meet her, and to see you again.

Yours, [not my usual signoff]
A.L. (Asshole Liar, if that's what you want my initials to stand for)

By that morning, my desire to inflict pain or knowledge on Rebecca had evaporated, and it felt rude and manipulative of Adam to treat me as though I were still the person I had been the previous night. In a way, responding to the email would have shown that I cared what he thought about me, which would have meant that I was **DEPENDENT ON THE OPINION OF OTHERS.** Sometimes not responding to an email is the only way to ethically engage with the universe. In any case, I didn't respond.

I didn't respond to his follow-up emails either. It became a weekly ritual: every Tuesday morning, an email from Adam. Each unreturned. Not returning Adam's emails was, in some ways, the closest I had ever felt to taking an action to stay true to myself.

Hey buddy,

I'm impressed that you keep ignoring me. Takes balls to be a dick for no reason. Keep doing it until you've proven to yourself whatever you need to prove to yourself. I'll keep writing.

Yours,
A.L. (Alien Lighthouse)

These emails from Adam continued up through the premiere of Ismail's play about him, which Ismail did wind up writing and which did star Leah. The two of them spent much of our sophomore year with Adam, preparing for the play. To get as full a sense as possible of the machine and how it affected people, they even took up my testimonial project. They kept on trying to get me to come with them to see Adam, and I kept on refusing. Rebecca intermittently expressed interest, but Ismail and Leah demurred from bringing her; no one was sure how Adam would react to meeting another Rebecca Hart.

By the time of the play's premiere in April, Ismail and Leah had gotten a lot of attention within NYU, and this play was much, much better attended than the first one I had seen with Rebecca. Rebecca and I were both in the audience for this one, too, but we technically weren't there together, since this was during another period when we were broken up and barely speaking. (We had a tense phone conversation about her attendance in advance: I considered Leah and Ismail my friends rather than our friends;

Rebecca pointed out that they both liked her better than they liked me, which struck me as true but still, somehow, irrelevant.) I arrived after her to find her sitting next to a dark-haired guy who looked like a more handsome version of me. He said something that made her laugh, though that didn't mean that they were there together, since the theater was packed.

Ismail's Adam was not exactly mine—his Adam was less ambiguously a Falstaff rather than a Rasputin, always straightforwardly well-meaning even at his most grandiose and garrulous. But it was hard to deny the clarity and force of Ismail's writing. I knew he had received some mentorship from Catherine Pearson, both on how to write dialogue and how to capture Adam, and this mentorship had clearly paid off.

One major caveat to the quality of the play: some of the diatribes against American culture—the "I don't know if the past was better, but the present is definitely worse" stuff—tipped heavily into speechifying, with long, didactic stretches about things like perfume ads and action-movie sequels, things so obviously terrible they were more interesting to defend than to attack. When I later read these passages again in press coverage of Ismail, it did seem to me that Ismail had soured on America in a troubling way. But, during the performance, I was focused less on Ismail's writing than on the brilliance of Leah's portrayal. Her impersonation of a portly sixty-year-old man should have been gimmicky at best, but she moved across the stage with calm command of his literal and metaphorical weight, and though her voice sounded nothing like his, it sounded more like him than he sounded like himself.

Were there messages from Adam to me? Maybe they were all in my head, or Ismail's, or Leah's. The play took the form of Adam convincing someone offstage to use the machine, and the names he named—Lennon, Chapman, Merdula, as well as the subjects of some of my testimonials—did not include mine. But it was hard to miss the significance of lines such as "I wish you could buy an insurance policy that would cover Protégé Abandonment" (nominally in reference to a different, fictional former protégé) and "Maybe there's only so much you can do for a boy rejected by his mother" (nominally in reference to a real user who had killed himself shortly after using the machine). Adam was trying to tell me that I had hurt him, and he was trying to hurt me in return, if only to get me to come back to him. It was probably the most moved I'd ever felt.

This time I was going to wait for Ismail and Leah. That also meant I was going to have to make awkward conversation with Rebecca, who, it turned out, was not there with the handsome dark-haired guy after all, which surprised me, since I had been certain that I was deluding myself into thinking that there was any chance they weren't together.

"Leah's getting really good," Rebecca said.

"So is Ismail."

"I wish he'd give her more to work with. She does a really good job walking around as an old man, but she shouldn't have to."

"It really pissed me off that he wrote about my mom and me."

"Maybe he wasn't thinking about you. Just because you're **DEPEN-DENT ON THE OPINION OF OTHERS** doesn't mean that other people have an opinion about you."

"Here we go."

"I'm sorry. I actually meant that to be comforting, but I know it didn't come out that way. Also, I've been meaning to tell you that I really liked your story."

"Really?"

I had given her a new story shortly before we had broken up. I had later decided the story was terrible and that it should be read by no one, but by that time, we were broken up and I assumed she would not read it anyway.

"Oh yeah, it's definitely the best work you've done. I know you wrote it when things were really bad between us; maybe that deepened your perspective."

I thought about the story again, and suddenly I could see how the characters were sharper than any other characters I had written. At this moment, Ismail came up to me from behind and hugged me.

"You've got to admit, I'm getting better," he said.

"Ismail, man, you're going to be the playwright of our generation." I had said this before but it had been puffery; now it seemed like I was making a very safe prediction, like saying that the earth would continue to rotate around the sun ten years from now.

"You were so great," Rebecca said, grabbing Leah and putting her face close to hers. "You were in total command up there. But you should play a woman next time. I'm kidding!" She hadn't been kidding, but I was glad she had said she was, so as not to imperil the evening. "Let's go get pizza."

Over pizza—which Ismail ate with one hand while making notes about the play with the other—Leah and Ismail said that they were going to Adam Lyons's apartment afterward to do a private performance for him.

"We tried to get him to come tonight, but you know him, he never goes anywhere," Leah said. "You guys should come!"

"Sounds fun," Rebecca said. "I'd love to meet Adam."

"No way," I said. "No way."

"'No way,'" Leah said, doing an impression of me that made both Ismail and Rebecca laugh loud enough to attract glances from the other NYU students gathered around. "'No way.'"

"Venter, man," Ismail said. "Your grudge against our dude is getting boring."

"'Our dude'?"

"He's totally our dude," Leah said. "He was so helpful when we were putting this show together. Although the main reason was probably to get to you. Can you even articulate why you refuse to see him?"

"I'm not going, and I don't have to explain myself. Coming, Rebecca?"

"I'm not your girlfriend anymore, Venter."

I had somehow forgotten this.

"All right, fine," I said. "Let's go see Adam."

CHAPTER

——— · · ◆ · · ———

26

As we approached Adam's building, I thought I saw Si Strauss walking in the opposite direction, but I couldn't be sure it was him, and besides, it wasn't as though I was going to flag him down for a chat. Adam did not answer when we buzzed apartment 7; that should have provided me with the excuse I was looking for, but I felt compelled to do this now, and it's difficult not to open a door when you have the key.

When we arrived upstairs, Adam was sitting on the floor, his eyes closed and his white-haired belly bursting out of his shirt buttons. I thought he looked like the Buddha, and though I chastised myself for this bit of cultural appropriation like the dutiful liberal arts student I was, nonetheless he looked so beatific I could not understand how I had ever doubted his peculiar divine inspiration.

"Is it okay that we're here?" Ismail asked. Adam opened his eyes and saw me before he saw anyone else.

"Is it okay that *I'm* here?" I asked.

He was always terrible at hiding his delight. "I'm glad Venter's here to see the show," Adam said. "And I'm glad to see you all brought a new friend. Thank you for visiting my humble apartment. Let's see if Leah can do something I've never been able to: do a convincing job of being me."

Leah repeated this, simultaneously charming Adam and beginning the show. Immediately, she was Adam again, so much so that the Adam who laughed and gasped seemed an intrusive Adam impersonator begging for attention. Ismail scribbled notes. I don't want to give the impression that I had placed him under any kind of informal surveillance, but I was standing right next to him, so I snuck some glances at what he was writing.

—L. thinks faster than you do, cut mercilessly and she will carry your meaning.
—Is this whole play a forced gimmick?
—Looking at her own breasts when talking about breastfucking—too easy a joke?
—Are you letting American capitalism off the hook?
—Revisit idea of prop arm? Maybe a whiteboard with erasable marker. We can use (velvet?) curtains to make it look like an arm.
—Only so far you can go with one character.

Midway through the performance, which Adam was without question loving, Leah-as-Adam did an impromptu version of "Your Mother Should Know," inviting Adam to get up and dance with her, which he did eagerly. If he was perturbed at the prospect of dancing with himself—and Leah stayed unquestionably in character—he didn't show it. Leah was dancing like Adam and Adam was dancing like Leah. This thought struck me so strongly that I was torn between the impulse to stop the dance so we could all talk about how brilliant my insight was, and the impulse to join in the dancing and not think at all.

While I was debating which of these to try, Ismail dropped his notebook on the bar and started dancing, too, removing his button-down shirt to reveal his **WANTS TO BLOW THINGS UP** tattoo. Now I wanted to start dancing, but I was afraid that doing so would make me look like a follower. So I just watched until Rebecca pulled me away and toward the purple velvet curtain.

The thought that Rebecca intended to use the machine dawned on me only very slowly—only as we were actually passing through the curtain—and to my great horror. When she took off her sweater I looked at her forearm and pictured the **OFFSPRING WILL NOT LEAD HAPPY LIVES** tattoo that she was walking toward, and I told her, as calmly as I could, that she should not be doing this.

"What? It's not like you've never seen me in a bra before."

I had been so focused on her forearm that I hadn't registered that her torso was bare except for her bra.

"That's the machine? It doesn't look as impressive as I'd hoped," she said.

"A lot of people say it's not the machine that's impressive, it's Adam."

"Adam? He seems okay. Funny, kind of like how my uncle is funny. I'm not sure what the big deal is, honestly."

Neither of us said anything for a moment, and then we started kissing. I started fantasizing about fucking her on top of the machine, and as our hands moved that seemed to be what she wanted, too.

Adam opened the velvet curtain. "About to have sex on my machine!" he said, laughing heartily. "That would be a first. Sorry I interrupted."

I hadn't fully taken off my jeans or underwear, but my embarrassment was probably as visible as my erection.

Rebecca was not embarrassed. "I'd like to use the machine now," she said.

"Is that a euphemism?" Adam asked.

"No. My name is Rebecca Hart and I would like to use the machine."

Adam looked to me for some indication she was joking. I looked at Rebecca for some indication of whether she had told Adam her last name out of defiance, or as a way of getting out of using the machine.

"It's just a name," Leah said, appearing through the velvet curtain.

Adam looked to Leah and then to me again, and as soon as he realized that Rebecca Hart was in fact Rebecca Hart, his face melted into a rage I had never seen before.

"You let a girl named Rebecca Hart get this close to my machine? Is this some kind of revenge you're trying to take on me, Venter?"

"If I'm going to kill my kids, shouldn't I know that?" Rebecca asked.

"If you're going to kill your kids, I don't want you within ten miles of my machine."

"That's all just silliness," Leah said, putting her chin on Adam's shoulder. "You should let her use the machine so she can see that she has artistic aspirations—*obligations*—that she's not fulfilling."

"I asked for the machine's opinion, not yours," Rebecca said. "And I wouldn't talk about not fulfilling artistic obligations if I were you."

"Excuse me? You just saw me give me the performance of my life, *twice*."

"Playing an irrelevant windbag," Rebecca said. "A total waste of your energy."

"This irrelevant windbag wants all of you out of his apartment," Adam said. "Now."

"Adam," I said, "we were all just fucking around."

"Exactly. And this is not a place for that. If you haven't noticed that no matter what the appearances might be I am above all always serious, you haven't noticed anything. You were right to cut off contact, Venter. Let's stay estranged this time."

Angry at Adam and each other, Rebecca, Leah, and I made our way glumly through the apartment. At the doorway we were joined by Ismail, who had been in the bathroom. I told him that Adam was an asshole, and he agreed, though when I tried to elaborate both Rebecca and Leah disputed my version of events. I could tell Ismail was taking notes in his head, workshopping his play, and it made me hate him.

"Writing makes you a bad person," I said to Rebecca in the cab uptown. "It stops you from actually being in the world."

"I think that's bullshit," she said. "It's bullshit if you have talent. And you do. Listen, Venter. A friend of my dad's is letting me have his apartment in Hell's Kitchen this summer, while I intern at the UN. I want you to live with me and write a novel. I want you to do nothing but write a novel. I'll cover rent, groceries, whatever. Don't argue. You're **DEPENDENT ON THE OPINION OF OTHERS**, and my opinion is that you can and should do this."

Now that she mentioned it, this seemed like exactly what I should do.

CHAPTER

——— · · ◆ · · ———

27

So that summer, Rebecca had an internship, I had a novel that she was sure I could write, and we had an apartment, albeit one that belonged to a friend of her father's, who had left a great deal of food behind along with a Post-it note exhorting us to enjoy it. On our first night in the place, we had vigorous and prolonged sex, in the course of which she shoved every appropriately sized vegetable in the kitchen inside herself, and also rubbed her (by then quite juicy) vagina on the arm of the sofa, against the standing lamp, and, in an impressive split, down the center of the glass coffee table in the living room while I lay underneath and gazed up. She got herself off, finally, by rubbing her clit up and down the long turquoise spine of a coffee table book about Majorca. I say finally, but she then wanted to put her pussy on each individual page of the book. I pulled her down to the carpet, both because by this point I was extremely aroused and because I was concerned about paper cuts. I pushed into her and it felt the way truly great thrusting can, like the mucous membrane of the world is helping you break through itself into something new and less petty.

"Come in the ice-cube tray," she said.

"Huh?" I said, not only because she was on the pill and I usually came inside her.

"The ice-cube tray," she said. "Open the freezer and come in the ice-cube tray."

"Can't I just . . ."

"GO."

I hopped up and trotted the twenty feet from the living room to the freezer. My first instinct had been to open the freezer door and masturbate into the empty ice tray while it was sitting right there partially covered by frozen enchiladas, but obviously I wasn't tall enough to do that, so I took the ice-cube tray out and put it on the counter. Rebecca grabbed my dick from behind with one hand, and with her other hand grabbed the ice-cube tray and turned on the faucet for a few seconds before shutting it off. Then she dropped the tray in the sink and stroked me hard. I was so turned on by whatever was happening that I came almost immediately, spraying and then dribbling into the ice-cube tray. Carefully, Rebecca put the ice-cube tray back in the freezer, and then she told me to go down on her on the floor.

There's nothing more **CLOSED OFF** than for a man to think that his own ejaculation means that sex is over, and though it probably is **DEPENDENT ON THE OPINION OF OTHERS** to think about how hypothetical other people would judge my sexual performance, I nonetheless redoubled my effort to turn in credible cunnilingus.

Surprisingly, this worked, or seemed to. Maybe she was so aroused that my poor showing didn't matter. In any case, within a couple of minutes we were both into it. After I was done she nuzzled happily against my chest for a long time before jumping up again and pulling a Sharpie from her purse. She wrote **VENTER'S ADORING SLUT** on her forearm, attaching a little heart to the final **T**.

I kissed her deeply, and then she told me that she wasn't done. She told me to close my eyes, and when she told me to open them, she was holding glasses of whiskey for each of us, with ice cubes only in hers. She swirled the ice cubes around, waiting for them to melt. Waiting was threatening the mood, so she drank the whole thing in one gulp, ice cubes and all.

"Yes!" she said, raising her hands in the air and shaking her breasts more than enough to make me want to continue our evening. "This place is fucking *mine!*"

For the first time in my life, my body felt like something more than a duffel bag for my neuroses. Rebecca and I had had sex before, of course, but we had never *become* sex in the way we just had. Or maybe we had, but I hadn't noticed it because up until now I had been too **DEPENDENT ON THE OPINION OF OTHERS** to actually inhabit my body. This was the last time I would think about any of those words; from now on they would be illegible on my arm, as though I had gotten tattooed with Chinese characters I couldn't read, as did so many Americans I had long disdained but now understood. The worst thing about words is that they mean something.

W hen I woke the next morning, Rebecca was in the bathroom, scrubbing at her arm as though it were cheese she was trying to grate. I had seen plenty of people scrubbing at their arms trying to get words off, but this was the first one that broke me.

"I'm sorry," I said. "I'm sorry about what we did last night."

She put down the sponge and turned off the water. "I'm not sorry about what we did. I just wish I had used a different marker. Whatever, I'll just wear a shirt and a blazer instead of a dress. That's probably what I should do anyway. You've forced me to be a man, Venter, and for that I thank you." She pecked my cheek and jogged past me, and got dressed very quickly. After asking me to make sure I did the dishes, she was gone.

I was extremely angry about the way that she had just treated me, even though I couldn't exactly say what was wrong about the way she had treated me, or even what that way was. All I knew was that what had happened, whatever it was, was too emotionally intense for me to start working on my book. I was tired, and also unsure about whether Rebecca felt that I had exploited her the previous night, which I did not think I had, although the most exploitive men are always certain that they are not exploiting anyone. Maybe what I should write about was whether or not I was an exploitative prick. But I could already tell I was going to write this in a stream of consciousness that would be an obvious rip-off of David Foster Wallace, who had visited Adam's apartment in the early nineties but decided at the last minute not to get a tattoo, an incident that inspired many irritated monologues from Adam, in addition to the nineteen-page footnote in *Infinite Jest* in which Don Gately almost gets an epiphany tattoo.

Now that I had all summer to write my novel, I was once again debating whether I wanted to use the epiphany machine in my fiction, or whether to use my personal experience at all. The answer, I knew, was no; I wanted to write from empathy rather than narcissism; I wanted to explore the world of other people, even—contrary to Ismail's argument—people very different from me. Maybe I could look again at the testimonials and take out all references to the epiphany machine, to make the stories more universal, and then combine them into a great symphonic novel.

I felt a kind of creative intelligence growing within me, and felt certain that as soon as I started typing, I would never stop. For that reason, though, I decided I should probably do the dishes right then, just to get them out of the way. This made me resent Rebecca for giving me a task that would distract me from writing my novel, though, of course, it was a very reasonable task, a very reasonable request, and the fact that I resented it probably meant that I was a misogynist, and I was probably a misogynist due to unresolved anger over my mother's abandonment, although blaming my mother for my misogyny was obviously misogynistic.

Around four o'clock, I did the dishes, and at four-thirty I started writing. At a quarter to five I started thinking about Rebecca's imminent return home and wondered whether she had stopped off to get some new lingerie. I was still wondering at six, at seven, at eight. After that, I found a Gristedes and bought a microwavable "Asian Chicken" meal. Rebecca came home around midnight, very drunk, with one girl and three guys in her internship program. I joined them in the living room, and one of the guys, a Norwegian, asked me whether it was true that Nancy Reagan had gotten an epiphany tattoo and whether the tattoo had had some impact on her husband's nuclear-weapons policy. Then I went to bed and tried to sleep.

This set the tone for the summer. Days and weeks like this.

One afternoon, unable as usual to think of anything to write, I took an aimless walk and ended up somewhere in SoHo. I heard my name spoken in a European accent. It took me a minute to place the voice and the face, but then both revealed themselves to me.

"Vladimir Harrican, right?" I said. "I'm surprised you remember my name."

"It's an unusual name," he said. "And I met you in an unusual place. Though I haven't seen you there recently."

"Adam and I had a falling-out."

"Yes, I was sorry to hear that. Have you given any more thought to my offer?"

"The offer of helping you convince Adam to agree to mass-produce the machine?"

"That is the one," he said.

Given how badly my writing was going, the thought of a job in which I would participate in making something, rather than being the sole person in charge of not making anything, seemed more appealing than it had in the past. But this particular job made even less sense.

"I don't have any influence with Adam anymore," I said. "If I ever did."

"Nonsense. Now he misses you. In your absence, you have more influence than ever."

I thought about this, thought about trying to talk to Adam again, being associated with the epiphany machine, being thought of as a sellout who went corporate before he had even really tried to become a writer.

"No, thanks," I said. "I'm just not interested."

Vladimir did what looked like an imitation of the Adam Shrug, though maybe it was just a shrug. "Okay. So what have you been up to?"

Somehow I was not prepared for this question. "Oh, I've been, um, working on a novel."

"Ah! Good. Keep writing if that's what you want to do. I once wanted to be a writer myself. Just make sure you get enough aerobic exercise. The best research suggests that creative work is impossible without it."

"During the school year, I run all the time in Riverside Park." This was not a total lie. I often tried to get in the habit of running and would run two or three or even four times in a week before stopping and letting months go by before exercising again.

"Do more. My grandfather used to tell me—in Russian, of course— that you can always do more than you think you can."

The mention of his grandfather made it impossible for me not to ask the questions I had on my mind.

"Why are you so obsessed with the epiphany machine? Is it because of your father?"

His face changed, but only for a second. "My family's experience has given me an understanding of Adam's talent for reading people, yes. He made my father see himself as the factory drone he was. I think we'd all be better off if everyone saw themselves for who they were. Including you, Venter. Have a good day."

Somewhat dazed from this conversation, I wandered down Houston and wondered again whether Harrican was Steven Merdula. In the days that followed, I replaced not-writing while sitting in my apartment with not-writing while walking around SoHo, in the vague—and, even to me, inexplicable—hope that I would run into Harrican again. I didn't, but one day I did run into two other people I knew: Leah and Ismail, whom I hadn't seen all summer.

"I've had an epiphany about my epiphany," Ismail said. "I was using my tattoo, **WANTS TO BLOW THINGS UP**, as a wall against my acting ambition. So now I'm going to blow up that wall."

This was a little melodramatic, but I was happy to hear him say it.

"We're in the early stages of thinking about a new play," Leah said.

"We're hoping to just record lots of our conversations over several years, and let characters develop who will blend in with our 'real' selves."

"I'm also going to immerse myself in my Muslim heritage," Ismail said. "I've been thinking that an artist has to work from within a solid tradition of wisdom."

"In the meantime," Leah said, "we're planning a reverse-gender adaptation of *Much Ado About Nothing* set during the Florida recount. The strange ways of the ballot and the strange ways of the heart will be metaphors for each other. I'll be playing Benedick, he'll be playing Beatrice."

"I was thinking we can litter the stage with chads," Ismail said. "We can leave a ballot on each seat."

Ismail jotted that down in a notebook, and then started talking about plans to do a production of *The Merchant of Venice* set at Camp David, with Ismail playing Shylock and Leah playing Portia.

"That will be subversive because I'll be playing a Jew," he said.

Ismail liked the word "subversive," as did everybody else I knew who liked art.

"Ismail is also working on a play he won't tell me about. He gets up in the middle of the night and types away."

"It's not ready for you to see it yet," Ismail said.

They were bursting with so many ideas that I was starting to feel jealous, not to mention acutely aware that I was spending the summer failing to write a novel for no reason other than that my girlfriend had told me I was talented.

"It's hard to imagine the two of you being so happy if Ismail hadn't gotten that tattoo," I said.

I had intended this all but consciously as a random shitty remark that would make me feel better for the few seconds before it made me feel worse, but Ismail appeared to take it earnestly, and smiled broadly.

"You're totally right, Venter," he said. "If you hadn't pushed me to get a tattoo that day, I would be a miserable Palo Alto pre-med. This amazing collaboration that I have with Leah would never have happened. We don't thank you enough."

"To Venter!" Leah said. "Hey, where's Rebecca?"

"I have no idea. We're kind of on the rocks."

"Nobody cares. Let's give her a call."

Within a couple of hours, the four of us were drinking in the apartment that I was by now more or less platonically sharing with Rebecca. Rebecca arrived already drunk, and we all got drunker, and also high on some marijuana Ismail and Leah had gotten from Adam, as the night went on.

"How are the diplomats?" Leah asked Rebecca, drawing out the word "diplomats" until Ismail and I laughed.

"I'm having the most fun I've ever had. This is what I'm meant to be doing."

"Maybe you can write a novel about the UN."

"I don't want to write a novel. I want to be the U.S. ambassador to the UN one day."

"You won't have any real freedom. You'll have to do whatever the president tells you to do."

"Doesn't sound too bad to me."

I could see in Leah's face the decision to change her whole attitude about something. "You know what? This is great. I'm so happy you've found something you like."

"We've all found something we like," Rebecca said. "Hey, listen, I've got a fun idea. Let's all fuck, right here in the living room."

"Genius," Leah said. "Should you strip first, or should I?"

"I'm serious. You and I obviously want each other to be happy, and what's a better way for each of us to make sure the other is happy than to fuck? And don't get me started on Venter and Ismail. They've obviously wanted to do each other for, like, their entire lives."

"Rebecca, come on," I said.

"You don't actually want to fuck me," Leah said.

"How do you know? How do I know? Maybe I'm joking, maybe I think I'm joking and I'll realize years from now that I was serious, or maybe I think I'm serious now and I'll realize years from now that this was just a stupid stunt that ruined a bunch of relationships I cared about. Let's stop thinking and fuck."

"Rebecca, let's get you to bed," I said.

"Don't pretend you don't want to suck Ismail's dick."

"Rebecca Hart, truth-teller!" Leah said. "You're scared of everything in the world, so you're pulling this shit to make yourself look brave."

"I'm pulling this shit so we can stop having endless boring conversations about art and just lick each other's pussies like we obviously want to."

"Let's go, Leah," Ismail said.

"See? The boys don't want to talk because they know they should be stuffing their mouths with each other's dicks instead."

"*Enough*," Ismail said.

"Have fun tonight, Venter," Leah said. Rebecca proceeded to describe what the four of us should do to each other until Leah and Ismail shut the door behind them.

"Are you happy?" I asked.

"I'm happy that you'll be sleeping on the couch tonight."

The next morning she apologized, and the next night we slept in the same bed, though we did not touch each other. The morning after that, she received the following email from Ismail:

Dear Rebecca,

I feel like I have to tell you that you are the embodiment of everything that is wrong with America. Nothing is important to you except chasing any experience that strikes you as momentarily "interesting" or "fun." You don't produce anything yourself, but do whatever you can to make Leah feel bad for being "just" an actress rather than a writer as well, which totally ignores who she wants to be as a person. You also show no respect for my love for Leah, and try to poison her against me by questioning my sexuality. I don't even think you're actually attracted to her; maybe you just want to make her feel uncertain about herself, or maybe you want to absorb some fraction of her massive talent and drive, or maybe you're just bored and will do absolutely anything to entertain yourself, regardless of the consequences, or maybe all three. Like so many Americans, you worship sex but don't understand it. You think you're a "free spirit," but you have no control over either your fears or your impulses. You're a horrible person and you deserve the misery that you're condemned to.

Rebecca showed this to me in tears as she was getting ready to leave and said that Ismail was absolutely right. I told her what I thought was true: that Ismail's email was offensive and totally inaccurate, and that he had said what he said only because he was angry. When she got home, she boiled water for tea and announced that Ismail had no idea what he was talking about and that she never wanted to talk to him again.

That night we had sex that made it obvious that we no longer belonged together. It was so obvious that we were broken up that she didn't bother to break up with me while we were living together, which would have posed logistical complications. We both knew that it was over, totally over, and so we could spend the rest of the summer laughing with each other and kind of enjoying each other's shortcomings instead of regarding them as punishments from God.

The first week we were back at school we avoided each other; we ran into each other the following Monday in line for the Taco Bell in our dorm's food court, so there was no way to avoid having lunch and agreeing we were broken up. It might have been the perfect breakup had the world not popped in.

*Ziad wanted to become a pilot since he was five years old. He
didn't care whether he would be a civilian or a military pilot.
He was crazy about airplanes. The only books he ever bor-
rowed from the library were about airplanes. I stopped him
from being a pilot. I only have one son and I was afraid that he
would crash.*

> —**SAMIR JARRAH**, father of 9/11 hijacker Ziad Jarrah,
> quoted in *The Wall Street Journal*, September 18, 2001

*Even with the benefit of hindsight, Jarrah hardly seems a likely
candidate for becoming an Islamic extremist.*

> —*The 9/11 Commission Report*

A boy wants to take a cockpit to the top of the world. The buildings
would look small if he ever looked down, which he never, ever
would.

A boy wants to take a cockpit to the top of the world. The tight-
est of spaces, suspended in the greatest expanse.

A boy wants to take a cockpit to the top of the world. But for now
he is in Beirut, eye to eye with the bullets that mark the ground
floors of the buildings he wants to fly above.

A boy wants to take a cockpit to the top of the world. But for now
he is in Beirut, and there is a Palestinian refugee camp a few blocks
from his house, where, he has heard it said, the Jews force his brothers and sisters to live like pigs.

A boy wants to take a cockpit to the top of the world. But for now he is in Beirut, and there is only so much longer that he can pretend that his bedroom is a cockpit at the top of the world.

A boy wants to take a cockpit to the top of the world. But for now he is in Beirut, and there is a library that has many books about airplanes. A book is not a cockpit, but maybe it is a way to get to one.

A boy wants to take a cockpit to the top of the world. Ziad's family is not religious. They do not believe there is any world other than this one, and so the top of the world is the top of the world.

A boy wants to take a cockpit to the top of the world. His father tells him he cannot be a pilot, for it is too dangerous. He is his father's only son, and he must choose a profession that will not get him killed.

A boy wants to take a cockpit to the top of the world. Another boy might defy his father, become a pilot despite what his father says. Ziad does not.

A boy wants to take a cockpit to the top of the world. He attends a Christian private school. A few years ago many of the boys in that school would have thought any Muslim worthy of death. Now religion hardly seems to matter. What lies beneath the sky is confusing.

A boy wants to take a cockpit to the top of the world. The Christians do make jokes about Muslims, but Ziad's father tells him not to mind, for jokes are not important.

A boy wants to take a cockpit to the top of the world. His father moves to the country, but Ziad stays in Beirut. There are many good things now in Beirut. Alcohol, women, nightclubs.

A boy wants to take a cockpit to the top of the world. There are moments on the dance floor when it feels as though Ziad has done just this.

A boy wants to take a cockpit to the top of the world. And look what he is doing instead: taking language courses in a small town in Germany, learning the German words for "sky" and "airplane."

A boy wants to take a cockpit to the top of the world. Instead, elderly Germans yell things at him he does not understand but does understand. Here, his skin is dark.

A boy wants to take a cockpit to the top of the world. Ziad does not spend much time in his room. He goes to the beach, looks at the sun over the water and the sand, and wishes for something to wrap himself up in, to hold him tight. He drinks a lot of beer.

A boy wants to take a cockpit to the top of the world. He talks to a girl, a dentistry student named Aysel. They talk more.

A boy wants to take a cockpit to the top of the world. His cock is in Aysel's pit.

A boy wants to take a cockpit to the top of the world. No dirty pun can diminish them or what they have. They are high, they are high, nothing could feel better or be better, this is what the songs are talking about when they talk about being "above the clouds." Why would he be a pilot when he has this?

A boy wants to take a cockpit to the top of the world. She helps him learn German. They pore over their textbooks until late at night. They laugh and laugh.

A boy wants to take a cockpit to the top of the world. Now that he knows the language, he can figure out the jokes. The jokes that the Germans can no longer make about Jews, they now make about Turks. He is not a Turk but they do not know or care, since to them he looks like a Turk. Aysel is a Turk and he hears what they say about her. He would like to knock out their teeth, but Aysel is being taught to remove teeth only in particular ways and under particular circumstances. She tells him that what they say does not matter. They drink beer, they go home, they smoke pot, they have sex.

A boy wants to take a cockpit to the top of the world. He dreams of his house in Beirut, the bedroom that he pretended was a cockpit. When he wakes up, he thinks of the Palestinian refugee camp.

A boy wants to take a cockpit to the top of the world. Another dentistry student is also a preacher. Even in class, Aysel says, this student is loud, full of opinions that have nothing to do with the mouth, though his mouth is always open wide. And yet there is something about him and what he says. He conducts services in a small cinderblock mosque known as "The Box." Aysel does not want to go.

A boy wants to take a cockpit to the top of the world. The Box is very dark and the services last for a very long time. At midnight, Ziad wants to leave and drink beer, but the dental student preacher yells at him, tells him to stay. Ziad does not know why he complies, but he does. The dental student preacher continues talking, and slowly something happens to the room. By the end, which must be three in the morning, Ziad feels as though he has been suspended high in the sky in a very small space.

A boy wants to take a cockpit to the top of the world. He goes to the Box again, and then again.

A boy wants to take a cockpit to the top of the world. This world is nothing compared to the next, and yet what happens to Muslims in this world cannot be tolerated.

A boy wants to take a cockpit to the top of the world. It is Islam or Aysel. The Box or the box. This joke makes him feel cruel, but sometimes to do God's work it is necessary to be cruel. He tells Aysel that they cannot see each other anymore.

A boy wants to take a cockpit to the top of the world. He cannot sleep for the lack of Aysel. He cannot pay attention in class or even during services. He asks Aysel for forgiveness, and they are reunited.

A boy wants to take a cockpit to the top of the world. Aysel's clothes show too much skin. She talks too much. She drinks too much. She is not a suitable companion. She must be corrected or forsaken.

A boy wants to take a cockpit to the top of the world. He loves her and he is sorry for the things he has said. He loves her and wants to study dentistry like her. He will be going to Hamburg to study dentistry like her. They will live apart but stay together.

A boy wants to take a cockpit to the top of the world. A mouth is like a cockpit. It is a small space and there will be pleasures in learning to control it. But there is nothing more repellent than what is inside a mouth.

A boy wants to take a cockpit to the top of the world. A mouth is like a cockpit at the bottom of the world.

A boy wants to take a cockpit to the top of the world. Aysel's mouth is not like a cockpit at the bottom of the world.

A boy wants to take a cockpit to the top of the world. They marry but continue to live apart. Aysel insists that he sign a contract stating that she is entitled to continue her medical studies. Later he will try to make her quit her medical studies anyway; she will take the contract to an imam, who will side with her.

A boy wants to take a cockpit to the top of the world. Cover yourself, Aysel.

A boy wants to take a cockpit to the top of the world. When Aysel visits him, he does not introduce her to his new friends in Hamburg because they would not approve of the way she dresses, or of her.

A boy wants to take a cockpit to the top of the world. Of his friends, the obvious leader is a man so rigid and humorless it is difficult not to laugh at him. How can you laugh when there are people dying in Palestine, this man says. Once, they all hear this rigid and humorless man urinating in the bathroom. When he comes out they point at him and mock him, and he blames what has happened on a faulty door made by Jews. He is not joking. Of course he is not joking.

A boy wants to take a cockpit to the top of the world. He wants to dismiss this rigid and humorless man as the buffoon he appears to be, but he keeps thinking about the Palestinian refugee camp a few blocks from the bedroom he pretended was a cockpit.

A boy wants to take a cockpit to the top of the world. His friends live together, but he lives alone. Living with the others would mean giving up sex with Aysel; it would mean giving up Aysel altogether.

A boy wants to take a cockpit to the top of the world. He says to Aysel's friends that today he is with them, but tomorrow he will kill them. He is trying to scare them, of course, but he does not know whether he is trying to scare them only because he is bored.

A boy wants to take a cockpit to the top of the world. He hits Aysel.

A boy wants to take a cockpit to the top of the world. Aysel writes to tell him that she has had an abortion.

A boy wants to take a cockpit to the top of the world.

A boy wants to take a cockpit to the top of the world. He tells her he is going to return to Beirut, to figure out what he wants to do with his life.

A boy wants to take a cockpit to the top of the world. He does not go to Beirut.

A boy wants to take a cockpit to the top of the world. Aysel hears rumors that he has gone to Afghanistan. Panicked, she makes phone call after phone call to try to find him. She receives phone calls from men she does not know who tell her that Ziad is fine. This does not ease her worries.

A boy wants to take a cockpit to the top of the world. She receives a letter from him with a Yemeni postmark. He says he misses her. He says he wants to have a child with her. He writes the word "child" in three languages.

A boy wants to take a cockpit to the top of the world. He shows up at Aysel's door, his arms filled with gifts, including a skirt much shorter than ones he once told her were too short. For the first time in a long time he does not have a beard, so it does not scratch when they kiss.

A boy wants to take a cockpit to the top of the world. He will not tell her where he has been or what he has been doing. But he seems relaxed. She senses that some battle has been waged in his mind between her and his terrible friends, and that she has won. There is more good news: he has decided what he wants to do with his life. He is going to fulfill his childhood dream and become a pilot.

A boy wants to take a cockpit to the top of the world. Aysel is ecstatic. She imagines their life together. They will finally live together while he studies flying. Then she will be a dentist, he will be a pilot, they will have children. They could live in Istanbul, in Beirut, anywhere where the skies are occasionally blue and the teeth inexorably rot. What could be more perfect?

A boy wants to take a cockpit to the top of the world. There is a message on the answering machine for him from a flight school in Florida. Aysel is furious; he explains that he can get his license more quickly in the United States than anywhere else.

A boy wants to take a cockpit to the top of the world. He is the first to arrive in Florida, living by himself and at long last sitting in an actual cockpit. Not quite an actual cockpit, a flight simulator, but the cockpit will come soon. Maybe some part of him hopes that the others will die in a plane crash over the Atlantic, and he will be left alone in America, but this does not happen and the others arrive.

A boy wants to take a cockpit to the top of the world. He logs flight hour after flight hour. He does not want to stop logging flight hours.

A boy wants to take a cockpit to the top of the world. With some friends he has made in flight school, he flies to the Bahamas. He sits with them and watches the sun over the ocean and the sand and the girls in bikinis rub suntan lotion on each other, and he wonders why such a sight is supposed to offend. The rest get very drunk, and they ask him to fly them home.

A boy wants to take a cockpit to the top of the world. It is a very small cockpit, a very small plane, a very short flight, but nonetheless it is a cockpit and a plane and a flight. The controls, they are all in his hands, and the wings are in the sky because of what he has done. The nose does as he tells it. He looks down at a cloud and wonders whether God is watching him, and for just a moment he does not care.

A boy wants to take a cockpit to the top of the world. He moves in with two of his classmates, sleeping on their couch. Or rather not sleeping, because he is thinking of what he loves, flying and Aysel. He loves talking to his classmates. They are certainly more fun than the others, particularly the rigid and humorless man whom he cannot avoid forever.

A boy wants to take a cockpit to the top of the world. Maybe it is not too late to back out, to refuse to go through with the plans.

A boy wants to take a cockpit to the top of the world. One of his classmates questions his flying ability. He does not respond well.

A boy wants to take a cockpit to the top of the world. His father has heart surgery. He flies to Beirut to visit. He tells his father he is living in America and learning to be a pilot. His father is worried but says he is proud of him. America and the sky: What better places were there, really? On his way back to Florida, he stops in Germany to see Aysel. He tells her he wants to have children soon so that his father can see them before he dies.

A boy wants to take a cockpit to the top of the world. Children scream and throw crayons throughout the flight back to Florida. There is an attractive woman in the seat next to him. His father is probably fine.

A boy wants to take a cockpit to the top of the world. The rigid and humorless man keeps pushing back the plans, which means that Ziad does not have to make a decision, and he has to admit he finds this agreeable. He is surprised to find himself becoming just another lost, floating American, but he is not sure he dislikes it.

A boy wants to take a cockpit to the top of the world. Plans, all plans, start to look childish. All he has to do all day is sit in a cockpit, exactly what he has always wanted to do, and yet he is now bored by his own dreams. He lets the others know that he is out. He expects that he will be killed, but he keeps on waking up alive. Perhaps they have not planned for this contingency. He goes to Nevada, to California.

A boy wants to take a cockpit to the top of the world. America is too big and uncontained. Maybe they are always taking more and getting bigger because they are looking for some tight, secure space they have overlooked.

A boy wants to take a cockpit to the top of the world. He has forgotten where he is when he stops in a diner for sausage and eggs and requests bacon in addition. A few tables away, a man starts talking about his time in the Gulf War. The waitress thanks him for his service, as though she has any idea what he did there. Ziad considers taking his knife and slitting both their throats. She admires a tattoo on the man's biceps. A real marine's tattoo, she says. You're not like one of those fancy New York types with an epiphany tattoo.

A boy wants to take a cockpit to the top of the world. This is not the first time he has heard of epiphany tattoos. But it is the first time he has felt confused enough to consider getting one. Any tattoo is forbidden by Islam, which makes getting one terrifying, and possibly appropriate.

A boy wants to take a cockpit to the top of the world. New York is full of very tall buildings, of course, but the building that houses the epiphany machine is only seven stories tall, and the apartment where the machine is kept is only on the second floor.

A boy wants to take a cockpit to the top of the world. The man who appears to be in charge of the epiphany machine, whatever it is and whatever that means, is very warm and welcoming. He is talking about how the worst thing you can do is make assumptions about people. You don't know people, the man is saying; that's what the machine is for. Ziad slowly realizes that the man is a Jew despite the innocent-sounding surname, but that hardly fazes him anymore. America is full of them, after all. The man talks about breast-fucking. Ziad wishes he could introduce this man to the rigid and humorless man. He accepts a glass of the man's whiskey, and then accepts another.

A boy wants to take a cockpit to the top of the world. Adam leads him through the velvet curtain; he is surprised to find, on the other side, a dentist's chair and a sewing machine. Perfectly symbolizing what Aysel is and what she should have been.

A boy wants to take a cockpit to the top of the world. I don't think I would be here, Ziad says, if I hadn't fallen in love with the wrong woman.

A boy wants to take a cockpit to the top of the world. I hear that a lot, Adam says.

A boy wants to take a cockpit to the top of the world. The needle is the greatest pain he has ever felt. It is worse, somehow, even than the most rigorous and demanding of the training in the camps. The needle is in his arm and it is not coming out. Maybe he has fallen victim to an elaborate Jewish plot to assassinate him. Okay, then.

He is in a small room in a small building, but there is no such thing as small martyrdom.

A boy wants to take a cockpit to the top of the world. **WANTS TO BLOW THINGS UP.**

A boy wants to take a cockpit to the top of the world. Yes, yes, this is all he has ever wanted. Now if only the Jew will let him out.

A boy wants to take a cockpit to the top of the world. Be careful, Adam says as he lifts up the arm or the neck of the machine with an oven mitt. There's probably only one thing in your life you want to get rid of.

A boy wants to take a cockpit to the top of the world. He looks back over his shoulder at the towers as he drives over the George Washington Bridge. It's not fair that the towers belong to the rigid and humorless man; it's not fair that the rigid and humorless man is the one in charge. But that's the way it is. He will pray to God to chew his pride so that he might swallow it. And Ziad will have the Capitol building, the seat of American government! Which—the thought makes him smile—looks like a giant breast. He buys a pre-paid calling card from an all-night convenience store and lets the others know he is fully in, fully committed.

A boy wants to take a cockpit to the top of the world. On the morning that it is to be done he is thinking of Aysel. Suddenly he realizes that he cannot do this, he cannot leave her, at least not for good. He will go back to sleep, he will let the others do whatever they do, and then he will go back to her. He calls her to find that she has just woken and is getting ready for her day. I love you, he says. I love you. I love you. I will see you soon.

A boy wants to take a cockpit to the top of the world. He hangs up and looks at his tattoo. How silly it is, how silly religion is, how silly anything must be if it needs words to be expressed. He feels total commitment to Aysel in his heart. He continues to feel total commitment to Aysel when he gets out of the shower. But he knows, because he has learned at least something about himself, that sooner or later he will not feel total commitment to Aysel in his heart. She deserves better than him, just as the world deserves better than domineering, sweet-talking, abusive, fickle America.

A boy has taken a cockpit to the top of the world. Symbolically, the box cutters were unfortunate; he wanted to close himself in rather than open something up. But now here he is, sealed in the open sky. No more doubts, no more regrets, only up and down, the only things that would still exist without words. He can hear the commotion in the cabin, he can hear the passengers coming for him, he can sense that he will not reach America's breast any more than he will ever again reach Aysel's, but in a sense it does not matter. He feels kinship with them now, the people who will kill him and whom he will kill; they share a tomb and they share a sky, and in the great tiny box of the world's mind, all of them will always be in this cockpit.

CHAPTER

✦

28

That morning, I woke briefly to the sound of car alarms or firetrucks or something, but when I was in college, it took more than an emergency to get me out of bed in the morning. When I woke up for good it was nearly ten. As always, the first thing I did was check my email. Adam had sent me a message at 8:57 a.m.

Hi, Vent. I've been thinking about it and I'm really sorry about that night you came by. You had just missed Si Strauss, lucky you, and seeing Si Strauss always gets me out of sorts for reasons I'm not even sure the machine could explain.

Not that I'm expecting a response or anything, but I do think it's a little funny to hear on the radio this morning that Monica Lewinsky is taking psychology classes at Columbia. Instead of giving head, she'll learn how to shrink one! Good for her, I guess. A blowjob is no breastfuck, but it will still do somebody a lot more good than therapy or probably even my beloved device for that matter if you ask me, which you probably won't.

Sorry if that sounds bitchy, buddy. Can't help it if I miss our chats. If you ever want to resume them, you know where to find me.

Yours,
A.L. (You can call me Al)

P.S. Holy shit, I was just about to press send when I saw on the news that a plane hit the World Trade Center! You should see the pictures.

The bit about the plane hitting the World Trade Center piqued my prurient interest but did not especially alarm me, since I assumed he was referring to a single-engine plane that had somehow gone off course. Before I could check out the pictures, I got an IM from Leah.

Have you heard the news?

You mean about a plane hitting the world trade center or about monica lewinsky taking psych courses at columbia?

There was a long silence from Leah, replaced finally by a message in italics saying *UhyeahLeah is typing.* This was up for a while; then it was replaced by *UhyeahLeah has entered text.* Then a message appeared.

jesus CHRIST you're an asshole

Then she signed off, and none of my other friends were online. I switched over to the *New York Times* website, where I saw the towers and the fire that would transform the buildings into ruins that I suddenly realized would stand as husks of themselves for thousands of years. I refreshed the browser and one of the towers had fallen. I refreshed the browser again and the other had fallen.

I don't know exactly what I did after that—most likely, I stared at my computer and pressed things that made things appear. I spoke to my father briefly. Then I got up and walked to the common area, where good friends and people I could barely tolerate and people I was too intimidated to talk to had gathered to come face-to-face, for the last time in history, with a sight commensurate to their capacity to gather around a single box and cry. Within an hour or so, I had heard the name "Osama bin Laden" for the first time, and instantly he had been my enemy since before I was born. We were all around twenty years old, legally adults only because the law takes pleasure in asserting things that are manifestly untrue, but we all agreed that this event had automatically and truly transformed us into men and women, hoping that by pronouncing each other adults we could magically increase the number of people capable of protecting us.

Somebody walked in whose father had been on a flight that originated at Logan Airport, and I felt a grief much more real than any I had felt or could imagine feeling. This feeling of grief did not leave me when we discovered that the kid's father was fine.

As the day went on, I wandered through campus, hugging acquaintances I would not have bothered to say hello to the previous day. Cesar Solomon, whom I had barely spoken to since we had lived together as freshmen, solidly embraced me.

"Today's a day that shows you who you really are," Cesar said. "I just want you to know that you are not **DEPENDENT ON THE OPINION OF OTHERS.**"

I tried not to show him how much it meant to me that he had said this, and we wandered together and were joined by other wanderers who convened in front of the library, on which the names of famous writers were tattooed. We all agreed that reality was real now. Though it would have been impossible to say out loud that we were grateful that this had happened, gratitude is exactly what we felt for the event that transformed the unreal feelings we had only sort of been feeling the previous day. There were many ways to interpret what was happening to us, which made it critical that we all come together and interpret it the same way: that we were innocents and we were under attack, that the smoke from downtown portended war, that the war would make us more serious, and that we were lucky to be made more serious.

I walked into more groups and more group hugs. I looked around for Rebecca but was overall relieved not to see her. Neither of us reached out to the other, both of us probably realizing that we would likely get back together if we spoke that day, and both of us finally realizing that that was not a good idea. I also decided not to contact Leah or Ismail, for reasons I could not quite articulate, but the events of this day seemed to give license to irrational decisions. I wandered into a vigil as night fell on what had after all been just one more day I had spent thinking about myself.

Over the two weeks that followed 9/11—which, I wrote in an email around that time, had been the *true* epiphany machine—I drifted along with the calls to rise to the historic occasion, at least insofar as rising to the historic occasion meant not going down into the subways. I spent most of my days surfing the web instead of doing my reading, which, even though this was exactly how I had spent my days prior to 9/11, now felt like a different activity altogether, one imbued with the national purpose of reading articles about how much national purpose everything was now imbued with.

I was going through these thoughts in a loop when two men knocked on my door and announced that they were with the FBI.

When they showed me their badges I felt an intense urge to cower, which I swallowed out of some kind of primal urge not to make a joke of myself.

"Please come in," I said, which I knew from my father I was never supposed to say to law enforcement. "How can I help?"

"Sweet tattoo," one of them said. "Where did you get it?"

I had opened the door wearing a short-sleeved shirt. Always a mistake. "Um, downtown."

"Downtown? At the World Trade Center? Couldn't have been recent."

"No, it was at this place . . ."

"Oh, you got it at a place. Places are my favorite places to get things."

"It's an epiphany tattoo. I got it at Adam Lyons's apartment on Eighty-fourth Street."

Another thing my father had told me was that if I was ever questioned by law enforcement or by a lawyer, I should answer questions as literally as possible. If someone holds up a pen and asks if you know what it is, you're supposed to say "yes," not "a pen." This was probably the most useful advice he had ever given me, and I was not following it.

"Do you know Adam Lyons well?"

"I used to know him a little."

"A little? We hear that you used to be his right-hand man."

"Right-hand man? I hung out at his place when I was in high school."

"And you were dependent on his opinion."

"No. Maybe. But that was a long time ago."

"Whose opinion are you dependent on now?"

"I'm sorry?"

"Back when you were dependent on Adam Lyons's opinion and you were hanging out at his apartment a lot, do you recall meeting a man named Ziad Jarrah?"

"The 9/11 hijacker?" I had heard the name over the previous two weeks. Jarrah was the lead hijacker on Flight 93, the plane that had crashed into a field in Pennsylvania following a passenger revolt.

"Ziad Jarrah used the epiphany machine," one of them said.

"Wait," I said. "You're saying that one of the 9/11 hijackers used the epiphany machine?"

"Good listening-comprehension skills. Now I can see why they let a former cult member into the Ivy League. Were you present when Ziad Jarrah used the machine?"

"If I was, I certainly don't remember him."

"You might remember the tattoo, though. We discovered his severed arm in the wreckage. Bruised and bloody, to say the least, so some of the letters were hard to read, but it said **WANTS TO BLOW THINGS UP.** Sound familiar?"

I felt like I had been turned inside out, and my arm was now inside my stomach.

"I really don't think I met Ziad Jarrah," I said.

"Doesn't answer my question. Do you remember people talking about that tattoo?"

"Not that I can recall."

"Do you remember anyone else receiving that tattoo? **WANTS TO BLOW THINGS UP?**"

I knew that if I gave the FBI his name, I would be condemning Ismail to, at the very least, intense interrogations. And Ismail was gentle, sensitive, not much more suited to interrogation than I was.

"What does it matter?" I asked. "The epiphany machine is a hoax. This is like asking me if I know anyone who got the same fortune cookie that Hitler got."

"Technically it would be more like asking if you know who got the same fortune that Hitler got, not the same fortune cookie."

I knew that I was being toyed with, but I didn't know what to do about it, so I didn't say anything.

"Cowed into silence by logic? The FBI isn't so interested in fortune cookies. But if a guy gets a tattoo that says he wants to blow things up, that's something we're going to give a second look."

"But Adam's guests . . . epiphany machine users . . . don't choose their tattoos," I said. "Do you think **DEPENDENT ON THE OPINION OF OTHERS** is the tattoo I would have *chosen*?"

"Cult leaders often have deep insight into personality. If he thought somebody might want to blow things up, maybe he might have been right."

"Or he might have been wrong," I said. "Or **WANTS TO BLOW THINGS UP** might be vague and open to interpretation, like every other epiphany tattoo."

"I know about three thousand people who wouldn't think Ziad Jarrah's tattoo was open to interpretation."

I sat down on my bed, thinking about that number.

"Listen, Venter. Whoever you're protecting, you don't really know him. You want his approval, you want him to think well of you, so you haven't noticed what he's hiding. Imagine you pass up this opportunity to tell us about him, and then he does something terrible. What then? What if he decides to blow up a school bus? Can you imagine the faces of those kids in their last moments? Can you imagine their parents? Can you imagine what their parents would think of you?"

In my mind, I watched a braver version of myself look these men in the eye and tell them I was immune to this fear-mongering bullshit. But I also, as though on another screen in the multiplex of my mind, watched Ismail. Everything that he had done now seemed secretive, furtive, the behavior of an angry, violent youth trying to conceal his anger and violence. These two men had taken my life and shined a new light on it, and now I was looking at it their way. I looked at the floor and mumbled that I did not want to talk to them anymore.

"So you do know someone who received that tattoo?"

"I don't want to talk to you anymore," I said. "I don't have to talk to you anymore."

"It's actually not entirely clear what you do and don't have to do anymore. The law isn't exactly tattooed on anybody's arms at this point."

I was terrified, but I was not going to give up Ismail. "Please leave my dorm room. Otherwise, I'll call security."

"And you think that security will throw out FBI agents who are interrogating a terror suspect?"

"Excuse me?"

"If you know of someone with this tattoo and won't give us his name, then some might wonder whether you're giving aid and comfort to a terrorist."

"There's no reason for you to wonder that!"

"We're not saying that *we* would wonder that. You seem like a solid young man who wants to help his country, but is too **DEPENDENT ON THE OPINION OF OTHERS**—if not on the opinion of the guy who got the tattoo, maybe on the opinion of some of his professors who are so dogmatic about due process that they'd keep clutching the Constitution while all of America burned around them. Or maybe you're dependent on the opinion of friends who just don't like the idea of cooperating with 'the man,' even when the man is the only one protecting you. *To us*, you seem like a solid young man who has gotten some bad guidance. But how will you seem to others?"

"So you *are* going to investigate me?"

"You tell us. Should we investigate a guy who's protecting a terrorist?"

I felt many emotions, the most powerful of which was an intense wish that somebody else was making this decision.

"Look," I said. "One person I used to know got that tattoo. But there's no way he could be a terrorist."

"And his name is?"

I gave them Ismail's name and told them how to find him. The agents gave me a look that told me they liked this answer, and then they asked me if I had any other names. I did not, but if I did, I would have named them.

"One other thing: Did Ismail ever show any tendency to do something violent in the name of Islam?"

"No. I mean, there was one time when he started praying while he was driving us over the Tappan Zee Bridge and threatened to drive us off it, but that was just a joke."

They looked at each other, and I immediately regretted having said anything.

"It was just a joke. He was just making a point about life being meaningless. Or death being meaningless. I mean . . ."

"Thank you. You've done a real service for your country today."

"You're just going to talk to Ismail, right? You're not going to arrest him for a tattoo, are you?"

"We'll talk to him," one of the agents said. They left, and as soon as I closed the door, I sat on the edge of my bed and stared at my tattoo, trying not to understand that what had just happened was the simplest and oldest story there is: I had betrayed my friend.

Eventually, I left my room to walk to a party. I hugged people who did not know that I had just delivered a good man into Hell, and who if they did know would probably think that I had done the right thing.

"**DEPENDENT ON THE OPINION OF OTHERS?**" said some guy who was handing me a beer from the fridge. "I like that. It shows how connected we all are now. Cheers, man."

I hated this guy while I drank his beer. I knew that before the end of the night I would somehow convince myself that I *was* some kind of hero, but for the moment at least I had a little bit of clarity, even if I had nothing else. Whether the machine was real or fake, whether Adam was just some good-hearted dude who had found a magic device in a trash heap or the cynical deceiver his tattoo advertised, for that moment I knew who I was and what I deserved.

CHAPTER

◆

29

A week passed and I heard nothing, except for the rustlings of life failing to return to normal. I think it was already October, maybe we had already invaded Afghanistan, when I got a phone call from Ismail's mother.

"He's staying with you, isn't he?" she asked.

"Mrs. Ahmed. Good to hear from you."

"Don't give me that. I worked hard to keep the two of you apart, but I knew I could never succeed. Ismail is sleeping in your room, and the two of you are . . . Just put him on the phone. Now."

"I don't know what you're thinking, but you shouldn't worry." Neither half of this sentence was true, though it was true, on multiple levels, that she should not have been worrying about what she was worrying about.

"If he's not with you, then where is he? He hasn't attended classes or checked into his dorm in days. Leah hasn't seen him. He must have told you something. You're his best friend." Her voice gave way to panic.

"I'm sorry," I said. "I haven't heard anything from him." The feeling of superiority that had been roused by her homophobia had evaporated, and now I was doing what was done only by the most egregious liars and by witnesses who followed my father's advice: saying only things that are literally true.

She was sobbing now. "Then where is he? Do you think somebody just beat him to death and left him in a ditch? Because he's a Muslim?"

"There's absolutely no reason to believe that," I said, though this did sound like a more likely explanation than the idea that the United States government had jailed him without so much as informing his mother. I didn't want to think that my friend was dead, but there was something attractive in not being responsible for whatever had happened.

"You've always been such a good friend to him," she said. This was not true, and she could not have believed it. But she was so terrified for her son that she must have found comfort in thinking that Ismail had a good friend in me. I told her that I was sure he was fine, and that I would call her if I heard anything. I knew I had been lying when I said I was sure he was fine, but I hoped that he was indeed fine.

My hope came to an end one late October morning when I booted up my computer and found this temporary tattoo across the *New York Times* homepage:

STUDENT'S PLOT DISRUPTED

The article described how Ismail Ahmed, a theater student at NYU, had been apprehended with a tattoo matching that of 9/11 hijacker Ziad Jarrah: **WANTS TO BLOW THINGS UP.** For years, Ismail had made contributions to charities "linked" to Al Qaeda supporting "jihadists" in Bosnia and Chechnya. I remembered those charities, which Ismail had taken a job at Blockbuster to send money to. It didn't seem likely that they were in any way linked to Al Qaeda, and if they had been, it seemed almost impossible that Ismail had known about these links. There had to be more, there had to be more. Apparently, "plans" had been discovered on Ismail's hard drive to detonate a series of bombs on the Queensboro Bridge during rush hour. As far as I could tell, those "plans" consisted of a draft of a play about a Muslim student in a creative writing workshop who had submitted a draft of a play about two Muslim students debating whether or not to detonate a series of bombs on the Queensboro Bridge during rush hour. "According to sources close to the investigation, Mr. Ahmed's girlfriend and close collaborator, Leah Marx, was unaware of the existence of this play." There were "reports" that he had once started praying while driving over the Tappan Zee Bridge, threatening to drive himself and a passenger off the bridge. There were also indications of "increasing investment in Islamic identity and of distaste with American culture" as well as "plans to cast himself as Shylock in a production of William Shakespeare's *Merchant of Venice*, widely considered one of the most anti-Semitic works in the Western canon."

If this was all the FBI had found, they would never have arrested him. They must have found more, they must have found actual evidence of an actual plot that they couldn't yet release to the public. If they had, then I had saved lives. If they hadn't, then surely Ismail would be released or acquitted.

Except for the strange fact that it was not clear that Ismail was going to be given a trial.

Apparently, since his arrest—which had taken place in secret, several weeks earlier—he had been held as something called an "enemy combatant" in a naval vessel off the coast of South Carolina. He had not been given access to a lawyer, and there were no plans to grant him that right in the immediate future.

This was horrifying—an obvious assault on the basic tenets of the American judicial system—but there was no way that he had been apprehended simply because of his tattoo. America was not a totalitarian dictatorship and I was not a movie villain. Ismail *must* have been participating in an actual plot. Evidence *would* be released one day, once the authorities judged the releasing of that evidence to be safe. After all, the evidence against Ismail would probably implicate other terrorists who were still at large and active, and releasing the evidence against Ismail would alert those terrorists that they were being monitored and help them evade capture. Once all of the terrorists Ismail had been in contact with had been captured—and maybe once all the terrorists that *those* terrorists had been in contact with had been captured—then the evidence against Ismail would be released. And if no evidence against Ismail was ever released, that itself would be evidence that Ismail had been in contact with so many evil people, or that those people had been in contact with so many evil people, that the web of evil people could never be untangled, and if Ismail had been in contact with that many evil people, then his own evil must have been massive.

It was true I had seen no evidence that Ismail had ever been involved in anything like this, but then again, We Are All Unknowable, Et Cetera. To think you know anyone, I reminded myself, is the height of hubris.

The alternative to accepting this logic was accepting that Ismail had, with my assistance, been put in a dungeon for no reason at all. I chose the first option.

I was a hero, I decided.

The important thing was that I had spoken up before it was too late; yes, I had spoken up in time to save the lives of countless people who might otherwise have been murdered by my suicide-bomber best friend. In that sense, I had even saved Ismail's life, since now he would not be able to blow himself up. His mother would one day thank me.

Calls started coming in from reporters, but I ignored them. Calls also started coming in from Leah, and I ignored those, too, though I couldn't ignore her when she called up to my room from the security desk. I was afraid she would attract attention, so I told the guard to send her up.

I held the door open while I waited for her, and I got some suspicious looks from people on my hallway who had hugged me on 9/11, and I thought I probably deserved those looks for having been friends with a terrorist. I tried to smile at Leah when I saw her, but she did not smile back. I got her into my room and shut the door as quickly as possible.

260

"You told them about Ismail's tattoo, didn't you?"

"Lots of people at NYU must have known about that tattoo."

"You're the one who told the FBI about it."

"I'm the one they asked. What was I supposed to do? If I had lied, they might have thought I was a terrorist."

"And you need them to think well of you because you're so fucking **DEPENDENT ON THE OPINION OF OTHERS.**"

"Am I dependent on the FBI having the opinion that I am not a terror-ist? Yes."

"Ismail's dependent on that opinion, too."

"And if he's innocent, I'm sure they'll let him go."

"*If* he's innocent? You know what that tattoo meant."

"I thought I knew what it meant."

"Are you seriously this much of a piece of shit?"

"If they're holding him, they must have *something.*"

"Yeah, they have a tattoo and a play that he was writing. Apparently that's enough."

"Why wouldn't he show you the play?"

"Venter."

"They must have more."

"You're **DEPENDENT ON THE OPINION OF OTHERS.** Does it bother you that I think you're an evil, stupid, pathetic little bitch who ruined my boyfriend's life?"

Saying this seemed to make her feel better, but then sobs ripped apart her face. I put my arms around her, and to my surprise she let them stay there.

"They questioned me for fifteen hours yesterday. They wouldn't let me have a lawyer. Who knows what they've made him say."

It was impossible not to ask myself where Ismail was at that second, and what was being done to him. But there was no way to know for certain that he was not being treated well.

After a moment, Leah seemed to realize that I was touching her, and she swatted me away like I was a rat crawling on her shoulders.

"I hope there is another terrorist attack," she said, "just so you can burn in it."

And then she was gone, and I cried more or less nonstop for two hours. Then I decided to go to a party I had heard Rebecca and her roommates were having in their suite, probably because I was in the mood to make another bad decision.

As soon as I arrived, I got the sense that everyone had just been talking about me. Nothing necessarily odd about that; after all, I was the host's ex-boyfriend. People kept on backing away from me whenever I tried to join a conversation, again not wholly inexplicable. I stood in a corner by myself fingering a lime slice into a Corona Light when Rebecca came up to me.

"So. My ex-boyfriend's best friend is a terrorist. That's not going to look very good on my State Department disclosure forms when I apply for an internship."

"Why would you put that on a form? It's not like you dated Ismail."

"You want to be as far away from somebody like that as possible."

"Well. Now you are."

"I reread that email he sent me, and it's scary. It shows a definite hatred of female sexuality."

"Maybe he was just angry."

"*Maybe* that email didn't strike you as so terrible because you weren't its target."

"Maybe you're just over—"

"*Maybe* you shouldn't finish that sentence. *Maybe* you should have reported Ismail as soon as he got that tattoo."

"I didn't think he literally wanted to blow things up." It occurred to me that I still didn't think that. I was certain that Ismail was innocent, if "innocent" is even an appropriate word for someone who hasn't even been accused of anything specific. But I tried to remind myself that just because

I was certain about something did not make it true. Only a few hours before, I had been certain that Ismail was a terrorist. For once, the worthlessness of my certainty was comforting.

"What if that really is what it meant, though?" Rebecca said. "They're not just holding him because of a tattoo."

Our mutual need to believe this—our mutual need to believe that our friend was not being persecuted without cause—was so strong that I thought we were about to kiss each other. But then she turned away.

"So why is your dad defending him?"

I put down my Corona Light. "What?"

"Your dad was on CNN saying that Ismail is a close personal friend of his family and that this is a gross violation of American values."

"My dad barely knew Ismail and hasn't spoken to him in years," I said. "My dad has barely spoken to me in years."

"Cults are cults, that's all I'm saying." This non sequitur came from Rebecca's roommate, a red-haired chemistry major who had never liked me.

"What's that supposed to mean?" I asked.

"The epiphany machine is a cult that defies reason to give people a sense of ultimate meaning. The same thing is true of Al Qaeda."

I said that I had heard enough of this and returned to my room, where I called my father.

"Venter!" he said, sounding truly happy to hear from me. "We're going to fight this and we're going to win. I've been on the phone ever since I heard. I've been finding out that a lot of the smartest lawyers I know are, inconveniently, cowards who have no interest in standing up against the total dismantling of the rule of law. I'm probably too close to the case to take it myself. But we'll find someone. We're not going to abandon your friend."

"Don't call him my friend, Dad. Why are you on TV reminding people that I know a terrorist?"

There was silence on the other end for a few seconds, and then some very disappointed sighing.

"There's no reason to call him that," he said. "And no matter what, he has the right to a lawyer."

"You're acting like we still live in a world that has room for law."

"That's the only way to act."

"They wouldn't have arrested him if he weren't guilty."

"Venter, come on. I know there's a lot of pressure right now to believe some ridiculous things about what we should be doing as a country, but you can't seriously be *this* **DEPENDENT ON THE OPINION OF OTHERS**."

I hung up the phone.

The next week, I was called in for a meeting with a dean who told me that a number of students had reported that they "did not feel safe" with me living in their dorm or attending their classes; there were two or three weeks when I thought that I was going to be kicked out of school for my association with Ismail. But like so many things, this just stopped being mentioned.

A *Time* magazine article made an argument similar to the one Rebecca's roommate had made, except it drew a closer connection: "There is a reason why Ziad Jarrah and Ismail Ahmed were drawn both to the epiphany machine and to Al Qaeda. Both cults, after all, hinge on the mortification of the flesh, and tell their members that this mortification will take them to paradise."

And so on. Other articles drew connections between Ziad Jarrah and Mark David Chapman, or between Ismail and one or both Rebecca Harts. There was even speculation—some of it from relatively reputable sources—that Adam himself had somehow been involved in 9/11. This speculation led to his harassment by the media, who'd begun waiting outside his apartment.

"It's not my fault my machine works," Adam said in one interview. "Maybe if more people came to see me, and came to see me earlier, they could get the help that they need and terrible things like this wouldn't happen."

A lot of people got mad about this and demanded that Adam apologize. He did not, and refused renewed calls to share epiphanies with law enforcement.

"Every epiphany is different and specific to the person who receives it," he said. "There are a lot of different ways to want to blow things up. Like this kid, Ismail, that they have locked up somewhere—I know him, he's a good kid and he's innocent. But nobody cares about my opinion, they only care about the machine's opinion, even though they think that I am writing the epiphanies—care to explain that to me?"

Adam had not sent me any more emails, but I felt I had to say something to him about this. I wrote:

A lot of grandstanding on TV, but what about what you do to people with **DOES NOT UNDERSTAND BOUNDARIES** tattoos? Maybe Ismail is getting what's coming to him, just like you think those people are getting what's coming to them.

After sending this, I felt very agitated, so I went downstairs to the dorm food court to get some Taco Bell. When I came back upstairs, I had received this response:

I know our friend is not a terrorist, and I also know that all those people with **DOES NOT UNDERSTAND BOUNDARIES** tattoos deserved what they got. Not all of us are **DEPENDENT ON THE OPINION OF OTHERS**, buddy.

Mine,
A.L. (Qaeda, if you think the way everybody else thinks, and obviously you do)

CHAPTER

—— · · ◆ · · ——

30

My father devoted all of his (very limited) free time to Ismail's defense, such as it was. He would not be allowed to defend Ismail because of conflict of interest issues, though these issues proved irrelevant since Ismail was being denied any kind of lawyer at all. I was extremely angry with my father about this, but I spent winter break in Westchester anyway. I was terrified of being attacked in Manhattan, either by Al Qaeda or by people who were angry at the epiphany machine and wanted to take it out on me. (Some drunk, fratty types had tried to knock down my door one night.)

My father had turned my room into what amounted to a giant filing cabinet—papers everywhere—so I slept in what had been my grandmother's room, the house's second master bedroom. I spent a lot of time draping myself in the bright, itchy afghans she had painstakingly knitted throughout my childhood. I realized how extraordinarily fortunate I had been to have had an intelligent woman devote herself to taking care of me, and I realized, too, how little I had appreciated it.

I was occasionally aware that I was thinking about my grandmother as a way of not thinking about Ismail, but feeling sad over someone you've lost is a very effective way of distracting yourself from what a prick you are. Or maybe I'm just speaking for myself.

On Christmas Day, Leah rang the doorbell, holding a cardboard box under one arm.

"I'm not here to see you," she said.

"I'm glad you're here. Whatever the truth is about Ismail, we should be here for each other."

"Venter, this box is heavy and I'd like you to get the fuck out of my way." I did as she asked and tried to take the box from her, but she yanked it out of my reach and carried it to the dining room.

"Mr. Lowood, I have some documents for you," she called out. The door to my father's den slid open.

"What are these?" I asked.

"Ismail's emails to me. A lot of the writing that he's done in the last few years."

"And what are you hoping to prove with all this?"

"I don't know. That he was a human being, maybe."

"Being a human being isn't going to count for much in court," I said. "And besides, Ismail has been refused a lawyer."

"Leave us alone, Venter," my father said, entering the room. "We have work to do."

Exiled as though I were half my age, I had nothing to do but watch television. At some point that day, or at any rate that week, I saw Adam's commercial for the first time.

The commercial, which looked like it had been shot using incredibly cheap equipment, showed Adam standing in the epiphany room, patting the machine like it was a child or a dog, and holding a coffee mug that, for all I knew, did not contain whiskey.

"You've heard a lot about this baby in the past few months, and not all of it has been good," he said. "In fact, none of it has been good. It's all been very bad." There was a dissolve now to one of those gauzy shots of the World Trade Center that were already becoming the second-most common images of the new century, right after images of the planes hitting the buildings. A few notes of soft patriotic treacle played on the soundtrack. "Just like those in our government, I think day and night about what I could have done to stop that tragedy. Of course there's no way for me to go back in time. But here's something I can do."

Adam put his hand over the sweat stain on his left shirt pocket.

"For the next six months, I will refuse all donations. I will not accept a dime from anyone who comes to see me to use the machine. A monster used my machine and it told him he was a monster. New Yorkers are strong, and right now they need to hear that they're strong. So come let the machine tell you how strong you are, in a way you won't forget."

Big smile, missing tooth, dissolve to black, next commercial.

Well, I thought, Adam's done now. This will not salvage the machine and will lead to many attacks on Adam for using a tragedy to gin up publicity.

Those attacks did come—but so did many people eager to use the machine.

The New York Times, April 25, 2002

IN CURIOUS OLD SHOP, SOLACE FOR WOUNDED CITY

BY ALICE GRAVES

When a friend suggested to Lydia Sardi that she use the epiphany machine to help treat the anxiety and depression she had been experiencing in the wake of the September 11 terrorist attacks, her first thought was that she should never speak to this friend again. After all, the controversial device—which tattoos cryptic koans on the arms of its users, koans praised by proponents as important, possibly supernatural wisdom and derided by critics as generic platitudes—had been in the news because it had been used by Ziad Jarrah, one of the terrorists who perpetrated those very attacks, as well as by Ismail Ahmed, an NYU student detained in connection with a plot to blow up the Queensboro Bridge.

But two weeks later, after a string of particularly debilitating panic attacks caused her to miss work for three straight days, Ms. Sardi, 38, a pulmonary nurse who lives in Washington Heights, decided to try the device. She looked up the Upper East Side address of Adam Lyons, the guru who for decades has kept the epiphany machine in a dedicated room in his apartment.

Expecting to be the only person using the epiphany machine in the middle of the afternoon she chose for her visit, Ms. Sardi encountered a line outside Mr. Lyons's building that extended down the block.

"I guess there are a few million people in New York right now who will try adventurous solutions to feel better," Ms. Sardi said.

The number of New Yorkers who have used the epiphany machine in the last few months might not be quite that high, but Ms. Sardi is certainly not alone.

"I went out to dinner last weekend with some friends, and I looked around the table and I saw that I was literally the only one without an epiphany tattoo," said Jennifer Dayles, 26, a management consultant. "They had all been so frazzled, just like me, and now they seemed a lot better. So I got the address, hopped on the 6 train, and got in line."

On a recent Saturday night, Ms. Sardi and Ms. Dayles drank whiskey together at a "salon night" at Adam Lyons's apartment. The purpose of salon nights, which Mr. Lyons hosts at least twice a week, is for those who have used the machine—or "guests," as he calls them—to gather, talk about their tattoos, drink alcohol, and bring friends who might be interested in using the machine themselves. Of the approximately two dozen attendees who filed in and out throughout the night, twelve had used the machine, and of these, eight had used the machine since September 11 of last year.

Throughout the night, Mr. Lyons, 61, told stories, listened to stories, drank whiskey, and showed every sign of having the time of his life. This is a sharp turnaround from a few short months ago, when he appeared irritable and defensive when approached by reporters, almost all of whom wished to discuss Mr. Jarrah or Mr. Ahmed.

Taking a swig of her drink, Ms. Dayles proudly showed off her tattoo. "**PRETENDS TO FEEL SORRY FOR SELF TO JUSTIFY EASY LIFE** isn't exactly what I would have chosen to have permanently inscribed on my arm," she said. "But it just makes what comes next, **BUT IS STRONGER THAN TERRORISTS**, that much more believable."

The last phrase of this tattoo was identical—some might say suspiciously so—to the last phrase of the tattoo received by Ms. Sardi: **TAKES PLEASURE IN PUTTING IN NOT QUITE ENOUGH EFFORT BUT IS STRONGER THAN TERRORISTS**.

Accusations that the tattoos are generic have plagued the epiphany machine since its heyday in the 1960s and 1970s, when John Lennon and other spiritual seekers found guidance in a device that claimed to have insight into their souls at a time when traditional sources of authority appeared to be collapsing. But never before has the device used identical language for so many of its users within such a short time frame.

Michael K. Severn, a professor of psychology at the University of Minnesota, said in a telephone interview that the appeal of this language should come as no surprise.

"People are terrified right now and looking for comfort. The epiphany machine's secret has always been that however nasty its judgments may be, they're still easy answers. Add this new phrase to those easy answers, and you have a perfect moment for the machine."

Asked about this comment at the Saturday gathering, Mr. Lyons appeared unfazed.

"There's a very simple reason why the machine has been saying a lot of New Yorkers are stronger than terrorists: it's because there are a lot of New Yorkers who are a lot stronger than terrorists."

Another attendee, Tyler Bryce, 33, a computer programmer, echoed Ms. Dayles's assessment that the machine's often unpleasant personal judgments lent weight to its rosier outlook on security.

"If Adam Lyons just wanted to tell people a happy story, that's what he would do. Instead, the machine takes a hard look at you and is honest about your strengths and weaknesses," said Mr. Bryce.

Appearing agitated, Mr. Bryce lit a cigarette, with which he almost burned the sleeve he proceeded to roll up.

"Look at this! **KNOWS CLAIM TO HAVE BEEN CHEATED IS ITSELF CHEATING BUT IS STRONGER THAN TERRORISTS**. Now, I really do believe that I was cheated out of a dot-com idea I had in '96, but I do have to admit that the machine is right that I sometimes dwell on it as a way of avoiding my other responsibilities. That level of insight makes me confident that I am also **STRONGER THAN TERRORISTS**."

Mr. Lyons dismissed all objections with an insouciant flick of his cigar.

"There have always been people convinced that I'm the bad guy. I broke up the Beatles, I made your mother abandon you, I killed John [Lennon], I turned your wife into a lesbian, I caused AIDS, I made a couple women named Rebecca Hart kill their kids, 9/11 is my fault. People who insist on seeing me as a monster should just remember that Van Helsings come and go, but Dracula lives forever."

The accusations surrounding Mr. Lyons and his machine caused a steady roll of laughter around the bar. The only attendee who expressed any reservations was a young woman who said that Mr. Lyons seemed awfully cavalier about making 9/11 jokes. Mr. Lyons gave a pronounced shrug and protested that he was not making fun of the victims of 9/11, but rather those, primarily in the media, who suggested that 9/11 was in some way his fault.

He and the woman, who declined to give her name, continued to bicker for several hours. In the end, he persuaded her to follow him behind the velvet curtain at the far end of the apartment to use the device that is said to have inspired the Beatles song "Happiness Is a Warm Gun."

Fifteen minutes later, she emerged from the velvet curtain with a tattoo. It read: **HIDES IN PROPRIETY BUT IS STRONGER THAN TERRORISTS.**

CHAPTER

———··◆··———

31

Anything that I learned in college after Ismail's arrest could easily fit on to my forearm. Most likely, it could fit on my pinky. I more or less stopped paying attention in class and doing my reading, even during a seminar I took my senior year on the work of Steven Merdula, though I did pay close attention to Merdula's chapter on Andrew Blue, since the actual Blue was experiencing renewed popularity, frequently cited in the aftermath of 9/11 as a model of strength and vision. My final paper for that class argued more or less what Ismail had argued years earlier—that Merdula's portrait of Andrew Blue as a crazed anti-Semite whose foresight was a matter of luck amounted to puerile libel, libel that ignored both the depth of Blue's learning and the careful thinking evident in Blue's every turn of phrase. I also said something about the "strange cosmic justice" inherent in the fact that Richard Reid, the famous proponent first of disastrous war and then of appeasement, was finding his name echoed in that of the terrorist who attempted to detonate a bomb in his shoe. My professor—whose interest in Merdula and the epiphany machine had led her to an interest in me that quickly dissipated—gave me a B−, saying that I hadn't sufficiently engaged with Merdula's underlying themes and that my reading of Blue was "marred by fealty to currently fashionable journalistic trends." I did take some validation in the fact that, about a month or so after I got that B–, an article in *The Atlantic Monthly* argued the same thing that I had argued, adding "the idea that Blue, a man allergic even to superstitions far more durable than those that have arisen around this hokey hunk of tin, would ever have used such a device, let alone paid the slightest attention to whatever arbitrary platitude it happened to scribble on his arm, is a patently sinister absurdity." The piece added that it was "unsurprising that at least two jihadists have used the epiphany machine; it is jihadists, not Andrew Blue, who possess the medieval credulity and barbarism that would draw someone to Adam Lyons's needle."

Most of these last two years in college I spent thinking about Ismail. Sometimes I would prepare a monologue that I would deliver when he was released, something about how I had been scared, both by the FBI and by the prospect of terrorism, and that I had never even for a moment seriously thought that he was a terrorist. This fantasy would end with him either sticking a knife in me or embracing me, either of which, I suppose, support the argument that I was homoerotically obsessed with him.

Other times I would spend hours on the Internet reading everything I could find about Al Qaeda and Islamic terrorism, and I would feel certain that Ismail was in fact guilty—that his email to Rebecca suggested a man who hated women, that his suspicions of American culture, which on the surface I agreed with, were in fact the tip of a much more dangerous iceberg—and I would fantasize about the lives I had saved that otherwise would have perished on the Queensboro Bridge, even imagining mothers thanking me for saving their children, if they could somehow know that their children would have been on the Queensboro Bridge at the time that Ismail would have blown it up had it not been for my intervention.

Early in my senior year, past the first anniversary of the attacks and approaching the first anniversary of Ismail's detention, I got a call on my dorm room phone from a man who asked me to hold for Vladimir Harrican. I held, and when Vladimir came on the line the first thing he said was that there was a job with my name on it at an organization he was starting.

"I don't want to have anything to do with the epiphany machine anymore," I said. "I just want to forget it. I certainly don't want to have anything to do with mass-producing it."

"I'm not interested in mass-producing it at the moment," he said. "My thoughts have changed a lot since 9/11. I'm not immune from the general flow of things in that regard. Ziad Jarrah and your friend Ismail have made it clearer to me than ever that Adam Lyons knows something about human nature. I want to use what he knows to save lives."

"I'm sorry?"

"I've started an organization to put pressure on Adam to make epiphanies public. I think you could be helpful in that regard."

"How so?"

"You know more than anyone else about Adam Lyons and Ismail. Except perhaps for Ismail's girlfriend, and she refuses to take my calls. You can tell your coworkers about what Adam does, who Adam is. You can give us insight that we can transform into results. Usually when I talk about 'results' I'm talking about profits or stock price, but now I mean stopping terrorists and saving lives."

Knowing what Leah would think of me if I agreed to accept Vladimir's offer made me doubt that I could accept it. Knowing what my father would think of me made me know I could not.

"Absolutely not," I said. "And I don't ever want to hear from you again."

"Maybe you're not the person I thought you were, Venter," he said, and while I was trying to figure out whether he meant this as a compliment, he hung up.

I continued to drift about for the rest of my senior year, one minute thinking that Ismail was innocent and it was my duty to try to free him, the next minute thinking that he was guilty and that it was my duty to accept Vladimir's offer. No minute did I spend doing anything productive.

Honestly, all I wanted was definitive word on Ismail's guilt or innocence to magically appear on my arm.

What appeared on my arm instead was fire. Just a little fire, but a little fire is enough.

Shortly before graduation, trying to blow off steam from my fear of my own total lack of post-graduation plans, I was running in Riverside Park—one of my many abortive attempts to make a habit of doing so—when an old man called out my name. The surprise of hearing my name was enough to slow me down, though I wasn't going very fast to begin with and was mostly worrying about what all the people who were passing me were thinking about how slow I was going. The man who had spoken was wearing a rumpled suit and smoking a cigarette, and looked like he hadn't showered or slept for several days, so I thought that I had misheard and he hadn't actually said my name.

"You work for the epiphany machine," he said. My picture had been circulated online briefly after 9/11, so I figured that that was how he recognized me.

"Not exactly," I said. "And not for years."

"You were friends with that terrorist, Ismail Ahmed," he said.

"'Friends' isn't the right word."

"Are you a terrorist, too? Let me see your tattoo."

In retrospect, I'm still shocked that I was so eager for this random disheveled man to feel assured that I wasn't a terrorist that I complied and extended my arm, which he proceeded to burn with his cigarette. I screamed and looked for help, but there was no one in that stretch of the park except for a young boy chasing pigeons, and his father watching him do so. They were too far away to hear or just didn't want their day interrupted.

"See that man?" asked the man who had just burned me. "That's what my son should be doing. Playing with his own boys. Instead, my grandsons are dead, and my son is in prison. Because you people hid a monster. That's what you people do. You hide monsters."

"What are you talking about?"

"You don't even know, do you? Go home and look up Devin Lanning. He should have been named Devil Lanning, but it's Devin Lanning. D-E-V-I-N L-A-N-N-I-N-G. Want me to burn it into your arm?"

"I got it, thanks."

He walked away, slowly enough that I could have tackled him. I certainly could have filed a police report. But he seemed to think I deserved what he had done to me, and I had the unnerving sense that he was right.

I did as he asked. I went home, did some googling, and discovered that the man who had assaulted me was probably the father of Jonathan Soricillo. Jonathan Soricillo's twin sons—so, the grandsons of the man who had assaulted me—had been discovered in the woods, each of them raped and murdered. Certain that his neighbor Devin Lanning was guilty, Jonathan Soricillo tied up Lanning in his basement, poured gasoline on him, and lit him on fire. A terrible story, of course, but I couldn't see what it had to do with me. It wasn't until the eighth paragraph that I saw that Soricillo said that Devin Lanning had an epiphany tattoo. Soricillo, who had seen the tattoo only in his fit of murderous rage, said he was unable to remember what the tattoo had said, but that it suggested that Lanning should not be trusted around children.

I sent Adam the link and asked him whether Devin Lanning had gotten a **DOES NOT UNDERSTAND BOUNDARIES** tattoo. He responded:

I remember everyone who gets that tattoo, and I don't remember the crisp in question. My guess is that the father was just trying to use the machine to justify the horrible thing he did. Easier to understand him than it is to understand most people who use the machine to justify the horrible things they do. *Cough, cough.*

A.L. (Absolutely Lucky (to be rid of you))

It was Adam's response that was self-justifying bullshit. The neighbor had obviously gotten a **DOES NOT UNDERSTAND BOUNDARIES** tattoo. Adam hadn't noticed or had decided to ignore it, and as a result, he had allowed this pedophile to rape and murder these two little boys. My thinking was solidified when Adam sent another email a few hours later.

> The more I think about this the less sure I am that this guy Devin Lanning didn't use the machine. Ever since 9/11, my mind has been tearing holes in itself, and maybe this guy got through one of those holes.

A minute later, he followed up again.

> Honestly I didn't mean "this guy got through one of those holes" as a double entendre. That would be disgusting. This whole thing is disgusting. You have no idea how terrible I feel.

I looked at my arm, now purple with the burn. In a way, *I* had allowed this pedophile to rape and murder these two little boys. Whether the machine possessed some kind of supernatural knowledge, or Adam was a preternaturally strong judge of character, I knew that people who get **DOES NOT UNDERSTAND BOUNDARIES** tattoos were pedophiles, and I had done nothing to protect the children those pedophiles would harm.

I wrote a short email.

> OK, it's time to share epiphanies with law enforcement.

He responded immediately.

> Can't do it, buddy. Privacy's a bird. You let it fly away and it's gone forever.

I typed a long email in response to this, but deleted it.

I took another run through Riverside Park, hoping to see the man who had burned me, so I could apologize to him. But he wasn't there. He probably didn't want to hear from me, at least until I had done something to make this right.

A feeling settled in me as I glided past tree after tree that I had not felt in a long time, or maybe ever. As I tried to identify the feeling, I looked past the trees at the river and the cliffs of New Jersey, at the river and the cliffs that had been here before New Jersey, before New York, before—no matter what its true origin story was—the epiphany machine. I looked at the river to the bottom of which Ismail had once threatened to take us— probably jokingly, but not definitely, since after all no joke is ever definitely a joke. And that is when I realized what the feeling was. Joy, certainty, purpose, the sudden possession of knowledge available to all but accessed by only a few—if I hadn't yet learned that all of those things were the same, then I truly had wasted all the time I had spent thinking about epiphanies. I knew what I had to do, and I knew that I was going to do it.

Did it occur to me that this feeling was actually just my relief at hiding from guilt and doubt, a choice of the widely approved pursuit of child molesters and terrorists over the wildly unpopular and probably doomed attempt to free a man considered a terrorist? Of course this occurred to me. Every epiphany contains an opposing epiphany. Which is why I acted as quickly as I did, before I—or someone else—could change my mind.

CHAPTER

✦

32

Vladimir Harrican's offices looked westward, over Manhattan but mostly past it. The buildings were just so much tall grass to be bent aside and the cliffs of New Jersey that I had stared at on my run were anthills to be stomped as Vladimir surveyed the vast plains of America that, as far as he was concerned, were still virgin territory and his to conquer. Or perhaps he believed that his conquering would be so beneficent that he would erase all the conquering that had come before. He would wake the country up from the nightmare of history, cradle it to his chest, and say that it was all right, Daddy's here, it was just a dream. Until then, there was a s'mores station in the waiting area. Graham crackers, dark chocolate, and marshmallows that could be roasted over the plexiglass-protected firepit in the center of the lobby. When I was led into his office, Vladimir was unhappy to hear that I had declined his assistant's offer to make myself one, and he lectured me for two minutes on the underrated health benefits of dark chocolate.

"Nothing else we could talk about today could be as important as dark chocolate," he said once that lecture was over. "But tell me the second-most important thing we have to cover."

Simultaneously insulted and disarmed, I stammered a bit before coming to the point.

"I saw something in the news that I wanted to talk to you about," I said.

"The guy who burned the sicko who killed his kids," he said.

I was totally shocked. "How did you know?"

"The epiphany machine prophesied it on my arm. Just kidding. I have somebody keep track of all news related to the epiphany machine."

"Epiphanies should be made public," I said.

"A clear point of view, clearly stated. But before we get there, let's back up a bit. Why did you come here?"

"Because I want to accept the offer you made. The one about working to make epiphanies public."

"Okay, let's back up a little further. The epiphany machine asks two questions of us. What are they?"

"I don't follow."

"Sure you do. The epiphany machine asks two questions of us: Will you believe the truth about yourself if it is presented to you, and what will you do about it? Of these two questions, only the second is interesting, since plenty of people know the truth about themselves but do not have the energy and, in most cases, any real desire to alter their habits in any way. Now, people who do improve their behavior for the better have some things in common. What are those things? You must have noticed when you were taking those—what did you call them?—testimonials."

The truth? The truth was that I had observed no pattern, had learned nothing.

"They make a clear decision to change?"

"Why are you offering your insight as though you're asking a question? Is it because you're **DEPENDENT ON THE OPINION OF OTHERS**?"

"They make a clear decision to change."

"Did you ever make a clear decision to change?"

"I think so?"

"You 'think so'? And have you changed?"

"No, I guess not."

"People who actually improve after their epiphanies are people who make a decision *not* to change."

"I'm sorry?"

"You are who you are. That's why the epiphanies are in ink."

This suddenly struck me as obvious.

"Why get the epiphany tattoo?" he asked. "So that you can stop trying to change. So that you accept yourself. You accept yourself if you're a person like me, a person of superior abilities who needs to remember not to feel guilty for accomplishing so much more and earning so much more than other people, although in my case I've always known that and have never needed to use the machine. You accept yourself if you're a person like my father, a man whose extraordinary gifts were outmatched by his overwhelming need to be told what to do. As strange as I find it for my father to have given up the career of an acclaimed violinist for the career of an anonymous factory worker, I recognize that he fulfilled his specific destiny. You, too, should accept yourself as you are. You have nothing like my father's gifts, but otherwise you're a lot like him. You're a guy who is decently intelligent but can't make up his own mind and will be much happier if he fulfills his destiny by following somebody's orders, instead of beating himself up all the time about not being the lone-wolf genius he wishes he were. You came to me because you need to follow someone's orders, and you know that I am the person whose orders you need to follow."

The truth of this insight struck me immediately, so much so that it put me in a defeated and obsequious mood. But I reminded myself that I had come here because I was certain I had a mission.

"I'm not going to sit here and take this," I said.

"Of course you're not," he said. "Because you can't accept what the machine told you. You're what Adam calls 'a waste of ink.' Adam is an extraordinary observer of human personality, and if you would simply admit to yourself that you are **DEPENDENT ON THE OPINION OF OTHERS**, then you could get down to the important work you should be doing."

"Good-bye and fuck you."

"Is that what you would say to a kid who's soon going to be molested by a guy who **DOES NOT UNDERSTAND BOUNDARIES**? 'Good-bye, kid, and fuck you'?"

I had never heard anyone other than Adam talk about the **DOES NOT UNDERSTAND BOUNDARIES** tattoo before. I did not say anything, but I also did not leave.

Vladimir smiled and took a bite of a dark chocolate candy bar that he apparently kept in his desk. "I have somebody who analyzes data for law enforcement who noticed that a bunch of child molesters arrested over the last few decades have had **DOES NOT UNDERSTAND BOUNDARIES** epiphany tattoos," he said. "I'm guessing that Adam, whether he's aware of it or not, has some kind of sixth sense—sick sense?—for child molesters, so this is the tattoo he's choosing for them. He also has some kind of sense for terrorists, which is why he chooses **WANTS TO BLOW THINGS UP** tattoos for them."

Again, I did not say anything, but I also did not leave.

"This is where the epiphany machine's usefulness becomes a bit tricky," Vladimir said. "We don't want child molesters and terrorists to just accept themselves. But that doesn't mean that the machine has no purpose for them. Child molesters and terrorists need—probably, in many ways, *want*—to be destroyed, and the machine can destroy them.

"Now, let's get to the real reason why you're here. You're upset about Devin Lanning, that you didn't stop him when you had the chance, and you're right to be upset about that, but there's something that bothers you more. You go back and forth on your friend Ismail. Some days you're certain that he is a terrorist and that he's getting what is coming to him, other days you're certain he is innocent and you're essentially a Judas who didn't even get thirty pieces of silver. So you want to work for an organization that is dedicated to making epiphanies public, meaning that you'll be working against Ismail and people like him, because by making this kind of commitment you'll be convincing yourself that Ismail is guilty. Right?"

I knew that this was exactly why I was here. "That's not why I'm here," I said.

"Venter. Of course it is. And of course it's natural to feel conflicted about what's being done to your friend, and to feel confused about whether he's guilty. You're looking for certainty that he was planning to destroy that bridge, so that you can sleep at night knowing that you did the right thing."

"I haven't slept a full night in a really long time," I said.

"Because you haven't found that certainty yet. September 11 raised the stakes for everyone, and your tattoo is out of date. You're no longer **DEPENDENT ON THE OPINION OF OTHERS**; you're **DEPENDENT ON THE CERTAINTY OF OTHERS**. Who can offer you that certainty? I can. I'm a very smart guy, Venter. All day long, I look at information and decide who's telling the truth, who's lying, who is a grand visionary, and who is a deluded moron. I'm so good at it that it has made me billions of dollars. Billions. I've looked a lot at your friend Ismail's case, and do you know how much doubt I have that he was planning a terrorist attack? Zero. He has been arrested and has not been let go. I can list about ten million ways in which the American government is stupid and wrongheaded, but it wouldn't keep a man in captivity without trial unless it had evidence that had to be kept secret for many reasons that we can clearly imagine."

"I've been thinking along the same lines," I said.

"You've been thinking along similar lines, but you've also been thinking along opposing lines. 'What if the government messed up? What if hysteria in the wake of the attacks led the FBI to arrest a man for nothing other than a tattoo some people say is magic?' You'll never be able to decide which of those two sides is right, so your mind is a field on which you watch those two sides toss the ball back and forth, with no real system of scoring and no point at which the game is set to end, except for your own death."

"My father used a similar metaphor once about keeping score. He took me to a cemetery and . . ."

"Your father's a smart man, but he's misled by what he wants to believe. He wants to believe that people are complicated enough to deserve rights. But they're not. Each of us has a very simple role to play. My role is to use my judgment. My judgment is among the best that the world has ever seen, and I have judged your friend to be guilty. It's good that you're crying, because this is important. Don't you want to share in my certainty?"

He reached into a drawer and pulled out a box of tissues whose sole purpose appeared to be given to people whom Vladimir had just made cry. I took one and wiped my eyes and blew my nose.

"I do," I said.

"Good. Remember that. There will be times when you'll have doubts and you'll want to leave. But never forget that if you leave, all you will have will be doubts."

"I won't forget," I said.

"Excellent. Go see Carol in human resources; she'll take care of you from here. Make sure to get a s'more on the way out."

I threw out my soaking, snotty tissue in the bathroom, started crying again, went through a few more tissues, and then headed out into the lobby to put a piece of dark chocolate between two graham crackers. I dropped a couple pieces of dark chocolate on the freshly buffed floor, but nobody who passed by seemed to mind, since this was obviously a freshly buffed floor that would soon be freshly buffed again. I stared into the furnace and watched the flame thicken and thin and thicken again. I thought about putting my hand into the furnace and burning myself alive the way that James does in the Merdula book. I could see the flames on my arm; I could feel the terror but also perhaps the relief that that pedophile must have felt as **DOES NOT UNDERSTAND BOUNDARIES** was about to be consumed. Perhaps word would find its way back to Ismail that I had killed myself, and that would bring him some comfort, wherever he was.

CHAPTER

—— ·· ◆ ·· ——

33

My first day at Harrican's nonprofit—Citizens for Knowledge and Safety—consisted of an orientation and of getting situated in my cubicle. The following two weeks consisted of me sitting in a conference room alone with the deputy director of Citizens for Knowledge and Safety, answering questions about the epiphany machine and Ismail. At the end of those two weeks, the deputy director, highly unsatisfied with the information I had given him, insisted that I sit in a cubicle and write down my experiences.

It would be a report, he said, but it would also be a memoir. It would tell the story of the machine through the story of my life. He did not mention a deadline. That was a mistake.

Writing has never been easy for me, and I certainly did not find it easy to type the story of my life in a cubicle, a perfect post at which to listen to my coworkers talk about the epiphany machine all day, trying with their every sentence not to give away what the machine would have written on their arms had they ever gotten tattooed.

I kept a Microsoft Word document full of my guesses.

- Steve, the executive director: **ABANDONED HIS MOTHER WHEN SHE GOT SICK**
- Franklin, the deputy director: **HAS BEEN CHEATING ON WIFE, STILL CONVINCED HE IS A VICTIM**
- Kristen, an outreach coordinator: **KNOWS THAT SHE WOULD STILL HATE HERSELF EVEN IF SHE HAD PERFECT PARENTS**
- Lisa, an accountant: **HOPES THAT HER JOKES ABOUT EMBEZZLING AND MOVING TO THE BAHAMAS COVER HER CONSTANT FANTASIES ABOUT EMBEZZLING AND MOVING TO THE BAHAMAS.** Or maybe: **TRIES TO CONVINCE SELF THAT SHE IS TOO MORALLY UPRIGHT TO EMBEZZLE, BUT KNOWS THAT SHE IS JUST TOO FEARFUL**

Every day that I showed up to work, I felt certain that I had, in fact, absorbed Vladimir Harrican's certainty. I felt certain that I was not betraying my friend with every minute I spent in this office. I felt certain, too, that I was not jealous of Cesar Solomon. My freshman-year roommate had, unbeknownst to me, been writing fiction throughout college. Less than one year after we graduated, he published a celebrated debut novel. *The Asperger Syndrome* told two parallel stories: one, set in Croatia during World War II, told the story of Hans Asperger, a medical officer with the Nazi army who has not yet discovered the condition that will be named for him, and the other, set in contemporary New Jersey, told the story of a Jewish teenager with Asperger's syndrome. *The New York Times Book Review* had likened Cesar to "a Steven Merdula with a taste for meticulous research and historical accuracy." I thought that the book sounded extremely stupid, and I hated myself for not having written it. I read every blog post and review I could find about it. In most cases, I read the negative ones two or three times. Then I read the book and I thought it was excellent. I reread the negative reviews to convince myself I was wrong. I reminded myself that I wasn't trying to write fiction and that if I ever decided to try to write fiction again, it would be better than Cesar's, though maybe not as popular, since what I would write would be tough, unconcerned with pleasing readers and critics. But for now, I was doing something more important than making up stories.

Of course, I didn't really believe any of this, however much I tried to. What I actually believed was that *Ismail*, were he not locked up who knew where, would be a better writer than Cesar. Ismail would have written a great play by now or would be well on his way to writing one. He had been making such progress in his writing, and that progress had been halted, possibly forever, by me.

No. He had halted his own progress. By deciding to become a terrorist.

The Soricillo twins. The people that Ziad Jarrah had murdered. The people Ismail would have murdered had I not stopped him. I had to think of them whenever I had doubts. Certainty is a habit and a skill, and I had to practice.

When I had been at Citizens for Knowledge and Safety for almost a year, I explained in a staff meeting—attended by Vladimir Harrican, a notable event even though he was attending only by conference call from many floors above us—that I would need another year to complete a memoir about the machine thorough enough to be used to combat the machine. Franklin, the deputy director, said that if I was truly **DEPENDENT ON THE OPINION OF OTHERS** I should probably speed it up so they didn't all think I was lazy and dim. The remark hurt, and so did the general laughter it elicited, primarily because I was convinced I was lazy and dim. Everyone looked at the plastic triangle at the center of the conference table, waiting for Vladimir's voice to waft through it. Vladimir was silent for long enough for me to wonder whether he had been paying attention, or if he would fire me, and so give me a reprieve.

"This is why Citizens for Knowledge and Safety has yet to make progress against Adam Lyons," Vladimir said, to murmurs of agreement.

"None of you understand the importance of working and working until you've gotten something right. Venter is to be given all the time he needs."

Apologetic mumblings, shame on everyone's faces. By the end of the day, all my coworkers had convinced themselves and were trying to convince each other that they had always supported my project and approved of the amount of time it was taking me to complete it.

"Franklin thinks he has all the answers," said my coworker Kristen, "but he has never appreciated your talent." Kristen had laughed appreciatively when Franklin made his disparaging remark.

My victory did not make me happy; nor did I find it invigorating to be surrounded by coworkers who were **DEPENDENT ON THE OPINION OF OTHERS**. But I had decided that I was doing quality work, and quality work takes time.

After three months, during which I had done almost no work at all, I saw Rebecca for the first time since graduation. She was sitting at a table in Bryant Park, wearing a peach sundress and holding a highlighter above a massive textbook like an expert hunter waiting for the right moment. She was so absorbed in her work that I hesitated to call out to her, and even wondered whether it was really her, or someone who looked like her, but who was more studious, more beautiful. The more I thought about it, the more I realized that she had always been studious and beautiful, and I had only intermittently noticed it.

"Rebecca," I called out finally. This caught the attention of another woman, presumably named Rebecca, but it did not catch the attention of the woman I still thought of as "my Rebecca."

"Rebecca Hart." As soon as I said the second word I flinched, annoyed at myself for calling attention to her full name, but the other Rebecca had returned to her scone and no one else looked up, the world having abandoned Rebecca Hart for other demons. I said "Rebecca Hart" again, and this time my Rebecca looked up. I'll never forget the look on her face when she saw me, a look of total relief and total love that totally confused me.

I sat down beside her, and the first thing she told me was that she loved law school, but feared becoming a corporate lawyer. She was hoping to get a job in human rights.

"Every day I thank whatever god is responsible for the epiphany machine," she said. "I know I can never have children, so I know where my focus needs to be."

"You don't actually believe that you're going to kill your children."

"I don't actually believe that, because I'm not going to have children."

"*Rebecca.*"

"*Venter.* It's been a while since I've said that, that's fun. Look, do I think it's *likely* I would kill my children? No. Do I think it's possible? I mean, it figured out our friend was a terrorist, so that's a pretty compelling track record."

"Are you making fun of me?"

"Absolutely not. Honestly, I find it difficult to make fun of anything anymore, given all those emails from Leah."

"What emails from Leah?"

"Oh, I just assumed she's been emailing you, too. She sends me long emails two or three times a month about what a horrible monster I am for refusing to stand up for Ismail. She's been writing a play criticizing the War on Terror, and I've told her that she should focus on that rather than on harassing me. I stopped responding a long time ago, because she won't listen to reason, and she doesn't seem to be bothered by that hateful email he sent me just before 9/11. She really doesn't email you? Don't you work for Vladimir Harrican now?"

"She's probably written me off as beyond redemption." There was no need for me to have said "probably." My father was in nearly constant contact with her as they both worked to free Ismail, and they met for the regular dinners one might expect of a father and adult child who live in the same city. He had let slip in a phone call once that Leah thought I was "beyond redemption."

"And that probably bothers you, because you're **DEPENDENT ON THE OPINION OF OTHERS.** Which brings us back to the original point: the epiphany machine is real, Ismail is guilty, and I will kill any children I have." She spread her arms wide to assert, at once mockingly and sincerely, that she had proven her point. "And now that we've covered that, I might as well mention something else. I've been thinking about getting in contact with you for a while."

"About what?"

"I've been on a lot of dates with a lot of guys. Usually it goes terribly. But I dated two guys for a month each, and both of those guys mentioned offhand that they one day want to have kids. I told them I refuse because of the Rebecca Hart thing, and they . . . don't get it. This has led me to believe that you're the only guy for me. You don't get it either, but at least you get the machine. Plus, I miss you."

She put her hand on mine, and it did feel electric. A major reason why I loved Rebecca, and by far the biggest reason why we fought all the time, is that we tended to reflect our confusions back at each other. Right now it seemed absurd to think that the machine knew anything, or that Adam knew anything, or that Vladimir knew anything. Ismail was innocent, and I had devoted my life to persecuting him. "I'm doing terribly," I said. "The best friend I've ever had is in Hell because of me."

She took her hand away. "Venter, when you get dramatic like this you're really evading responsibility. I'm not in Hell. I just think we should try getting back together. Jeez."

I thought about correcting her mistake. I also thought that if I did not correct her, but we wound up having sex, I would feel guilty. I also thought that if I corrected her because I did not want to feel guilty if we had sex, that would be presumptuous. I worried about various combinations of correcting her and not correcting her and having sex and not having sex until, that night, on the pretext of helping her unpack, I met her at her new apartment, where we did not unpack, I did not correct her, and we did not have sex.

Our not having sex, I should be clear, was not for lack of trying. We started kissing almost as soon as we walked into her apartment. I'm not exactly sure when the word "impotent" entered my mind, but as soon as it did it might as well have been tattooed on my dick and all over Rebecca's body, because I saw it everywhere. Panicked, I told myself to stop thinking of the word, but of course that just made me think about it more.

Despite this, when we stopped trying, I said I didn't know what was wrong with me, as though the diagnosis were mysterious.

"I'm just happy to be with you again," she said, nuzzling my neck and pulling one and then two of my fingers inside her. I enjoyed touching her. Afterward, we wrapped our legs around each other, both confident that we had found what we needed to find.

We got back together, and I continued to have difficulties getting erections. (I know, I know, it was hard to get hard. Ha, ha, ha.) It's not that we never had sex, but when sex worked, it usually worked only after many stops and starts, and sometimes I would lose my erection while inside her, a very big death indeed.

"I think it's because I feel guilty about Ismail," I said to her after one failed attempt. "I can't think about anything else."

"Why do you feel guilty about Ismail?"

"He wouldn't be where he is if it weren't for me."

"He wouldn't be where he is if he weren't a terrorist."

"There have been reports that he has been tortured."

"Well, he shouldn't be tortured."

"That doesn't make you mad? He was our friend."

"We never really knew him, obviously. I spend all day reading about women being raped and hacked to death. I just don't have any spare room in my heart for a terrorist who's being made uncomfortable."

"I still think it's why I'm too depressed to have sex."

"Are you sure that's the reason? Maybe you need to accomplish more professionally."

I sat upright in bed. Suddenly, I realized that this was exactly what I needed to do. Rebecca always had a knack for knowing what I should be doing at any particular time, even if I failed to do it, as with that summer when I failed to write a novel. I had not been disciplined in practicing my certainty; I had let my certainty get flabby.

I needed to practice my certainty by accomplishing something. Rather than sit at my cubicle trying to get started on the memoir, I needed to take a concrete step to stop future Ismails, future Ziad Jarrahs, future Devin Lannings.

I was right that I was impotent because I felt guilty, but I didn't feel guilty because I was persecuting Ismail; I felt guilty because I was acting impotently, not doing enough to stop people like Ismail.

This was the sudden realization I needed. This one, I was certain, would stand. An embarrassing double entendre, but a crucial one.

"I've actually been thinking that I'd like to write a more direct call to action," I said. "Rather than just write this endless memoir, I should write something that convinces people that epiphanies need to be made public."

"I was thinking you should get back to writing fiction," Rebecca said.

I barely even heard this, because I was already thinking about the project that I was sure would bring me praise. I arrived at work the next morning ready to begin it, but as soon as I booted up my computer I discovered that Steven Merdula had published, in the literary journal *Needle Quarterly*, his first short story in many years.

Never to Be Doubted

BY STEVEN MERDULA

Somebody must have been telling lies about Ismail A.

Maybe this joke occurs to Ismail shortly after he is lifted off the sidewalk in front of the Tower Records near NYU and thrown into an SUV, in a movement so assured that any passersby who have noticed probably think he is just any college student, being ushered by friends off to adventure. He is handcuffed and hooded. His first thought is that this is Al Qaeda, perhaps here as part of some campaign to execute random Muslim apostates on the streets of New York. But his captors have American accents, and like many people with American accents, they shout at him and do not listen to what he says in return. What is happening to him is awful, it is hellish, it is, yes, Kafkaesque, but he tells himself it is also that most American of things: OK.

Perhaps when he is released, he will write an adaptation of *The Trial*, one that entwines his own experience with that of Josef K.'s.

Or perhaps he makes no plans. Perhaps he already knows that what has him will not let him go.

When the SUV stops, he demands—for the first time, partly because his mouth is covered with cloth, and partly because he is always slow to say what needs to be said, this is precisely the quality that draws him to write plays—to speak to a lawyer, to speak to his parents, to speak to his friend Venter's lawyer father, to speak to Leah. His captors do not respond, but shove him out of the SUV and then push him, from the best that he can hear and smell, into a building. A hallway, an elevator. He calls out "Leah," not because she will hear but because he needs the sound of the name "Leah" to fill the space he cannot see.

He hears a door lock behind him, and then he hears nothing else for a long time. Ten minutes? An hour? Ten hours? He cannot tell time in a hood, but this will all be over soon. It *must* be over soon; his country may be inhaling hysteria along with ash, but it is still his country, one in which there are things that the government will not permit itself to do.

"Leah," he says to the darkness. If he were writing a play, he would squish out this sentimental moment, but he is not writing a play. He can see her in front of him; it is like she is there.

And then it is not like she is there. What is there now is darkness. Not the absence of light but a physical thing. The darkness is like a brick wall, or like water.

Finally, he hears the door open. "When were you first contacted by Ziad Jarrah?"

"Who?"

"Or was it Atta?"

"Can you take this hood off, please?"

"I'll take the hood off if you're honest with me and tell me when Atta contacted you."

"Why are you doing this to me? You have to let me see! You have to let me know what time it is, and when I will be allowed to speak with a lawyer."

"When did you first learn about the September 11 attacks?"

"Right after the planes hit, just like everybody else who lives downtown."

"Don't pretend. I can't help you if you're not honest."

"I want a lawyer."

"When I send you to Hell, you will have seventy-two lawyers."

The darkness pressing down on his shoulders does not improve bad jokes.

"One will be fine. But I want one now."

"Have it your way. We'll send a lawyer soon. Keep your eyes open."

The door closes and does not reopen for a long time. Ismail longs to read something, anything, even just the tattoo on his arm, over and over.

When he realizes that he is here because of his tattoo—**WANTS TO BLOW THINGS UP**—he is surprised that it has taken him this long to figure it out. For the first time in a minute or an hour or a day he feels hope. He bangs on the door and says he wants to speak to someone, and then keeps saying it until the door opens.

"Venter Lowood," Ismail says. "He's the one I got this tattoo with. It just means I wanted to 'blow up' my relationship with my family. Venter will vouch for me." He could have mentioned Adam Lyons or Leah Marx, but he assumes they know about Leah, and he is not certain he trusts Adam. "V-E-N-T-E—"

"Venter Lowood is the one who told us that you're a terrorist."

Hearing this makes Ismail long for silence.

"You're lying," he says. "Venter is my friend. He would never tell lies about me."

"Venter Lowood chose his country over a terrorist." Then the door shuts again.

Of course Ismail should knock again, ask them to ask Adam Lyons. But he is too depressed to do anything now. As much as he does not want to believe it, he knows how comically easy Venter must have been to manipulate. Venter Lowood—Venter, both of whose parents used the machine; Venter, whose mother abandoned him and all but left him to die of exposure on top of the machine; Venter, who nonetheless used the machine and received the tattoo **DEPENDENT ON THE OPINION OF OTHERS**. Until a moment ago, Ismail had long considered Venter his best friend, despite how fragile and suggestible he was, because anyone could see that Venter was fundamentally a smart and good-hearted person who had been unlucky enough to have a horrible, selfish mother. Ismail had even allowed Venter to convince him to use the machine, maybe in part to boost Venter's confidence, to make him feel accepted. But someone else, someone looking to round up as many terrorism suspects as possible—CIA, FBI, someone— must have made Venter feel accepted.

Somehow Ismail feels a rush of affection and sympathy for Venter—affection for the late nights they spent talking about Kafka, sympathy for this poor guy who had been abandoned by his mother and as a result searched for whatever authority might approve of him—and then that rush is gone. Almost immediately, he feels a painful nostalgia for the time—surely it is not quite gone, surely there are a few seconds or a few centuries of that time left—when he felt anything at all for anyone other than total, vibrating hatred for Venter.

Sometime later—there is no saying when, or at least Ismail cannot say when—he is grabbed by the shoulders and pushed somewhere, and then pushed somewhere else. Doors open and close, beyond his hood there is some hazy suggestion of brightness, but then this brightness is extinguished forever as a door slams shut behind him, and now he realizes he is in a vehicle and that vehicle is moving. Finally, there are the sounds of a helicopter, the feeling of air and the smell of the sea, the sensation of being lifted, and Ismail suddenly realizes that he will be dropped into the sea. The government will not want to admit that it has held him for days or weeks or hours on nothing but a tattoo, so he is going to be dropped into the sea and forgotten forever.

But he is not dropped into the sea. The helicopter's whirring, which reminds him very slightly of the whirring of the epiphany machine, slows and stops, and then he is alone and it is quiet again. He is alone, he is taken somewhere, it is quiet for a long time. He would like to be stronger but he weeps into his hood and he begs to be let go.

"I can't help you unless you're going to tell me the truth." The same voice that spoke to him hours or weeks ago.

"The truth is that I'm innocent."

"That is not the truth we're looking for."

The cloth chafes and he tastes it in his mouth, and he thinks, They are going to suffocate me, I am never going to be allowed to breathe again, much worse, I am never going to be allowed to speak again. But he is not suffocated with his hood. It must have gotten stuck in his mouth on its way off his face, because his hair is pulled and then the hood is removed.

Immediately it is too bright to see. He can barely see the outlines of the four men in the room with him, and he can see nothing of their faces, which are obscured by strange translucent plastic rectangles, strange translucent plastic rectangles he will see many more of.

These men remove the rest of Ismail's clothing.

He shuts his eyes so that the darkness to which he has become accustomed will return, and he asks the men when he will be granted access to an attorney. There is no answer, save for thudding feet and a slamming door.

There are three things in the room: a toilet, a sink, a steel frame that looks like a bed. But it cannot be his bed, because there is no mattress. Surely they would, at the very least, give him a mattress.

They have not given him a mattress. This is his bed.

It doesn't matter, though, because he cannot sleep, no matter how tired he may be. It is too bright to sleep. He calls out asking for the lights to be turned off, but the lights are not turned off.

At some point, it is made very cold. He shivers, he is naked, he asks for heat and for clothes and there is no answer. The lights are turned off. He can't even see enough to find his bed, though it wouldn't matter if he could, because it is too cold to sleep. Then it grows warmer, warmer, and warmer, and then far too hot. It is dark and hot, dark and hot, dark and hot, dark and hot.

If there were a clock, he could not see it, but he wishes that there were one, its presence would be reassuring.

Bright and cold bright and cold bright and cold dark and cold dark and cold dark and cold.

He imagines Leah, he imagines holding her. He imagines Venter, too, he imagines hitting him in the face. He imagines finding Venter's mother and strangling her.

When he is released, he and Leah will turn this into a play. He imagines Leah's intelligent, furious eyes as she paces around a stage that they will make to look exactly like this room. Leah will play him, she will inhabit him, she will make the audience feel what it is like to be here right now.

It is bright and hot. It is bright and hot. It is bright and hot. His eyes hurt and his skin feels so sweaty and disgusting and he wishes he could take his body off.

It has been two days, three days. He does not know whether they bring him three meals a day or one meal every other day. If there are rules in this place, he has not been permitted to know them.

A man enters and this man starts talking without offering Ismail clothes or a shower.

"Who came up with the plot to blow up the Queensboro Bridge?"

"What?"

"Atta? Bin Laden? Khalid Sheikh Mohammed?"

"What are you talking about?"

"We found the plans to blow up the Queensboro Bridge on your computer."

The man's words are confusing, either because the words are confusing or because Ismail's mind is deteriorating, or both.

"May I have some clothing?"

"You can have some clothing when you start being honest. We can't trust you to cover yourself up if you also cover up the truth."

"I don't know what you're talking about."

The man slaps him.

It is still difficult to believe this is happening.

"You were going to incinerate everyone who happened to be on the bridge. School buses. Ambulances. Mothers returning to their children at the end of the day."

"Are you talking about my play?"

"Don't bother trying that. The whole 'playwright' business was a lie."

"Who told you that? Venter? None of it's true."

"We have many of your friends in custody. They've all told us the truth."

"I wrote a play. Fiction. Fiction. There's a difference between reality and what's made up."

"We have some of your writings in which you say that, given that the world is itself a fiction, there is in fact no such thing as fiction, there is only reality."

"Huh?"

The man starts to recite something, and its source is mysterious until it is not: it is from a paper that Ismail wrote for a literature class. The paper was called "*Don Quixote* and the Uncertain Nature of Reality."

For the first time in this time that cannot be measured, Ismail laughs.

"The murder of innocent people is funny to you?" the man asks. "We have the minutes from your meetings with your co-conspirators in which you discuss your plans to launch an attack on the Queensboro Bridge."

"The minutes from my meetings? You mean the dialogue from my play?"

"Keeping up that lie won't help you improve your treatment. Only telling the truth will improve your treatment."

"I am telling the truth."

The man was silent for a long time. "Do you think America is an evil country?"

"No, I do not believe that." To Ismail's surprise, this is still a true statement.

"But the United States is detaining you without charge, denying you access to a lawyer, stripping you naked, subjecting you to extreme temperatures, depriving you of sleep. The United States would have to be *certain* that you are its enemy to justify what it has done. If you are innocent, a country that would do what it is doing to you would unquestionably be evil. If you are saying you are innocent, you are saying the United States is evil. And if you believe the United States is evil, then you are an enemy of the United States. So whether you are saying you are innocent or guilty, you are saying you are an enemy of the United States, and we are required to continue treating you this way."

"I have nothing to say," Ismail says. This, again to Ismail's surprise, is also a true statement.

Without saying anything else, the man leaves. The heat is turned up again. Other men come in, grab Ismail's arms, shackle him, and chain him to a wall.

His arms are raised and he cannot lower them. He can look down at his nakedness, he can look around the room at this empty cell, he can look and see his tattoo, extending up toward the heavens, though it will not reach the heavens, because God will stop Ismail's arm in the atmosphere, and the arm and the tattoo and Ismail will be incinerated. Then perhaps God will incinerate all tattoos—there is good reason why tattoos are forbidden by Jews and Muslims, they are filthy, disgusting things that make it impossible to ignore just how filthy and disgusting the body itself is. Then perhaps God will incinerate billboards, graffiti, Qur'ans, Bibles, all books, anything with words. Adam and Eve ate from the tree of knowledge rather than the tree of life, which they would never have done had God made them correctly in the first place. Words are the worst thing about the universe, they are even worse than bodies. The word "naked" is even more disgusting than nakedness itself. The ability to read is nothing more than a euphemism for the ability to misread.

It is cold. It is dark. It is painful. It is cold. It is dark. It is painful.

The man comes again, with a needle, and Ismail is sorry that he has ever seen a needle—pens, needles, penises, anything that can be used to mark or puncture or penetrate should never have been invented.

"This is truth serum," the man says, just before he jabs it into Ismail's raised arm. Ismail knows or comes as close as he can to knowing that there is no such thing as truth serum, but he hopes that it is real, for then he will tell the truth, and if he tells the truth then he must know it, and if he knows the truth then surely he can tell it to himself. The first truth will have to be the truth of where he truly is. In an insane asylum. On stage with Leah. It cannot be true that he is where he is.

He is slapped by his interrogator. His interrogator tells him that he must tell the truth, that he has no choice, and he does his best, he tries to tell the interrogator the truth that the interrogator is looking for, but the truth now seems hazy, out of reach.

Truth and lies, like brightness and darkness, no longer look different, or rather they only *look* different. He can hear in his torturer's voice increasing panic, fear that he is torturing an innocent person. But nothing will come of this, because the torturer will not be able to tolerate the knowledge that he is torturing an innocent person, and therefore Ismail will be guilty.

The torturer leaves, assuring Ismail that he will return. It is cold. It is hot. It is dark. It is bright. The seasons are evoked and parodied as though Ismail is on stage. He is on stage and he will be on stage. Leah will be him with him. Venter and Venter's mother will both be in the audience, and at the end of the play Ismail will call them to the stage. Venter and Venter's mother will assume it is a joke, a gag about breaking the fourth wall, but Ismail will keep insisting until Venter and his mother find it more embarrassing not to take the stage than to take it. He will help them both up, Venter will start crying, overwhelmed by this gesture of forgiveness, and then Ismail will pull a knife from his pocket and slit Venter's throat, and then he will slit Venter's mother's throat. Their blood will mingle as it flows off the stage and they will try to grab each other's hands, but Ismail will kick their hands away from each other, for each of them deserves to die alone. And then Ismail will slit Leah's throat and slit his own throat, because he and his love both deserve the truth, and the knife is the only implement that can bring forth the truth.

But none of this will happen, because that would constitute a story, and he has been removed from the realm of stories.

It is dark. It is cold. It is hot. It is bright. It is cold. It is dark. It is bright. It is bright. It is bright. It is bright. It is bright.

CHAPTER

──── · · ◆ · · ────

34

I read this at my desk in a state of mounting fury. What did Steven Merdula, that anonymous coward, know about me, or about my mother, or about Ismail? He had obviously read the handful of interviews Leah had done in the weeks after Ismail's arrest, and had obviously read—and believed—the most salacious accounts available on the Internet of Ismail's treatment. Merdula had combined this small amount of information with a total blind faith in Ismail's innocence that thoroughly contradicted, even betrayed, the suspicion of certainty that marked Merdula's best work. It was also, I thought, written badly.

The rest of my workday consisted of trashing this piece with my co-workers; every half hour or so someone else would pop up from a cubicle to share a thought on something else that was wrong with the piece, or another psychological theory for why Merdula had gone so wrong. A lot of people suggested that I sue, and I said that I was definitely going to, but I already knew that I absolutely would not, since nothing Merdula had written about me was exactly untrue, and I didn't want to sit through depositions that would establish that fact. (Merdula and the editors of *Needle*

Quarterly had probably counted on my making this calculation. There are few feelings worse than knowing that you're going to do exactly what your enemy wants you to do.) I called Rebecca in the afternoon and she was as outraged as I was, though most of her outrage was directed toward Leah, whom she was convinced had given Merdula additional information. Rebecca and I each wrote emails to Leah, who responded in one email to us both that she had not spoken to Merdula, nor did she know who Merdula was, but that as far as she was concerned, Merdula had let Rebecca off way too easily by not mentioning her, and had let me off way too easily by making it sound as though I were the victim of an evil, abandoning mother, when it was more likely that my mother had abandoned me because I was evil. Also, Ismail thought Kafka was overrated and would have thought Merdula's entire approach gimmicky and annoying. She concluded:

> I'm actually glad that Ismail won't be permitted to read this shitty story. I do kind of like the ending, but, Rebecca, I'd swap you in for Venter's mom, just like Venter has. Let me know if the two of you want to get your throats slit on stage at my next performance.

The next morning, I was, if anything, even madder, so I wrote an angry email to Steven Merdula and sent it to him care of *Needle Quarterly*, even though I knew there was no chance he would respond. To my great surprise, he responded by the end of the day.

> Dear Venter,
>
> You are a badly lost young man. You must know that your friend is entirely innocent of wrongdoing and is the victim of injustice that—to use a rare legal term that actually evokes rather than obfuscates human experience—shocks the conscience. The mean-

ing of Ismail's tattoo, to the extent that a phrase as vague as **WANTS TO BLOW THINGS UP** has any meaning at all, clearly refers to benign rebellions against family and convention. What little I have learned about you in investigating Ismail's case suggests that you are of at least average intelligence, so you must grasp this. Perhaps you are at the mercy of the hysteria that has seized so many, but your particular fealty to this hysteria is notable in that it has led you not only to betray your friend, but to betray him over and over again, forty hours every week. Mr. Harrican is a lot like you—at the mercy of a multigenerational family struggle with the machine that influences his behavior in ways that he does not understand—and I think that working for him is reinforcing your worst tendencies. My theory—one that may offend you but that I hope you will give the consideration it deserves—is that you are "playing up" to your tattoo. You are exaggerating the degree to which you are **DEPENDENT ON THE OPINION OF OTHERS**, and so you are acquiescing to the baseless belief held by so many that Ismail is a terrorist, despite your personal knowledge that this belief is wrong.

I feel sympathy for you given the many strikes against you, starting with your mother, who by any reasonable standard sounds like a terrible woman. So far, the miserable life you have lived cannot be said to be entirely your fault. But you must take control of what you do from now on. It is not your fate to acquiesce. Do your best to free Ismail, and do it now.

With concern and good wishes,
Steven Merdula

This email, and its nasty remarks about my mother, made me angrier than I had ever been. I wanted to throw my coffee mug at my laptop, but I didn't want to be known for having an anger problem, so I took the mug into the breakroom and threw it on the floor, an aggressive act I could plausibly claim was an accident.

Surprisingly, almost nobody outside my office seemed to read Merdula's story, because nobody wanted to read about torture. The episode left me unharmed, but with my commitment redoubled to writing what I knew I needed to write.

[DRAFT]

Sponsored Content

Paid for by Citizens for Knowledge and Safety

AMERICAN PORTRAIT: BILLY H.

Let's imagine a boy named Billy H., who likes to dig in his parents' backyard looking for dinosaur bones. At night, he clings to a stuffed purple triceratops that he once found in his parents' attic and without which he cannot go to sleep. The man who lives by himself next door, a Mr. M., has an epiphany tattoo that says **DOES NOT UNDERSTAND BOUNDARIES**, a tattoo that is correlated with child molestation. Mr. M. is canny enough to wear long-sleeved shirts exclusively and has evaded the attention of Billy H.'s parents, of local law enforcement, and of other community leaders. One day Billy decides to ring Mr. M.'s doorbell to ask whether he can dig for dinosaur bones in his backyard. Mr. M. says that Billy would be more than welcome to do so, and that in fact he has heard rumors about dinosaur bones in his backyard, so Billy will have a lot of work to do and should first come inside for a glass of lemonade.

Imagine if Mr. M.'s telltale tattoo had been in a database, allowing law enforcement officials to keep track of whether he had, say, moved next door to a child. Unfortunately, Billy lives in a country that will defend an abstraction called "privacy" even if that means delivering him into the hands of a man who means him the worst of harm.

But let's say that Mr. M. does not mean Billy the very *worst* of harm. Let's say that Billy is only molested, rather than molested and murdered. He graduates high school and college with excellent grades, though also with persistent social and particularly sexual difficulties. Perhaps he pursues graduate work in paleontology at Columbia University, and pursues it successfully. One beautiful spring day, on that campus's storied steps, he strikes up a conversation with Angela R., who is pursuing an MFA in fiction. They share a taste for worlds that either no longer exist or never did. On their fifth or sixth date, he tells her of his molestation, and she listens with great sympathy but does not, as other girls have tended to, treat him like a wounded bird. As they both near completion of their thesis work, they move in together into a small apartment in Astoria; there are promises of postdoctoral fellowships and the strong prospect of a tenure-track position for him, and impressive publication in *The Paris Review* and *Granta* for her.

On the morning of their graduation, Billy puts on his cap and gown and looks forward to hugging his parents, looks forward to telling them that despite all that has happened he has forged a meaningful, fulfilling, and joyful life, something he could never have done without their unwavering support. Though he has blamed them in the past, he understands that they would have done anything that they could have to save him from Mr. M., if only they had known about Mr. M.'s tattoo.

Seeing Angela in her cap and gown, Billy tells her, quite truthfully, that she looks beautiful. He takes her hand, and together they walk to the subway. A train arrives just as they reach the top of the steps, as though it has been chartered just for them. As soon as they sit down, Angela puts her head on Billy's shoulder, and they both gaze at the Manhattan skyline. She is reaching up to brush his tassel out of his eyes when they are both suddenly reduced to bloody bits of viscera.

Several hundred other people on board the train are blown apart immediately, or burn to death slowly, each of them with their own families, hopes, delusions, triumphs, disappointments, and aspirations.

It will later be discovered that the bomber had an epiphany tattoo that read: **WANTS TO BLOW THINGS UP**.

Perhaps there are valid reasons to keep epiphanies secret. Perhaps these reasons outweigh the right of Billy H. not to be abused as a child and murdered as an adult. But if you believe that they do, we would ask: Would you want to be the one to tell Billy's parents—who, as the bomb goes off, have just arrived at Columbia University to celebrate with their son—how they will be spending the day instead?

CHAPTER

35

I handed my father this piece when I met him for dinner at an Italian restaurant adjacent to Grand Central where I knew he frequently dined with Leah. It had been many months since I had seen him; the dinner had been my suggestion, mostly so I could show my father what I had written. He read it while we waited for our bruschetta. I wasn't sure whether I was picking a fight or whether I was irrationally hoping that he would approve of my work, but as he read his face appeared to be doing something that I could describe only as "beaming with pride."

"I know you think I did everything wrong when I raised you," he said when he was finished, "but I must have done *something* right to raise a son capable of writing such high-quality horseshit."

"Thanks, Dad."

"The compliment is genuine. Reading this, it . . . it *does* something to me. I should want to laugh you out of this restaurant for writing something this contrived, cloying, cynical, shameless. But somehow I'm actually *moved* by this nonsense. Where are they publishing it?"

"They're not publishing it. They told me to write shorter, not to use writers as characters, and to try for a more straightforward tone. But they said they're cutting it down and using it as the basis for a thirty-second commercial. They're very happy."

"That's very good. I'm very glad that they're happy with you at work."

I squished a dry piece of bread into a tiny bowl filled with olive oil. "Are they happy with *you* at work?"

My father, despite his conflict of interest, was informally advising Ismail's defense team—"defense team" seemed like a strange term for the group of lawyers trying to force the government to actually file charges against Ismail that they could defend him against, but it was the closest term available. Whatever those lawyers should be called, my father's law partners wanted him as far away from them as possible.

"They'll probably be even less happy with me once they've seen the commercial based on your piece," my father said. "Hell, when I read this, even *I* think: How could that bastard Isaac Lowood place the rights of child molesters and terrorists above the life of Billy H.? I want to give myself a lethal injection for serving as an accomplice in the murder of this dear sweet boy, this cherubic Billy H., and if someone were to say that I can't be given the death penalty for participating in the murder of a character in a sentimental paranoid fantasy, I would sue them for making defamatory comments about Nonexistent Americans."

"Enough, Dad."

"Is it enough? Do you have any idea what you're doing by working for Vladimir Harrican? If I were someone who had not been following the debate closely and I saw something like this, I would be in favor of forcing Adam to make epiphanies a matter of public record. I would be in favor of *requiring everyone to get epiphanies.* This is going to solidify the idea that just because Adam looks at you and thinks you want to blow things up—which even *he* says can mean a lot of different things—that means you're a terrorist. You'll be wrecking Ismail's life all over again."

"Come on, Dad. Nothing I write could ever have the impact you're talking about. Poetry makes nothing happen."

"Right, but this isn't poetry. This is ad copy. Ad copy can make a whole lot happen."

Of course, I had written it because I wanted to make something happen. I wanted to make sure that no one ever again met the fate of the Soricillo twins or the victims of Ziad Jarrah, murdered by men who had already been caught by the epiphany machine.

"I hope you're right," I said.

"If," my father said, "you care about the childhood friend who, because of you, was tortured and who, because of you, continues to sit isolated in a cell, or for that matter if you care about anything at all, you will quit this job tomorrow morning."

"If I quit, then I'll have to live off of you."

"There are worse things than living off your father, you know."

This was so surprising that I asked him to repeat it. He did not repeat it but instead said: "Destroying the lives of the innocent, for instance."

"Are you offering me money? Because I'm not going to take it."

"Why not? I've always known that you're very talented, and even though you're using your gifts for evil right now, this proves it. Quit your job and write. It's why you're here on earth. It's also why Ismail is here on earth, from everything I hear, but unfortunately I can't immediately put Ismail in a position to write. You, I can immediately put in a position to write. Giving you money was why I have made way too much of it for way too long. If anything is supposed to happen, it's this."

"I'm sorry, but I just want to have a job. I want to have *this* job."

And I did. Waking each morning with a clear purpose for the day, firmly believing (much of the time) that my work had clear value, getting paid a salary that it would not have humiliated me to publicly admit—I took such delight in all of these things that the unhappiness I had felt for so long had transformed into an exceedingly rare kind of unhappiness: one that could be lived with.

"Why are you doing this, Venter? Why did you show me this?"

"Because it's work I've done and I want to share it with my father."

313

"I think you gave it to me for a different reason. I think you knew that once I read this indecent filth you're writing for that indecent man, there would be no way that you could remain my son."

"I thought you said you thought it was good."

"I do think it's good! That only makes it worse. You seem to find *fulfillment* in destroying your best friend. Do you?"

"I find fulfillment in exposing terrorists. If Ismail weren't a terrorist, he wouldn't still be locked away."

"Do you know what it's been like for me these past few years, hearing stuff like that from people I respect, and from one person I love? Hearing over and over that people are guilty because they've been arrested? Hearing that something is true just because it's written on somebody's arm? And now people are saying that even if Ismail was innocent when he was arrested, he has to be kept a prisoner because he's surely been turned against the United States by now. Can you empathize with what it feels like to hear that nonsense presented as hardheaded logic? It makes me feel like I'm the crazy one."

"Maybe you are."

This was the closest to crying I had ever seen him. "Well," he said, putting his napkin down. "Then I guess we have nothing more to say to each other. The machine was wrong about Ismail, but it really was right about me. I never should have become a father. Nothing I can do about that now except wish you the best. So long."

He stood up and turned away, leaving Billy H. at the table along with money for food and tip. "Oh, one more thing," he said. He pulled an envelope from his pocket and dropped it next to my bread plate. "I brought these for that problem you're having with Rebecca. You'll want to take one pill one hour beforehand. There might be a bluish tint to your vision, but that's okay. My doctor says it works better on an empty stomach, but I don't know whether that's true because I've never used them. My doctor hands out free samples to all of his male patients over fifty."

By now I could make out the outline of little triangular pills pushing against the envelope.

"Dad," I said. "Are you giving me Viagra?"

"I can't be your father anymore, but I still want you to have a tolerable life."

"How did you know that Rebecca and I are having problems?"

"'Problems' is the wrong word. You have a medical issue and I'm offering a medical solution."

"Rebecca called you and told you?"

"I wouldn't have to embarrass us both like this if you had just gone to the doctor with Rebecca like she asked."

I felt torn between wanting to run away and wanting to burrow a hole deep in the ground and never leave it.

"This is such a betrayal," I said.

"*This* is such a betrayal? Don't you see that after everything you've done I'm still trying to help you? Don't take them. Don't worry. They're the last thing I'll ever give you."

Now he was on his way and he was really gone. Hatred for my father and Rebecca sloshed in my stomach along with too much bread.

I walked out into the lobby, which echoed with the steps of the handful of late commuters. I could now claim the distinction of having been definitively rejected by both of my parents, one in infancy and one in adulthood—a stronger indication than anything else in my life that I was marked for the great, special destiny of which I desultorily dreamed.

I suddenly realized that what I had needed was a clean break from everyone I had thought I loved. My father, Rebecca: I would continue to be dependent on their opinions for as long as they were in my life.

Rebecca did not pick up her cell phone, so I left a voice mail breaking up with her.

I stepped onto the escalator that would take me down into Grand Central proper and then release me into a city that, however many humiliations I had suffered in it, was still an only slightly sagging breast of the new world. I was impotent before my twenty-fifth birthday, and yet a great glad light shone from within me, because I knew, with total serene certainty, that I would never see Rebecca or my father ever again.

CHAPTER

— · · ✦ · · —

36

Rebecca and I were married three years later, in July of 2009. The wedding was held in Brooklyn Bridge Park, which offered a spectacular view of the Manhattan skyline, at least theoretically—our wedding day was rainy and foggy and we couldn't see much. Our guests couldn't hear much, for that matter, with our vows drowned out by the D train. I was grateful for that, because what I had to say was only for Rebecca, and were the sorts of truths that become lies if too many people hear them. I told her that she had made me a much better person, much more relaxed with myself, and she had done this by giving me someone to care about more than I cared about myself. Because of her, I told her, my tattoo now really was false, because she had liberated me from caring about the thoughts of anyone other than her, and what she thought was so important that the word "opinion" was completely inadequate. I kissed her and then we were married.

I felt better than I ever had before—certainly better than I had felt when I swore off Rebecca three years earlier, a moment that, given how much I loved Rebecca right now, I was very grateful had passed.

After leaving my father that night at Grand Central, I had wandered around New York until, deciding that I had no real friends left with whom to stay, I found myself at the apartment of Cesar Solomon. I had the address because I had been invited to his housewarming party, but had not gone because I did not want to be asked how it felt to have once been the roommate of a now-famous novelist. My image of his apartment included lots of shiny silver surfaces, a vast kitchen and a vaster couch, and a roster of women wearing only Cesar's button-down shirts. The reality was that Cesar's apartment, though it was bigger and nicer than mine, was not all that much bigger or nicer than mine, and there were no women, at least when I arrived. There was not even the sound of furious typing, followed by a groan of frustration at the interrupting knock at the door. Instead, Cesar just looked wan, depressed, unlike I had ever seen him.

Cesar explained that he was having a crisis of faith, both in his fiction and in fiction in general. He had come to the conclusion that fiction no longer had any power to affect anyone's consciousness, if it ever did. He needed to find a new way of engaging with the way people thought. It occurred to me to be disappointed in this banal crisis, and also once again to wonder what Ismail would have written by now, whether it would have been better or at least more searching than what Cesar had written, but I decided I wanted to be more generous to Cesar and to not think at all about Ismail. Also, I reminded myself, Ismail's plays hadn't even been all that good. After Cesar and I had talked for two hours—during which I said almost nothing—he told me that he considered me the best friend he had ever had and one of the smartest people he had ever known, and I thought again about our friendship, which suddenly seemed much deeper and more rewarding than it ever had before.

I crashed on Cesar's sofa for two months, through a flirtation with my coworker Kristen. On our first date, at a diner in Brooklyn, I ordered chicken fingers and a milkshake. We joked about how this is what I would have ordered when I was a child (pound cake was not on the menu), and I made a bunch of other easy jokes, and she laughed and seemed very much into me. All I could think about was how Rebecca would have been pushing back against my shtick and how much I missed that already. I went on some more dates with Kristen, and then she suggested that we do something crazy and move in together, so we did. Kristen and I talked about some studies that suggested that one's mid-twenties were the optimal time in one's life to get married. A few months passed, and we talked about how other studies suggested that waiting until one's thirties was much better, both for happiness and income, and of course we also talked about how all these studies were meaningless, since the only thing that mattered was whether Kristen and I were in love, though actually that wasn't the thing that mattered, since passion never lasted, and according to many studies what really mattered was a solid foundation of friendship, though it couldn't just be friendship, since there also had to be a solid foundation of passion. Kristen wound up going to graduate school in sociology across the country, and I wound up getting back together with Rebecca, who took me back and dismissed our most recent breakup as an understandable aftershock of my final falling-out with my father.

Now I was married to Rebecca, the ceremony was done, and it had almost been perfect. *Almost* because I had, until the very second the rabbi told us we were married, somehow managed to harbor the hope that I would catch a glimpse of an aging, fox-fur-clad woman on the carousel, watching the wedding from a distance, and that I would know instantly that this was my mother. But no such old woman was anywhere to be seen.

The absences of my father and mother left their very different marks, but for the most part, in the immediate aftermath of the ceremony, as people were congratulating Rebecca and me and I was looking at Rebecca's beautiful, happy face, I was thinking about how happy I was, and also about the remarkable fact that thinking that I was happy was not destroying my happiness.

Then I noticed Ismail's mother coming toward us, her graying hair uncombed, her white dress unwashed.

"I curse you! You must face justice!"

I looked around, trying to see whether the guests were on her side or mine, but none of them seemed to notice, and they just kept chatting among themselves, making only the most obvious jokes about sex. She got closer and continued to yell at me, and then I realized that it was not Ismail's mother but merely a crazy homeless woman. I breathed in relief, as anyone can survive being yelled at by a crazy homeless woman, regardless of whether the crazy homeless woman is right.

Ismail had finally received a trial, of sorts. Though the government did not even try to charge him with actually planning an attack, Ismail was convicted of material support for terrorism; according to the government, some of the money that he had earned at Blockbuster in high school to send to Bosnia and Chechnya had ended up in the hands of, if not Al Qaeda, then other jihadist groups. Ismail had been silent throughout the trial, refusing to speak even to Leah or his mother. The sentence was a staggering seventeen years. I somehow took this as validation for having turned Ismail in in the first place. Lacking the courage of my convictions, I took courage from Ismail's conviction.

Perhaps it was imperative that I face justice. But I would never face justice and so I faced my bride instead.

Apart from a handful of Rebecca's friends and my coworkers at Citizens for Knowledge and Safety, the receiving line consisted almost entirely of Rebecca's family, who would be my family now. But the people in her family were as pleasant as any people, which is to say not very, but tolerably. And, in Rebecca, I had all the family I needed.

My new bride and I were sharing a lobster dish with some sort of creamy sauce—a secret joke about our sex life, which had long since returned with full vigor and no more than half a Viagra—when my new father-in-law got up to give a toast.

"For much of the last decade I've lived with one big question," her father said. "What did I do to drive my little girl into that guy's scribbled-on arms?"

He looked around for laughter and he got it, including from me.

"Of what did I give her too much or too little?" he continued. "Love? B vitamins? Exposure to death? Should I have stopped her from quitting the field hockey team? Why, when I raised her to be an independent woman in control of her own destiny, did she fall for this cult reject?"

This time when he looked around for laughter, he did not get it. He was attacking me, but I still felt sympathy for him. There's nothing sadder than not getting a laugh.

"Skip the toasts and stick to ears, noses, and throats!" some cousin shouted out, and *this* got a laugh.

"Let me finish," her father said. He took off his coat and handed it to the DJ, who accepted it because he did not know what else to do. Then he removed a cufflink and let it clank onto the floor. "So then I suddenly realized: all I had to do to get my questions answered was ask the epiphany machine!"

He pushed his sleeve up and held his arm high.

DISGUISES REGRET WITH CONTEMPT

He proceeded to say a lot of things about how this sounded like a generic cliché, but it was absolutely true of him. He said how relieved he was to have this out on his arm instead of cooped up in his head. He said all the things I had heard so many people say, each thinking it had never been said before. I was fairly certain that he was insulting me, whether he consciously intended to or not, but since he and everyone else were looking at me expecting to feel moved, I tried to feel moved.

"Most important," her father said, "this tattoo has made me realize how lucky I am that my daughter has found such a wonderful man, who is **DEPENDENT ON THE OPINION OF OTHERS**. For a long time, I thought this dependency was a mark of cowardice, of an inability to think for himself, but now I know that I was simply projecting onto Venter my own unhappiness with the path my professional life has taken. I always wanted to become an Augustine scholar, but I never tried, because I was afraid of rejection and failure. I thought that Venter's tattoo suggested personality flaws similar to mine, that my daughter would end up with a husband as spineless as her father.

"Nothing could have been further from the truth. The fact that Venter is **DEPENDENT ON THE OPINION OF OTHERS** has led him to the highest peaks of bravery and of selfless accomplishment. If he had followed his own instincts, he might have tried to cover up for his best friend, unable to admit that his best friend was a terrorist." Rebecca's breathing changed; she was not happy that he was bringing up Ismail. "But Venter is **DEPENDENT ON THE OPINION** of the American people, and this led him to do the right thing and turn his friend in. This same dependency on the opinion of the American people led him to give up his self-centered dreams of being a writer and devote himself instead to the selfless if not especially lucrative cause of exposing terrorists and child molesters before they can hurt people.

"And now, Venter will be **DEPENDENT ON THE OPINION** of the most important people of all, his new wife and their future children, all of whom, I am confident, will always have the highest opinion of him."

Now there was very loud applause, including from Rebecca, who probably wanted to get this over with as quickly as possible. I stood up and applauded hard, surprised to find that I was crying.

Then, to delighted gasps from everyone assembled, my father-in-law ran across the dance floor, climbed up onto our table, and extended his arm for me to join him. Nobody else in the room seemed to think he was insulting me so probably he wasn't, and besides, everyone thought I should do what he wanted me to do. I took his hand and, trying not to step on any plates, joined him on top of the table. I quickly realized that the crowd was not going to let me get out of undoing my cufflink and rolling my sleeve up, so I did that, too.

Flashes from cell phone cameras assaulted my eyes, which gave me an excuse to close them and imagine myself as the brave man my father-in-law had spoken of.

TESTIMONIAL #92

NAME: Ismail Ahmed

DATE OF BIRTH: 10/07/1981

DATE OF EPIPHANY MACHINE USE: 07/25/1999

DATE OF INTERVIEW BY VENTER LOWOOD: N/A (Letter Written by Ismail Ahmed to Venter Lowood from ███████████████████████ ███████████████████, Date: ██████████

(Redacted by Order of the United States Department of ████████)

██

████████████████████████████████████ wedding ████████████

██

███████████████████ wedding ████████████████████████

██

██

██

██

██

██

██

██

██

███

██████████████████

███

██████████████████████████

██

██

███

████████████████████

██

███████ wedding ████████████████████████████████

███

███

███

███

███

████████████████████████████████

██████████████████████

CHAPTER

— · · ✦ · · —

37

I returned from my honeymoon determined to compel Adam, at long last, to make epiphanies public. I wanted to prove that my father-in-law's belief in me had not been misplaced.

There was no question that, up until now, Citizens for Knowledge and Safety had accomplished almost nothing. My father had not been completely wrong all those years ago about the ad—the commercial loosely inspired by what I had written had generated some hysterical cable-news segments calling for use of the machine to be required of all teachers to make sure that they weren't pedophiles. But as often happens, what we had expected to happen simply did not happen. Probably the most tangible effect of that ad, at least according to a blog post, had been an apparent uptick in wealthy parents requiring that prospective nannies use the machine, at the nannies' own expense, before permitting them near their children. So far, there had been no real momentum toward forcing Adam to divulge the epiphanies. That, I was determined, was going to change.

I was writing Adam an email to this effect—telling him that he was going to have to turn over epiphanies, that I was going to make sure of it myself—when our executive director looked over my shoulder and said that any communication I had with Adam was subject to a review process. My email was commented on and revised by the executive director, the communications director, and an intern who was said to have "a gift for conversational tone in formal email."

The process wound up taking three weeks. The result received this response from Adam:

Dearest V[D],

Since you're **DEPENDENT ON THE OPINION OF OTHERS**, maybe it's not such a good idea to give us so many reasons to think you're a prick.

Maybe not mine but sure as hell not yours,
A.L. (At a Loss—for why I wasted so much time on you)

My sense of clarity, purpose, and urgency was once again clouded. For the next week or so, I still fretted about the children that Citizens for Knowledge and Safety was failing to save, but mostly I fretted over whether to get lunch at the Quiznos across the street or the Pret A Manger a few blocks away.

I remember distinctly that I had just chosen Quiznos and returned from lunch to settle in for a long afternoon of avoiding mostly uninteresting work by looking at completely uninteresting things online when the office erupted in a "Holy shit!" chorus.

The New York Times was reporting that real-estate billionaire Si Strauss had been arrested. Apparently he had been accused of sexually abusing at least a dozen boys whom he had met through his baseball charity.

One of my coworkers, sounding a little winded, asked me if I had gotten to the eighth paragraph yet.

The eighth paragraph stated that when Si Strauss had been arrested, slightly after dawn in his apartment, he had not been wearing a shirt, and on his forearm was a faded tattoo that read: **DOES NOT UNDERSTAND BOUNDARIES.**

I thought back to his testimonial. Of course he had lied about his tattoo. Nobody gets a tattoo as nice as **BURNS WITH DESIRE TO MAKE A DIFFERENCE.** For a couple of minutes, I believed that I had known the truth all along.

The next morning, I woke up thinking I should write to Adam again. Instead, I checked the news and discovered that he had killed himself.

Adam Lyons is taking a walk through Central Park, trying to ignore the proximity of Strawberry Fields, when his phone buzzes with the news that Si Strauss has been arrested. In the minutes afterward, it is unlikely that anyone notices the ashen old man taking slow, painful steps, as the park is full of ashen old men taking slow, painful steps. Maybe there are three or four who recognize Adam Lyons as the magic-tattoo dude, and another one or two who recognize him as the Man Who Killed John Lennon, but no one says, "Hey, your patron is a pedophile." No one emerges from the bushes with a baseball bat to give him what he deserves.

Or maybe *this* is what he deserves, to walk unrecognized through the city that is so different from the one to which he introduced the epiphany machine, and yet has been so unaffected by it. The park would have fallen first to the muggers and the junkies and second to the blissful jogging bankers even if he had left the machine in the trash heap.

Did Adam know what Si Strauss was doing to the kids in his baseball charity? We do not know the answer, any more than we know whether Adam in fact faked all the epiphanies, or what really happened to him in his past. But I suspect a shameful answer: he knew and he did not know, just like everyone who came to him.

There was one thing that Adam did unquestionably know—he knew, just before Si Strauss received his epiphany all those decades ago, that Si was an angry rich kid who, if he was happy with his epiphany, could solve Adam's legal woes. Adam also knew that Si, as he was settling into the epiphany chair about to be tattooed, babbled strangely about the children he watched beneath his office window. Perhaps more crucially, Adam continued to know this immediately after Si Strauss received his tattoo, and for years afterward. Eventually, Si ceased to be a rich kid who could solve Adam's legal woes and became a rich man who often did solve Adam's legal woes—as well as create some legal woes for people Adam didn't like—but the basic facts remained the same: Adam knew what Si's epiphany was, and he said nothing.

With good reason! What did **DOES NOT UNDERSTAND BOUNDARIES** mean, after all? It sounded like a compliment. It *was* a compliment. No one who achieved anything worthwhile understood boundaries. Certainly, Adam never understood boundaries: the boundary between huckster and prophet, the boundary between deceiving someone and enlightening them, the boundary between never lying and lying with every word. Not even he was sure whether the machine was real. He would often get a sense of what the machine was going to write before it wrote it, but that did not necessarily mean he was unconsciously guiding the epiphanies; it could just mean that whatever entity was writing the epiphanies was giving him, clearly its chosen emissary, some advance notice.

True, two men before Si who had received **DOES NOT UNDERSTAND BOUNDARIES** tattoos had later been arrested for what they had done to children. This had made Adam paranoid about that tattoo. Eventually, Adam started taking matters into his own hands—or more precisely the hands of some guys he had known growing up—but that had led to beatings for at least four people who were almost certainly innocent. Probably innocent. He couldn't be sure, which is why, or part of why, he never said anything about these false positives to anyone who worked for him, though surely they must have known that a one-to-one correlation of tattoo to villain was too clean to be true. One man had been crippled in his beating, and afterward no evidence could be found against him other than his tattoo. If the machine was not real, all

Adam was doing was ordering the assault of people about whom he had some nebulous negative feeling. True, Adam cringed every time Si mentioned his baseball charity, which he did all the time, but hurting or exposing Si might very well be hurting or exposing an innocent man. It would also mean putting an end to all the good work that Si was making it possible for Adam to do. And yes, true— *yes, true*—Adam had worried about what the downfall of Si might mean for the machine's reputation.

Now the machine's reputation was ruined forever. For the last several years, Adam has thought it would be worth it for the machine's reputation to be ruined, if a ruined reputation meant a free Ismail. But Ismail is still locked up and the machine's reputation is ruined anyway.

It does not seem very long ago that Adam first discovered the machine. It does not seem very long ago that Adam was a child, himself a potential victim for earlier incarnations of Si Strauss. Adam spent his childhood as a literal kid in the candy store his father owned on the Lower East Side. Candy Lyons. Adam's father said that he changed the family name to Lyons from Loewenstein because it sounded better for the store, evoking child-pleasing images of lions made of candy, ferocity made sweet, as well as rhyming with "dandelions," which is every child's favorite flower even though it is a weed. Uncle Yoav, a rabbi, said that Adam's father "changed his name to please the goyim," but for much of Adam's childhood that seemed okay, since the goyim came to Candy Lyons, and the more goyim came to Candy Lyons, the more candy there was for young Adam Lyons. What's in either a name or a rose when one has sweets? Adam spent his childhood days growing happily fat, ringing up customers and swiping candy, all while listening to the backroom whir of his mother's sewing machine, on which she sewed ever-larger clothes for him.

Then, slowly, Adam learned what had happened across the ocean when he was a toddler, and it made him want to spit out every piece of candy he was given. He looked at the goyim who came into his father's store, and he wanted to ask why they had waited until the last possible moment to lift their chocolate-stained fingers for his people.

"Your name is Adam Loewenstein," Uncle Yoav said, "and you are a man of the Jewish people."

"My name is Adam Loewenstein," Adam said to his father, "and I am a man of the Jewish people."

To Adam's disappointment, his father did not slap him. He merely gave a big shrug. "I have this store, and your uncle Yoav has his synagogue, but we are both giving people the same thing: distractions."

"Distractions from what?"

"From the fact that it's all a big nothing. Some people say life is a joke, but they're wrong. Jokes have a point."

Adam asked Uncle Yoav about this, and Yoav gave an identical shrug and said: "Your father only says life is meaningless because it's easier to say that than it is to face the truth, which is that he is a man of the Jewish people, just as you are."

This word "truth" held great power for Adam. He sensed that there was indeed such a thing as truth, submerged but waiting to be brought to the surface, on which it should be written in big letters so that everybody could see it. He returned to his father. "My name is Adam Loewenstein and I am a man of the Jewish people," he said.

Again his father shrugged. "Better cut out the bacon and the cheeseburgers."

Maybe only to prove that he could, Adam did cut out the bacon and the cheeseburgers, and started spending every Friday night at the synagogue where Uncle Yoav was a rabbi.

A curious thing happened with Adam's Jewish education. There was so much tradition, and so much commentary on the tradition, that Adam felt constantly confused. The Book of Ecclesiastes sounded exactly like Adam's father—all is vanity, there is nothing new under the sun. Adam wished that there would be something in the Torah or the Talmud—or *somewhere*—that would sum everything up. Of course this was Adam's fault—Yoav told him that he had eaten too much of his father's candy, that he had gotten too used to the American sweet tooth, to the American taste for easy answers—and he strived to be more like Uncle Yoav.

"You want to be just like Uncle Yoav?" his father said. "Here." He reached behind the counter and tossed Adam a pair of dice. "Hope you're better with these than he is."

Adam was twelve by now, only a few months away from his bar mitzvah, old enough to understand that his uncle was a gambler, and perhaps he did understand that—certainly, when he and the other boys practiced reading the Torah for Uncle Yoav, he understood that those big men sitting in the back row were not there to hear Adam's stumbling Hebrew. But it was nonetheless a surprise, shortly before Adam's fifteenth birthday, when Adam's father informed him that they had to sell Candy Lyons to pay for Yoav's gambling debts. It was somehow less of a surprise when, less than a year after that, Adam's father dropped dead of a heart attack.

"You killed my father," Adam told his uncle when he came to sit shiva.

"Candy killed your father. Candy and bacon and cigars and whiskey. But mostly it was not having faith in God."

"You bankrupted my father, you killed my father, and now you insult him?"

His uncle shrugged widely. Since he was very young, Adam had been imitating this shrug that his uncle and father shared. Now he could not seem to shake it.

"You're a smart kid and you read a lot of books," Uncle Yoav said.

"You should have figured out by now that gambling is God's vice. He makes bets that people can be good, and He keeps losing bigger and bigger, but He hasn't left the table yet."

Adam imagined himself strangling Yoav right there in the living room. Instead, Adam said nothing and did not move, and Yoav excused himself to console Adam's mother. Adam's mother had always found Yoav distasteful and irritating, and that did not change after the death of Adam's father. One thing that did change: his mother, who had spent so much time cheerily scolding children in their store for buying too much candy, now spent all of her time hunched over her sewing machine, mending clothes for people in the neighborhood for a pittance, while Adam dropped out of high school to work as a short-order cook.

The job was hot and the hours were long, and Adam was amazed at the amount of fat and sugar and salt it took to persuade people to nourish themselves. Did they really hate life so much that they had to be blackmailed with a rush of pleasure just to agree to sustain it?

Dice held great appeal for the other guys who worked at the diner, but none for Adam, so when his shift was over, he would go home and sit at his typewriter until he could see streaks of dawn light over the alleyway below his Upper East Side window. Under the influence of Hemingway, Adam hoped to type one true sentence after another until those things linked together to form a novel that would make him famous and earn him enough money to buy a house for his mother, where she could sew or not sew as she pleased. But he found that everything he wrote was dead.

Soon he found that his mother was dead, too. Actually, he found his mother dead, slumped over her sewing machine, her cold nose pressing a piece of cloth. Adam called Uncle Yoav and asked for money for the funeral, but Yoav said no, it would be better for Adam's character to pay for the funeral himself.

Adam could have screamed in anger. Instead, he silently hung up the phone and carried his mother's sewing machine back to his apartment, picked up his typewriter, carried the typewriter and the sewing machine to a pawnshop along with some of his mother's jewelry, and had her in the ground by sunset the next day, as required by Jewish law. The next morning, he resolved never to follow Jewish law again.

Now he started playing dice. Amazing, the way the other guys would say certain words they thought were lucky or turn their hats a certain way, as though what they were hoping for was not a few bucks but a demonstration that someone or something out there cared whether they won a few bucks. For Adam, the appeal was the reverse: he reveled in the randomness. Throwing dice in an alley was a beautiful, even artistically noteworthy concentration of the randomness of the world. Throwing dice was a joke without a point, and that was what made it worthwhile. Another thing that made it worthwhile was that he won. A lot. So much that if he ever started keeping track, which he wouldn't, he was pretty sure he would find that he was doubling his salary from the diner. So much that the other guys thought that he must be cheating.

Mostly out of boredom, he took a second job, as a mover. One day, Adam was one of two men carrying a bed for a girl who was moving out of her parents' apartment and into one she would share with a roommate. While the other mover watched television with the roommate, Adam was invited into the bed he had carried.

Shira knew more than Adam did—she knew where to go in Greenwich Village to hear poetry and music, she knew that Joyce was better than Hemingway, and Kafka better than Joyce. He wanted to think she was wrong, but then he read Joyce and Kafka and he saw that she was right. He focused on the word "dead" in "The Dead"; he focused on what Gabriel Conroy learned, and thought about whether it might have made a difference if Gabriel had learned what he learned decades before he did.

Stop playing dice, Shira said. But God was sending him some kind of message, something about chance and fate, and Adam needed to learn to read it. A few months later, Shira moved in with a dentist in Greenwich Village. (Years later, Shira and the dentist moved from Greenwich Village to Greenwich, Connecticut, as it became more acceptable for Jews to do so. Shira and the dentist had three children, none of whom, as it happened, ever used the epiphany machine.)

Adam played more dice.

On the evening of his twentieth birthday—October 9, 1960—Adam won twenty dollars and got very drunk. Walking home, he wandered by a trash heap in an alley, and his eye was caught by what looked like a pink baby's blanket wedged between two garbage bags. This is understandable, as our eyes are made to be caught. But they are also made to wriggle free, and he should have seen very quickly that there was no baby discarded in the garbage. And yet now he was pawing at the blanket, trying to get a hold on it but knocking over the garbage instead. Within a minute, he had a banana peel in his hair and an antique sewing machine in his arms. There was no reason for him to think the sewing machine was the one that had belonged to his mother, the one he had sold to pay for her funeral. There was no reason for him to cradle the sewing machine like it was a baby.

If his forearm had not ended up beneath the needle, many lives might have been very different.

FIRST MAN TO LIE ON

Adam had long ago stopped believing in God, and yet he was immediately flooded with a feeling that this had been sent to him by something that was at the very least God-adjacent. The same God-adjacent thing—maybe the same lowercase *g* "god"—that had led him to win at dice. Adam had indeed been lying down on his responsibility to lead a meaningful life, and this god had come to show him the way.

He carried the heavy machine the few blocks to his Eighty-fourth Street apartment, examined it, figured out how the ink was loaded, and then he sank down on his bed, heavy and giddy with the weight of the knowledge of how he was going to spend the rest of his life.

He talked about the machine with a few guys he played dice with, on the theory that some of them would suspect he was supernaturally favored because he won so frequently. He made plans to meet a few of them after work one evening. One guy genuflected, and then another guy punched him in the face.

"So you decided to make fun of us by getting a tattoo bragging that you cheat," one of them said, while the fist of another one landed on his nose. More fists landed on his stomach, his eyes, his mouth. He was probably lucky to lose only one tooth.

It took him a couple of weeks to heal, and then he got a job at a different diner. As though God (or the machine's god) were testing him, around this time there was a scare around the city that tattoo parlors were spreading hepatitis B, and though this was not true, tattooing was outlawed in the city. Adam tried to make friends in the underground tattooing scene that cropped up in the aftermath of the law, but every tattoo artist thought he was a crank, a crazy person. He found ways to get needles and ink—thankfully, standard needles and ink worked in the machine and did not, as he feared the first time he loaded it, destroy it—but he had a strong sense that suppliers were overcharging him and an absolute certainty that there was nothing he could do about it.

Adam asked for a late shift at the new diner, and he looked for lonely people who showed up and sat by themselves. He chatted with them, and eventually he invited them back to his place for whiskey. He got punched by a few men who thought he was making a pass at them; he disappointed a few other men who thought he was making a pass at them; and horrified several more who interpreted their tattoos to mean that they were queer. (In later years, he received grateful letters from members of each of these three groups for helping them come out.) Other men were told that they delayed their lives with fantasies of glory, or were compounding the misery of their lives by blaming those close to them for it, or were dependent on the opinion of others. (And two or three, yes, were told that they did not understand boundaries.) Only a few women used the machine in the early years, but of those who did, some were told that they had the strength to embark on careers they had dreamed of, or to leave men who beat or stifled them, and if Adam was a bit too proud of this, perhaps we may forgive him.

Users experienced pain, of course, but Adam also recognized in them a gambler's high. There was great excitement in giving yourself over to something, of closing your eyes and letting chance, a lover, artistic inspiration, heroin, or anything else have its way with you. Those few moments between settling in to the chair and reading the tattoo—that was the most life in many lives.

Or a few lives. The total number of users in the first four years did not surpass one hundred. Though some (mostly mocking) attention was given to the mimeographed flyers he put up around the city—with a drawing of the machine and the words "THE EPIPHANY MACHINE—EVERYONE ELSE KNOWS THE TRUTH ABOUT YOU, NOW YOU CAN KNOW IT, TOO"—for obvious reasons he could not put his address on the flyer, and so apart from those he approached himself, users found him only through rumor and word of mouth. He probably would have died an obscure New York curiosity—or a New York curiosity even more obscure than the one he did die as—had it not been for a concert performed at Shea Stadium on August 15, 1965.

Adam was entirely uninterested when he heard that the Beatles were playing a massive concert in Queens. Adam was an obsessive fan of Dylan, had seen some of his earliest performances in Village cafés, and had even approached him on two separate occasions about the machine, remaining a fan even after Dylan responded both times with open disdain. Adam also enjoyed and admired the Stones. But the Beatles, with their candy sound, held no appeal for him.

The Beatles did hold appeal for Lillian Secor, a recent high school graduate who had shaved her head and gotten an epiphany tattoo mainly to get any kind of tattoo, to horrify her parents and even her friends, and had found herself transformed by her tattoo, **HORRI-FIES TO CREATE LOVE**. Read one way, this was just the dismissive nonsense she ignored from her parents—that everything she did she did only for attention—but read another way, it told her that her refusal to do what was expected of her, to dress the way people wanted her to or do her hair the way people wanted her to or talk the way people wanted her to, was not solely an expression of anger, as even she thought it was, but rather a way to create love, a way to convince people to love things they were not expected to love, including themselves. This made her relax, at least a little bit, at least enough to attend a Beatles concert with thousands of identically screaming girls, where she intended to hand out flyers about the epiphany machine. She did not intend to run onto the field to hand one to John Lennon. But the love the crowd had for him was so intense that she wanted to create more of it—and if she ran onto the field, she would horrify the crowd in a way that would just make them love John more.

It is possible to find an interpretation of virtually every Beatles lyric from *Rubber Soul* onward as an insult or a paean to Adam Lyons—he is Father McKenzie in "Eleanor Rigby," he is Eleanor Rigby in "Eleanor Rigby," he is Doctor Robert, he is the sugar-plum fairy, he is the egg-man, he is the walrus, he is the fool on the hill, he is the holy roller of "Come Together." That the epiphany machine and John's penis are the twin subjects of "Happiness Is a Warm Gun" is almost universally accepted.

Most of these interpretations are probably nonsense, but in any case, John inspired many people to use the epiphany machine. (The precise number is lost to history; Adam never maintained a good record system and managed to lose the record book maintained by Rose Schuldenfrei Lowood, his assistant from 1972 to 1980.) It was almost impossible to stop the machine from attracting almost weekly attention from the tabloids, almost all of it fearful and alarmist. And it was absolutely impossible to stop the lawsuits.

Which is why Si Strauss had been so important. That day that Si showed up at his apartment, Adam thought he was finished. Then Si agreed to use the machine, and Adam saw the future that did in fact come to pass, the future in which Si covered Adam's legal bills and made it possible for Adam to enlighten more people. And then Adam saw Si's tattoo.

There was nothing Adam could have done—it's not as though Si would have been arrested or even questioned had Adam gone to the police. Instead, Adam continued to help people—even Uncle Yoav, who came for a tattoo in late '68 or early '69. Yoav told Adam that young American Jews had, just like young American goyim, gotten themselves stuck in the quicksand of endless questions, and if Yoav was going to help them get out, he would have to step into the quicksand, and thus Yoav's tattoo, under normal circumstances a serious offense against God, would be not only justified but necessary. The metaphor was nonsensical, but Adam felt a family affinity for nonsensical metaphors, and he felt a family affinity, too, for Yoav, an adrift gambler helpless before his compulsions, who needed an excuse, any excuse, to get a tattoo that might possibly set him on the right path.

NEED NOT HATE HIMSELF FOR NOT BEING AS GOOD AS HIS BROTHER

Yoav was angry about this tattoo, as so many were angry about their tattoos, but it did help him give up his gambling, and when he died he and Adam were friends.

Adam and John, too, were friends when John died. Most people forgot that, because John so often renounced Adam. He renounced Adam in favor of the Maharishi, and then, after a brief visit to the Maharishi, renounced the Maharishi in favor of Adam. At another point John renounced Adam for Arthur Janov and primal scream therapy. John decided that he had learned exactly the wrong lesson that night at Adam's after Shea Stadium, and that what mattered were not his fans' arms but their screams, the way their screams drowned out all of his stupid, pointless words and instead got straight to the loud bleating center of human need and desire. But eventually all that screaming started to sound to John forced and hollow, while his tattoo still looked almost as fresh as ever. Adam always knew that John would return; after all, Adam was fairly certain that without the epiphany machine, John would never have been drawn to the show of an artist known for her enigmatic phrases, most of them short enough to double as epiphany tattoos, or even shorter. Adam was certain that, without the epiphany machine, John would have never fallen in love when that artist handed him a card on which was written the word "Breathe." Adam tried not to be offended when John told him how this word and the word that Yoko's exhibit required him to climb a ladder and use a magnifying glass to read were far more brilliant, far more fundamental, than anything the epiphany machine might write. Breathe. Yes. These, John told Adam not only to hurt him, were the only words that mattered.

Adam saw John and Yoko only very rarely once they moved to New York, though they were only a park away, but unlike so much of the world he always liked Yoko. (Yoko, for her part, seems to have thought Adam was funny and charming, though she has always refused to believe that even Adam himself intended the machine to be taken seriously. She regarded Adam as an artist, though perhaps one who might be well served to move on to a new work, rather than repeating himself over and over on new arms.) Adam felt very warmly toward both of them when, in December of 1980, a pudgy young man who couldn't stop talking about John Lennon came to use the machine. It wasn't unusual for a young man to come see Adam and talk a lot about John Lennon; nor was it unusual for a tattoo to be repeated. Adam even hoped that the young man would find motivation in receiving the same tattoo as his idol, and do something useful with his life. If he had known what Chapman's mountain was, or what kind of nothing Chapman saw from it, he would have slit that lonely and terrible man's throat without hesitation.

And then there was Si and his baseball charity. Yes, Adam had sensed what Si was, even if he had always refused to admit this to himself. This is why Adam kept Si away from his guests and from Rose Schuldenfrei, and would certainly never let him anywhere near Lennon. What happened to the boys that Si hurt is not Adam's fault, exactly, but Adam, for all his dismissive remarks about anything too long to fit on a forearm, has read a great deal of literature, and literature has exactly one thing to teach us: that it is our deepest and highest moral obligation to accept punishment for things that are not exactly our fault.

Adam spends the rest of the night drinking whiskey while sitting on the floor. He thinks for a long time about Venter Lowood, that poor lost boy who had no one to guide him. Then he pushes the curtain aside to enter the epiphany room one last time.

He lays his head down on the machine, sideways, so that his left ear touches the base. **FIRST MAN TO LIE ON**, indeed. He grabs the arm or the neck of the machine and prepares to pull the needle through his right ear.

In an ideal world, he would be able to read what the epiphany machine will write on his brain, but in an ideal world, the epiphany machine would not need to write anything at all. So he will have to dream the message to himself, as the needle passes through his ear on its way to write the last words to which Adam will fail to listen.

CHAPTER

— · · ✦ · · —

38

It was not easy to read about the suicide of a man who still meant a great deal to me, particularly given the grisly nature of the suicide. According to news reports, first responders had, in order to free Adam's corpse from the machine, been compelled to break the machine into several pieces. "Nothing supernatural was found inside," wrote a journalist who thought he was being funny. Rebecca comforted me and did not try to lecture me about how Adam had shielded a pedophile for many decades and so deserved to die miserable and alone. The next morning, I got a very unexpected email from my father, the first in three years apart from perfunctory congratulations on my wedding, inviting me to a funeral service he had organized for Adam.

The service was held in a small basement theater in the East Village. There was no one at the box office, though the door was open. No one in the lobby, either. I thought that I might have the wrong address, but I pushed through into the theater itself. At first that looked empty, too, but then I saw the back of a woman's head. It looked like Leah. It was Leah.

It occurred to me, briefly, that this was an elaborate plot to kill me.

"I didn't think you'd be here," I said.

"Adam spent the last several years trying to help Ismail," Leah said, without looking at me. "And playing him made me come into my own as an actor. I'm grateful to him, and I always liked him. I liked him enough that I'm distressed to see someone he hated at his funeral."

"Not many of us get to curate our own funerals."

"That sounds almost like something he would say, except clunky, and somehow totally wrong. All that time you spent with him, and you have no idea who he is."

I didn't want anyone to walk in to us arguing. "I've heard good things about your show," I said.

Leah was doing a one-woman show—probably in this theater, I now realized—called *Jane Payne*, the real-life code name given to a female CIA agent who photographed the mutilated genitals of a terrorism suspect whom the CIA had rendered to Morocco for torture. Leah's dream had become to use theater to bring American torturers to justice, and to free Ismail, among others. I had checked some blogs and the reactions to the play were quite positive, though I didn't know for sure how things worked in the theater world, and whether people only said positive things and blew smoke up each other's asses all the time like in most other professions.

"Thanks," she said. She explained that the rabbi my father had hired had gotten cold feet because of Adam's tattoo, because of his flagrantly blasphemous attitude toward the religion of his birth, because of his sacrilegious founding of his own quasi-religion, and because of the fact that his lifelong patron was a pedophile whom Adam had shielded.

"When you put it that way," I said, "it sounds like he shouldn't get a Jewish funeral."

For the first time since I had walked in, she met my eye. "I'm not your wife, the one with the baby-murderer name," she said. "I don't find you or your jokes cute or charming. You're a monster who put the love of my life in prison for no reason."

This was a cruel thing to say, but I could not exactly say I did not deserve it. My father arrived and hugged Leah, and then he looked at me, and we were both unsure whether to hug, so we didn't. He apologized for being late—a judge had kept him longer than he had expected and then he had to make arrangements for Adam's body to be cremated, since no living relatives could be found who were willing to take responsibility for it.

He put his briefcase on one of the cheap, squeaky seats and then surveyed the auditorium.

"Seems awfully empty, huh? Well, I guess this is what we were expecting . . ."

With more grace than I could have managed, he took the stage and made us his audience.

NAME: Isaac Lowood

DATE OF BIRTH: 08/14/1951

DATE OF EPIPHANY MACHINE USE: 09/19/1974

DATE OF INTERVIEW BY VENTER LOWOOD: N/A (Eulogy for Adam Lyons Delivered on 09/20/2009)

I first met Adam when I was pursuing a Ph.D. in sociology at Columbia. I was younger than any of my classmates because I had skipped a grade in school, and I felt pressure to find a perfect subject for my dissertation, one that would allow me to display my brilliance. I was fascinated by the success of this man who seemed to be operating a religion out of his apartment, a religion to which he had attracted at least one of the most famous men on the planet, along with many others whom no one could argue had been driven insane by paparazzi flashbulbs. I should say that I did not think John Lennon was insane. I thought he was the world's greatest living genius, and if he thought there was something special about the epiphany machine, there must be something to it. Or maybe I was just tired of reading thick academic books and dense academic articles and wanted to read Adam's forearm koans for a little while. I started searching for him by seeking out downtown tattoo parlors, which were themselves generally not easy to find, and when I did find them, I was reliably sworn at, since almost all tattoo artists hated Adam. Not infrequently, they threatened to do something like tattoo "Dumb Fuck" on my ass if I didn't leave quickly enough. After a particularly humiliating encounter, I got on the subway feeling so demoralized that I couldn't even concentrate on my assigned reading, couldn't do anything except stare at the big bright graffiti that was all over the subway in those days.

This is when I noticed: "GO KNOW YOURSELF IN THE BIBLICAL

SENSE, ADAM LYONS!!! RUBICON EPIPHANY CORPORATION, 235 e. 84th st. Apt. #7 = THE GATES OF HELL. DON'T GO!!!!"

Adam always denied that he was the one who wrote that, and he might even have been telling the truth, but saying a place is Hell is of course an irresistible advertisement. I might have gone even if I hadn't already been looking for it.

I did not have any real plans for what I was going to do, or whether I was going to tell Adam that I was there to conduct research on him rather than on myself. I felt so nervous as I approached Eighty-fourth Street that I think I might have kept walking past the building and found a different dissertation topic if I hadn't fallen into step with a blond woman in a fox fur coat. I barely noticed her at first; on the Upper East Side in the seventies, it was hardly uncommon to see a blond woman in a fox fur coat. I'm not sure if I registered that she was on her way to the epiphany machine, but I may have, since word was that the machine was popular among bored rich girls. I do remember that she was the first one to speak; she said that she could tell from the way I was breathing that I was on my way to see Adam Lyons.

I said that I was, but that I could take a detour if she had another destination in mind—the closest I've ever come to earnestly using a pickup line, and, appropriately, she rolled her eyes at it. She told me to just come up to Adam's and have some whiskey, and she gave me this smile that was the sexiest thing I've ever seen.

Anyway, Rose, whose name I now knew, took me up to see Adam, and the place did not have the hypnotizing effect on me it has on so many—I thought, *This place* is supposed to be the navel of the world? *This place* captured Lennon's mind? I looked at the line to use the machine and saw somebody coming out holding a gauze pad to his arm chanting the old mantra "This isn't true! This isn't true! This isn't true!" I think his epiphany had something to do with expecting his wife to be his mother, or something similarly generic.

It took me a moment to notice the man who was draping a meaty arm around this man's shoulders. The man with the meaty arm was saying: "Don't worry about whether it's true. From now on, just look at what you do, look at how you feel about what you do. Just look: that's all the machine tells you to do."

Of course, that was the first time I saw Adam Lyons. I wound up staying well after everybody had left to chat with him and Rose. That night is when I first heard about his enthusiasm for breastfucking, his hilariously absurd theory that T. E. Lawrence was assassinated by the British to cover up the fact that he was gay, his fear that the CIA was trying to assassinate him, his preference for Dylan over Lennon, and his continuing disappointment that Dylan would not use the machine. But mostly I talked to Rose while Adam smoked a few joints. Adam knew how to get out of our way while not getting so much out of our way that we felt uncomfortable or pressured. We talked about how she had been taking care of her mom since her dad died, and about her decision to quit law school to work for Adam. That did not make a lot of sense to me, and I thought she might be brainwashed, but she said that law school taught you to use words to win a game, whereas Adam wanted you to stop playing games with words. That probably should have sounded cultlike, but I was so enamored of her that I thought there might be something to it. Toward the end of the night, they showed me the machine, and I was so scared that I blurted out that I was there to investigate the epiphany machine as a potential subject for my dissertation. To my surprise, Adam was flattered and said I could come to visit the apartment whenever I liked and take notes.

The next night I had dinner with Rose, and of course I was struck by her extraordinary wit and intelligence and Queens accent. At one point, she made a reference to "war-torn Europe," and I said that that phrase was hackneyed—mostly because I thought that girls liked it when you're smarter than they are. She told me that the next time I belittled her would be the last time I saw her. Believe me, I never belittled her after that.

I think that initially what I had in mind, Venter, was not entirely dissimilar from the testimonial project that you did for a while—I think

Adam may have asked you to do that in part, or maybe entirely, because of me, either to get my goat, or because he thought that, as my son, you would be a good candidate to do the work that I talked about doing. I did interview a few people, but I lost all those tapes long ago. Mostly I tagged along with Rose and did whatever she did—chat with people waiting in line and assuage their fears, occasionally put up cryptic flyers around the city, harass tattoo artists who were doing fake epiphany tattoos.

I was just in love with Rose and following her around like a besotted puppy. But I was genuinely amazed by the impact Adam seemed to be having on the lives of most people who used the machine. More than one heroin addict came by and got a tattoo that said something like **THIS IS THE ONLY MARK THAT BELONGS ON THIS ARM**, and I can think of three separate junkies who kept coming back and seemed to have gotten clean. Husbands stopped cheating on their wives, often because of something they had been told about their fathers. I was on board in every way. According to forms I filled out for my department, but also in my own mind, all of this was field research. I think even in Adam's mind I was doing field research. He talked to me a lot about his past, and he never suggested that I use the machine.

And then one day I stopped calling Rose or stopping by Adam's apartment. I couldn't think of any real reason; I just didn't feel like going anymore, or writing a dissertation about the machine, or continuing to date Rose, so I just stopped going and started looking for another dissertation topic and another girlfriend. I also changed my number so Adam and Rose couldn't call me.

Three weeks later, Adam showed up at my apartment. Venter, Leah, both of you knew Adam, so you're fully aware how rare it was for Adam to leave his own apartment, let alone show up unannounced at anyone else's. The first thing he said was: "Rose would kill me if she knew I was here." The second thing he said was: "I think you should use the epiphany machine." I told him that of course he thought I should use the epiphany machine; his entire trip was telling people that they should use this device he had found in a trash heap. He told me that if that was what I thought, then I hadn't been paying attention at all, because his role was to stop people from using the machine unless they felt absolutely compelled to use it and were using it for the right reasons. I had never seen him turn anybody away, so this struck me as standard cult-leader hogwash. I didn't tell him so, since I figured that if I did, he would just throw cult-leader hogwash on me, and then he would repeat the process until I was so drenched in hogwash that I would mistake it for clean water and start bathing in it and drinking it. So, instead, I told him that I didn't need to use the machine, because I already knew what my epiphany would be: **CANNOT COMMIT TO ANYTHING**. I had run away from the epiphany machine, not the first dissertation topic I had run away from, and I had run away from Rose, definitely not the first girl I had run away from.

Adam started shaking his head about midway through this, and by the end, he was doing a full, untethered Adam Shrug.

"You think my machine would waste its time talking about your commitment problems? Commitment problems are like the sniffles: everybody gets them sometimes, most of them aren't worth paying attention to since they usually go away on their own, and if they are worth paying attention to, that's only because they're symptoms of a much deeper problem. Do you go to a surgeon and expect him to hand you a tissue? I thought you were a smart guy. What the epiphany machine will tell you almost certainly has to do with your father."

I protested that I had only mentioned my father to him once or twice.

"Exactly," Adam said. "That's exactly what gives you away. You're training to become a professor, just like your father is a professor, so clearly you must have a very strong tie with your father."

I told Adam that my father, as a mathematician, had an extremely low opinion of sociology, which he called "a let's-pretend-it's-science science." He loved to remind me that I had once wanted desperately to be an astronomer, had even given lectures on the constellations at my hometown planetarium throughout high school, but I just hadn't been good enough at math to be an astronomer. I had been good enough at math to handle statistics, but not good enough at math to be an astronomer. So I had given up questions about the biggest systems in the universe for questions about the smallest ones. That was how my father had put it, anyway. Of course, I could have pointed out that *he* was hardly the world-famous mathematician he desperately wanted to be, that the only teaching job he had been able to find was at a terrible college in Indiana, meaning that his students actually *needed* him, but all he ever did was complain about how stupid his students were—he used that word constantly, his students were stupid, stupid, stupid, and of course he called me stupid, too. His stupid students and his stupid son—*they* were keeping him from greatness. For a long time, he blamed anti-Semitism for his lack of success, so he changed his name to Lowood from Loewenstein—we have no relation to Adam, Venter; I've investigated the issue—but anti-Semitism had nothing to do with it. And when my mother was diagnosed with terminal cancer when I was in college, my father saw that as the perfect time to lock himself in a room and finish the great mathematical opus he had delayed throughout his entire life, leaving me to care for my mother. I've never really been able to explain how that felt, sitting by my mother's side, doing whatever I could to comfort her, while my father stayed at home and "worked." Of course I did not understand what he was working on, since, as he loved to remind me, my mathematical skills were not up to that task. And of course he never finished. He died about a year after my mother, leaving his room cluttered with pages and pages of what one of his colleagues described to me at his funeral as "gobbledygook." I punched that colleague in the nose—he was talking about my father, after all, and at my father's funeral, no less—but what he said had pleased me.

In short, I told Adam, I hated my father, so nothing I did had anything to do with him.

This engendered in Adam a very, very big Adam Shrug. I knew what it meant even before he did it—of course I was obsessed with proving that I was better than my father, so obsessed that it was stopping me from committing to any relationship that might keep me from greatness, in just the way that my father thought his own personal relationships kept him from greatness. And my desire to find the perfect dissertation topic was stopping me from finding any dissertation topic.

All of this was obvious, but it is the obvious things that we are least likely to see. I thanked Adam for showing all of this to me and told him that I didn't think it was necessary for me to use the machine, since I had just had this gigantic, gigantic epiphany.

"It's in pencil," Adam said. "Let's go write it in ink."

So I went back with him to his apartment and I went through the pain and fear and my tattoo said **SHOULD NEVER BECOME A FATHER**.

I said that that seemed awfully harsh, and Adam said that it was possible that it meant **SHOULD NEVER BECOME FATHER**, meaning that I should not become *my* father—it was possible that the indefinite article was just a smudge, so it was indefinitely an indefinite article. On the other hand, Adam said, it might mean that I would be able to lead a happy and productive life only provided that I did not have a child, since the wound in my soul from my own father would cause me to be an equally bad father. I didn't like this at all, and like many people who have just used the machine, I deeply regretted having done so.

"Look at it this way," Adam said. "At least you can be with Rose."

I immediately went to Rose's house, introduced myself to her mother, and asked her permission to marry her daughter. She called up to Rose and told her that one of the moonbats from her moonbat religion was here. Then I asked Rose to marry me, and she laughed and said she wasn't remotely ready to get married, but she was perfectly happy to take a walk. We took a walk past St. Aloysius, the Ridgewood church she had attended as a child. I showed her my tattoo, still covered in Saran Wrap, and she said that it was perfect. She wanted to work with the epiphany machine for the rest of her life, and children would be a distraction from that.

Adam got erratic in the late seventies. I don't want to psychoanalyze him in light of what we've learned in the past few days, but now I wonder whether he had learned something about Si Strauss, and took to cocaine as a refuge. Or maybe Si Strauss just bought him a lot of cocaine, and cocaine did what cocaine does. But it was more than that. Through the sixties and most of the seventies, Adam had thought his device was going to solve everything, he thought it was going to end war and sexual repression and all the varieties of self-loathing that make people so horrible to each other. By the end of the seventies, he was realizing that he was not going to rewrite the world, and it made him angry. I started to find Adam disappointing in ways that I didn't think had anything to do with my dad.

Even meeting John Lennon was disappointing—not disillusioning the way meeting your idols is supposed to be. He was just pleasant and charming and unremarkable and eager to use jokes to cut off subjects he did not want to talk about and a little tedious whenever he was *not* joking, just like everyone else in the world, and I was not transformed by the presence of his genius in the way I had once naively hoped to be.

In any case, the machine stopped being fun, and I started to worry more and more about what would happen in a society in which everybody's secrets were written on their forearms, and my graduate study wasn't getting any more interesting—slowly, I came to see that the entire reason I was doing graduate work was to try to prove something to my dad. So I dropped out and entered law school, with the vague intention of providing Adam with legal help when I graduated, but really I just wanted to get away.

Then Rose got pregnant. Adam wanted us to get an abortion, ostensibly because of my tattoo, but really, I think, because he was scared of losing Rose. Which I can understand, because I, too, was always scared of losing Rose. But Rose and I wanted a child at this point. Adam was mad—he kept on telling Rose it wasn't too late, it wasn't too late, it wasn't too late. Then, when Rose was six months pregnant, Mark David Chapman killed John Lennon, and we decided that we had just had enough.

What was tattooed on me had catastrophic effects on my relationship with you, Venter. I spent a couple of decades seesawing between trying to prove the tattoo wrong and just trying to accept what it told me, and at times that made me as poor a father to you as my father was to me, a fact that I'm tempted to say kills me, except that it doesn't, because I'm alive and so are you, and I'm so glad we have time to spend together. Even if we don't spend it together, even if you decide that you never want to see me again after tonight, I am grateful that we have the time to squander.

We have no more time with Adam, and you may be wondering why I have spent so much of this eulogy criticizing him. I've said what I've said because he would want me to tell the truth, and everything I've said is true, but there is always more to the truth than what is said. At the risk of betraying the legal profession, there may be such a thing as the whole truth, but it certainly cannot be told. What I can tell you is this: I am grateful for you, Venter, more grateful than I am for anything else in my life. Though I do not approve of what you do, I cannot help but be filled with happiness simply by your existence. Without Adam, there would be no you. Adam or his device—the difference between them is, finally, trivial—made me look at the truth about myself, about how terrified I was of becoming my father. Not only that. The fateful indefinite article, my scarlet A, played a very productive trick on me. It made me think that as long as I did not become a father, it was safe for me to commit to love, and that is what allowed me to commit to Rose, and then, against its explicit advice but maybe in accordance with its implicit command, to have you. In a sense, Venter, the epiphany machine created you. I cannot imagine a higher accomplishment.

CHAPTER

————— ·· ◆ ·· —————

39

My father's speech left me in tears, and to my surprise, it also left Leah in tears. I jumped onto the stage and hugged my father, and unlike every other hug we had ever shared, there was nothing hesitant in it.

The three of us went to a bar across the street, a bar where there were many older and many younger people, and none of the three of us looked out of place. Leah talked about some plays she had seen, which she said she was disappointed by for their lack of political engagement, then she started talking to my father about a conversation she had with one of Ismail's lawyers about a possible appeal, and then she looked at me and stopped herself. She said she was going to bring whiskey shots for all of us. I had never known that my father had been left alone with his mother while she was dying, and knowing this made his shielding me from my mother's mother dying make much more sense to me, so I asked for more details, and I also asked for more details about both of his parents, since I had heard very little about either one. Eventually, Leah returned, and she toasted Adam and his enthusiasm for breastfucking. She drank her shot, slammed the glass on the bar, and clapped her hands together.

"Well, thanks so much for this incredibly shitty night, guys."

"What's the matter?" my father asked. He put a hand on her shoulder that she pushed off.

"Sometimes I think the problem *is* me, sometimes I think that I should just accept that the love of my life is a terrorist, because the government says he is, and they wouldn't say that if he wasn't. I thought that at least you understood, Isaac. I thought you understood what it means that Ismail is still in prison for no reason. I thought you understood how terrible that is."

"I do."

"So how can you be so chummy with the son of a bitch who put him there?"

"Don't use that word about Rose."

"Are you serious? I wasn't even thinking about Rose, it was just a random, totally inadequate insult for Venter, but are you serious? It bothers you that I would use the word 'bitch' to describe the woman who abandoned you with an infant son who obviously grew up very, very wrong?"

"My wife is my wife, my son is my son."

"A clock is a clock, right, Venter?"

"Venter is my son," my father said. "That's all I need to know."

"That can't excuse everything. That can't excuse the fact that he destroyed Ismail."

"Maybe if the world were a fair place it would not, but it isn't, and it does."

It took me a second to realize that this was the nicest thing my father had ever said about me. It took me a little bit longer to realize that, when Leah walked away and my father did not follow her, this meant that he had chosen me over her, his misguided son over the surrogate daughter with whom he had bonded over the past several years. This did not strike me as a wise choice, but it was one that meant a lot to me.

"I'm hungry," he said. "Do you think we can find a diner around here that serves pound cake?"

CHAPTER

· · ◆ · ·

40

The week of Adam Lyons's death was also my last week at Citizens for Knowledge and Safety, which was being dissolved since it was no longer necessary. One by one, we were being called upstairs to be fired. Most of the meetings were with HR; for some reason, probably because he wanted to yell at me personally for how little I had accomplished, my appointment was scheduled with Vladimir Harrican. Sitting at my cubicle, waiting until it was time for me to go upstairs for my appointment, I received another email from Steven Merdula. It was simply a forwarded article with the plainest of attached comments: "Seen this?"

Somehow I knew what the link would be before I clicked it. The case that had prompted me to work for Citizens for Knowledge and Safety had been based on a lie. Jonathan Soricillo, his conscience apparently stirred by the news about Si Strauss and Adam Lyons, had admitted in prison that he had raped and murdered his sons. He had murdered and immolated his neighbor, Devin Lanning, in order to frame him. Everything Soricillo had said about Lanning's epiphany tattoo had been a lie; Lanning had never gotten an epiphany tattoo, **DOES NOT UNDERSTAND BOUND-ARIES** or otherwise.

Reading this made me react as Merdula must have known it would. I went to the men's bathroom and cried and threw up. Then I looked into the mirror. Mirror, mirror on the wall, who's the most pathetic stooge of all?

I thought about breaking the mirror, picking up a shard, and cutting out my tattoo. I pictured myself doing it, and then pictured myself doing it again. But I couldn't actually do it, so I headed to the elevator, my tattoo intact.

When the elevator doors opened onto Vladimir's floor, I crossed paths with an old man in a suit who looked shocked and embarrassed to see me, a young man about to be fired. Little did he know how little concerned I was with my fate; I was thinking instead about Lanning and the Soricillo family. So much were they on my mind that this old man, despite his expensive suit and perfect grooming, reminded me of the grandfather who had burned me in the park, the grandfather who had endured so much tragedy and was now learning that his own son was a monster beyond all reckoning.

"Are you Steven Merdula?" I asked Vladimir as I walked into his office.

Vladimir laughed. "I'm sorry, what?"

"Are you Steven Merdula? Have you been fucking with my head this whole time?"

"That's two questions. The answer to the first is a definite no."

"I know you're going to fire me. But first I have something to say."

"You think I'm Steven Merdula and you think I'm going to fire you. You're not the prophet your mentor was."

Vladimir proceeded to offer me a job as the director of content at the Rubicon Epiphany Corporation, which he was acquiring from the chaos of Adam Lyons's estate.

"I want you to keep doing what you've been doing," Vladimir said. "But now the emphasis will be different. You'll be telling the stories of people who have had their lives transformed by the machine in a positive way. Like the testimonials you were doing when you and I first met."

"Why? Adam Lyons is dead and the epiphany machine is broken."

"We're releasing a new version soon. It will be linked to users' Internet history."

"Sorry?"

"The websites they visit, terms they type in to search engines, emails they send, preferences they express in various ways—it all gets fed into an algorithm, and the algorithm generates an epiphany that it then tattoos on the user."

"That sounds evil."

"Adam Lyons had a rare gift; that gift was why I admired him and why, until the day he died, I always harbored hopes that he would one day come around and agree to work with me. That's part of why I hired you, his supposed protégé. His gift was that he *listened* to what people thought they were saying, but he *heard* what they were really saying. That's what the Internet does. Of course, the Internet does it a lot better."

"You could name this device anything. Why call it the epiphany machine?"

"I happen to like the name and the design. And I have a sentimental family attachment."

I didn't want to hear any more about this idea, which sounded doomed. Besides, I had a pressing matter to discuss that, since he was not Steven Merdula, Vladimir might not be aware of. "Devin Lanning was innocent."

"Yes, so I've heard. Assuming that Jonathan Soricillo is telling the truth now, which is a big assumption. But we can't get everything right, can we?"

At this, he gave the worst shrug that I, a connoisseur of shrugs, had ever seen in my life.

"We should officially apologize for everything Citizens for Knowledge and Safety did," I said. "We should apologize to the family of Devin Lanning. Most important, we should proclaim unequivocally that Ismail is innocent and must be immediately released." It was not until this moment that I suddenly realized I knew that Ismail was truly, unquestionably innocent.

Vladimir did not follow my logic and asked me to take him through it.

I tried to build an argument that Vladimir would respond to. "You want people to have positive associations with the machine. Because of the work we've done—the work I've done—a lot of people associate the epiphany machine with terrorists and child molesters. Breaking that connection might make people feel better about the machine."

"No. The epiphany machine can keep people safe from predators like Ismail and Devin Lanning, and it's important for people to remember that, so you'll keep telling those stories. They just won't be the emphasis anymore."

"But Devin Lanning was innocent. We just said so."

"*You* just said so. I don't know. And in the public imagination, he's a predator who got what he deserved, but should have been stopped earlier. From a marketing perspective, that's what we have to work with. So that's the perspective you'll write from."

"No. I refuse."

For the first time since I had known Vladimir, he looked genuinely surprised. "This is one of the most important innovations of our time. Do you want to be known as the guy who passed up a chance to take part in it?"

"I don't care how I'm known."

"We both know that's not true. I'm the only person who's ever believed in you," said Vladimir. "Just think what people would think about you if they knew how ungrateful you are."

I thought again about the man at the elevator. "The man who accosted me in Central Park. The man I thought was the Soricillo twins' grandfather. You hired him. You paid him to burn me."

Vladimir smiled. "I didn't tell him to burn you. He added that. I think he was frustrated. He had been going to Riverside Park every day for weeks. You told me you ran there all the time. I should have known you exaggerated."

"Why? Why did you do that?"

"I knew you needed a little push to come work for me."

"The murder of the boys, you didn't . . ."

Vladimir's laugh reminded me how high the ceiling in his office was. "Venter, don't be ridiculous. I learned of the murder of the two boys and of Devin Lanning the way I told you I did, from someone on my staff. I thought it would help you see the importance of working for me."

"Why am I so important to you? I don't know how to do anything."

"I'm beginning to finally see that. I think I'm having an epiphany of my own, right here in this office. My father's tattoo told him to **MAKE DIFFERENT USE OF HANDS**, and you know what that use was? To hold me. My father was a great violinist and could have been a greater one still, but instead he gave his career up to hold me until I was ready to stand on my own. Adam Lyons tricked him into doing that by playing on my father's proletarian delusions. This made me look at Adam Lyons as a kind of god, no matter how much I denied it to you and myself. Or maybe I viewed him as my real father. I thought I needed him for what I needed to do, and I thought you could help me get to him. And maybe, in some strange way, I thought of you as a kind of little brother. A shiftless, unimaginative little brother who needed to be guided. But Adam was never necessary to the machine. That's the biggest mistake I've ever made; it delayed my development of the real epiphany machine by years. The second biggest mistake was thinking you could be of any use to me whatsoever. Go, get out of my office. Go see what people think of you now that you're no longer working for Vladimir Harrican."

"Their opinion of me probably won't be any worse than it already is," I said. "Freedom's just another word for everybody thinking you're a schmuck."

I had a s'more on the way out.

NAME: Matthew Cole

DATE OF BIRTH: 02/10/1982

DATE OF EPIPHANY MACHINE USE: 10/09/2011

DATE OF INTERVIEW BY VENTER LOWOOD: 12/01/2014

Three years after we broke up, my ex-girlfriend sent me this email:

> You're nothing but a lying, manipulative loser.

She knew that the worry that I was a loser had been a major facet of my life since I was a child, so her use of that word was itself manipulative. No one is as reliably correct as a hypocrite.

A crazy woman, this ex-girlfriend of mine. The entire time we were together, she badgered me to use the machine, even though, right there on her arm, were written the words **BADGERS PEOPLE TO PUSH THEM AWAY BUT IS STRONGER THAN TERRORISTS**. About two years after we broke up, so about one year before she sent me this email, she sent my mother an email that said:

> I'm really offended that you're not my friend anymore just because your son and I are no longer having sex.

Here I am not lying, but I am manipulating you. This is the line I always use when I want to demonstrate to someone beyond a shadow of a doubt that this ex-girlfriend is crazy. When I tell that story, I can count on a gasp, and if you get a gasp when you want a gasp, you know you've made your point, particularly if your point is that a woman is crazy, which is something people tend to want to believe. But the truth is that I had done lots of things to make my ex-girlfriend crazy. I had told her I wanted to stay friends, then did not return her calls and emails; I had told her I needed a break from talking and would contact her in a few weeks, then did not contact her for months.

Now I'm trying to manipulate you again. I'm trying to demonstrate to you that I'm self-critical, that I've reformed. Confession is basically manipulation, at least for me, and since I'm the only person whose consciousness I have access to, I have to assume that everybody else thinks the way I do.

I cheated on this girlfriend many times while we were together. She was going to school in Boston and I was living in New York, so I had plenty of opportunity. Mostly, I was just miserable with myself, stuck in a cubicle job I despised because I knew I was perfect for it; it was an ideal job for a man who didn't really want to do anything. I didn't even really want to cheat on her, but after all, a man has to do something. On the bus to visit her, I would strike up a conversation with a girl—something I was not usually good at doing—and I would tell her that my girlfriend had used the epiphany machine and was trying to coax me into using it as well.

"You shouldn't use that thing," the girl would say. "The epiphany machine is a cult."

"I know," I would respond. "But my girlfriend says that I shouldn't judge the machine without using it first."

"That's insane! You have to join a cult to figure out whether it's a cult?"

We would argue about this back and forth, and I would manage to get the girl's number and meet up with her back in New York, or in Boston when my girlfriend had a class. Once I got a handjob right there on the bus, underneath a blanket the girl had packed. Another time, I had sex in the disgusting restroom of the disgusting Chinese restaurant where the bus stopped. My girlfriend used to react with mock-horror when I told her that I had eaten at the buffet. "Ugh, I can't believe I kissed you after you ate that." So I took particular pleasure when she said this after I had licked that girl's clit (or at any rate the general vicinity of her clit—in my defense, we only had a few minutes and she hadn't shaved). There was an entire year when all the energy of my soul was focused on cheating on my girlfriend in the sleaziest, most soul-depleting ways possible.

Now I'm manipulating you *and* lying to you. None of what I just said about cheating was true; I've never cheated on anyone in my life. A few weeks after she sent me that email about me being a loser, my ex-girlfriend sent me an email apologizing. She was mad, she said, and she was trying to hurt me. But buried inside that email was the accusation that I had cheated on her several years earlier. I responded, truthfully, that I had never cheated on her, and she responded that she had no reason to believe me, since I had admitted to her that when I was a teenager I had been a pathological liar. This was infuriating, in part because it was, in a twisty way, entirely fair.

I've gotten back at her just now, sort of, by lying to you and saying that I did in fact cheat on her. And really, it's disappointing, after you've broken up with someone, never to have cheated on them. If the relationship doesn't work out, you might as well have had some exciting cheating sex. Or at least I assume cheating sex is exciting. I've done a lot of lying, which is the worst part about cheating, and the only part I know.

The way I actually spent those bus rides was reading, by which I mean staring at a page while thinking. "Thinking" might be too exalted a word for the scroll across my brain: **WHY CAN'T YOU BREAK UP WITH YOUR GIRLFRIEND, YOU WORTHLESS PIECE OF SHIT? WHY CAN'T YOU BREAK UP WITH YOUR GIRLFRIEND, YOU WORTHLESS PIECE OF SHIT?** Finally, she broke up with me for being too passive and for needing too much reassurance. She begged to get back together with me after she moved back to New York, because other men in New York were so much worse than I was. After my relationship with my next girlfriend followed exactly this pattern, I decided that maybe I should use the epiphany machine after all.

By this time, I had come to a point in my life when what little integrity I still sensed in myself felt like it was slipping away, so submitting to the machine did not seem terribly unreasonable. I used the new model of the machine, the one that actually works, the one that's connected to your Internet history. Obviously you can see my epiphany, and even if you hadn't seen it before you came up to me on the street, you probably could have guessed it just from the story I've told.

Now when I date, I date with this tattoo. It's not a great tattoo to have in the winter, because I'm bundled up and the tattoo isn't immediately apparent when I'm first talking to a girl, so I have to make a decision about whether I'm going to mention it up front or whether I'm going to wait until we go home together and I'm taking my shirt off. Either way, it tends to kill the mood to discover this tattoo on the cute-ish guy you're either considering hooking up with or in the first stages of hooking up with. Summer's much better, because everybody is showing their arms anyway, and these days there are usually at least three or four epiphany tattoos in any given crowd, usually more, and since almost all of them sound bad, none of them really sound bad. My tattoo can be a conversation starter rather than a conversation ender.

That's even more true with Epyfa. The girls who see my tattoo on that dating app and then contact me are interested in how I deal with the tattoo; they tend to be the best girls, smart and curious and with low self-esteem. I can make some self-deprecating jokes about my craven, caddish past, and about how I've moved on and have committed to not lying anymore. I get them home, we have a great time, and I go on a date with a different girl the next night.

Some Saturdays I have two dates, one for brunch and one for dinner. Then I'll say I had a great time, I'm totally going to text you. And if I feel like it, I will. If I don't, I'll say my mom's dog got sick and I went home for the weekend to help her take care of it. Then, weeks later, if I feel like seeing that particular girl again, I'll text her that my mom's dog died, and I had gotten really close to it, so I had been grieving and that's why I hadn't been in touch.

See, when most people get an epiphany as bad as mine, they try to contort themselves to change. They try to be different. I, on the other hand, have embraced who I am, and I've discovered that there are ways to really enjoy your life when you're a **LYING, MANIPULATIVE LOSER**.

CHAPTER

——— · · ◆ · · ———

41

I felt very proud of myself for having stood up to Vladimir, and also terrified by the question of what to do next. Simply losing my job due to circumstances beyond my control had been a relief. Choosing not to accept Vladimir's offer obligated me to do something important. Actually, it obligated me to do what I was obligated to do anyway: free Ismail. Somehow.

The first thing I said to Rebecca when she came home that night was that Ismail was innocent, that I had been persecuting him for years for no reason. Without responding, she put her bag down, poured herself a glass of pinot grigio, and—one of the first times I had ever seen her do this—burst into tears.

"I know," she said. "I've known for years. But I didn't want to admit that to myself, because I have no idea how to help him."

"I want to do something to help him," I said.

"Great. What? Whatever you want to do, I'll fund you to do it."

Her corporate-law job made this an eminently achievable goal.

I tried brainstorming out loud, but none of my ideas sounded very impressive even to me. She didn't respond, and after a while she seemed to stop listening. Finally, her eyes, red from crying, lit up with an idea.

"Write a book," she said. "You've always wanted to write, and I've always known you're incredibly talented. So why don't you write a memoir about your relationship with Ismail? I'll support you while you write."

At first, I thought she was just making a bitter joke. Writing a book seemed more like self-indulgence than self-sacrifice.

"Make it clear what a smart and decent person Ismail was. *Is.* People just hear his name and assume he's guilty. Make people realize that he's a real flesh-and-blood human being. Be honest about your role in what's happened to him. You'll be doing penance for what you did to Ismail, but you'll also be fulfilling yourself as a person. You've always wanted to write and you *should* write. This is perfect."

I was not certain that I had always wanted to write. I had always wanted to think of myself as a genius—or at least as someone who could compete with Ismail—and writing had always seemed a way to do that. But apart from what I had written for Vladimir Harrican, I had barely made any attempt to write since college.

But Rebecca's faith in me made me think I had talent after all.

There was a part of me, of course, that knew just how **DEPENDENT ON THE OPINION OF OTHERS** I was proving myself to be by making my first serious attempt to become a writer just because Rebecca told me I should, but there was a bigger part of me that was happy to take Rebecca's money and sit at home with my computer all day.

Maybe that previous sentence does not do me justice. When I first sat down to write about Ismail, I did so in good faith and with great energy. Rebecca was excited about the project, my father was excited about the project, I was excited about the project. I thought about calling Ismail's mother and telling her what I was doing, maybe even interviewing her, but I thought she was more likely than not to blow me off, or maybe take legal action against me. So I just decided to sit and write what I remembered about Ismail.

Unfortunately, sitting at home with my laptop turned out to mean reading blog posts about the problematic portrayals of women in popular culture in one tab and watching porn in another. After a few months, I joined a writer's space in Long Island City, near the apartment Rebecca had purchased for us. The writer's space was called The Oracle Club, a name that carried uncomfortable echoes of the epiphany machine, though the owners, a dispiritingly gorgeous couple named Julian and Jenna, claimed not to have been thinking of the device when they chose the name. Neither of them had epiphany tattoos, which led me to devise a theory that truly beautiful people had sufficiently high self-esteem that they did not feel the need to use the device, a theory that lasted me through the first five pages of an essay, until I realized that the idea was ridiculous, and that of course beautiful people use the machine all the time, and that many beautiful people have extremely low self-esteem. I deleted the file and tried to write about Ismail, but I couldn't think of any interesting de-tails, which made me feel annoyed that I had not kept a notebook as a teenager. Or rather, I was annoyed that I had kept a notebook as a teenager, but had hardly written anything in it beyond a handful of abstract pseudo-intellectual gibberish, like that thing about how my bed felt so empty that it felt like the grave. I wished that I had "kept a notebook" in the way that I now defined "keeping a notebook," meaning making concrete observa-tions about what I saw from day to day. I wished I had the discernment to spot important details and the discipline to write them down. In other words, I wished I were Ismail. I was certain that if the situation had been reversed, if I had been in prison and Ismail had been writing about me, he would have done a much better job turning me into a convincing charac-ter on the page, a thought that made me feel envious and resentful, and also extremely guilty, since I had deprived the world of a great talent and substituted my own mediocrity.

I began and abandoned several more projects until I remembered "The

Undead," the mashup I had written in high school of "The Dead" and *Buffy the Vampire Slayer*. I asked my father to find it and send it to me. He did so—"I had to go through about ten boxes in the attic, but it was worth it. I read it and this is great. I *always* knew you were a genius!"—and when I read it again, I was amazed by the insight and the passion, by the humor and the honest emotion, by what a good writer I had been in high school. Getting it published, I reasoned, would be a good way to establish my name, after which I could more easily get people to pay attention to what I wrote about Ismail. Rebecca read "The Undead," and she loved it so much she jumped up and down and shouted, though the next morning she reminded me not to lose focus and to keep writing about Ismail. I took four months, lengthened it, polished it, and then sent it off to a dozen agents. I received exactly one response, which read: "Not bad, but the whole drop-vampires-into-classic-literature thing peaked a couple of years ago."

After this, I was severely depressed and spent my days at The Oracle Club brooding over the fact that I had had at least some talent and had wasted it, while Julian, a published and respected novelist, typed happily and constantly at the desk next to mine. Jenna, an astonishingly gifted and prolific portrait painter, worked downstairs. Their three-year-old son tap-thumped back and forth between them, making a fuss until they agreed to play *Sgt. Pepper's Lonely Hearts Club Band* for the millionth time on their antique record player. It made me uncomfortable to find such a great fan of the Beatles in this toddler—this tiny child who grabbed my knee and shouted "JohnPaulGeorgeandRingo" every time I made myself some French-press coffee. This struck me as Adam's way of haunting me, but I had signed up to work at a place called The Oracle Club, so perhaps I was looking for Adam to haunt me. In any case, a large percentage of my time was spent watching this child dance to this old record, all the history and cultural significance of which he was blithely unaware. I wished I could once again feel that total absence of self-consciousness, and I knew that I would, but only when I no longer had a self to be conscious of, a prospect I found terrifying and, maybe for the first time, near.

These thoughts would often swirl around in my head while I stared at my computer in The Oracle Club. Passersby would look at me through the window, and, not knowing that I could hear them, would speculate about what the place was and what I was doing.

"Is this a library? Is that guy real? Is he a statue?"

"It's a zoo for unemployed people."

Believe me or don't believe me, but I tried very hard to write about Ismail.

One morning when I couldn't make myself sit at my computer—there were many such mornings—I took the train into Manhattan to walk around the Upper East Side, near Adam's old neighborhood. Where Adam Lyons's old building had been, there was now an empty lot and green construction barriers. This was where my parents met, where my personality had been formed or revealed or both, where I had led my friend into ruin, where I had spent countless hours with a man whose voice I would never get out of my head or off of my arm. But none of those things amounts to a legal claim on property.

I looked down the street and could see my father catching up to a woman in a fox fur coat. I could see myself and Ismail coming up the street, pizza and dreams on our tongues, Ismail's arm still bare. Turn around, Ismail, have another slice and then get on the train. I looked again at the empty lot and wished the building had been leveled decades earlier, and also wished that the building was still there and would stand until the end of the world. I looked again and felt annoyed that construction barriers are always green, lulling us into thinking of renewal, a return to the earth, rather than the imminent appearance of another sterile condo.

But it was not a condo that replaced Adam's building, which I discovered had been purchased and leveled by Vladimir Harrican. It was the flagship Epiphany store, to which people would come to use the new "smart" machines, which, applying a proprietary algorithm to a user's Internet history, crafted a general summary of life trajectory and personal proclivities.

Four other stores appeared in New York shortly afterward: one on the Upper West Side, one in SoHo, one in Williamsburg, one in Park Slope. Each store was a giant glass cylinder that was mostly empty space. "It's supposed to look like a forearm, but it looks more like a dick," somebody wrote online. There were terminals where users registered and synced their Internet history; there was a s'mores station. In the middle of the store were translucent orange plastic chairs that resembled catcher's mitts; the chairs vaguely suggested some kind of elegant future, however uncomfortable they were to sit in in the present. Users waited in these chairs until their names appeared in epiphany font on a giant digital board in the center of the room. Beneath this board were massive screens displaying live feeds of the store's "epiphany stations," at which "epiphany artists" guided needles onto skin. The stations themselves faced the street, so passersby could stop and gawk at each tattoo as it formed, thrilling to the reactions of the users reading their tattoos for the first time.

Soon, the only time there wasn't a user in the epiphany station was the time it would take an epiphany artist to change needles or ink, or the five-minute break epiphany artists were permitted every two hours. Every chair in the waiting area was filled, and there was a line of users down the block. As much as Vladimir disliked altering his vision even slightly, he agreed, once cold weather hit, to install another row of chairs in each store to reduce outside waiting times. "We don't want anybody's arm to freeze off before they can get their tattoo," he said.

There were many impassioned articles and posts decrying the total surrender of privacy that these new machines signified, but soon these articles and posts sounded stodgy, irrelevant, of concern only to the old, to the paranoid, to the belligerent, to everyone with something to hide. Who else would not be curious?

Vladimir put the matter this way, in a statement that was scandalous for the year or so before it became accepted wisdom: "If you're afraid of the machine, maybe we should be afraid of you."

Many who proclaimed themselves (and may have honestly considered themselves) early risers and diligent workers were informed that they **PREFER SLEEP TO LABOR**. Because the machine revealed personality traits that job candidates might not volunteer in job interviews, employers started requiring prospective employees to receive these tattoos—what to the recipient of a tattoo might appear to be a violation of privacy, after all, was to everyone around that recipient useful data. Within two years of the first appearance of these machines, it was essentially impossible to get a retail job without one, since stores believed that they were an excellent way to identify potential thieves. Early consensus that white-collar professionals should avoid the machine at all costs, on the theory that tattoos and office jobs did not mix, soon gave way to advice that getting a tattoo before one's company required one would demonstrate openness and self-confidence, unless of course the tattoo said that you were **CLOSED OFF AND SELF-DOUBTING**, in which case, well, you might as well know. Soon coworkers were reaching over cubicle walls to show each other their tattoos and speculate about what was being kept secret by those who declined to roll up their sleeves.

The New York restaurant industry was a holdout, largely because so many of its employees were aspiring actors who did not want to get tattoos that would ruin whatever chances they had of one day "making it." But soon enough, patrons demanded tattoos on waitstaff to ensure that their waiters did not have heinous hygiene and were not prone to taking revenge on complicated special orders by, say, ejaculating in the soup. (Even Julian, the proprietor of The Oracle Club, who moonlit as a waiter at a high-end brunch spot on the Upper West Side, was compelled to get a tattoo, though his tattoo was the enviable **WILL NOT STOP WILL NOT LOSE FOCUS**. Some people have all the luck, or all the merit, while the rest of us try desperately to convince ourselves that those two are not the same thing.)

Soon, too, audiences came to expect that even actors would have epiphany tattoos; a lack of which came to suggest caginess, a suspicious unwillingness on the part of actors to share themselves with their fans. Today, magazines speculate about why certain stars refuse to receive or display epiphany tattoos, what affair or proclivity they might be hiding.

Some political pundits have suggested that, during the next presidential election campaign, candidates be asked on the debate stage to roll up their sleeves and show their tattoos. But I think that these pundits are joking, at least for now.

It sounds from the way that I am writing this that I was deeply engaged with these changes as they were occurring. Nothing could be further from the truth. When I first heard about the stores, my reaction was to dismiss them as Harrican overreach. Rebecca and I both laughed about them, which was nice, since, with the hours that she worked at her law firm, we hardly saw each other anymore and so had little opportunity to laugh about anything. I lost track of the new machine almost entirely for a period in which my mind was preoccupied by an Iranian-American documentary filmmaker named Roxanne Salehi.

CHAPTER

· · ✦ · ·

42

Roxanne emailed me proposing an interview for a project she was doing about post-9/11 terrorism prosecutions; I looked her up and saw that she was a highly respected filmmaker. I thought that talking to her about how guilty I felt about Ismail, and about how certain I now was about his innocence, would be good for Ismail and good for the book I was writing about Ismail. She came to interview me early one morning at The Oracle Club, and as her assistants set up lights, she seemed reluctant to look me in the eye. She asked me a few general questions about the machine, about my friendship with Ismail, about the day that Ismail used the machine, about the day that the FBI came to interview me about Ismail, about Ismail's fate, about Citizens for Knowledge and Safety. I sensed that my answers were terrible, but the truth was also terrible, if in a slightly different way.

When I watched the documentary, which also prominently featured interviews with Leah and Ismail's mother, even *I* hated myself, this shifty little weasel who can't take responsibility for having destroyed his friend's life. And then, The Phone Call, overlaid on a still photo of me with Ismail circa 1998: "Hey, Roxanne, it's Venter, I've been thinking about that stuff I said, and I'm really worried about how it will make me look. I mean, not that I only care about how I will look. I think that it will help Ismail if I look good, if that makes sense?"

As the credits rolled and Netflix suggested something else that we should watch, Rebecca said quietly, "It's not that bad," and then she said she had a lot of work to do and had to go back to the office. I called my father, who was not pleased that I had talked about the case on camera without a lawyer present. Though he had declined to be interviewed, he did not come off well either. The interview with Leah made my father's choice to stand by his son look like an act of corruption rather than an act of love, though of course it was both.

Within a weekend of the documentary's release, it was declared a cultural phenomenon by people who declare things cultural phenomena. I was excoriated on television, I was excoriated on podcasts, I was excoriated everywhere on the Internet.

```
Too bad venter is DEPENDENT ON THE OPINION OF
OTHERS since literally everyone in america
thinks he sucks!!!!!

he's the one who should be in prison

do we have any evidence that venter lowood
did NOT collaborate with osama bin laden?
```

I wanted to—as an Internet comment recommended I do—crawl into a hole and let maggots eat me while I was still alive. Somebody threw rotten eggs at the window of The Oracle Club while I was writing; then somebody spray-painted **DEPENDENT ON THE OPINION OF OTHERS** onto the windows. Julian said he didn't want to ask me to leave, which I interpreted to mean that I should leave. I started spending all my time in my apartment.

And for the first time in many years I was happy. I was exposed as the terrible person I was—the opinion of others was now the correct one. More important, Ismail would be freed, or at the very least his sentence on the trumped-up charges against him would be radically reduced—that much seemed assured. Ismail's mother was interviewed on the *Today* show along with Roxanne Salehi and several legal experts, notably not including my father. Roxanne said she wished that the reaction to her documentary had been focused more on Ismail and less on Venter Lowood, but nonetheless she was pleased that it had resonated, and confident that the American people now understood it was unfair to jail someone for a tattoo.

Rebecca's reaction was similar to mine. She was ecstatic that Ismail would soon be free; she considered it worth the price of having people shout things at us in the grocery store. For months, we had the best sex we'd had since college.

And we waited, and waited. There was a lot of discussion in the media of possible legal avenues for Ismail, but it seemed that, even though everyone agreed that they hated me for caring what they thought about me, there was still widespread disagreement about what should be done about my friend.

"After all," somebody wrote online, "there's no clear evidence that Ismail is not a terrorist. And if he wasn't a terrorist when he was arrested, how can we be certain that this experience hasn't made him one?"

I wrote an op-ed calling for Ismail's immediate release. The op-ed was debated online for a few days, it seemed like it was important, and then somehow it just seemed to be forgotten.

Then a Muslim man, an immigrant from Pakistan, opened fire on the café car of an Amtrak train as it pulled away from Wilmington. The shooter had a **WANTS TO BLOW THINGS UP** tattoo, and though the tattoo was not an epiphany tattoo—he had tattooed himself, quite amateurishly—and though this obviously had nothing to do with Ismail, nonetheless it ended any remaining public discussion of Ismail's fate.

Eventually, weeks and months went by without anyone attacking me on the Internet. I was surprised to find that I missed being attacked, maybe because I was so **DEPENDENT ON THE OPINION OF OTHERS** that I preferred negative opinions about me to none at all, or maybe because I knew that I fully deserved even the worst of the attacks. In either case, I felt once again like I had suddenly realized something: that other people's opinions actually do not matter, even when the world would be a better place if they did matter. I hoped I would never suddenly realize anything ever again.

I threw myself into a new writing project, or an old one, sorting through testimonials from machine users, and adding my thoughts and experiences. I also tried to collect new testimonials about the new model of the epiphany machine, and though I did do a handful of interviews, it was difficult to find willing subjects, since a Google search of my name revealed only people attaching nasty comments to my name. Maybe worse for my prospects was that Cesar Solomon, who had given up trying to write a second novel, had instead taken the job that Vladimir Harrican had offered me. Anyone who wanted to publicly discuss his or her experiences with the new epiphany machine could do so through Cesar's site, so there was no reason to talk to me.

NAME: Cesar Solomon

DATE OF BIRTH: 10/01/1981

DATE OF EPIPHANY MACHINE USE: 01/12/2013

DATE OF INTERVIEW BY VENTER LOWOOD: 10/15/2016

I've always felt bad that you fell out with Adam Lyons because of me. The epiphany machine struck me as weird—that iteration of the epiphany machine continues to strike me as weird—but the only reason that I insisted you break with Adam was that you were my roommate, and I was afraid that your involvement in the epiphany machine would reflect badly on me. I was eighteen just like you, man. Eighteen-year-olds don't know anything. You don't need magic or an algorithm or anything else to tell you that. I'm not sure it's my fault that you thought I knew something, but I still feel guilty about it. At least from time to time.

Honestly, though, I'm impressed with what you've done with your life. At least until recently, you had contributed much more to the world than I had. Of the two of us, I won greater esteem, but you *deserved* far, far more esteem. What did I do? I wrote a pretty good novel. It made a lot of people think. What did it make anyone *do*? Maybe it made a couple of people with Asperger's feel better about themselves, but I don't think so; it was too nuanced, too ambivalent, too insistent on showing every last goddamn side of every last goddamn thing to make anyone feel better about anything. It made a bunch of people with Asperger's angry that I was speaking for them; that was pretty much the most tangible effect it had. Consider what you were doing at the same time. I know you don't want to hear this, but the work you put into Citizens for Knowledge and Safety helped keep your friend Ismail where he belongs. You say that he's innocent, but honestly I think you're once again letting other people do your thinking for you. Why do you think he's being held? As part of some massive but simple conspiracy that is one day going to be revealed on somebody's arm? Give me a break.

But we're not here to talk about you, we're here to talk about me. Okay. I've always been driven to make art and to reach as many people as possible. These are fundamentally contradictory impulses, no matter how much we'd like to pretend otherwise. I sold a lot of copies of my novel, awards were shoved into my arms like they were children somebody was trying to get rid of, and that all felt incredibly, incredibly empty. You may or may not have heard this, but I fell in love with Catherine Pearson at AWP, a writer's conference. We were both on panels that we didn't go to. We stayed in bed the entire time. Unimaginable bliss. I asked her to marry me on the last day. She said she was never going to get married again, certainly never to another writer, not after her marriage to Carter Wolf, but if I wanted to meet her in Rome that summer I was welcome to. I did meet her in Rome, and we had what are still the six best weeks of my life, followed by the worst several months. We're both very popular writers in Italy, so we'd go out to dinner and get treated like John and Jackie Kennedy, and then we'd spend the rest of our time in our hotel room, writing for the few hours each day we weren't having some iteration of sex. I still wasn't making any progress on my manuscript, but I cared less than I usually did. Catherine, on the other hand, was writing a ton, and I felt jealous of her, but it also turned me on like nothing else. I'd spend the entire afternoon under her desk, eating her out while she wrote. She'd type furiously, I'd work her into an orgasm, then we'd repeat. The sound of her typing around and above my head was a challenge, so I'd do my best to get her so aroused she couldn't concentrate, and she would take her increasing arousal as a challenge to concentrate more intensely, and her concentration would increase, and she'd write and write and then have an incredibly powerful orgasm, and then we'd start again. Afterward, I'd read what she had written during these sessions, and it would be full of typos and inconsistencies and need to be substantially rewritten, but the power, the essence would be there. Then we'd switch and I'd write while she was giving me a blowjob, but I couldn't concentrate on anything other than the blowjob, a fact that made me feel bad about my writing, which in turn made getting a blowjob much less fun than eating her out. I think I was starting to learn that the particular way in which I could be useful to the world did not involve making art.

Sorry, I got carried away there. You probably want to edit that out. But do what you want.

The time came to leave Rome, and we had a difference of opinion: I wanted to stay together, and she did not. She said we could have a good fuck every year at AWP. I said no, absolutely not, I wanted all or nothing, if we weren't together I never wanted to see her again. Then I saw her a few months later at AWP and begged her to come to my hotel room for one fuck, that's all it had to be, one fuck. She said no, she said it would be cruel to fuck and run given how obvious it was that I was still in love with her. She was right, it would have been cruel. I wish she had been cruel.

To get under her skin, so to speak, I said I was going to use the epiphany machine. I knew this would annoy her, because I knew that she hated the new model of the epiphany machine.

I got so wrapped up in my sex life with Catherine just now that I haven't even talked about the role of the epiphany machine in our relationship. Early on, of course, I had noticed that she had an epiphany tattoo—I had read about her tattoo somewhere, or maybe you had told me, long before I had ever met her—but I didn't think very much about it. By that time, I had lost my teenage need to establish and broadcast my superiority to a false system of knowledge; I just figured, okay, this is something she's into, that's fine. Even in the first days we spent together, she talked a lot about how much she loved and respected Adam Lyons, how she thought he got a bad rap for his association with Si Strauss, and I was silent about the fact that I had met Adam.

In Rome, Catherine talked about how much the machine had energized her, about how it had led her to do what she most needed to do in

life. She also said that the new iteration of the machine was "catastrophi-
cally impersonal," which, to my mind, is another way of saying "objective,"
"data-driven," "accurate." But she'd go on and on about how the new machine was betraying Adam's vision by behaving like, well, a machine.

In any case, when I saw her again and threatened to use the new machine, I had no intention of actually letting that thing write on my arm. I
just wanted to piss her off. Instead, she pissed me off, by kind of cocking
her head at me and saying that I *should* use the machine. I asked her if she
was daring me, and she said no, absolutely not, okay, well, maybe a little,
but for all she knew it might do me some good.

I cursed at her, I said the word "bitch" in a non-fun way for the first
and definitely only time in my life, and then I called a car and had it drive
me to the nearest Epiphany store. The tattoo impressed me so much that I
called Vladimir Harrican, told him that I didn't want to be a novelist anymore, was impressed with his device, and wanted to work for him. He
didn't believe it was me—actually, at first he thought I was you, playing a
prank. But he called me into his office, I ate his s'mores, and we hashed out
a job for me, basically the job that he offered you a long time ago.

What I do all day is find people who have used the epiphany machine
and ask them to write down their stories, which I then feature on our website, although to be honest I could easily run the site on unsolicited sub-
missions alone. People are really eager to talk about what happens to them,
even when you think they should feel humiliated. But why *should* they feel
humiliated? Why should anyone feel humiliated because of who they are?
If you **WILL SPEND ANY AMOUNT OF MONEY TO FEEL COOL
FOR A FEW MINUTES**, then be proud of that. Be proud of the money
you're funneling into the industries that are supporting your feeling cool
for a few minutes, whether that's the fashion industry, the alcohol industry, your local cocaine dealer, the independent bookstore from which you
buy a ton of novels you never read, whatever it is. Be proud of the fact that
you value that feeling of connection to a community over the pointless,
probably incoherent ideal of personal integrity you might think you should

value. Don't feel ashamed of your behavior, unless your epiphany tells you that you **CANNOT STOP FEELING ASHAMED OF OWN BEHAVIOR**, in which case you should take pride in the fact that you're ashamed. Shame is basically hypocrisy redirected against yourself—it's holding yourself to a higher standard than you're capable of meeting, rather than holding other people to a higher standard than you're capable of meeting. So be proud of reaching for that standard you can't meet, and be proud of beating yourself rather than other people up over the standard! And if you *are* a hypocrite, if what's on your arm is **EXHORTS OTHERS TO COMMITMENT AND FIDELITY BUT CANNOT STOP SENDING DICK PICS**, then take pride in the happiness you'll bring to anyone whom you inspire to achieve commitment and fidelity.

These are the kinds of conclusions that I encourage my writers to make. I want people to accept themselves as they actually are—which is what makes me so mad when I get a fake testimonial, when someone attaches a photo of someone else's arm and then makes up a story. A story that is not true deforms our understanding of what is possible, and therefore is quite harmful to the world. I was so miserable when I was a fiction writer because invented stories almost inevitably lead to good guys and bad guys. Only true stories can make people love each other and themselves.

That's why the testimonials I publish are so helpful. I also have a staff of people who write paid advertisements for the machines, listicles and that sort of thing, but those are less helpful, either for the writer or for the machine. Your testimonials were helpful, too; they provided the model for mine, which is why I agreed to sit for you rather than write one of my own, although now that I'm sitting here I'm wondering whether you have an ulterior motive. What is the point of *this* testimonial? You got me to do it by praising me, by making me think you looked up to me and envied me, but now I'm wondering whether you're trying to trick me into making me feel bad about Catherine again. Talking about her makes me feel like I'm about to fall apart, and I haven't felt like that in a very long time.

I didn't even feel bad when I ran into Catherine last year at a mutual friend's reading, and while we both sipped terrible white wine out of flimsy plastic cups, she told me that I was a traitor to the machine, to art, to the human spirit, and to her. I was also the "handmaiden"—a term she meant to be offensive, as though I would be offended to be likened to a woman or to someone who does things for other people—of Vladimir Harrican and the American capitalism that he is for some reason supposed to embody.

This is so much bigger than complaints about capitalism. The forearm is a clean surface to write on; what's really important is the line beneath it, the line that runs from the brain to the fingers and empties into devices that we can track and measure, and so can be truly seen for the first time in human history. If that benefits Vladimir Harrican, what do I care? He was the first person to figure out what the machine could be made to do, so he deserves whatever wealth comes to him as a result. And I don't buy that it necessarily benefits American capitalism. A basic tenet of American capitalism is keeping people ignorant of what they're not really suited for, so that they think if they buy *just one more thing* everything will be awesome. American capitalism, at least in its worst forms, is in direct opposition to the new epiphany machine, as far as I'm concerned.

I said this to Catherine, or as much of it as I could before she turned her back on me and started talking to somebody else. If I were still a fiction writer, I'd probably slow down on that moment and describe the way the bookstore light looked in her hair as she walked away or some nonsense like that, all to create the impression that I miss her and long for her love, for her approval. Instead, I can just look at my arm and *see* all that, encapsulated by a concise assessment of my personality based on analysis of hard data.

My tattoo says what I've basically already told you it says. **DEPENDENT ON THE OPINION OF OTHERS.** I'd like to use the classic villain's line here—we're not so different, you and I—but that wouldn't be true, Venter. We're very different. I've suggested to Vladimir and to the engineers that a future model of the epiphany machine should include "happily" or "unhappily." Obviously everybody feels multiple ways about the way that they are, but there's almost always a dominant feeling about whether the way they are is good or bad, and that dominant feeling is a much more important part, both internally and externally, of who they happen to be than is who they happen to be. I am ***HAPPILY*** **DEPEN-DENT ON THE OPINION OF OTHERS.** If I were you, I'd try to be more like me, but I'm not you, and now we both know it.

Sponsored Content

Rubicon Epiphany Corporation

Posted October 10, 2014

14 THINGS PEOPLE WHO HAVE USED
THE EPIPHANY MACHINE ARE TIRED OF HEARING

1. Why would you choose to get a tattoo that says that? *I didn't choose it, okay? It chose me.*

2. The epiphany machine? Isn't that just like a fortune cookie? *Um, maybe you might have a point if fortune cookies were INSIGHTS INTO PEOPLE'S SOULS rather than lame ADVICE?*

3. I think I know myself better than some hocus-pocus machine does. *Hmmm, interesting. Why don't we ask the people around you how well you know yourself?*

4. You just got that tattoo for attention. *Yeah, you got me. I paid for a needle to dig painfully into my skin just so that YOU and people like you would start unwanted conversations with me on the subway about my body.*

5. See? You admit it! You CHOSE to put that tattoo on your body. *Look, I didn't choose to get THIS tattoo, but I did choose to get A tattoo. I chose to acknowledge that, because I am a human being, my understanding of myself is inevitably cloudy, and the epiphany machine's needle is one tool I can use to puncture those clouds.*

6. Are you saying that if I don't get an epiphany tattoo, then there's no way that I can know myself? *Gah, I just said it is ONE tool! There are lots of others. The epiphany tattoo is just the one that works for me.*

7. How about astrology? Only wingnuts pay attention to astrology, and I don't see how an epiphany tattoo is any different from a horoscope. *I tend to be very brooding, contemplative, and cautious, not really Gemini traits, so reading my Gemini horoscope doesn't really tell me much. But I have a lot of friends who read their horoscopes every single morning and won't make any important decisions without them. You know why? Because that works for THEM. It's an unbelievably big universe, and there are lots of ways to figure out how our unbelievably tiny selves fit into it.*

8. But by your logic, how do you know you're not just deluding yourself by not acknowledging that you have Gemini characteristics? *Just because I acknowledge that I need SOME help discovering my true self doesn't mean that I just walk away from the sense of myself that I have put together through hanging out with myself for my entire life. Any honest approach to the truth is going to be a collaboration between internal observation and external feedback.*

9. If I joined a cult, I don't think I'd advertise it on my body. *Sometimes people tell you this while wearing a Yankees jersey AND a Yankees cap.*

10. That tattoo is so vague it could apply to anyone. *Right, but it DOES apply to me.*

11. Can I touch your tattoo? *Ugh, seriously? NO. Like, as a general rule, maybe don't ask strangers if you can touch their bodies because you find them weird or exotic, okay?*

12. Does the tattoo, like, burn through your clothes if you start to forget about it? *People who ask this need to stop watching Indiana Jones movies on repeat.*

13. Why do you want the worst stuff about you on the out-

side of your body, where everyone can see it? *Why do you want the worst stuff about you on the inside of your body, where everyone can see it?*

14. Forget what this machine says. What's really wrong with you is . . . *See, this is what's really behind every anti-epiphany thing you hear. Everybody always wants to tell you what's wrong with you. Because we all know on some level that there's SOMETHING wrong with us, we tend to give these people a lot more credit than they deserve. Once you get an epiphany tattoo, what you really need to work on is written on your forearm, so any other criticism just slides off your back.*

There is no evidence that the second Rebecca Hart ever read my book. There is certainly no evidence that it was in any way responsible for her killing her children. But she did say, after she murdered her children, that she wanted to be as famous as the woman who shared her name, and my book had increased general chatter around the machine. The slightest possibility that my book played the slightest role in her carrying out the murders sometimes makes me wish that I had never been born, or at least that I had never become a writer, and had instead made myself happy with some ephemeral pursuit, such as raising a child.

But the second Rebecca Hart is not my fault. The fact that she said she murdered her children for "fame" suggests that she is grasping for a word or a handful of words to tattoo on the chaos of whatever is in her that made her kill her children, just as the rest of us are. "Curse," "brain chemistry," "a society that systematically drives women insane," "a book by Steven Merdula": these are all just words, used as incantations to make order flicker before it disappears again.

I had more words to add to these about the first Rebecca Hart; about the second I have none. Choose your own words to describe her. Tattoo them on your forearm. Chant them out loud. See if they can make order stick around. When you find that they can't, feel free to write me a letter that I will not read.

CHAPTER

—— · · ◆ · · ——

43

Rebecca told me she was pregnant by telling me she was going to get an abortion.

"I want to kill the baby before I can kill it," she said. She said she wanted to go have a drink, and though I was tempted to stop her, I did not. She came home very drunk and said she wanted to have the child.

She told me that she had had drinks with her boss, Julie, who told Rebecca something that she had not previously told anyone at the firm: that her ex-fiancé had broken up with her after the epiphany machine told him that he, as he put it, had to marry a Jewish girl. This left Julie depressed for a very long time, but eventually she found a man she loved and was now married with three children in addition to being senior partner. And she had long since realized that her ex-fiancé was a pompous, cowardly ass who would have made her miserable. Julie said that she had hated the machine for years, but now she was grateful because Joshua's use of the machine had, very circuitously, led her to exactly where she wanted to be. Maybe the whole Rebecca Hart thing had just led Rebecca to become a mother at exactly the moment that was right for her.

"If I kill our kid," Rebecca said, "maybe you can write a book about *that.*"

I was certain that Rebecca was not going to kill our child, and I told her so, and I told her I was happy. And I was happy. I posted online that Rebecca was pregnant, and people I barely remembered congratulated me. High school acquaintances who had written horrible things about me on their personal pages after Roxanne Salehi's Ismail documentary congratulated me, said that this news was exciting, included many exclamation points. Almost everyone agrees that becoming a parent is what life is for, and that was what I was doing.

My happiness about becoming a father did not, perhaps predictably, last. I imagined my child asking the very reasonable question of what Daddy did for a living, and having no better answer than that Daddy was still writing his book, a book that would never end and that would include every lesson that every human being had briefly thought they had learned, and simultaneously distill everything that all these people had learned into one short phrase to be tattooed on the forearm of humanity. I imagined her blinking in response.

One day in Rebecca's third month of pregnancy, I googled Ms. Scarra's name and discovered that she had hanged herself in prison two years earlier. I took a long walk and found a construction site, where I tried to feel some of the emotion that I was fairly certain I had felt the last time I stood by a construction site, the one at Adam's old building. Then I returned to my laptop and stared into the infinite space of which I was some kind of ridiculous little king.

Kulturkampf, September 23, 2016

WE WHO ARE ABOUT TO DIE FEEL
A LITTLE CONFLICTED ABOUT *DOUGLAVICH*

BY ANNA VILLANUEVA

I would like to report that *Douglavich*, the Vladimir Harrican biopic and debut fiction film by the renowned documentarian Roxanne Salehi, is an effective critique of the epiphany machine. Over the past several years, Harrican's efforts to squelch the project out of his obsession with his own privacy have been almost as intense as have his efforts to flush out any privacy for anyone else. The same person who wants every keystroke to leave a mark on the stroker's arm would prefer that the basic facts of his own background not be known. Harrican's lawsuits against Salehi were so numerous that it sometimes seemed that not even one day could go by without a new one. That the film was produced and has received even paltry art-house distribution is a minor miracle.

If anyone seemed equipped to take on Harrican, it was Salehi, whose doc-umentary *Ismail*, about accused terrorist Ismail Ahmed, made it clear not only that Ahmed is entirely innocent of wrongdoing or even wrong-thinking, but that Harrican has been instrumental in Ahmed's continued persecution.

Unfortunately, the film serves mostly to further mythologize the already vastly over-mythologized Harrican. Taking as its title Harrican's hated patronymic, *Douglavich* focuses on Harrican's early childhood and troubled relationship with his father. In the opening scene, British violinist Douglas Harrican uses the earlier, much sketchier incarnation of the epiphany machine operated by the perverse, later disgraced guru Adam Lyons and is inspired to leave his fiancée and the West to defect to the Soviet Union. Douglas, in the film as in life, then marries Anya, the daughter of a party leader named Anton

Vasiliev. The three proceed to engage in screaming matches for most of the rest of the film, as gifted young Vladimir looks on and is molded into a sociopath obsessed with his family demons and with making the epiphany machine his own.

The problem with this approach is that we cannot help but feel sorry for Vladimir, and we leave the film impressed with his ability to triumph over his trauma and launch the great venture we know is to come. A more effective critique might focus not on his dark personal history, which makes Vladimir unique among contemporary captains of the tech industry, but on his bland professional focus, which makes Vladimir look banal and typical. Every tech billionaire wishes, like Vladimir, to collect as much information as possible about the innermost souls of everyone on the planet, because that information can be used to reap unfathomable profit, but mostly because they just want it. Vladimir's true shameful se- cret is that he is the most boring thing of all: just another man who wants to know everything.

It's probably necessary to disclose here that this will be my last post for this blog, which has itself been purchased by Harrican, who has been buying up media outlets large and small. (If you know of any jobs for outlets not yet owned by Harrican, please email me!) As of Monday, this blog will be folded into a site run by Cesar Solomon, formerly a respected novelist and now a Harrican hack, at which point this post, and all others pertaining to Harrican and the machine, will likely be deleted. I think this makes me more hostile to Harrican and therefore predisposed to be sympathetic to Salehi, but I suppose it's possible that I am already identifying with my captor and am doing Harrican's work by criticizing a work that attacks him. Harrican and I: I don't know which of us has written this post.

CHAPTER

◆

44

In Rebecca's last weeks of pregnancy, there was a huge resurgence in her libido. Maybe her fear that she was going to kill our baby expressed itself in arousal, or maybe she just got horny while she was pregnant, as a lot of women do. In any case, I responded in full force. Maybe *I* was afraid she was going to kill our baby, but I don't think I was. Maybe what I was writing in support of Ismail had removed the guilt from my body, or at least diluted it to manageable levels. True, on any given day I was mostly not writing, and what I was not writing was unlikely to help Ismail even if I managed somehow not to not write it, but at least I was no longer actively working against him. Guilt, misery, and a dead child seemed like what I deserved, but given a choice between what I had and what I deserved, I would take what I had. And what I had was the living room rug below and my wife on top of me, her person-filled stomach bouncing down on my Doritos-filled one.

One morning, after a particularly intense bout of fucking, I took one of thousands of showers I have taken that have not removed my tattoo, though it did a decent job with the lube. Toweling off got me hard again and I hoped that Rebecca would be ready for another round. Instead, she was on the phone with her father, arranging for him to come pick her up and take her to the hospital.

"I thought our birth plan was for me to get an Uber," I said.

"I trust my father more than I trust Uber drivers."

I felt a rush of affection for her, and a rush of respect for her recognition that I was not to be trusted with even trivial tasks once they became important. I also felt a rush of pride in myself for not being offended at her realistic assessment of me.

Rebecca, having examined both the thinness of the evidence against epidurals and the lowness of her own threshold for pain, asked for a shot as soon as we reached the hospital. Her friends had tried to pressure her into some kind of natural birth, and I was glad that she had resisted; I was glad that she was not **DEPENDENT ON THE OPINION OF OTHERS**. As a needle was prepared by an old man in green who, despite my squinting, looked nothing like Adam, Rebecca told me that she had called Leah—"I wanted her to be here more than I wanted you to be here, I think"—but that Leah had hung up without responding. After the epidural was administered, I excused myself to find a vending machine, and I wandered around the halls for a long time, thinking seriously about walking out and never coming back.

CHAPTER

— · · ✦ · · —

45

I was still wandering around the hospital hallway when I got a text from my father saying that he had arrived. After a lot more wandering, I found him standing by a vending machine and deep in conversation with a white-haired woman. When he saw me, he took a deep breath, and he put his hand on the woman's back. It was only then that I noticed that she was wearing a faded fox fur coat.

"Venter, there's someone I'd like you to meet. Though technically you've met."

"Rose," she said, extending her hand to me in a businesslike fashion. "But we've corresponded under my pen name. Steven Merdula."

I put my hand on the vending machine, blotting out the SunChips.

"You're joking," I said.

She smiled, and I saw either Adam or myself in her smile.

"When I chose the name, back in the eighties, it was almost impossible for a female writer to be taken seriously. From what I understand, it's a little better today, but not much."

I looked at my father to see whether this was some kind of prank, but if there is one thing I can recognize in my father's face, it's when he is not joking.

"You abandoned me to become a famous writer," I said to Rose.

She gave what had to have been a conscious Adam Shrug. "Men have been doing that to their children for centuries."

"There will be plenty of time to talk about all of this later," my father said. "But right now, Venter, we have some very big news. Your mother and I are getting back together."

"What?"

"We ran into each other about a year ago at a Film Forum screening of *Taxi Driver*, which we saw together with Adam when it was new," my father said. "We couldn't hear the movie that time because Adam kept on talking about how he had tattooed half the cast and crew one night. This time we heard the movie. We've been dating since."

"Dating since?"

"I saw her as we were going into the theater and I almost left. But I didn't. I sat a few rows behind her and watched the back of her head the whole time. Which was a creepy thing to do. It made me feel a little bit like Travis Bickle. But I couldn't stop looking at her. I've never wanted to stop looking at her. I invited her out for a drink afterward, mostly so I could yell at her, and I did yell at her, but we just kept talking, and I felt what I hadn't felt in decades, but also had never really stopped feeling."

"And I felt the same way," Rose said. "After I left you, Venter, I moved to Phoenix and moved in with Georgette Hoenecker and Lillian Secor, and I helped run their French restaurant when I wasn't writing. I loved my life. The two of them got married a little over a year ago, now that they finally can, and I got ordained online so I could officiate their wedding in the restaurant. The wedding was so beautiful, and it made me realize that I had to end my life with someone who loves me. I moved back to New York, telling myself it was because I missed New York, but really it was because I missed Isaac. If I hadn't run into him there, I would have called him eventually."

"You've been dating for a year and you didn't tell me?"

"I wasn't sure I wanted to see you," Rose said to me. "You've lived your life disgracefully."

It did not even occur to me to contest the charge. "And whose fault is that?"

"Whose fault do you think it is, Venter?"

I could get lost in the hospital again, I could flee the hospital, New York, Rebecca, our child, but I couldn't escape the fact that I knew the answer to this question. "Mine. Who I am is my fault and no one else's."

"I couldn't stop myself from coming today. I wanted to meet my granddaughter. And whatever else you are, you are my son. Even reminding myself about the terrible things you've done can't stop me from needing to see you, whether or not I want to."

"What a moving statement of motherly love."

"It's more than you deserve."

This was true.

I turned to my father. "So you knew that she was Merdula this whole time?"

"She only told me that first night after the movie. But it wasn't a surprise. I've strongly suspected for decades. Haven't we talked about this before?"

"No, Dad. We haven't."

"Huh. I guess it just never came up."

It occurred to me that I could start a long feud with my father over the fact that he was so distracted that he had never discussed with me the possibility that my mother was a famous pseudonymous writer, but it also occurred to me that I could also not do that, and just let the issue go. I could ask lots of people for their advice on how to proceed and get many conflicting opinions, or I could ask no one and just accept my father as he was.

It also occurred to me that it was completely fucking obvious that my mother was Merdula and I should have figured it out years ago.

"Tell me about Rebecca," Rose said.

"I don't deserve Rebecca," I said. "I don't deserve my child. I deserve to be in Hell for what I did to my friend."

"Neither your mother nor I disagree with you, exactly," my father said. "But Hell does not exist, and your daughter is about to."

I looked at my mother, her sweet ashen face, and I knew for the first time both that I had always hated her and that I had no supportable reason to.

"Tell me about Rebecca," my mother repeated. I suddenly realized that I knew nothing about Rebecca. I hoped that this would be the rare sudden realization that I would not forget and would do something about.

I turned my back on Isaac and Rose and looked at the waiting area. There were expectant grandparents and siblings and friends of the new parents. Many of those around my age had tattoos from the new model. **DEVOTES EVERY SPARE MINUTE TO HONING SKILLS** on the arm of a young woman reading an economics textbook; **DESPERATE TO APPEAR COOL** anxiously jabbing at his cell phone. The epiphanies did not seem as penetrating as those I remembered from Adam's era, but I was aware that this was most likely nostalgia.

NAME: Rebecca Hart Lowood

DATE OF BIRTH: 11/18/1981

DATE OF EPIPHANY MACHINE USE: N/A

DATE OF INTERVIEW BY VENTER LOWOOD: 01/06/2017

I was seven when I heard about the first Rebecca Hart. I was sitting on the floor in my father's office, stabbing my doll with a curette to remove her earwax, when my father introduced me to a patient as his daughter, Rebecca. "Oh, Rebecca Hart? Like that cunt who killed her kids?" My dad threw the guy out, probably the only patient he ever threw out. He wouldn't tell me what the word meant or what the guy was talking about, only that he was a bad man and I shouldn't worry about what he was saying. I didn't worry about it, exactly, but I couldn't get that phrase out of my head.

After asking an older girl who asked her mom and reported back, I figured out exactly who Rebecca Hart was and more or less what a cunt was. I remember thinking that my dad should have done more than throw his patient out for saying that word in front of me; he should have killed him. I remember thinking that maybe Rebecca Hart had murdered her children—her sons—because she was afraid they would end up like my dad's patient and was taking necessary precautions. After all, my dad's patient had a mother, and I can't imagine she would have been pleased to learn that her son would grow up to be a man who would use that word in front of a seven-year-old girl. So I wrote a story about a girl superhero who flew over our town, saw this man on the street, swooped down, embraced him tightly, flew up to the sky with him still in her arms, showed him buildings down below, and whispered in his ear about the amazing things she could see and hear women doing inside those buildings with her superpowers of sight and hearing. While he was crying about how much better all these girls were than he was, she dropped him over the Atlantic Ocean.

When I showed it to my mother, tears came to her eyes and she said that it was very sweet. That is not, to put it mildly, what I intended it to be, so the message that I took away was that I should not be a writer, because I had no talent for making people understand me through things I had written down.

All of this obsessed me for a few days and then it was out of my mind for years. Rebecca Hart's crime was mostly faded by the time I heard about it—sure, like a faded tattoo, knock yourself out with that metaphor, Venter. "Rebecca Hart" was still what everyone deserves: a name that's easy to forget.

The second Rebecca Hart changed that. I had just finished my math homework—*plus* the even-numbered questions that the teacher hadn't even assigned—when I turned on the television and saw the anchorwoman talking about Rebecca Hart, who was now the second woman with that name to drown each of her children in the bathtub after receiving an epiphany tattoo that read **OFFSPRING WILL NOT LEAD HAPPY LIVES**. My first thought was: "Damn, this is how I'll be known at school."

As I predicted, the next morning I was greeted by taunts about the previous night's news. Not quite as I predicted, my math teacher didn't even give a shit about my math homework and instead just wanted to give me a hug and tell me not to worry about my name. I was annoyed, because I had done a really good job on that math homework.

"Rebecca Hart is my hero," I said. She released me from the hug, and then I was by myself and in need of an explanation. I imagined a witch beside me telling me to say what I had said. I imagined this was the same witch from my story—by now I had learned that the approved word for "girl superhero" was "witch"—and this witch had also told the two Rebecca Harts to kill their kids. I didn't have much of an opinion at all about Rebecca Hart, or even know which Rebecca Hart I was referring to—the first one or the second one—but whichever one I was talking about, I did have a strong affinity for her, and the thing that's annoying about having a strong affinity for anyone you are neither related to nor want to fuck is that you have to explain it.

"Her kids were boys," I said. "They probably would have done something to deserve it."

Within the space of something like twelve hours, I had gone from "Math Nerd" to "Girl Who Shares the Name of a Baby Killer" to "Girl Who Shows Disturbing Tendencies and Needs to Be Placed Under Surveillance." Suddenly teachers talked to me differently. I was used to teachers talking to me differently, but instead of talking to me like I was the one smart friend they had in a group of hostile morons, they started talking to me like I was an unfamiliar dog that might bite.

I don't know what my teachers thought I was going to do. Maybe they were worried that I was going to have my first kiss, get pregnant, and, then, in the middle of gym class, while performing a dance that some other girls and I had choreographed to "Rhythm Is a Dancer," expel the baby from my vagina and immediately strangle it with the umbilical cord.

So that's what I did.

A few months earlier, I would have found any excuse to hide in a corner of the gym and read while I was supposed to be practicing the dance, and when I had to perform, I would have made it clear with every resentful rhythmic jerk of my leg that I was too good for this. But feeling myself the object of fear made me feel much more energetic, much more intensely and even exclusively *physical*, than I could remember ever feeling before. The other girls were much prettier than I was and they were much better dancers than I was, but I danced much better than they did, because as I danced I imagined delivering and killing my baby. As we practiced, the girls tried to sap my confidence by making fun of me, by whispering about me loud enough for me to hear, but I did not care. On the day of the performance, nobody—not the boys, not the girls, not the mildly pervy gym teacher—was looking at anybody but me. I was united with the imaginary baby that I was giving birth to and killing; it was part of my body, and so was the dance. There's a good reason why dance is so closely associated with witchcraft. Or at least there was while I was dancing underneath a middle school basketball hoop.

Immediately after the dance, I ran home and tried to write down what had happened, but the words on the page didn't come close to evoking what I felt. For the second time, I swore never to become a writer.

I thought that my name and whatever came over me during that dance would be the two things that I was known for, but fairly quickly, people at school forgot to be afraid of me. My essential mildness also asserted itself around this time—incompatible tendencies toward aggression and timidity made me vague and dull, as they do for most teenagers. I think I daydreamed from time to time about getting pregnant just to live out the urban legend of killing my baby at my prom, but nothing could have enticed me to go to my prom.

Am I being glib? Of course I'm being glib. But I think I did actually believe that there was a curse on my name, that there was a witch who would materialize if I ever did have a child and entice me to kill it. Or maybe I just made myself believe that, to ensure that I would remain unencumbered by a child. Sometimes the most cunning thing you can do is believe the worst about yourself.

Almost as soon as I got to Columbia, I started hearing rumors about a guy in our freshman class who had used the epiphany machine, who even worked for Adam Lyons. I don't think I would have let myself get interested in you in the first place if I hadn't been taking a disappointing creative writing class, the professor of which, Carter Wolf, had nothing to say about my work other than that I should try to choose more serious topics than witchcraft. That was the third time I decided not to be a writer, and I directed my energy toward stalking you.

I don't know what I was expecting—either somebody who was immaculately dressed, suit and bow tie and buzz cut, or somebody in smelly rags and really long, unwashed hair. Instead, you just looked like a regular slob, like every other college boy. I thought you were cute, okay? I didn't expect to ruin my goddamn life over you.

You and I were on and off for so long, and somehow that consumed almost all the energy I had in college. I mean, I had interests and I pursued them, and I was smart and I excelled, but I was thinking about you pretty much the whole time. Somehow I got the idea that you were a brilliant writer, though as I'm telling you this story right now I'm starting to realize that the only reason why I told myself you were a brilliant writer is that *I* wanted to be a brilliant writer, and I just handed you my ambitions and hopes as though that would make them stop calling out to me in the night.

Remember when that news anchor gave a speech at our graduation about how his best moment in college had been reading *Ulysses*, and he talked about Molly Bloom's closing line "yes I said yes I will Yes," and he basically exhorted us to say yes to life? At that point you and I had broken up long ago, but I remember sitting a few rows behind you and looking at the back of your neck throughout the ceremony, thinking about how sorry I was for you, how much it sucked for you to be so lost. But as the news anchor started talking, I started feeling sorry for *him*, because here is a guy who has been incredibly successful throughout his entire career, but who like everybody else just has to please other people all the time, and so you try to give pleasing other people the pleasing spin of "saying yes to life," and you do that so well that people ask you to give a speech to college graduates, and obviously you're not going to tell them that life is basically a long, incredibly boring avant-garde play in which you watch your own brain trying to figure out what other people are thinking about you, and you, the audience member, are given this one line to shout out at your brain over and over, "Relax and be yourself!" but obviously your brain can't hear you, which is too bad, because if it could, it would calmly explain to you that none of this matters very much, because soon enough "yourself" won't be anything at all, except maybe heartburn for a worm. Wormburn. Obviously you're not going to tell college kids *that*; they want you to make uplifting noises while they tune you out and brood over all the beautiful people in the crowd that they have just spent the last four years failing to fuck. So you recite something about saying yes to life, and you get all excited because you can tie it to *Ulysses*, which is totally appropriate, because maybe a few kids, while they're brooding about those people they failed to fuck, will hear the word "Ulysses" and then spend a few seconds brooding over failing to read *Ulysses*. And I thought: Jeez, I hope I can just get my brains fucked out for the rest of my life, if only so that I never accomplish anything that would inspire somebody to ask me to give a graduation speech, or to say anything at all. To silently fuck until I am dead, that was what the purpose of life seemed to me to be at that moment, Venter, and I felt so grateful to no longer be in a relationship with you, so that I could get to the fucking that I hoped might make my life just a tiny bit fucking satisfying. Then I felt annoyed at myself for spending my graduation ceremony—*my* graduation ceremony—thinking about you and the news anchor, two men I did not care about. Throughout my childhood, even though for the most part I didn't think I was going to be a writer, I had thought that any purpose my life found would have something to do with finding words for the world other than the words that men were always carving into it, and here I was thinking about two men, with no idea what to do with my life other than to spend it fucking, hardly a terrible idea but hardly an original one, either. The witch had left me.

A major problem with my plan to have a lot of sex: I'm like you, Venter. I live almost completely in my head and that makes it difficult to enjoy sex all that much. Whenever I'm having sex, I'm *thinking about* sex, how I wish I were better at it and how I wish the circumstances were hotter. You're supposed to say yes, yes, yes, you're supposed to try to connect with the other person. That's why I took improv classes for years, even though I'm pretty sure you never noticed even after we got back together. In improv classes they talk a lot about saying yes. Not only yes but "yes *and*." It's not enough to affirm something; they make you add to it. Exhausting, totally not me.

I think the appeal of the epiphany machine and my name is that I wouldn't have to say yes to this awful experience that you're supposed to say yes to, the experience of having kids. I married you in large part to never have kids. Another reason I married you is that we kind of see the world the same way, meaning hazily, through this thick filthy scrum of our thoughts about ourselves. The difference between you and me? I think about myself all the time just like you do, but I also think about my work.

I'm not going to kill my kid. Obviously. In retrospect, I don't think I ever thought I was. On the one hand, I thought the witch was going to swoop in as soon as I gave birth; on the other hand, I knew she was going to stand me up.

Now get your fucking iPhone out of my face and stop recording me. I've given you enough. I'm not going to keep translating the sense that my life makes for me until it makes sense for you. I'm not going to talk about Leah and how much she meant to me. That's for me. You know what else is for me? Me. Almost anything could be tattooed on my arm and I would recognize it as a murmuring from the deepest part of my soul, because at some point or other I've wanted everything; I've wanted to be everyone. There have even been rare occasions when I have wanted what I am supposed to want and have wanted to be what I am supposed to want to be: respectively, you and myself. That's the entire reason the machine seems to work; anything that you can claim is in somebody's head has probably been there at some point. People feel a shock of recognition at the truth, but they feel a shock of recognition at a lot of other things, too.

I've already given you myself, Venter. It's too much to ask me to tell you who that is. I won't do it. No I'm saying no I won't No.

EPILOGUE

I write this as my daughter is about to turn one year old. Rebecca and I are still together. Though it is impossible to know what anyone else's relationship is like, it does not seem unreasonable to guess that our relationship is in the lower fifty percent of relationships. I do know that raising Baby Rose as a stay-at-home dad has been the only time of my life that I can truly say has been worthwhile. I love bouncing Baby Rose around in my arms through our apartment at three in the morning; I love taking her out on the balcony to gaze out at the UN building. I love the falling sigh she makes when she stops crying, like the deflating of a balloon three times her size. I love the dainty, nearly polite way she shakes spaghetti from her fingers. I love it when she bites the arms of any adult we introduce her to, as though she is checking to make sure they are not counterfeit. I love watching television with her in my lap, particularly what seems to be her favorite show, a self-consciously "gritty" new CIA drama, which stars an old friend of her father's: Leah. As the eponymous hero of *Jane Payne*—theoretically but not actually based on her play—Leah plays an agent who tortures terrorists, all of whom are guilty, because her character is never wrong about what is in people's souls. One critic wrote, "If the show endorses torture, at least the waterboarding is swimming in feminism." Leah's dream had been to star in something that would attack America's war on terror, something that would open the audience's eyes to the evils of torture and of subverting the judicial system. She got much closer to her dream than most people do.

Often I walk Rose down the Long Island City riverside, recently converted from a dock into a park carefully constructed to suggest bliss, a lovely way of living. Occasionally I imagine that there are whispers about me. Even in the unlikely event that I am right, and I am being judged, and judged harshly, for having nothing else to do with my time or life but raise a child, that could not dampen my commitment to Baby Rose. Never have I felt less **DEPENDENT ON THE OPINION OF OTHERS**.

Well, there is one person whose opinion I'm dependent on—Baby Rose's. I want her to think, many years from now, that I was a good father to her. This is an opinion I am grateful to be dependent on.

I also have another Rose, my mother, at my side on many days to help me with the baby. In the mornings, my mother sits on the living room sofa with a laptop and writes—she, or rather Steven Merdula, is finishing a second book about the epiphany machine—and in the afternoon, she sits with me and the baby. She has barely held a baby since she held me, and yet she has an effortlessness with Rose that I am jealous of, and am ashamed to talk about in my parenting classes—as I write that, I realize I am still, to some degree, **DEPENDENT ON THE OPINION OF OTHERS**. I think I'm also jealous of Baby Rose, as strange as that sounds, because she will grow up knowing my mother. But I try to put all of this out of my mind, since Rose's presence will be good for my daughter. And it's good for me, too, to have adult conversation every afternoon, however strained that conversation may sometimes be.

"Why didn't you ever at least, like, check in with me?"

"That would have just made it harder."

"It didn't seem to bother you to make things harder for me."

"Actually, I meant it would have made things harder for me. I was pretty sure that you were what mattered most to me, and I didn't want to have to keep abandoning you over and over again. And if I came back to you and then found out that I had abandoned my writing, and that *that* was what mattered most to me—well, it wouldn't have been good for either one of us if that's what I had found."

"Is that supposed to be heartwarming? Because it makes you sound even more self-centered."

"You asked me a question and I answered it. Staying away and doing my work and letting you develop on your own seemed like the best option."

"If you hadn't left me, I wouldn't have gotten tattooed. And if I hadn't gotten tattooed, Ismail wouldn't have gotten tattooed."

"That's possible. Why are you putting it like that?"

"I'm putting it like that because it's the truth."

"You put it like that because you're trying to cause me pain over something you know I feel guilty about. There was a time when I held myself personally responsible for what you and the state did to Ismail. It's all over that story I wrote about him, probably the weakest thing I've ever written. But it's not my fault at all, as we've already discussed. You're your own person, Venter. You may be **DEPENDENT ON THE OPINION OF OTHERS**, but you have no one but yourself to blame."

I suppose I should leave this part out, as my mother and I reached something close to resolution on this back at the hospital. But there's no such thing as resolution, no such thing as closure, no such thing as an insight that makes the past less painful, and as a recovering epiphany addict I should be honest about all this. What she said made me mad, which made me storm into my bedroom, which in turn woke the baby, who let out a sharp, angry cry. My mother beat me to the baby, and almost as soon as she picked her up the baby was quiet, and then giggled as my mother recited a passage she had memorized from *Ulysses*. The scene looked so perfect, and it occurred to me that the world would have been better had I never existed, had Rose skipped me entirely and gone straight to Baby Rose.

On many afternoons, we are joined by my father, semiretired and having, like the culture itself, mostly abandoned his desire to fight for privacy. He and my mother get along so well that I wonder what it would have been like had they stayed together throughout my childhood. There is no way to know how my life would be different had she stayed; there is plenty of reason to think it would have been worse. She might have locked herself in a room and written a story imagining that she had abandoned me when she wanted to. She might even have written that novel in my voice.

This book, which I have completed while Baby Rose naps, will be my only book, assuming it is even published. Publication does not look likely, considering that when I was writing it I thought the major appeal would be Ismail. I doubt there's anyone in America who still thinks that Ismail is guilty of anything, and that is precisely the reason why he will stay in prison, at least for a long time; seeing him free would mean seeing what we have done to him.

Nor is there likely to be much interest in the testimonials that I gathered for my project, almost all of which tell of experiences with Adam Lyons's machine. As the new machines grow more and more prominent, Adam Lyons's device seems like a quaint curiosity, of interest primarily to tedious old men obsessed with Beatles trivia.

Baby Rose does have one parent whom I believe is fated to achieve literary glory, sooner rather than later: Rebecca. While she was on maternity leave from her firm—a shockingly ungenerous three months—Rebecca wrote several stories, and my mother read them and reread them and said that they were brilliant. Now that Rebecca has gone back to work, she wakes up impossibly early to write for two hours every morning, and once a week she and my mother go to a café to discuss Rebecca's stories. One of these stories will be published in a forthcoming issue of a prestigious journal in which I always dreamed of getting published—sometimes so dreamily that I barely wrote for years at a time. Last month, she signed a two-book contract for a collection of short stories, to be followed by a novel.

Yesterday afternoon I took Baby Rose to see the Whitney Museum's exhibition *Arming the Self: The Epiphany Machine in American Life, 1960–2018*. Much of the exhibition consisted of photos of epiphany tattoos, some disembodied, others as part of full-figure portraits. There were photos by amateurs and photos by professionals, Polaroids taken in 1975 and iPhone selfies taken last year. Roxanne Salehi's documentary was playing on a loop.

"Hey, you're the guy from the documentary! You suck!"

I gave this guy a nasty look, which he captured in a photo. "Free Ismail!" he said, probably the caption he would use when he posted that photo online, where it would be liked, widely shared, and promptly forgotten.

In the center of the hallway, three people sat with their bare arms entangled; a sign below them, printed in Adam's font, read: **MEET MICHAEL BRANDON AND SHANICE FEEL FREE TO STARE AT THEIR TATTOOS BUT THEIR TATTOOS WILL STARE BACK.**

Through Brandon and Shanice, I saw a lifelike sculpture of Ismail's mother on the deck outside. This struck me as tasteless until she pulled her arms tightly against her chest to keep warm, and I realized that it was actually Ismail's mother. She saw me before I reached the glass doors (on which were written the words **OUTSIDE IS STILL INSIDE THE EPIPHANY MACHINE**), and she stared at me with an expression I could not even read as disgust.

"There are a million reasons why I shouldn't keep coming here, starting with the fact that I can barely afford the admission fee, because I lost my job," she said as I opened the doors. "But, also because I lost my job, I have nothing else to do with my days. They gave everybody the choice of getting an epiphany tattoo or resigning. I wasn't going to let that thing near my arm."

"I'm sorry," I said. "Tell me what to do and I'll do it. I'll do anything to make this right."

"There is something you can do, and you know that there is. But you also can never know what it is. That's the closest you'll come to punishment. Not nearly close enough. My best wishes for your daughter."

And then she walked away.

Baby Rose made a gurgle that sounded like a question. To stop myself from sobbing I pointed out some buildings to her, in this city that Adam Lyons once dreamed of changing. I walked with her to the plexiglass barrier that halted any patrons tempted to leap to their deaths in distant sight of the Hudson River and the Statue of Liberty. I thought about Ismail and his joke about driving us into this very river, north of here. If we had gone over the bridge that day, my arm would have been clean when I gave it to the water. Maybe it would have been severed somehow in the wreckage, and it would have floated all the way down to this final stretch of New York, where it would have bobbed and pointed to the sky, a miniature version of the massive faded green arm above it, suggesting only promise and possibility, without words to limit either.

The way we were constantly learning and forgetting things—the way that I constantly learned and forgot my culpability for what had happened to Ismail is only one small example—made me feel that the human race was pitiful and should be annihilated. I looked up at the blue sky and I hated everything underneath it, including this tiny child who would soon ask me why the sky was blue. It occurred to me to hurl my baby over the plexiglass, to bring about the fulfillment of any number of prophecies, and to bring upon myself the calumny and disaster I deserved. Baby Rose would hit the pavement and become part of the pavement never knowing the words that described her.

Of course, many prophecies had already been fulfilled. My father should never have become a father, and my mother had abandoned what mattered most—her sense of decency—to accept as her son a man who had betrayed his best friend.

Baby Rose reached up and put her forearm in my face. Terrified of myself, I kissed her forearm and took her back inside the museum.

Current trends suggest she will get a tattoo when she turns eighteen, or maybe even earlier, if only to fit in with friends who might look at her askance if she refuses. But maybe she will refuse. Maybe she will seek out Ismail's mother—or even a finally freed Ismail. Or she will just watch the documentary. Even the broadest outlines of the case will be enough to make her hate me. Stronger than my father and mother, my daughter will never allow me to win her back, leaving me with only my tattoo.

I kissed the top of her head, and then kissed it again, and again, as though if I kissed her head often enough I could stop any negative thoughts about me from forming in it. Eventually she started to wriggle hard enough that I could see I was smothering her, my kisses pushing her face into my forearm. I eased up and she cried a nasty cry, still staring at my forearm, as though she could read my tattoo. I tried to murmur soothingly, but she wailed louder, drawing attention, and out of embarrassment, I looked over her head at another looped video installation. Titled *The Epiphany Machine Is Good; The Epiphany Machine Is Bad,* it consisted of interviews with people on the street giving their opinions about what the epiphany machine meant for human hopes, while the words they spoke were inscribed on the screen, not disappearing like normal subtitles but instead inching up until they obscured the faces of the people who spoke them. Then the words obscured each other, blending together until they covered the screen as one unreadable tattoo.

ACKNOWLEDGMENTS

My agent, Monika Woods, and my editor, Alexis Sattler, are brilliant readers who made this book much better than it would have been otherwise. They are also tireless advocates. I am immeasurably lucky to work with them both.

I am lucky as well to have many friends who provided invaluable support and feedback. Angelica Baker read many drafts with great insight. I am indebted also to Tara Isabella Burton, Will Chancellor, Scott Cheshire, Ryan Joe, Courtney Elizabeth Mauk, Maxwell Neely-Cohen, Abby Rosebrock, Yvette Siegert, and Chandler Klang Smith.

Much of this book was written at The Oracle Club in Long Island City. Special thanks to Julian Tepper, Jenna Gribbon, and Matthew Gribbon. (Of course, the portraits in this book of The Oracle Club and of Julian and Jenna are pure fiction.) Thanks to Bryce Bauer and Tyler Wetherall. Thanks also to Sandra from the Long Island City UPS store.

Of many books that were helpful, particular gratitude is due to: Terry McDermott's *Perfect Soldiers: The 9/11 Hijackers: Who They Were, Why They Did It*; Philip Norman's *John Lennon: The Life*; Dave Schwensen's *The Beatles at Shea Stadium: The Story Behind Their Greatest Concert*; Larry

Siems's *The Torture Report: What the Documents Say About America's Post-9/11 Torture Program*; and John Michael Vlach's *The Afro-American Tradition in Decorative Arts*. *The 9/11 Commission Report* and *The Official Senate Report on CIA Torture* were also useful.

Few things in my life have been as important to me as the friendship of Michael Seidenberg. What he has created in Brazenhead Books can never be satisfactorily described or repeated.

My writing—along with everything else in my life—would be impossible without the love and support I have consistently received from my mother, Barbara Gerrard, my father, Michael Gerrard, and my brother, William Gerrard.

Thanks most of all to Grace Bello for all her help with this book, and for filling my life with love every single day.